Lost Legio IX

MW01125175

Lost Legio IX

The Karus Saga

Marc Alan Edelheit

This book is a work of fiction. Names, characters, places and incidents are either the product of the author's imagination or are used fictitiously. Any resemblance to actual persons, living or dead, or to actual events or locales is entirely coincidental.

Lost Legio IX: The Karus Saga – Book One
First Edition

Copyright © 2017 by Marc Edelheit. All rights reserved, including the right to reproduce this book, or portions thereof, in any form. No part of this text may be reproduced, transmitted, downloaded, decompiled, reverse engineered, or stored in or introduced into any information storage and retrieval system, in any form or by any means, whether electronic or mechanical without the express written permission of the author. The scanning, uploading, and distribution of this book via the Internet or via any other means without the permission of the publisher is illegal and punishable by law. Please purchase only authorized electronic editions and do not participate in or encourage electronic piracy of copyrighted materials.

I wish to thank my agent, Andrea Hurst, for her invaluable support and assistance. I would also like to thank my beta readers, who suffered through several early drafts. My betas: Barrett McKinney, Jon Cockes, Norman Stiteler, Nicolas Weiss, Stephan Kobert, Matthew Ashley, Melinda Vallem, Jon Quast, Donavan Laskey, Paul Klebaur, Russ Wert, James Doak, David Cheever, Bruce Heaven, Erin Penny, Jonas Ortega Rodriguez, April Faas, Rodney Gigone, Brandon Purcell, Steve Sibert, Tim Adams, and Brett Smith. I would also like to take a moment to thank my loving wife who sacrificed many an evening and weekends to allow me to work on my writing.

Editing Assistance by Hannah Streetman, Shannon Roberts, Audrey Mackaman

Cover Art by Piero Mng (Gianpiero Mangialardi)

Cover Formatting by Telemachus Press

Agented by Andrea Hurst & Associates

Chronicles of a Legionary Officer:
Book One: **Stiger's Tiger**
Book Two: **The Tiger**
Book Three: **The Tiger's Fate**

Tales of the Seventh:
Book One: **Stiger, Tales of the Seventh Part One**

Author's note:

Lost Legio IX and the tale it kicks off take place many years before *Stiger's Tigers*. Karus and Amarra's story is one I wanted to tell long before I introduced you to Stiger. There will be at least five books in this series.

Please keep in mind writing is a hobby for me and reviews keep me motivated and help to drive sales. I read each one.

I hope you enjoy *Lost Legio IX* and a sincere thank you for your purchase.

Best regards,

Marc Alan Edelheit, author and your tour guide to the worlds of Tannis and Istros

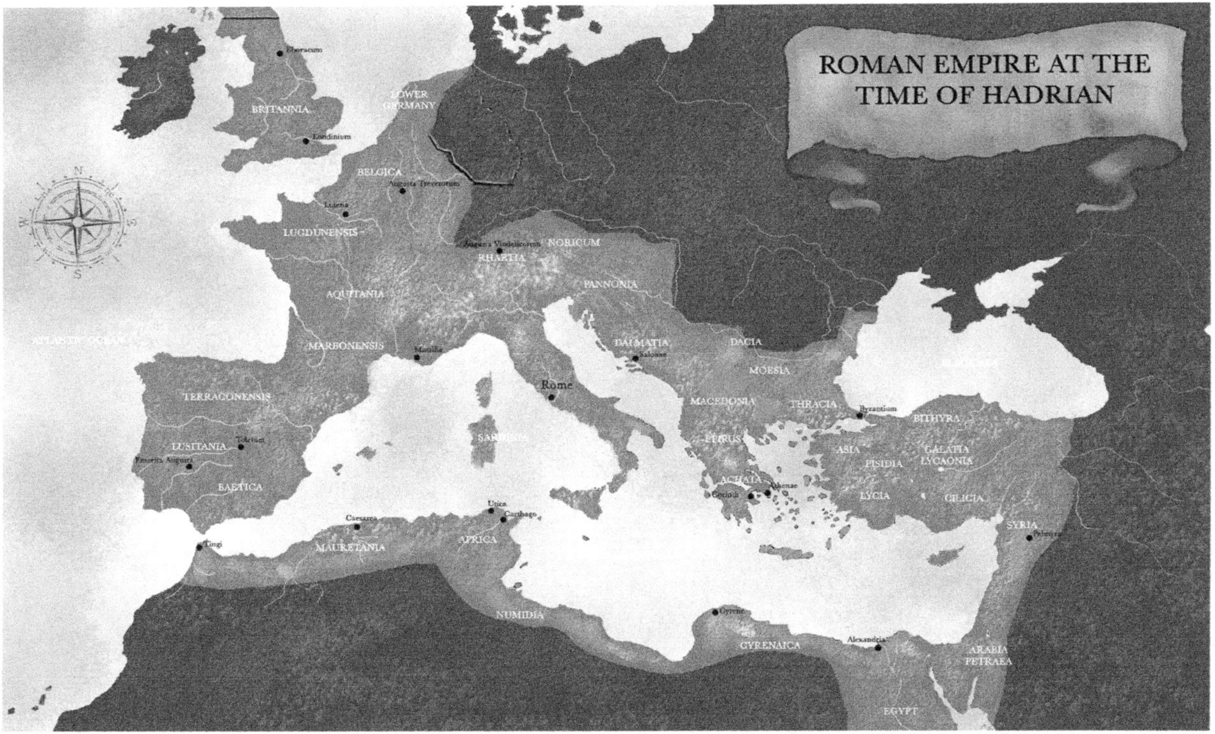
ROMAN EMPIRE AT THE
TIME OF HADRIAN
BRITANNIA
Eboracum
Londinium
LOWER GERMANY
BELGICA
Augusta Treverorum
Lutetia
LUGDUNENSIS
AQUITANIA
NARBONENSIS
Massilia
NORICUM
RHAETIA
PANNONIA
DALMATIA
Salonae
DACIA
MOESIA
MACEDONIA
THRACIA
Byzantium
BITHYRA
ASIA
GALATIA
LYCAONIA
PISIDIA
LYCIA
CILICIA
SYRIA
ACHAIA
Athenae
Corinth
EPIRUS
Rome
SARDINIA
TERRACONENSIS
LUSITANIA
Toletum
Emerita Augusta
BAETICA
Tingi
Caesarea
MAURETANIA
Utica
Carthago
AFRICA
NUMIDIA
Cyrene
CYRENAICA
Alexandria
EGYPT
ARABIA PETRAEA
N
S
E
W

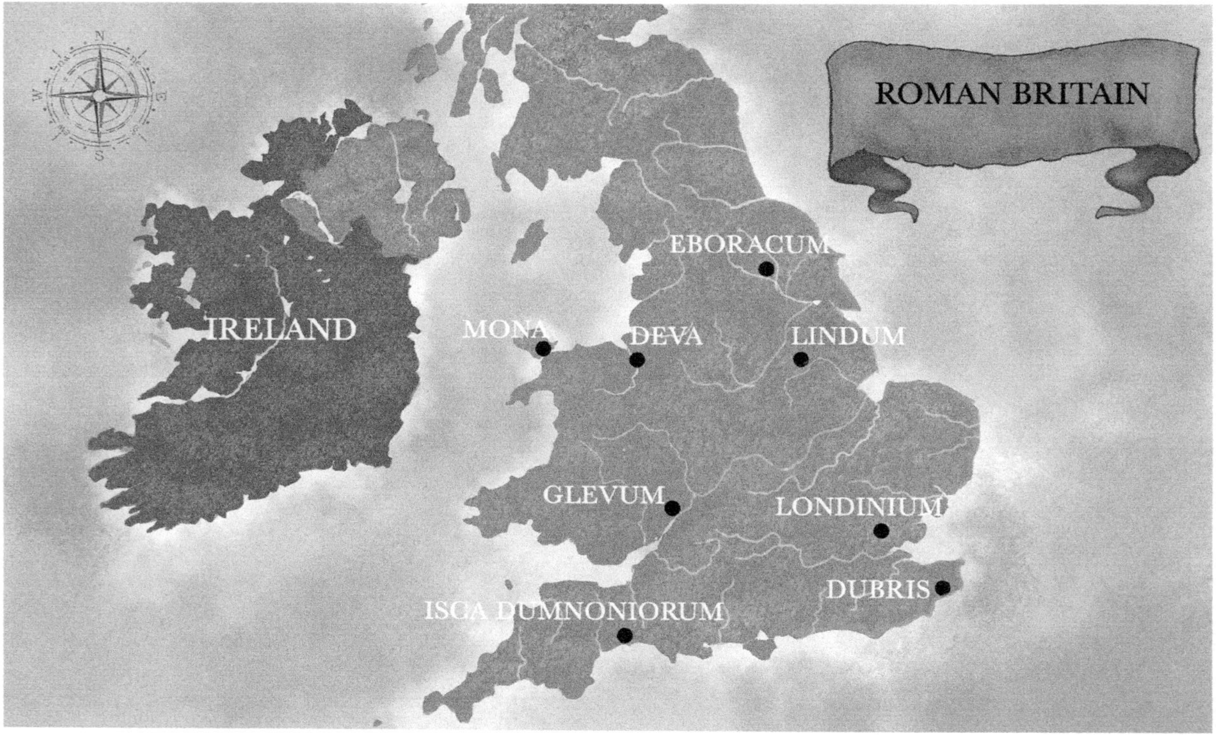
ROMAN BRITAIN
N
E
S
W
IRELAND
MONA
DEVA
EBORACUM
LINDUM
GLEVUM
LONDINIUM
DUBRIS
ISCA DUMNONIORUM

I would like to dedicate this book to my three little meatballs:
Isabella, Juliana, and Amelia Rose.

ORGANIZATION
NINTH LEGIO, HISPANA

Legionary Symbol: Bull

The Ninth was arranged into ten legionary cohorts of four hundred eighty men each, with the exception of First Cohort, which was maintained at double strength. Led by a legate, the Ninth, along with her five auxiliary cohorts, was a formidable combat unit staffed with professional soldiers who were highly disciplined and trained.

Senior Officers:
Legate: Vellius Rufus Julionus
Tribune: Crispinus Martialis Saturninus
Camp Prefect: Aquila Desidus Tarbo (Deceased)
Junior Tribune: Tiberius Garius Delvaris

Senior Centurions of the Legion:
1st Cohort: Lucius Grackus Lisidius Karus
2nd Cohort: Tacitus Cestius Dio
3rd Cohort: Balbus Bassus Titus
4th Cohort Gallus Felix
5th Cohort: Verran Flaccus
6th Cohort: Ulpuis Mettius (Recently Reconstituted)
7th Cohort: Manlius Varno

8th Cohort: Fadenus Artunus
9th Cohort: Melanda Frontinus
10th Cohort: Catus Didius

Allied Auxiliary Cohorts Prefects:
Ala Agrippiana Miniata: Cavalry Cohort – Tricianus Valens
First Nervorium Cohort: Light Infantry – Arminus Autun Otho
Second Vasconum CR Cohort: Light Infantry – Gordian Varno
Fourth Delmatarum Cohort: Light Infantry – Maximus Geta Haemus
Fifth Raetorum Cohort: Light Infantry – Cestus Pactus

Surgeon:
Anatolius Demosthenes Ampelius

Other Legions Characters:
Fadius, Titus, Akamas, Iamus, Pammon, Thoon, Saccus, Pulmonus, Janus, Ajax, Sextus, Arentus, Cestus, Macrinus, Arrens, Daemon, Marci, Crix, Mettis, Ternus, Serma, Ipax, Mika, Sadeus, Cleotis, Paro, Ganarus, Sextus, Marus, Argus, Drusus
Civilians: Keeli, Milza, Illya, Elena, Harikas, Cylenia, Lohert

Part One

Prologue

'For these I set no bounds in space or time; but have given empire without end.'

—Jupiter, Virgil's Aeneid.

"Why are we here, Blue?"

Opening his eyes, Blue took a deep breath of the crisp early morning air and then slowly released it. He thoroughly enjoyed the cooler climates. It almost brought him back to his youth, and the dank chill air of the underground. Almost.

Blue assessed his energy stores from casting the transference spell. It had taken him years to accumulate the energy he now held, and he dared not waste too much. Satisfied that he'd drained little of his reserves, he waved his staff and spun a masking shroud over the two of them before anyone noticed their presence. Such a minor spell barely drew enough energy for him to be bothered. Still, with all that he had planned and prepared for, it was unwise to squander too much, even insignificant amounts.

"This seems a place of no import," the other said with disdain as he glanced around them. "A military camp? Really?"

The morning light was still dim, and a misty fog swirled around their feet. The two stood in the middle of a central parade ground. A few strands of hardy grass poked up from amongst the moist, packed-down dirt.

"High Master of Obsidian," Blue crowed. "A grand title for a wizard of nearly godlike power, and yet such little patience. Aren't elves known for their placidity? Sometimes, my friend, Vera'Far, I wonder what went wrong with you."

Blue himself was a High Master, one of only a handful the gods permitted. In truth, the High Masters were disciples of their respective gods, and though both Blue and Obsidian were aligned in purpose, each answered to different masters.

"Rarokan, I will not be put off." Obsidian turned on him, robes rustling.

Blue offered the elf a flat look at the use of his given name. Despite his appearance, Obsidian was ancient. Yet like those of his race, he carried the timeless grace of youth. The only telltale signs of age were in the eyes. Deadened by time beyond end and, perhaps, Blue reflected, years of unremitting war. Both had suffered, and Blue had tired of it. It was why he had brought them to this forbidden place.

"Well, then," Blue said as he studied the other wizard. A sigh escaped his lips. "It has been an age since we last met. It seems you have changed little in that time, both in attitude and dress."

Blue, in an exaggerated manner, swept his eyes over the other wizard. Obsidian wore a well-cut midnight-black robe that seemed to flow down around him. The elf had grown out his hair. Black, silky, and shining, it was combed to perfection and had been pulled back into a ponytail, secured by a delicate golden clasp at the back of his neck. A thin gold circlet was perched upon his head. Blue had never seen his friend without the crown. It was encrusted with small azure crystals, which, in the early morning light, gave off a faint hint of a pale glow.

The elf brought his staff, a crystalline miracle that no mortal hand could have ever crafted, down with a soft thud on the soft ground. Etched with arcane runes, the staff throbbed with power, occasionally brightening, before settling back to a dull, somber radiance.

Blue considered the staff. Perhaps it was a true relic of the First Ones? The few who remained now called themselves the Noctalum and had once walked the worlds with the gods at their sides.

"Why are we here, Blue? Are you going to answer me?" Obsidian demanded as the mist, propelled by a gentle gust, swirled between them.

"Time has not mellowed your demanding nature," Blue said as he dragged his eyes away from his friend's staff. Most elves had a sense of humor; his friend here had never fully developed one. Nor did the elf seem to recognize irony when he heard it.

"Humor, I presume?" Obsidian let out an exasperated breath and thumped his staff upon the ground again.

Blue glanced down at the six age-gnarled fingers of his right hand gripped loosely around his own staff. Crafted by his own hand, Blue's staff was made from a simple Theoak tree. The staff was topped with a misshapen sapphire crystal that throbbed with a dull, sullen power. His staff was nothing compared to the elegance of Obsidian's, and yet in the right hands, it was just as powerful a tool. He flexed the thick fingers of his hand, each adorned by a large gold ring set with a crystal. These glowed brightly, almost fiercely. Small flashes of energy sparked and crackled from ring to ring in rapid, soundless discharges. Blue no longer felt the accompanying tingle that originated from his storage devices. He had lived with the feeling so long that he no longer paid it any mind.

"I should have expected nothing less from a dwarf."

Blue frowned at the insult. He was a Dvergr. Calling him a dwarf was an insult, but such petty words bothered him little.

"I fear any real humor would be lost upon you should I attempt the effort." Blue brought his free hand up to stroke his freshly shaved chin. "We come here because I willed it."

"Really? I fail to see why you would bring us to some army encampment?" Obsidian glanced around with a bored expression. Dozens of solid-looking stone buildings with arched tiled roofs hemmed in the parade ground. These structures were arranged in neatly ordered rows, with wide paved streets running between them. In the distance, sentries slowly and deliberately walked the length of a crenulated outer defensive wall. "I have seen others of a similar nature on a hundred different worlds. This is nothing new."

"This one is different."

Obsidian glanced around, feigning curiosity. "I do not see it."

Blue gazed at the nearest buildings—barracks, all of them. The soldiers stationed here were sleeping away the last remaining moments before their day began. He well knew their routine, for he had spent much time studying them.

"Welcome to Eboracum," Blue said, holding out his free hand and staff in an elaborate show. "Home to the Roman Ninth Legion, Hispana. I welcome you, my friend, to a world you have never been... Earth."

"What?" Obsidian looked over at Blue sharply, then closed his eyes. He waved his staff around in a slight circular motion. It flared with light before rapidly fading. The elf's eyes opened. Where a moment ago they had been deadened by time unending, Obsidian's eyes flashed with anger. "You fool! It is madness just to be here."

Blue smiled wryly back, which seemed to irritate the elf further. The other wizard's face colored, causing Blue to grin. Getting any type of emotional reaction from his friend pleased Blue immensely. Surprise was even better.

A horn sounded, shattering the early morning quiet. The two wizards turned to watch as the men, wearing only their gray service tunics and sandals, began to spill out of the nearby barracks. They rushed over to the parade ground where the two wizards stood and began falling into their respective formations. Officers followed their men out onto the parade ground. Junior officers carried wooden slates coated in wax for taking roll. The more senior officers who commanded each formation carried vine canes.

"Madness?" Blue asked with some amusement and deep satisfaction at having genuinely surprised his friend, which, he reflected, was not an easy task. He took another deep breath of the cool morning air and let it out slowly. "I think not."

"You dare meddle with a cradle world?" Obsidian asked, aghast, turning back to face him. "If that does not constitute madness, I should like to hear what does!"

"These Romans reign supreme over a sizable portion of this world," Blue said. "Long have I watched and studied them. Long have I admired their spirit and resolve." He paused, gazing at the legion, which had formed up around them, so close he could almost smell the foul breath of the men. Though he had never sired any children, Blue suddenly felt like a proud parent. He turned back to Obsidian.

"These Romans have built an empire that is most impressive."

"Why is that important to our needs?" Obsidian hissed with irritation. "Why risk it all? This place is forbidden to us."

"These Romans have managed to develop a mindset for domination and power that can only be dreamed of on most other worlds," Blue continued, turning away to watch the formations continue to assemble. "Their military operates much like a well-built and oiled machine might. It is highly disciplined and, when properly led, fairly unstoppable. This legion, the Ninth Hispana, is but a tiny part of that great machine... a small cog, if you will."

"Again," Obsidian lowered his tone, almost as if he feared they might be overheard, which was quite impossible given the spell Blue had spun, "I ask what relevance that information is to our cause, and the war?"

Blue ignored Obsidian and continued.

"These Romans over the last few centuries have managed to expand their reach greatly. They have subjugated entire peoples, dismantling some of the most powerful kingdoms and empires their world has ever known."

Blue paused a moment and glanced around with pride at the assembling legion. "They have developed an aggressive spirit that is quite unmatched in thirst for both conquest and glory. Despite incredible reversals that would have humbled other nations and peoples, these," he gestured at the legion, which had formed up around them, "took the punches and never gave in. Their spirit and resolve kept them going until their foes were either crushed or submitted to subjugation. Even those they do not rule bow economically to them, having become dependent upon the goods and services Roman civilization provides. They station their permanent armies—legions, they call them—upon the fringes of their territory. They do this not to provoke war, but to display their might in full view of their neighbors, who in turn fret that the Romans will turn their way. They are bold, I tell you."

Blue fell silent, preferring to gaze upon the legion. All his plans and efforts hinged upon these people. Obsidian considered Blue for a moment, before he too began studying the assembled formations of the legion. The two wizards watched as officers took roll and then began inspecting their men, a practice that rang with ritual.

"It is risky just coming here," Obsidian said with a heavy sigh, seeming to let go of his anger. "The gods may notice."

"Imagine if this empire had some direction," Blue said with a wave of his staff. "Imagine what it could do, what it could become."

"It is prohibited from interfering with this world's development," Obsidian said quietly. "The gods have mandated it. We should not even be here."

"Istros," Blue said wistfully.

"What of that backwater?" A scowl creased Obsidian's youthful brow, which caused his crown to shift slightly. "It has only one serviceable World Gate, which, if I recall, is sealed. The other, thanks to misguided members of my race, is inaccessible. Istros is nothing but a dead-end world with little value to anyone."

"The other alignments, including our enemies, think as you do." Blue turned to face his friend. "I tire of endless reversals and defeats. Giving up world after world to our enemies is intolerable. Tell me you feel as I do."

"We are doing all that we can." Obsidian reached a hand up to his gold and crystal necklace, absently toying with it. Though it was incredibly fine, and clearly made by a master of unparalleled ability, Blue recognized it as just another storage device.

"Are we?" Blue asked, arching an eyebrow. "Are we really?"

"What do you mean?"

"Though Istros is in your sphere of influence, I intend to make that world a strong point," Blue said. "On Istros our reversals will halt. Upon that world, with my design, and your assistance, we will eventually strike back."

"How?" Obsidian asked, irritation once again leaking into his voice. "There are no great empires on that world. It has been adrift for two thousand years. Though the people there are numerous, they are scattered into many individual kingdoms, hopelessly divided. There is no unifying influence. They have no concept of our war. The gods, for all intents and purposes, ignore them."

"I intend to change that," Blue said, flashing what he thought was a devious a smile at the elf.

"How?" Obsidian asked again.

Blue gestured with his free hand around them. "It is why we are both here."

Obsidian's eyes widened. He stumbled back a step.

"You cannot ask that of me," Obsidian said in a whisper. "You cannot be serious."

"I am," Blue said firmly, a feeling of deep burning rage rising up within him to match the resolve of his actions. "I tire of struggling so much for so little gain. It is time for drastic measures. Something must change, for our cause as it stands now is lost. The tide must turn, and if it will not do so on its own, it must be rolled back by force of will alone."

Obsidian was silent for several moments. Blue could almost sense the other's thoughts despite the implacable façade his friend worked so hard to present to the world.

"You think these legionaries can provide that backbone?" the elf said after some time, glancing around at the assembled legion.

"I do," Blue said in a near whisper. "I have arranged things nicely."

"Will not the gods stop you?"

"They dare not," Blue replied with an almost maniacal giggle.

"Are you so sure?"

"Direct interference would upset the order of things," Blue said, struggling to sober his tone. The vast quantity of power he was holding onto threatened once again to overwhelm him. With effort, he closed his eyes and tamped down the wave of energy that had bubbled up, and pushed it back to where it belonged, reserved for his call and need. The crystals on his rings flashed, and his staff's ill-shaped sapphire blinked with the effort. When he opened his eyes again, he saw Obsidian studying him with a calculating look.

"The order has been upset before, but never like this."

Blue shrugged. "It would be an escalation even they are not prepared to fully undertake."

"I don't know about that," Obsidian said. "I have my doubts."

"Imagine for a moment if this empire were pushed and permitted the run of this world," Blue said. "What greatness could they achieve? Should a Gate be opened to the next world, surely they would come to eventually dominate that one also. In the end, who knows how far it could go?"

"The gods will not permit a Gate on this world." Obsidian cocked his head to the side. "I am unsure exactly what you intend."

"True, they will not permit a World Gate, yet there still resides an ancient portal, one of the very first, and not far from where we now stand."

Blue saw the surprise register in Obsidian's eyes. It pleased him greatly, and he almost lost himself as his hold on the energy slackened. It was becoming a real effort to maintain control over the power, which continually threatened to overwhelm his will and sanity. In a few days' time, he would be free of the burden. Then would come a greater weight to shoulder. He was not looking forward to that.

"The gods will demand a price for your actions," Obsidian said. It came out almost as a whisper. "Are you prepared to accept their punishment?"

"They have yet to act," Blue said.

"What do you mean they have yet to act?"

"I have been working on this for a very long time, taking individuals and small groups from this world," Blue said casually. "Though they mean nothing to you, I have removed Carthaginians, Etruscans, Greeks, Assyrians, Medians ... the list of peoples goes on." He paused and once again glanced around at the assembled legion. "This, however, will be something a bit more ... substantial."

"All to Istros?"

"No, to Tannis," Blue responded with a heavy sigh. "An ancient portal still resides on that world. Sadly, one was never built on Istros, and if I rectified that oversight, it would be noticed." He paused for a moment to suck in a breath of the cold morning air. "Once on Tannis, these Romans would need to unlock the World Gate to Istros."

"Surely," Obsidian said, "there are better choices than Istros. It is so ... out of the way."

"There are no others," Blue said firmly. "Besides, that world's remoteness makes it the perfect choice."

"I don't like it."

"Neither do I," Blue said. "But I can see no other way. Very few of the ancient portals remain active. Sadly, most lead to places that would prove far harsher environments than Tannis."

"Can these ... these Romans make it?" Obsidian asked. "Tannis is slowly being overrun. Our enemy, knowing the dead-end nature of that chain, seems in no particular hurry."

"That will change once the Ninth arrives," Blue said matter-of-factly.

"That is an understatement," Obsidian said.

"The journey to Istros will be difficult and perilous," Blue said, "but there are ready allies in place."

"So, that is why there are dwarves on Tannis?" Obsidian looked closely at Blue. "It must have taken centuries to get them all the way out there."

"I have long planned this," Blue admitted with a slight shrug of his shoulders.

"I am beginning to see that. It would seem your ambitions are as unrivaled as these Romans'."

Blue nodded at that truthful statement, and the two were silent for some time as they watched the legionaries.

"Should they succeed and make their way to Istros," Blue said after some time, "they will have all the time they need."

"Should?"

"I shall give these Romans their empire without end, as their god has promised," Blue said, turning back to Obsidian. "And you, my friend, will help me. You will give them their push. You must send one of your wizards to this world to watch over them and guide things."

Obsidian turned away and cast his gaze around them. The roll had been taken, and the formations were being dismissed one after another. Men were streaming off the parade ground on their way to begin their daily routines.

"Only if you send one of yours," Obsidian countered. "Two wizards on Istros will increase the chances of success."

"I have already done so," Blue said with a sense of triumph. "He is on Tannis, as is a Knight of the Vass, and several Noctalum."

Obsidian glanced over at him with a raised eyebrow, and then nodded. "You realize that once the other alignments figure out what we are doing, they will move to counter us?"

"Yes, but, with luck, by the time they react," Blue said, "our momentum will have carried things too far along for them to easily stop us, particularly if the Romans make it to Istros. With your help, they will seal the Gate behind them and begin to dominate their new world."

Obsidian remained silent as he considered what Blue said.

"Once the Gate is sealed again," Obsidian said, "anything could happen. There will be no help available, and no going back."

"That is why we are each sending our best with them."

"Are you prepared for judgment?" Obsidian asked. "For the gods will surely demand it for removing this... this legion."

"You know better," Blue said with a frown.

"The question is, do you?"

"Once I have seen to the transfer, I will travel to Olimbos. There I will atone... for my sins," Blue said with a heavy sigh. Yes, he would go to the one world where the gods still walked the land and pulled strings from afar. There he would pay the price for his actions, even as he served the god he honored and loved. "Besides, traveling through space and time as we both do, you know it has already happened."

"Will you really climb that mountain?" Obsidian asked him, ignoring the last comment. Blue could almost detect a trace of sympathy in his friend's tone. "Willingly?"

"Indeed, I will." Blue hesitated. "I already have."

Obsidian was silent for some moments, his eyes on Blue.

"Eventually, another Dvergr will rise to assume my mantle," Blue added, filling the silence. "Until such time, you will have to carry on without me, but you will help me. Yes, my friend, Vera'Far, you will help me."

Vera'Far, the High Master of Obsidian, glanced over at Blue and, after a pause, gave a curt but firm nod. "I shall, Rarokan, High Master of the Blue. I swear by my god, and yours, I will indeed help you in this mad endeavor, but only because it may just work."

"Good," Blue said with a grim look, though he was deeply pleased. Everything he had worked toward for so long had hinged upon this one moment. Had Obsidian refused him, his plan would have stood little chance of success. Even now, with Obsidian's assistance, the odds were long. "I want to show you the champion I have selected. Though he has been but a soldier his entire life, he is a complicated individual for a human."

"Your champion?"

"Yes," Rarokan said as he turned and stumped off, leaving Vera'Far behind. He stopped several feet away and turned back. "I have also tied another and his subsequent line to destiny. You will meet them both, for, from time to time, they or their descendants will need assistance."

Rarokan turned away and continued walking across the parade ground. A heartbeat later, he sensed that Vera'Far followed, and with that, the endgame of his design had begun.

Chapter One

There was a loud rap on the hardwood door. Karus looked up from the scroll he'd been reading, feeling somewhat annoyed. He was seated at a rough wooden table scattered over with a variety of scrolls.

"Come," Karus called.

Karus sat back as the door scraped open to reveal Centurion Tacitus Cestius Dio. A wash of cold air from the outer corridor flooded into the already chill room.

"Am I interrupting?" Dio flashed Karus a lopsided grin.

"Yes," Karus said.

"Good." Dio stepped into the small room, closing the wooden door behind him.

Though spring had arrived, the morning temperatures were still quite bitter. The small brazier that sat in the corner of the austere room did little to combat the cold, even before Dio had opened the door. Karus had no idea how the locals managed to thrive.

Dio glanced about the small room. Karus followed his friend's gaze. Except for the table, everything was neat. Karus liked it that way. There were two simple trunks and a camp cot. A sputtering yellow lamp hung from the ceiling. Another lamp sat on the table and provided light for Karus to read by. A thin stream of black smoke trailed toward the ceiling, where the numerous drafts caught it and swirled it about.

Karus's armor, maintained to perfection, hung from hooks on the back wall, as did several spare tunics. His shield rested against a wall. It prominently displayed the bull emblem of the emperor's Ninth Legion, Hispana.

Dio's eyes scanned the floor.

Karus knew there was not a speck of dirt or a particle of mud present, unlike the rest of camp, where dirt seemed to cling to everything. He had swept it clean.

"Is this an inspection?" Karus was being ironic. Dio was junior to him in rank.

"For the legion's senior centurion, you read too much." Dio's gaze traveled back to Karus. Dio reached down and picked up one of the open scrolls, narrowing his eyes as he studied the script. "Is this Greek?"

"Yes," Karus said with a sour note, "it is."

Dio made a further show of examining the scroll, though Karus well knew his friend was unable to read it. As it stood now, Dio could barely read Latin, and only enough so that he could manage his duties. Being able to read and write was required for promotion to the centurionate. After a moment, Dio lost interest and laid the scroll back down upon the table.

"A proper soldier should not read so much," Dio said. "It is not natural for those in our line of work."

"Only a fool ignores the histories," Karus said, "particularly those focusing on *our* line of work."

"So, I am a fool then?" Dio asked with a hint of a smile.

"Let's just say you are my kind of fool." Karus began to roll up the scroll he had been reading, along with the others scattered about the table. No matter how much he desired to continue reading, he had duties to attend to. It was time he began his day. "You should try reading sometime," Karus suggested. "You may learn something for a change."

"How to speak, and read, like a Greek?" Dio chuckled. "No thank you. I am a soldier, not some dishonest merchant. Besides, thanks to your brother, you are now of the equestrian class, with aspirations of nobility. I understand from good authority that all respectable patricians learn Greek. So, I find it fitting in a way that you can read this stuff."

Karus spared his friend an unhappy look as he finished securing the scrolls of the book he had been reading. He tied each off with a bit of string. Satisfied, he leaned over, stool creaking, and carefully placed each into a small trunk, which was filled with similar scrolls.

"What were you reading?" Dio asked curiously when Karus snapped the trunk closed.

"Polybius's *Universal History*," Karus said. "I have all forty books."

"All forty," Dio teased him. "You sound rather proud of that."

"I am," Karus admitted, and it was the truth. It had taken him years to collect all the historian's books. They were now the pride of his collection, and he was quite confident another complete set did not exist anywhere in Britannia.

"What does old Polybius have to say?"

"A great many things," Karus said.

"Such as?" Dio pressed.

"I was reading on Governor Galba, and his tenure in Hispana specifically."

"Galba?" Dio said. "Never heard of him, though I guess our legion has something in common with him."

"He was a bit before our time." Karus stood. He groaned with the effort, using his hands to help push himself upright and off the stool. He massaged the old wound on his thigh a moment, then glanced up at Dio. "What say we grab some grub? While we do, I will tell you all about him."

"I thought you would never ask," Dio said.

Karus was already dressed. In truth, he had been waiting for Dio. Over the winter, as in others past, this had become their morning routine. Though these days Karus's responsibilities were greater, the two still made the effort to continue the practice. Karus was the legion's senior centurion, the primus pilus of First Cohort. Dio, on the other hand, commanded Second Cohort, and was that unit's senior centurion.

Officially, a cohort numbered around four hundred eighty men. A cohort was lucky to come close to that number. The emperor's legions were always understrength. This was due to a number of factors, some of which included death, disability, retirement, or sickness. Or, in the Ninth's current circumstance, a lack of recruitment.

First Cohort, Karus's own, was a double-strength cohort and, out of all the formations of the legion, was maintained as close to full strength as possible. The First was the backbone of the legion and boasted the greatest concentration of veterans. Not counting those on the sick list, Karus commanded nearly eight hundred men.

He glanced back at the spare tunics hanging from pegs on the wall opposite his bed. He considered slipping on a second one. It was not uncommon in cold weather for legionaries to wear multiple tunics.

A quick glance at Dio changed his mind. His friend was wearing only one tunic, and besides, Karus was of the opinion that the men should see their centurions as tough, unflappable bastards whom even the frigid morning air failed to disturb.

Dio led the way out of Karus's quarters and into the short hallway beyond. Unlike standard cohorts, Karus shared the barrack with the five other centurions from his cohort.

Each commanded a double century, which consisted of a hundred sixty men, instead of the normal eighty. The doors were all shut, as most elected to sleep until the morning horn called the legion to assemble.

The two men stepped out into the bitter cold of the quiet early morning. His breath steaming, Karus glanced up at the sky, which had barely begun to lighten. Within the next hour, the legion would be roused from its nightly slumber, the quiet shattered. They started walking in the direction of the officers' mess.

"I bloody hate Britannia," Dio hissed as a bitter gust of wind whipped down a pathway between the buildings. It struck Karus like a slap on the face.

The legion was stationed at Eboracum, a permanent garrison town. Eboracum represented the northernmost point in the empire. It was almost as far away from Rome as you could get, and as such, it seemed to Karus as if the High Command had more often than not forgotten them.

"It is too damned cold out, that's for sure," Karus agreed as the two men weaved their way between buildings, following the pathways of the fortified camp toward the officers' mess. "My days could be spent in warmth and comfort."

Dio glanced over at him, amused. "Sicily again? I can't ever see you retiring."

Karus grunted in reply.

"You," Dio jabbed a finger at Karus, "love your job too much, as do I. Though to be perfectly honest, on a bitch of a morning like this, a warmer climate has some appeal."

Karus chuckled.

Dio was right, of course, but in truth Karus was thinking more and more on retirement. He was nearing the age when his usefulness to the legion would come to an end. Karus found that he was beginning to think on his responsibility to family over that of the empire. He could not admit this, of course, but he found himself dwelling increasingly upon his life after the legion.

"Trade army life for one of comfort and indolence?" Dio waved his hand dismissively. "Bah, you'd be bored in a week, and you know it."

"It might take more than a week," Karus chuckled.

"At least you have something to look forward to besides your army pension and a plot of land in some poor veteran's colony," Dio said. "You know it's not every centurion that has a brother who is exceptional at business."

"I don't know about that," Karus said.

Dio shot him a skeptical look. "You are seriously trying to tell me your brother is not good at what he does? He grew a small, shitty farming interest your father left him into one of the largest plantations on the island of Sicily."

Karus shrugged, admitting defeat.

"That's what I thought," Dio said. "Your father raised two exceptional sons, I think. Both became very good at their respective professions."

"I will agree to that," Karus said, reflecting upon his brother's success. There was an open invitation for Karus to join him, to help manage not only the plantation, but the family's growing investments.

Karus had put in twenty-two hard years of service. With each passing year, his aches and pains increased. This past winter had been especially trying for not only Karus, but the legion.

"Too much mud, wet, and cold," Karus grumbled unhappily. His toes had quickly become moist from the numerous small puddles along their path, a result of the half-thawed mud.

"Agreed," Dio said as they reached the officers' mess. He pulled the door open and held it for Karus. Light and warmth flooded out, as did a number of voices. A brown camp cat with white paws had been waiting for the door to be opened. It darted in as Karus stepped through, with Dio right behind him. The other centurion slammed the door closed as a gust of sucking wind attempted to keep it open.

The officers' mess consisted of a medium-sized common room filled with well-worn tables, basic stools, and benches. A kitchen, complete with several ovens and a fireplace for cooking, had been added as an afterthought. The kitchen was separated by a simple wooden door, which had been wedged open so that the heat from the ovens could warm the common room. Compared to the chill cold outside, the warmth was more than welcome. Karus's fingers and toes began to quickly ache. As the door closed, half a dozen heads turned toward them, looking up from their meals.

"Morning, Karus." A grim-looking officer in his late twenties nodded a greeting. The man's face had once been fair, but was now marred by a myriad of scars, the result of the previous summer's campaign. Valens had once been an extremely personable and outgoing officer. Hard action and unfortunate luck—which led him into the hands of their enemy—had changed his outlook on life, and his view of the locals.

"Valens," Karus returned the greeting, nodding to the prefect. "And how is the Ala Agrippiana Miniata this morning?"

Valens commanded the legion's cavalry wing, an allied auxiliary cohort.

"Still sleeping the night blissfully away along with the rest of the legion," Valens replied. "Though soon enough I will have my boys in the saddle."

"There is nothing quite like a day filled with drill and exercise." Dio clapped his hands together and rubbed them for warmth.

"Entirely correct," the cavalry officer replied, raising his cup of wine in toast to Dio. "Train 'em hard and often is what I say."

"Valens," Karus said, "as a proper infantry officer I freely admit to a ready dislike for the cavalry. That said, I've always found your attitude toward drill and training your men toward perfection somewhat refreshing."

The officers in the mess chuckled, and Valens gave Karus another nod as he sipped at his wine. The young officer had long since earned Karus's respect, which was not an easy thing to do. Unfortunately, after his rescue, Valens had developed a deep-burning hatred of the Celts. Friend or foe mattered little to the prefect. He hated them all just the same.

Valens was seated with another auxiliary prefect, Arminus Autun Otho, who commanded the First Nervorium. The First was a light infantry cohort. Otho's men had distinguished themselves over the last few years, primarily working as skirmishers and scouts. Otho, on the other hand, was a recent appointment, having transferred over from Second Legion, which was stationed farther south. Karus did not know him all that well. He hoped to change that, as Otho seemed competent enough. Only time, and hard action, would tell the man's true worth.

Karus received a few other nods and a handful of greetings as he and Dio made for a common table that had been set with bread, cheese, and jars of wine. He poured himself a cup of wine, which he knew was well-watered-down. The officer's mess fee, a meager charge, paid for it. If he wanted better-quality stuff, he had to go into town and pay for it himself. Karus took a battered wooden plate, grabbed a half loaf of bread, and then poured himself a liberal helping of garum sauce from a jar. Dio did the same, but instead took honey.

They settled on an empty table with two benches along the back wall.

Karus saw Dio grimace as he dipped his bread into the sauce. Karus took a large bite and chewed thoughtfully as he contemplated his friend. It was the same old story.

"You have to be the only legionary I know who is not overly fond of fish," Karus commented out of the side of his mouth, chewing. He loved garum and for the life of him could not understand why his friend loathed the stuff. In Karus's mind, the sauce was a gift from the gods. It simply made everything taste better.

"I believe that real men were meant to eat animals that walk the land, not swim in the sea," Dio replied with a look of distaste.

"It isn't because you can't stand the taste of fish, is it?" Karus asked, deliberately dabbing up some more of the sauce with his hunk of bread. He took another bite and chewed, raising an eyebrow.

"Fermented fish sauce is a taste that I fortunately have never acquired." Dio wrinkled his nose at the ripe smell coming from Karus's plate and dipped his own bread into the honey before taking a healthy bite. "You know perfectly well that summer we spent on those bloody ships cured me forever of fish."

"There was plenty to eat, that's for sure." Karus grinned, thinking back to the time they had helped to hunt down a small band of pirates operating along the coast. "I miss rays, and boiled lobster."

Dio grimaced again, shook his head, and then changed the subject. "Tell me about this Galba."

"He was governor of Hispana a few years back." Karus took another bite and waited 'til he had swallowed before continuing. "He forced this tribe, the Lusitanians, to surrender. They were real tough bastards and had been a thorn in Rome's side for some time, interrupting the imperial silver and lead supply. They even killed tax collectors."

"The usual stuff then," Dio joked, then sobered. "Worse than the Celts we have here in Britannia, do you think?"

"Now that is hard to say," Karus said, taking a deep breath as he thought on it a moment. "It is possible they were worse, but I doubt it. Anyway, after a difficult campaign, our friend Galba managed by force to finally convince the Lusitanians to come to heel and negotiate."

"I like these stories," Dio said, "where hairy-arsed barbarians get it into their thick skulls that it's easier to simply submit to Roman authority than resist."

"Well, they did."

"Quite sensible of them," Dio said, taking a pull of wine from his cup and washing down some bread. "I wish our bloody Celts had as much sense, but assuming they had any would be charitable."

"Well," Karus continued, drinking a swallow of the watered-down wine, "Galba made some demands. The Lusitanians met them and came as an entire tribe—men, women, children, entire families—to the governor and his army to submit. At the agreed upon spot, Galba ordered his legion to surround the tribe and made them turn over all of their weapons." Karus paused as he thought on what it would have been like. Romans typically left conquered peoples armed. In a ceremonial surrender, the key figures usually handed over their weapons. It was far better to allow the tribes and local kingdoms to deal with internal problems rather than have the Romans police all issues, such as banditry, in a province.

"Once the Lusitanians had given up their weapons," Karus continued, "the governor ordered the legion to move in and put the tribe in its entirety to the sword."

Dio paused mid-chew, eyeing Karus for a long moment. He continued to chew, though more slowly. He swallowed.

"Women and children too?"

Karus nodded.

"That is a bad bit of business," Dio said quietly. "Maybe they *were* worse."

"Perhaps," Karus said and took a small bite from his bread. They were quiet for a few moments.

"I would not have enjoyed that task," Dio said, "even if these Lusitanians had it coming."

"Neither would I," Karus agreed, "but this act by Galba represented more than simply the act of wiping out an entire people."

"How is that?" Dio asked, cocking his head to the right slightly. "They were enemies of Rome, and apparently got what was coming to them. Otherwise, the governor would not have executed them all. Am I wrong?"

"Galba's decision was flawed," Karus said. "Once the Lusitanians had surrendered and agreed to submit to Roman rule, they were no longer our enemies. There is the practicality of reputation to consider."

"How so?"

"Don't you think it sensible for Rome to honor her agreements?"

Dio thought on it, and then nodded. "By honoring our agreements, no matter how much the bastards deserved it, you are saying that it would help with future negotiations?"

"Exactly," Karus said, pleased that his friend had grasped the meaning of Galba's betrayal, which had really been to Rome herself. Despite Dio being barely literate, he was sharp as a finely edged weapon.

"So, by going back on his word… other peoples and tribes might not be so willing to negotiate with Rome?"

"Which would likely translate into more fighting," Karus said.

"More bleeding and dying by our boys then?"

Karus nodded somberly.

"Then Galba was a fool," Dio concluded, chasing down some bread with a liberal dose of wine.

"It was indeed bad business," Karus said. "Polybius wrote it down—"

"Wait," Dio said, holding up a hand. "I think I've heard this part before. Long ago, he wrote it down so that future generations would not make the same mistake. Is that what you were about to say?"

Karus chuckled. "You know me only too well."

The two officers ate in silence for a bit.

A pretty woman in her early twenties emerged from the kitchen, carrying a small pitcher. She caught Karus's eye, and he flashed her a smile of greeting. Dio turned slightly as she placed the pitcher on the serving table behind them.

"Morning, Keeli," Dio said, waving at her with his hand holding the hunk of bread.

"Dio," she said in a soft voice and then returned to the kitchen.

"A nice girl," Dio said. "Easy on the eyes too. I can understand why Felix likes her."

"He finally got around to buying her," Karus said. Gallus Felix was the senior centurion for Fourth Cohort, another close friend and old comrade.

"About time too," Dio said. "They've been sweet on each other for far too long."

"He's saved for six months," Karus said. "When the headquarters staff gets around to it today, Keeli will be his."

"I suppose he still plans to free her?"

"Yep. He's also petitioned to the legate to make her an honest woman."

"Well," Dio said, raising his cup in a toast, "I hope they make each other very happy."

"They both deserve happiness," Karus said with a glance at the open kitchen door. "Though I rather suspect she will have her hands full with Felix."

"Has it occurred to you it might be the other way around?"

Karus chucked.

"How are those new recruits coming?" Karus looked at Dio as he took a pull on his cup of wine.

"The other freed slaves?" Dio asked. "Well, they just finished their basic training. Surprisingly, none washed out, which I suppose is as good a sign as any." Dio frowned. "To be perfectly honest, I was not expecting the manumitted when I put in the request last fall for replacements. I tell you, it's just not right enlisting freedmen. Our recruits should be citizens."

"They will be when they complete their service. You'd reject a hundred eighty fresh recruits?" Karus asked him, already knowing the answer. "Just because the emperor saw fit to free a bunch of slaves, who had earned it?" The emperor had made legionary service a condition of their freedom.

"Well, when you put it that way, of course not," Dio said. "I'd never question the emperor's wisdom. Freed slaves or no, we will make proper soldiers out of them."

"I have no doubt you will," Karus said, speaking out of the corner of his mouth as he chewed.

"It is a good thing we have some time," Dio said. "This winter was rough and the legion needs work."

"Nothing that can't be fixed with drill, exercise, and training," Karus said. "Though the campaign season is fast approaching." Karus paused to take a sip of wine. "You should feel lucky, you know."

"I should?" Dio looked up at him with an amused expression.

"Half of Felix's recent batch washed out," Karus told him. "The legate sent the washouts to an auxiliary cohort somewhere down south, near the coast."

"Seems like recruits these days just don't measure up." Dio made a disgusted look. "Kids today are all soft types, raised on the government's dole back in the capital and expecting everything to be handed to them. They don't understand that nothing worthwhile comes easy. They have an inkling we lead a life of adventure, and they want that, but are not willing to work for it. It is sad."

"We don't lead an adventurous life?" Karus asked with a sudden grin.

"Bah," Dio said and tossed the remnants of his bread back onto his plate. "We seem to get only weak-kneed, spoiled children or, worse, convicts... and now slaves. It's not like when we enlisted. I tell you, standards have fallen."

"I fear you are correct."

Karus had enlisted at age fifteen. His father before him had been a centurion, who had mustered out after taking a near-crippling wound. Raised on stories of legion glory, unlike his brother, Karus had known he wanted to be like his father. When he grew old enough, his father had seen to it that Karus had a place with his old outfit, the Ninth.

"Nothing worth doing comes easy," Karus said, quoting a saying that centurions were fond of telling their men. "Though I can think of a recruit who once thought he had all the answers."

"You and Centurion Sadius beat that out of me," Dio said with a straight face. "But, as only age can confirm, I now know I have all the answers."

Karus chuckled.

"Who got your two new centuries?" Karus asked, leaning back on his stool.

"Cestus took the Fifth, and Mika the Ninth."

"Good men," Karus said with approval, "solid soldiers, and suitable choices for centurions."

"Say," Dio said, lowering his voice so only the two of them could hear. "What is going on with Julionus?"

"The legate?" Karus asked, and his mood darkened. "Nothing that I know of. Why?"

"When old Tarbo died, you should have been promoted to camp prefect."

Karus dipped the last bit of his bread into the dregs of the sauce on his plate. He was deeply unhappy about this subject, and did not answer. The camp prefect was, technically speaking, third in command of the legion. The last camp prefect had caught sick over the winter and had not recovered. Tarbo had been a good man, someone Karus respected.

It had been over a month since the new legate had arrived. As the senior centurion in the legion with the most experience, Karus felt that by rights the position should be his. However, for some unknown reason, Julionus had put off appointing the next camp prefect.

"Tarbo was one tough bastard," Karus said, unwilling to follow the path Dio had started down. "I was sorry to see him pass from this world."

"He was a good man," Dio agreed, taking the hint and looking down at his plate. "Remember that time he caught me sneaking those girls into camp?"

"I do." Karus chuckled at the memory. "He should have busted you back to the ranks."

"Only he couldn't without embarrassing himself," Dio said with a matching grin, "seeing as how one of them beauties was the girl he'd been seeing, bragging on for months."

"She was a looker," Karus said, thinking back on a happier time. "What was her name?"

"Cylenia."

"He got a little angry over that."

"I'd say." Dio's grin grew wider. "I'd be mad too, if I found out my girl was a common prostitute."

A muffled horn sounded in the distance. Both men looked in the direction of the door, as did those other officers present. The officer of the day had given the order for the legion to be rousted.

"Well," Karus said, standing stiffly. He waited a moment for the discomfort in his thigh to subside, then gathered up their plates and empty cups. He placed them in a wooden bucket by the kitchen door. Most of the other officers in the mess were doing the same.

Dio stood and stretched out his back.

"Duty calls," Karus said loudly to those centurions who had not yet moved from their tables. "Time to earn your pay, ladies."

⚜ ⚜ ⚜

"The legate will be with you shortly," the clerk said. He spared Karus a bored glance, then returned to his stool at a small table cluttered with scrolls and tablets. The clerk picked up a bronze stylus and began writing on a wax tablet. A scribe to his left wrote using ink on vellum.

Karus chewed on his lip as he looked around the headquarters. Half a dozen scribes and clerks worked feverishly at various tasks. To his eye, they seemed unusually busy. He idly scratched an itch at the back of his jaw as he studied them. Something was on the wind, he was sure of it.

He strolled casually over to one of the tables, where two clerks were working diligently. Both were legionaries who had been assigned to the headquarters staff because they could read and write. Rarely would the legate's staff be asked to fight, and it was a good thing, as their kind generally went soft after a few years of sedentary work. The physical requirements, though the same for every legionary, saw these men repeatedly excused from regular training and drill, something Karus despised.

He glanced down at one of the wax tablets that had just been placed aside. Reading it upside down, Karus saw it was an order to the legion's cooks to prepare pre-cooked rations. Interestingly, it detailed how much each man was to receive: four days' worth of salted pork, a portion of dried beef, a measure of bacon fat, vinegar, salt, cheese, hardtack biscuits, and wine.

Hardtack biscuits were an unfortunate staple of a legionary's life. Hardtack had the unique ability to remain unspoiled for quite some time and was the perfect wheat ration for extended marches. Despite that, Karus hated the biscuits, but had to admit when rations were short it beat starving. The biscuits were so hard that it was nearly impossible to chew without first soaking in some water or wine. A few years back, Karus accidently discovered another use for hardtack when he had once used an uncut block of the stuff to brain an enemy unconscious during a difficult moment. The incident was still the talk of the legion.

He glanced toward the closed door of the legate's office and wondered what was going on. Had the legion received movement orders from the governor? Surely the campaign would not start so early in the year. The ground was only partially thawed, far from firm. It had only recently gone from being frozen solid to having a soft and wet top layer. This time of year, individual cohorts could easily move about if needed, but not the legion in its entirety. Any type of massed movement would prove problematic, as the local road network would hardly hold up under the strain. The only reliable roads were all legion-built, and those were far to the south.

"Can I help you, sir?" One of the clerks had looked up from his work. Karus glanced down on the clerk, who had flipped several tablets over so Karus could not read their contents.

"No," Karus said curtly and stepped away. Something was definitely up, and it was likely the reason he had been summoned to headquarters right after the morning parade.

Well, Karus thought, he would just have to wait on the pleasure of the legate to learn more. He placed himself near one of the large braziers that had been set in the corners, providing the room its warmth. From the terrible smell, Karus recognized coal as the fuel source.

Coal was one of the truly rare commodities of value that Britannia had to offer. It provided more heat than wood, but was expensive. While the legate got coal, everyone else had to make do with peat, dried cow droppings, or wood.

Karus leaned his back against the wall and settled in to wait patiently, allowing the brazier to share some warmth. One lesson the legion taught every recruit was how to hurry up, and how to properly wait, for those seemed essential requirements for serving the emperor.

Just moments later the door to the legate's office opened, and out stepped a Celtic noble, dressed in a rich fur cloak over a chainmail shirt. Karus blinked in surprise. He knew most of the local nobles. All of them were arrogant, though some had adopted Roman ways, including dress. This one he had never met.

The Celt, a man in his late twenties, was tall and heavily muscled. He looked every part the barbarian, complete with gold jewelry, tattoos, and long black hair tied off in a single braid. He had the way of a born fighter.

The man spared Karus a disdainful glance as he retrieved his sword from one of the guards by the door. The Celt slipped the long sword's scabbard over a shoulder before turning away and stepping through the door, leaving the legion's headquarters behind.

"Is Centurion Karus here yet?" The legate's high-pitched voice reached out from his office. One of the clerks scurried from his desk to the door.

"He is, sir." The clerk turned and hurriedly motioned for Karus.

"Well, man, just don't stand there. Send him in."

Karus was already moving before the clerk could say anything further. He stepped through the door into the legate's office. It was a large room, easily five times the size of Karus's own personal quarters. A table had been placed near the back wall and served as the legate's desk. Several large trunks lined the walls. As the legate had his own personal quarters, these, Karus assumed, were for important papers. Another smaller table with two chairs had been placed off to Karus's left. Two braziers, burning coal, smoked lazily at the sides of the desk, providing a modicum of heat and a mildly nauseating smell in the closed room. The small windows were shuttered to keep the cold out.

Wrapped up in a heavy blue cloak, the legate was seated behind the desk. He was a slight man, and the cloak hung awkwardly on his bony frame. Papers, scrolls, and wax tablets were scattered haphazardly across the table. The legate was bent over a small map, studying it intently.

Julionus reminded Karus of a bird. The man had a large hooked nose, similar in shape to a beak. His eating habits had only reinforced that impression. Karus and several of the other senior centurions had recently been invited to dine with Julionus. The legate had the most annoying habit of picking through his food with his index finger and thumb until he found a choice morsel that he judged worthy enough to consume. It was a delicate gesture, but oddly reminded Karus of how a crow picked at the flesh of the dead, looking for the tastiest portion.

Karus marched toward the table. He straightened into a position of attention and saluted.

"Centurion Karus reporting as ordered, sir."

"Close the bloody door," the legate roared around Karus at the clerks and then bent back down to his examination of the map. There was the sound of hasty footsteps behind Karus, and then the door scraped closed. Karus remained at attention. After a moment, the legate looked up and straightened.

"Stand at ease."

Karus relaxed a fraction. The legate was still relatively new to the legion. Karus did not know the man well enough to take any liberties, lest he offend his new boss. Vellius Rufus Julionus commanded the legion in the emperor's name. His word was law.

Karus's eyes took in the map, which detailed the region north of the Ninth's garrison. No matter what official maps claimed, just a handful of miles farther to the north, imperial authority, and civilization as Rome knew it, came to an abrupt end. And whether they desired it or not, the legions were here to pacify the tribes and bring civilization to the island the Celts here called home.

"You want the job of camp prefect?"

Karus blinked, considered his reply for a fraction of a second, and then gave a mental shrug. Honesty was in order.

"I do, sir."

"You feel you have earned it?" There was a scheming look in the legate's eyes.

"I do, sir." Karus wondered where this line of questioning was going. He kept his face a mask.

The legate considered Karus for a long moment, saying nothing further. Julionus had access to his military record. There was no need to recount his battle honors and justify his fitness for the position. Besides, he was primus pilus of First Cohort. Only one who had repeatedly distinguished himself could ever hope to attain such a prestigious and coveted position.

"We don't fully know each other yet," the legate said. "I have read over your service history, but it tells me little about the man himself."

Karus refrained from frowning. The service record, in his opinion, told much.

"What would you like to know, sir?"

"I would not dream of putting you on the spot." The legate studied him for another long moment. Karus was becoming irritated. Julionus was playing a game with him. For what purpose Karus could not fathom, so he waited.

"Your service to me will tell me everything I wish to know," the legate finally said. "Effective immediately, you are promoted to 'acting camp prefect.' You will handle this additional duty along with your current responsibilities, those of leading First Cohort. This will continue at least long enough for me to determine a suitable replacement for the First."

Karus blinked, at first unsure he had heard the legate clearly. He almost asked for clarification, but bit his tongue as he struggled to contain his rage. There should be nothing "acting" about the position. By rights it should be his. He swallowed and cleared his throat.

"Thank you, sir," Karus said, doing his best to keep the anger from his tone.

"Good, good. I see you are moved by my magnanimous gesture." The legate gave him a smile that smacked of insincerity. "In a month's time, after we have worked together under some trying conditions, I hope to make your appointment permanent."

"Yes, sir." Then what the legate said registered. The fighting season was at least two months off. Something was definitely up, and he was about to find out what. Despite his rage, Karus leaned forward slightly, eager to learn more.

"Karus, an opportunity has presented itself." The legate's eyes fairly shone with excitement. "The Caledonian tribes are gathering just to the north of us, here in this valley." The legate pointed to the map on the table.

Karus leaned over to examine the spot where the legate was pointing. The location was uncomfortably close to Eboracum. The terrain in that area was extremely rugged, with rolling, misty hills. Karus had led a few patrols through those same hills. There were two large villages in that valley and another just beyond.

Though not yet imperial territory, the previous legate had found it was best to show Roman strength by marching a cohort or two through the valley on a regular basis. In fact, that very same valley had claimed the entirety of

Sixth Cohort over the winter. The legion had learned of the Sixth's fate when they found the heads of the officers mounted on wooden stakes before the gates of the garrison.

Tarbo's death, coupled with the loss of an entire cohort, had been a body blow to the men of the legion. Morale had been low ever since, and it had not picked up with the arrival of the new legate. Karus knew in time it would recover, but he found he was increasingly tempted to submit his retirement request despite his desire to achieve the most coveted position a ranker could reach, that of camp prefect. He sensed the day fast approaching when he would finally put the life of the army behind him.

Karus looked back up at the legate. He had lost more than a few friends in that ambush and wanted some payback.

"They intend to launch an attack against us here, before the campaign season begins. I understand they hope to catch us before the might of the governor's army can assemble," the legate said.

"I would be shocked if they could overcome the walls of the garrison," Karus said matter-of-factly. "Our enemy fights better in the field than against fortified positions. Courage is no substitute for technical knowhow and discipline."

"Agreed," the legate said with a nod. "That is my thinking as well."

"Besides," Karus continued, "attacking us here won't help them."

"What do you mean?" A frown line creased the legate's brow, and he cocked his head to the side.

"Well, sir, they could easily enough besiege us," Karus said, thinking it obvious but working carefully to keep it from his tone. "There is plenty of loot to be had in the town outside the walls. However, our supply depots would allow us to hold out for some time. Once the ground hardens, the governor will bring up the rest of the army to lift the siege. They won't stand a chance and will ultimately be forced to flee back to their mountains with little gain to show for their efforts."

"Yes, exactly," the legate said with a snap of his fingers. "That is why we must strike first."

Karus blinked in surprise.

"Strike them first, sir?"

"Yes," the legate said, full of the excitement of the moment. "That is the brilliance of my plan. You see, we strike them before they are ready and have fully assembled. By doing so, and smashing what forces they have gathered, we can scatter them to the winds before they can move against us. That way, when the governor brings up the army, the summer campaign will have a much easier time of it, courtesy of the Ninth, of course."

Karus thought it through, and was silent as he did so. After a moment, he noticed the legate looking at him with an odd expression and realized he had been frowning.

Karus, like most of the legion, wanted payback for the Sixth. The only problem was that Karus felt anything but excitement at Julionus's plan. In fact, he felt dread at the thought of taking the field so early, and without any ready support. The Celts knew those misty hills and mountains far better than the Romans.

"Sorry, sir," Karus said neutrally. "I was just thinking it through."

"Yes, well," the legate said, looking down at the map again, before glancing back up. "It is a rather bold and audacious plan, isn't it?"

"Yes, sir," Karus said, and then a thought occurred to him. The legate was new to the legion. He was the authority in the region. He determined when, and where, the legion moved. However, surely even he would not act without the governor's direct orders. Had he even consulted the governor? Karus considered how best to approach the matter.

After a moment, Karus continued. "Sir, I am sure the governor will bless your plan."

"He will," Julionus said, glancing back down at the map. "Once I have won my victory."

"You have not informed the governor?" Karus was so surprised that the words spilled from his mouth before his brain could catch up.

"There is no time for that," the legate snapped, clearly irritated that Karus had questioned him.

Karus said nothing. Julionus was new to Britannia and was clearly looking to make a name for himself back in Rome. It was an old story, and a dangerous combination.

"If we don't march immediately," the legate said, visibly calming himself, "the opportunity will be lost. Waiting for word from the governor will take too long. Karus, this is a once-in-a-lifetime opportunity. Even Tribune Saturninus recognizes it. Surely you can see that we must do this?"

"Sir," Karus said, and gestured at the map. "I feel it only prudent to point out the ground is not yet firm enough for the entire legion to march. The roads to the north are poor and in short order will be reduced to mud. We will be unable to cover ground quickly. At best, we will be moving at a snail's pace. If that occurs, and I expect it to, the element of surprise will be lost. We know the enemy has spies in the town. They will get wind of our intentions the moment we march through the gates, if not before. Once we get into those hills, that ground up there is rugged, hard, and difficult. It is their ground, sir, not ours. They will be waiting. They will have the advantage."

"I have intelligence that they have only managed to gather a few thousand warriors so far," Julionus said.

"Regardless of whether they know we are coming or not, we should easily outnumber them."

"What if the intelligence is wrong, sir?"

"They are barbarians," the legate countered with a heavy breath.

"Who wiped out Sixth Cohort this winter, in that very same valley. They may be undisciplined barbarians who wouldn't know how to use a latrine if instructed in advance, but that does not make them any less dangerous. And, sir, they are incredibly dangerous."

The legate's look hardened. Karus realized that he had gone too far.

"Do you fear the enemy?" Julionus asked, a contemptuous expression crossing his face.

Karus resented the implication. "No, sir. But I do have a healthy respect for them."

"They are nothing but uneducated and illiterate barbarians," the legate said. "I have studied them extensively and met with their representatives, including their nobles. My intelligence sources are unimpeachable. We are prepared, and they are not. All it will take is one quick lightning strike to the north. They will not expect such a bold move, before the traditional coming of the campaign season. There is no way they can stand against the might of this legion, especially with me in command." Julionus paused for a breath. "You may not know it, but back in Rome I am considered something of a tactician."

Karus could not believe what he was hearing. The legate had no military experience that he was aware of. The man had not even served as a junior tribune. Rumor had it Julionus's connections, and a hefty bribe, had secured him his current post. Thoughts of Sicily came to mind. Karus considered for a moment submitting his resignation.

Would the legate even accept it?

His thoughts hardened. Karus loved the Ninth. The legion was his home, and she was going into danger—mortal danger, if Karus was correct. How could he abandon her now?

"Did you know that the emperor is on his way to the island?" the legate said.

"Hadrian is coming here, sir?"

"It is not widely known yet, but indeed he is." The legate picked a cup off of the table and sloshed the contents around a moment before taking a liberal sip. "Before I left Rome, barely three months ago, he told me himself." The legate paused. "I fully intend to present him with a victory. You, Centurion Karus, will help me deliver that victory."

"Yes, sir," Karus said stiffly. The legate saw only the glory of a victory, the adoration of Rome, and further advancement waiting within his grasp; perhaps that even included the purple toga. Julionus would not be the first legate to crave the emperor's chair. He was gambling with the legion and their lives on a fool's errand, and Karus did not know how to stop it.

"I have no doubt we will bring the enemy to battle," Julionus said, a fervent look in his eyes. "I have had the omens read. They are auspicious for a victory. The gods are on our side."

Karus said nothing.

"Have no fear. We shall prevail."

"Yes, sir."

The door opened, and both men turned.

"Ah," the legate said in a delighted tone. "Tribune Saturninus, I am so pleased you could join us."

The tribune had arrived with Julionus. He was young, in his twenties, and handsome. The tribune had a ready smile and wore an expensive, thick fur robe over his tunic. He was no different than many of the other tribunes who came to serve with the legion—rich, powerful, and well-connected. For Saturninus, serving with the Ninth was a stepping stone to public office or higher military command.

"It is I who am pleased, sir," Saturninus said. A clerk closed the door behind him. "Why, Karus, my favorite centurion, it is good to see you."

"Sir," Karus said neutrally. Since the first moment he had met Saturninus, the tribune had been nothing but friendly to him. That worried Karus, for Saturninus was clearly a player of politics, and such games were dangerous. Roman patricians rarely played nicely with each other. When their politics became violent, bystanders frequently suffered in their stead.

"I trust I have not missed anything?" Saturninus turned back to the legate.

"No, no," the legate said, waving a negligent hand. "It is nothing we did not cover last evening. I've just explained my plan to the centurion."

"And what do you think, Karus?"

"It is a bold plan, sir," Karus said, and Saturninus turned his gaze on Karus, regarding him curiously. He was half tempted to bring up his objections again, but common sense intervened. He remained silent.

"Yes, well," Julionus said, "I do have a talent for strategy."

The legate went to a side table, where there was a fine ceramic pitcher, and poured some wine into two cups. He then walked back and handed one to Karus and the other to Saturninus before picking his own back up from the desk.

"A toast, to our success and victory." The legate held up his cup and drank deeply. Karus hesitated a moment before taking a sip of the fine wine the legate had provided. He found it tasted like ash but, not being one to ever waste any type of wine, forced it down with a single gulp. The legate took back the cup with a disapproving expression.

Saturninus sipped his own. "A very fine vintage, sir."

"Thank you," Julionus said, looking down at his own cup. "Sentinum is my favorite wine. I brought it with me all the way from Rome."

"Sentinum, really?" Saturninus took another sip and appeared to savor it. "Perhaps you would be kind enough to spare me some? Good-quality wine is hard to come by on this miserable island."

The legate looked uncomfortable with the idea, and then caught Karus's eye. He flashed another insincere smile Karus's way.

"Fear not, Centurion," the legate said, returning the cup to the table with the pitcher. "I have planned everything out. We even have the benefit of local guides to show us the way. Between the legion and my overstrength auxiliary cohorts, we will have over thirteen thousand highly trained men. With such a powerful force at my command, the enemy cannot hope to stop us."

"Yes, sir," Karus said. He wanted to object, but it was not his place. The legate had made up his mind. Karus, no matter how much he disagreed, was bound to support Julionus in his mad fantasy.

"Serve me well, and when we return, the position of camp prefect will be yours," the legate continued.

"Thank you, sir," Karus said, almost biting the words out. *If* we return, he wanted to say.

"Very good," the legate said, seemingly pleased with himself. "I will have orders issued within the next few hours. We march in two days."

Two days? Karus was rocked by this news. His mind raced over all that would need to be done. Supplies had to be drawn from the depots. The legion's train had to be put together and packed. That alone usually took a week of careful planning, supervision, and work, especially after a long winter with little activity. Not to mention the time needed to check equipment and ensure that anything found deficient was repaired or replaced. There were a million things that needed doing, and with his new responsibilities, much of that would fall on his shoulders.

"Now, I am sure you have a lot to do," the legate said with another smile that Karus felt had been intended to reassure. It had the opposite effect. "You are dismissed."

Karus drew himself back up to a position of attention and saluted crisply. The legate did not bother to return his salute, but had turned back to his map and his fantasies. Karus eyed Julionus for a long second, then turned on his heel and left the office, remembering to close the door behind him. Before he closed the door, he saw Saturninus, cup in hand, walking over toward the fine ceramic pitcher.

Karus passed the clerks, barely noting their frenetic activity, and stepped out of the headquarters and into the street. The chill snap of the wind was a shock, yet Karus paid the cold no mind. He glanced around and saw Dio waiting for him just a few feet away. The other centurion had been leaning casually against the cracked, plastered wall of the headquarters building, flipping a silver coin into the air. A brown cat nosed its way around Dio's feet, rubbing itself on one of his legs before walking off. Clearly his friend was hoping for a scrap of news.

"That bad?" Dio pushed himself off the wall and approached with a trace of a lopsided grin. He rolled the coin absently over his knuckles. "You look like your pay was just docked."

"He promoted me to 'acting camp prefect'," Karus said. "And we march in two days."

"What?" Karus could see Dio was genuinely shocked at this news. "Is there trouble to the south?"

"No," Karus said and gestured in the direction the legion would be going. "We march north."

Dio was silent as he absorbed this new information. "In two days? The entire legion?"

"Yes," Karus said unhappily, and began making his way back toward his quarters. Dio fell in beside him, looking as troubled as Karus felt.

Karus's mind raced as they walked. He had to get not only his own cohort as ready as possible, but the entire legion. Just thinking over all that needed to be accomplished in the limited amount of time available made him weary.

"It's going to be a nightmare," Dio said. "The ground is far from firm. Add a few thousand sandals, carts, horses, and hooves... it will be a bloody quagmire. We won't be moving anywhere fast."

"I know," Karus said.

"Does the legate understand that?"

"I did my best to convey my concerns," Karus said. He was unhappy with himself for not being more assertive. However, he also realized that had he done so, the position of camp prefect would have gone to someone else. At the very least, the position was his, even if it was only in an "acting" capacity. As camp prefect, in the days ahead he might be able to do some good. Perhaps he might even be able to mitigate some of the potential disaster that he felt was in store for the legion.

"Are we to have any support?"

Karus stopped and looked over at his friend. There was genuine concern in the other centurion's eyes.

"No," Karus said heavily. "We will be on our own, with only our auxiliary cohorts."

"Madness," Dio whispered.

"Nevertheless," Karus broke eye contact, turned away, and started moving again. "Those are our orders."

Dio did not follow.

Karus took a deep breath of the cold bitter air as he walked. He resolved to make an appropriate sacrifice to the gods. If he did right by them, hopefully they would do right by him. A little fortune, he reasoned, might just come in handy.

Chapter Two

"Very impressive," Saturninus said amidst the solid crunch of many sandals.

"Yes, sir," Karus said, and in truth he agreed. They were standing just beyond the outskirts of Eboracum, alongside the main road that ran north. They were so close you could still smell the strong stench of habitation, piss, and shit mixed with smoke. The sun had just come up, and yet it was still bitterly cold.

The legion was marching one formation at a time out of the town and into the countryside. Hundreds of civilians had turned out to watch the spectacle. They cheered as each cohort, standards held proudly to the front, emerged from the tightly grouped buildings that had grown up around the garrison.

Children scampered about in excitement. They ran along in packs or marched next to the legionaries, pretending to be small soldiers. Others, in a more wretched condition, begged shamelessly for food or coin. Most were ignored. One who got too close received a swift kick from an irritated optio, which propelled the urchin face first to the ground. Picking himself up, he quickly gave the marching column some distance. All in all, it was nothing Karus had not seen before. Still, Karus reflected as his eyes roved over the scene, it was impressive.

First cohort had already passed them by, along with Second and Third. Fourth was coming out now, Felix at the cohort's head. No words were exchanged, but he saluted Saturninus and Karus. Each century behind him was arranged in neat, ordered blocks, the centurions in turn offering a salute as they passed.

As the men streamed by in ordered ranks, they shouldered their heavy marching yokes, which included a small pack filled with a few meager personal possessions, a saw and/or an entrenching tool, and haversacks stuffed with precooked rations. Most of their equipment was carried on the shoulder and tied or strapped to the yoke. This included cooking utensils and implements, canteens filled with either water or wine, a cloak, and a rolled up gray woolen blanket. Each also carried a stake intended for the fortified encampment that would be constructed at the end of the day's march. Shields in their protective canvas covering had been strapped to their backs. Combined with their armor, it was an incredibly heavy load, and Karus could feel the vibration of their steady tramp through his sandals.

Karus admired the discipline and precision. It was one of the reasons he loved the legion. All worked toward a common, unified goal: service to the empire. Eyes stayed fixed to the front as Felix's legionaries moved by, dressing tight with ranks close-ordered. Yet, just a few miles into the countryside, the marching order would be relaxed, as it always was when not on parade. The spacing for each unit would stretch out, giving the men a little bit of leg room for the long miles ahead. The men would be permitted to remove their heavy helmets. These would hang by ties from their necks. Talking would also be permitted to help pass the monotony of the march.

"The majesty of Rome is before us," Saturninus said in a tone that was both wistful and tinged with awe. "I love it so, and am proud to be part of it."

Karus glanced up at the dark and menacing clouds that hovered above. "That majesty is about to get rained upon."

Saturninus, loosely holding the reins of his horse, turned to Karus and frowned. The tribune, in his ornate armor, cut a striking figure in the early morning light. "Your mood is rather black this morning."

"Is it?"

Saturninus barked out a laugh. "Why, Karus, I do so enjoy your company. You could try a little harder at being more optimistic though. It is all about attitude, and you of all people should understand Fortuna notices such things."

Karus grunted and turned his gaze upon the Fourth.

"I wonder, were you out late celebrating with the low-hanging fruits of civilization?" Saturninus shot him a wink. "I certainly hope you were, as it will be the last you see for some weeks." Saturninus chuckled at his own joke and swung his eyes along the ramshackle buildings. "Civilization, if only Eboracum could be called that. What a shit hole."

"What was that about attitude, sir?"

Saturninus chuckled again, then sobered. "Seriously, Karus, what is it? Did you drink too much last night?"

"No," Karus said, letting out a long breath. "I was not out drinking. There was too much that needed doing."

"Then what ails you this fine morning?" Saturninus actually seemed perplexed. "After a long, hard winter, I would think you would be more than eager to march out after Rome's enemies."

"The ground," Karus said.

"What about it?" Saturninus glanced down at the dirt beneath their feet. They were standing on the edge of a farmer's field. Behind them, the remains of last year's crops rotted.

"It's wet."

"So?" Saturninus said. "It usually is at this time of year, especially here in the north. Gods, Karus, the snows only just melted. You should be happy we're not marching through two to three feet of frozen white."

"That's my point." Karus used a sandal and moved some of the dirt aside at his feet. It was wet, almost muddy. He scraped some more away until he reached a semi-solid layer. "A few inches down and the soil is still partially frozen. Add a little rain, thousands of feet, and this road before us will become a gods awful mess."

Saturninus glanced down again and then over at the legionaries marching by. He was silent for several long moments.

"Well," Saturninus said, "it's just a bit of mud. It can't be all that bad."

"A few miles to the north," Karus said, "that road becomes little more than a dirt track. I tell you, it will not hold up. If we are lucky, our advance will slow to a crawl."

"You think so, truly?" Saturninus turned skeptical eyes upon Karus. "Perhaps the road will surprise you."

"I only wish it were so," Karus said. "I told the legate as much."

Saturninus turned a surprised expression on Karus and barked out a laugh. "You really don't want to be camp prefect, do you?"

Karus was about to respond when the crowd cheered loudly and drew their attention. The legate was riding out from the town, several of his junior tribunes—most mere boys, spoiled brats of Rome's elite—riding just behind him. This was their first taste of military service.

The spectating crowd erupted again in a great cheer at the sight of Julionus, as they had the legion's Eagle some time before. The Eagle had already marched past with the First and was now out of view and likely some miles ahead.

Julionus was clearly enjoying the moment and waved back as he rode the length of the crowd, which shouted even louder. He slowed his horse and seemed to be savoring the moment, almost as if he were riding at the head of a triumph back in Rome. These days, only the emperor and his close family were permitted triumphs. Successful military commanders were instead awarded ovations, a lesser, more humbler form of a triumph.

Having reached the end of the crowd, Julionus spotted Karus and Saturninus along the roadside. He nudged his horse into a speedier gait and steered the animal in their direction. Karus stiffened to attention and gave a salute. Saturninus offered a lazy salute that the legate did not seem to mind.

"Ah, Saturninus," Julionus said in a pleased tone, "and Karus. A glorious sendoff, don't you think? A perfect start to my campaign."

"Quite," Saturninus said. "Only what you deserve, sir."

"True, true," the legate said absently, his horse sidestepping nervously as the crowd cheered again, at what Karus could not tell. Julionus glanced around at the men marching by. "We shall earn it though. There will be hard going ahead, including, I fear, bitter fighting. Still, we will shatter those uneducated barbarians to the north and win a great victory for Rome."

"The senate and emperor," Saturninus said, "surely will honor your tactical acumen with an ovation."

That brought a smile to Julionus's lips. "Ride with me, would you, Tribune? I would value your counsel on the coming campaign."

Saturninus mounted up as the legate turned his horse and nudged the animal ahead with his heels. He spared a curt nod to Karus. Julionus's party followed, like dogs after their master before the hunt.

"Cheer up, Karus," Saturninus said in a confident tone as he nudged his horse into a walk. "Even if it does rain on us and we have to fight through a little mud, the legate knows what he's doing."

"Aye, sir," Karus said with mixed feelings. "I am sure he does."

Saturninus frowned at that, but said nothing further as he turned away and followed after the legate.

Hands curling into fists, Karus watched the tribune ride off. His anger flared at the legate's recklessness. This entire expedition was a mistake, and yet there was absolutely nothing that could be done to stop it. The only thing Karus could do was do his duty and be ready for whatever came his way. He took a deep breath and slowly let it out. Karus relaxed his hands.

The last centuries of the Fourth had exited the town. A party of locals rode by next, working their way around the Fourth's trailing century and out into the field. One spared Karus a look as they clopped close by. These were the local guides the legate had spoken about. He was sure of it.

Karus recognized the noble he had seen in headquarters. The man looked just as disdainful, hostile even, but Karus got the impression he was being studied intently. Karus returned the other's gaze with equanimity and held it. After a few moments, the Celtic noble's eyes softened and he gave a nod that was almost respectful. Then the party was past.

Idly wondering what that was about, Karus glanced back at Eboracum. Shortly the Fifth would exit the town and then the newly reconstituted Sixth, whose job it was to escort the supply and baggage train. After these would come the camp followers and then the remainder of the legion's cohorts. The auxiliaries would come last. Karus took a deep breath of the cold air and let it out in a long stream that steamed. He then started forward after the Fourth, picking up his pace to catch up with the line of march and Felix. There were long miles ahead and he felt it would be good to start them with an old friend.

Karus glanced once again up at the low hanging clouds and then at the first of the misty hills in the distance. He wondered what was in store for his beloved Ninth, other than a miserable and difficult muddy march.

⚜ ⚜ ⚜

Karus scratched an itch on his chin as he drew a foot out of the sucking morass of mud that had once been a dirt track. Both of his legs were thoroughly caked up to the knees. The Celts called this a road, but having had a hand in the construction of a fair number over his long career, Karus knew better. It was little more than a dirt trail that cut through the stunted grass and scrub.

Thousands of feet had churned the way into a veritable sea of mud. The road followed a winding path north, snaking its way around the craggy hills of the region. Centuries of sheep herding and grazing had denuded much of the land, so the rugged, rocky hills bore only a scratch coating of inedible bushes and what passed for grass. It was a depressing sight.

Karus seriously wondered whether this land produced more rocks than crops, as evidenced by the numerous stone walls hemming in the fields they had passed as the line of march moved from valley to valley. The farms themselves were mean affairs, really nothing more than round stone huts with thatched roofs. There had been few animal pens, which meant the residents most likely kept their animals in the huts with them at night and during inclement weather. The handful of villages, filled with clusters of huts, were just as mean, the only difference being a stout palisade for shared defense meant to withstand the occasional raid by a rival tribe.

Karus took another difficult step, and his sandaled foot sank with a squashing sound. He had long since lost feeling in his feet and toes, but that was nothing he had not experienced before. As long as the temperature did not dip too low and he was able to thoroughly dry off his feet later, he would be fine. Numb feet were just another of the numerous discomforts a legionary suffered on a regular basis.

Karus had once walked more than six miles with a three-inch wound in the bottom of his left foot. He had even managed at one point during that painful ordeal to run. It had been either that or get left behind to the not-so-tender mercies of the enemy.

Worse was the surgeon's care, when his century had returned to camp. The surgeon, a kindly older man named Cleotis, had thoroughly rinsed the wound out with a vinegar solution. That had been incredibly painful. But what followed was worse. Cleotis had scrubbed the wound clean with a wool towel before once again rinsing it, and then sewing it up. There had been no milk of the poppy available. Karus had felt it all. If he could handle that, he knew he could easily tough it out with numb feet.

Karus glanced around. Fourth Cohort, with whom he had been marching for the past hour, slogged along next to him. As camp prefect, he had taken to visiting a number of different cohorts each day to help keep up morale, and also get a sense for the general mood.

The heads of the men were down, and there was little talking. Karus did not like what he was seeing. The legion had left Eboracum just five days before, and each day had proven a tremendous struggle. Karus sensed a growing exhaustion overcoming the legion. He was also beginning to sense apathy.

A man to his left abruptly slipped and fell face first into the brown mire. No one moved to help him up. They just continued to march by, one legionary even stepping over his fallen comrade.

"Easy there, son." Karus helped the legionary up, careful to not slip as he pulled the man to his feet.

"Thank you, sir." The legionary was covered in mud. He took a moment to wipe the mud from his face with a hand. Glancing over the man's armor, Karus knew he had a hell of a job ahead of him this evening to clean it. They all would.

"Paro, right?"

"Yes, sir." The legionary registered surprise that Karus knew his name. A few other heads turned at the exchange. Though his body was slowly starting to catch up with his age, Karus's mind was sharp as a tack. He prided himself in his ability to have instant recall, and a near perfect memory.

"Centurion Felix says good things about you." Felix had said no such thing. Karus simply remembered Felix dressing the legionary down during parade a few mornings ago.

"Thank you, sir." The man puffed up at that the compliment.

"Keep on marching, boys," Karus said loudly so that all of those within earshot could hear. "Only a few more hours left before we make camp and you will be out of this wretched mud."

The men let out a cheer at that. Karus nodded to himself with satisfaction. They may be tired, but they were the best dammed soldiers around.

"Come on, son," Karus said to Paro. He patted the legionary on the arm, and together they started forward again.

Tribune Saturninus clopped by, mounted on a fine brown horse, a handful of yards to Karus's right. The tribune was doing his best to ride where the ground was slightly firmer. Even so, his horse was having some difficulty with the ground occasionally giving way. It made for an uneven and disjointed ride.

Saturninus saw Karus, slowed his horse, and flashed a smile of greeting. In his tribune's armor, free of the grime everyone else seemed covered with, and mounted on a fine horse, he cut an impressive figure. Back in Rome, Karus was confident Saturninus's looks had made him popular with the women, at least the ones he did not pay.

"Karus, my favorite centurion," Saturninus said cheerfully, with a glance to the unit standard just ahead. A frown crossed his face. "I don't believe Fourth Cohort is yours, is it?"

"As camp prefect, they are all mine," Karus said, stepping over to the tribune, who had not stopped his horse. The pace was just slow enough for Karus to walk by his side. "When duty permits, I make a point to spend time with different units."

"I see." Saturninus tapped his jaw with his free hand. Karus noticed that Saturninus wore gloves against the cold. "Making the rounds, then? How very sensible of you."

"I think so," Karus said. "It allows me to check in on each unit—to spend some time with the men, and also their officers."

"You should really get a horse, you know," Saturninus said with a glance at Karus's legs, which were slathered in muck, and then winced in an overly dramatic manner. His horse slipped, and then sidestepped nervously. The tribune patted the neck of the animal in an attempt to calm it. "With a good mount, you would be able to get around easier, don't you think?"

With his new post, Karus could very well have requisitioned a horse. He was no stranger to riding, and with the money his brother had forwarded to him, he could have afforded a good-quality mount.

"I prefer to march with the men." Karus shrugged. "I might miss something if I spend all my time on horseback. Besides, I get paid for a living, sir."

It was the tribune's turn to shrug. Saturninus glanced up at the low-hanging cloud cover. It was a very gray day and was threatening to rain again. He then looked back over at Karus, and the smile was back.

"Lovely day, don't you think?"

"Exceptional, sir," Karus said, forcing enthusiasm into his voice. "I wish every day could be just as fine."

"Ha," the tribune chuckled. "At least there is one centurion in this legion who has a semblance of humor."

"I thought you enjoyed my company for my intellect?"

"I never said that," Saturninus said with mock seriousness. "Though to be perfectly honest, you are well-read, and about the only one worth having discourse with, the legate excepted, of course."

"What of the other tribunes?" Karus asked, referring to the legate's aides.

Saturninus waved his hand dismissively. "Not a thought in their heads, and sadly, they are without guile. Those spoiled children are not worthy of my attention, nor my wit."

Karus looked closely at the tribune. Though Saturninus had said the last in a lighthearted manner, Karus suspected there was truth in it. Saturninus came from a better family than the other tribunes on Julionus's staff.

Karus decided to change the subject. "Five days in, and we're fairly crawling along." He glanced back at the men doing their best to slosh through the churned-up mud just feet away. "The enemy knows we are coming, sir."

"Karus," Saturninus breathed heavily, looking about ready to say something. He pulled his horse to a halt, glanced around, and then leaned toward Karus. "Has it occurred to you the legate may be right?"

Karus was silent as he thought things through. "Right or not, it is my duty to carry out his orders."

"Spoken like a true centurion," Saturninus said, then gestured up the road. "If they are waiting for us, then there will be a battle. If the legate is right, everyone shares in the glory of victory."

"And if there is no victory?"

Karus studied the tribune's face carefully. Saturninus was difficult to read, but his eyes narrowed before he broke eye contact.

"Pray there is." The tribune nudged his horse into a slight trot, leaving Karus behind.

Karus took a deep breath and stepped off the muddy track onto a large rock. He stood there a moment, relishing the feeling of being out of the slime. A small rock-studded hill rose to his right, perhaps forty feet in height. The rock he was standing upon at some point had rolled down its craggy slope. He reasoned the hill would provide a good view of the surrounding countryside, and Karus decided he wanted a look.

He worked his way up, climbing and scrambling the last few feet to its summit. His legs, already tired, burned with the exertion as he climbed.

Karus puffed out heavy breaths that steamed in the cold morning air as he stood atop the hill's crest and surveyed the scene before him. The legion stretched out in either direction like a great long snake. The Ninth, along with her auxiliary cohorts, numbered almost thirteen thousand men. That did not take into account a like number of camp followers, skilled labor, and the contractors hired to manage the legion's main supply train. Karus put his hands on his hips as he studied the column. A legion under march was a massive undertaking, and the sight never ceased to impress him. When he retired, he would miss this.

"Just had to pull yourself out of the mud, didn't you?"

Karus turned to his left to see Felix making his way up the hill toward him. Standing a little over five feet ten inches, Felix was not a large man, at least by legionary standards. He was fit, trim, and hard as a rock. In the middle of this strange land, Karus found it comforting to see his friend.

Karus nodded in greeting to the senior centurion of the Fourth Cohort as he made it up the last few feet. Karus's thoughts were on the slow snaking movement of the legion. It was, as he had predicted, a snail's pace.

"A nice perch you have up here, Karus." Felix set down his marching yoke and straightened back up, stretching as he did so. "I saw you make the climb and thought I would join you. What brings you up here?"

"I wanted one last look before I make a decision on retirement."

Felix barked out a laugh. "Sicily again?"

Karus gave a curt nod.

"The legion is the only life for you, my friend. We both know it, no matter how miserable the conditions under which we serve."

"True," Karus said. Felix was right, of course. The legion was his life. But there would come a time when the legion would judge his use at an end.

"Remember that fight a few years back?" Felix said, apparently sensing Karus's melancholy mood. "The one where our old cohort was cut off and surrounded by a couple thousand Caledonians?"

Karus looked over at his friend, wondering where he was going with this.

"You remember that fight," Felix continued, "where it hailed?"

Karus nodded, recalling the desperate afternoon, the terrible weather of the day.

"A little mud is nothing," Felix said, gesturing down at the legion marching by, "compared to the conditions we fought under."

"If I recall..." Karus expelled a long breath. "First it rained, then snowed, and finally hailed frozen chunks of ice the size of a denarius."

"I can still hear the hail bouncing off my armor," Felix said, a faraway look in his eyes. "If only that ice had been real money, we would have cleaned up."

Karus chuckled. "We sure fought like we were protecting a treasure in that village. It was a good thing the palisade was still intact or..." Karus let his words trail off. There had been so many close calls over the years. It had left him wondering when his own fortune would run out. In a profession that saw the majority of his peers eventually crippled or killed, Karus had managed not only to survive, but prosper. As he looked down upon the column of march,

Karus wondered... did he have any fortune left, or would this campaign be his last?

"That was one tough day," Felix said. "A real bitch."

"Any day you can walk away from a fight is a good day."

"There were a lot of men who did not," Felix said quietly. "We both left comrades behind in that shitty little village."

"It was not a good day for them." Karus returned his gaze to the legion.

A moment later, a soft drizzle began to fall from the low-hanging gray clouds that scudded by overhead. The clouds were so close, Karus felt he could almost reach up and touch them. He glanced up, raindrops striking his face, and then, with a heavy breath, looked over at Felix with a sour expression.

"You just had to say something, didn't you?"

"Don't blame me," Felix said, holding out his hands. "This is the work of the gods."

"No doubt."

Karus's eyes were drawn to movement in the distance. About half a mile away, a squadron of cavalry was pursuing a handful of native horsemen. Felix followed Karus's gaze. In moments, both the squadron and natives were gone from view, having ridden over the crest of a small hill.

"I guess," Felix gestured at the legion moving slowly by beneath them, "there was no way the natives could have missed us."

"No," Karus said. He had been deeply troubled since they had marched from Eboracum. There was something ominous looming over the legion. He felt it in his bones. "They could hardly have missed us."

"What have our cavalry scouts found?" Felix asked, looking over at Karus.

Karus considered changing the subject, but shrugged mentally. Felix was a trusted friend, and he deserved the truth.

"We've been shadowed ever since Eboracum." Karus shot the other centurion a significant glance. "Our cavalry has done their best to drive the enemy scouts off, but…"

"It does not bode well for what is waiting up ahead," Felix finished.

"No, it does not," Karus said. "It is almost as if they were waiting for us to move out."

Felix glanced down at the ground, digging his sandal into the soft soil and displacing a tuft of brown grass.

"This is poor country," Felix said with an unhappy glance around. "There is not much to be had here other than slaves and those rocks that can be burned."

"Despite the look of this hard land," Karus said, "Britannia is rich in resources. There is lead, tin, coal, animal hides to be had, a constant stream of slaves for the plantations and mines. And, of course, those oysters you love so much. They fetch a high price back in Rome."

Felix grunted. "They live like animals and have so little. I just don't understand what drives them."

"Freedom," Karus said simply. "Religion too. The druids encourage them to fight for both."

"The druids are the real savages in this land." Felix spat on the ground in disgust. "We should kill them all on sight."

"We're to take them alive," Karus said firmly. "Make sure you remember that."

"The gods only know why." Felix kicked at the soft turf, sending a spray of mud and small stones down the hill. "If we fell into their hands, you know what they would do to us."

Karus looked over at his friend, and their eyes met. Since being posted to Britannia, both had seen the horrors and cruelties perpetrated by the druids, against not only Romans but their own people as well, particularly those friendly with Rome. The druids worked through terror. They seemed to revel in it, and anyone who was sane, in Karus's opinion, feared them.

"Dying would be the least of our concerns," Karus said quietly.

"Karus." Felix lowered his voice, though there was no one within earshot to hear them. "I have a very bad feeling about this expedition. The land around here is deserted, the farms and villages empty."

"Yes," Karus agreed. He had had half a dozen similar conversations over the last two days. "They are undoubtedly massed, waiting for us somewhere ahead."

"The legate knows this?" Felix asked. "And still we march on?"

Karus thought for a moment on how he wanted to phrase his next words. "The legate still believes he can catch the enemy unprepared. He is listening to his native guides."

Felix gave Karus a sharp look and worked his jaw, as if he had something to say.

"He does not listen to me," Karus added, before Felix could speak.

"What about Saturninus?"

"That man is nothing more than a young politician, practicing at war. I fear he only desires to further his career with an easy victory," Karus said.

"We may not be marching toward a victory," Felix said. "Have you seen the camp followers recently?"

Karus shook his head. He had been too busy over the last couple of days to check on them. He needed to do so. After the legion made camp for the night, he resolved to make it happen. The camp followers, like the men, needed to see him.

"The cold and damp conditions are starting to take a toll. It is only a matter of time before sickness begins to take root."

Karus glanced over at Felix, who looked as frustrated as he felt. Felix's new wife was amongst the followers. Karus could only wonder how his friend was feeling about that. This was one of the reasons why he had never taken a long-term woman, nor started a family. Besides, Karus did not like children.

"Why bring them?" Felix asked. "This was supposed to be a quick strike north. We defeat the enemy and return. They could have waited for us in Eboracum. Why bring them?"

"I don't know," Karus admitted. "The legate made that decision."

"We should send them back," Felix said. "Before it becomes too dangerous."

"I fear it already is," Karus said and turned to lock gazes with his friend. "We should all turn back."

"Perhaps you can try again with the tribune?" Felix suggested. "He might be able to reason with the legate."

"As I said, Saturninus hopes the legate is right," Karus said with a heavy breath. "I have had multiple talks with him about this to no avail. He is no military man. He can't see the trouble we are marching into."

"Then there is nothing to be done?"

"Not until we contact the enemy in some strength," Karus said. "Hopefully the legate will then see some sense and pull us back to Eboracum."

"Do you think he will?"

"I don't know."

Felix shook his head.

"That is why you must keep your men as ready as possible," Karus said. "We have no idea where the main body of the enemy is. They could be on us with little, if any, warning."

"Surely our cavalry will spot them first," Felix said. "Valens is out there, and if anyone can find the enemy, he can."

"We can only hope," Karus said. "Be ready for anything."

"I will." Felix turned his gaze down the slope at the men struggling through the mud. "My boys are already worn. A few more days of this and the legion will be blown."

Karus only nodded. He had figured as much himself.

The two men were silent for a while, each lost to their own thoughts. Fourth Cohort gave way to the Fifth, who had been assigned the supply train, along with the Ninth. Long lines of mules led by weary guides came first, then the carts and wagons. After a time, a cart became stuck beneath them, the mud and mire seeming to cement it in place. No matter what the teamster did, the cart remained immovable.

Centurion Veran Flaccus, the senior centurion of the Fifth, strode up and lent a hand, along with a dozen other legionaries working to free the cart. They heaved and pulled as the teamster vainly cracked the whip, attempting to get the mules moving. The cart stubbornly refused to budge. After several tries, the wagon abruptly lurched forward, wheels rolling only a few turns before the right wheel splashed into a large pothole and sank deeply. The mules came to a halt. The cart was once again stuck fast.

Flaccus, screaming invectives and oaths at the driver, led the legionaries forward. Karus realized this group of legionaries had been ensuring that this particular cart kept moving. He looked back down the line and saw similar scenes. Between each cart and wagon marched a small contingent of legionaries whose job it was to provide security and ensure their charges kept moving. Karus well understood it was hard and exhausting work, but it had to be done. Behind the train, somewhere toward the end of the column, came the camp followers and the legion's rearguard, perhaps three miles distant. Karus wondered how they were faring.

He took a deep breath. There were women and children there, along with whores, an assortment of merchants, and skilled labor. They were a headache the legion did not need. They required protection, which strung out the line of march farther than it needed to be and, in Karus's opinion, threatened the safety of the legion.

The cart below them was eventually pushed and pulled out of the pothole. Incredibly, it trundled on with no more difficulty, wheels kicking up flecks of mud. Flaccus and his men rested, breathing heavily as they watched the near miracle with surprise.

"Keep up the good work!" Felix called down to Flaccus, who looked up in surprise at the two officers.

"Gods, I hate Britannia," Flaccus called back, having caught his breath. "Karus, tell me how I get transferred out of this shitty province. A warmer climate would be good, I think."

The men with Flaccus laughed, which Karus realized was what the centurion had intended. Morale was low, and Flaccus was doing what any good centurion would—working to keep spirits up, even at his own expense.

"Just as soon as this leisurely march north is over, I will put in your transfer to Syria," Karus called back, getting into the spirit of things. "I understand the garrison there is always in need of good officers."

Instead of replying, Flaccus just looked up at Karus and Felix with a flat expression.

Karus knew that Flaccus had served in Syria and hated it.

"I think…" Flaccus said after a heavy pause, with a wry look at his men, "I will stick it out with the mud and Celts, thank you very much."

"Very sensible of you," Felix called down to him as Flaccus and his men started moving again. Flaccus waved a hand back in reply.

Felix watched a moment before he turned to Karus. "If you will excuse me, I will return to my men before they get too far ahead."

Karus nodded. Felix bent down and picked up his marching yoke. He started down the hill, passing a legionary who was working his way up toward Karus.

"Sir." The legionary saluted. "Beg to report Centurion Frontinus has another cart with a broken axle. He says there is no repairing it."

Karus closed his eyes and shook his head. That was the third cart they had lost today.

"Have him transfer the supplies as best he can to his men, the other carts, and any mules that can stand to handle additional weight. Anything that can't be taken with us is to be destroyed. Nothing of value is to be left behind. Is that understood?"

"Yes, sir." The legionary saluted and made off back down the hill. Frontinus led Ninth Cohort, whose place in the march was just behind Flaccus's Fifth.

Movement caught Karus's attention. In the distance to the east, he could once again see the enemy's mounted scouts. This time they were on a large round hilltop about a mile and a half away. With no sign of any of the legion's cavalry, the Celts were simply watching the legion slowly snake its way north.

Karus wondered for a moment where Valens's cavalry was, and then realized it mattered little. They knew this land far better than the Romans. With ease, the enemy scouts had been evading most of the patrols. Karus glanced to the north where the head of the column was out of view, having wended its way around yet another hill.

"How will you get out of this one, old boy?" Karus asked himself, and then started back down the hill to rejoin the column of march.

Chapter Three

Karus glanced around at the senior centurions of the legion and the prefects from the auxiliary cohorts gathered around him in a rough semicircle. The sun had yet to rise, and an early morning frost lay heavily on the ground. The camp where the legion had spent the night was rapidly being broken down in preparation for the day's march. Within the next hour, the Ninth would be on the move once again, leaving the remnants of the night's fortified marching encampment behind as the mark of their passing.

"Eighth Cohort will lead today," Karus announced, his breath steaming in the bone-numbing cold. His leg ached abominably, and he massaged it as he talked. "The Ninth will have the rearguard."

Frontinus groaned in an exaggerated manner. "Karus, we will be up to our waists before noon."

"It's just your turn to play in the mud, that's all," Karus told him.

"If you can call it that."

The trek had been so difficult that Karus had begun rotating the order of march after the first few days. The lucky cohort at the head had it the easiest, as the ground had yet to become churned up into a sucking, glutinous quagmire. Those at the rear were not so lucky. Since the legate had delegated this duty to him, Karus felt it was only fair that all the cohorts shared in the misery, and so the rotation had begun.

"The Eighth thanks you," Centurion Fadenus Artunus said with a wink over to Frontinus.

"Second in line will be the Seventh, Sixth, Fifth, and so forth," Karus continued. "First will guard the supply train, along with the Second."

Dio nodded his understanding.

"Tenth will provide security for the camp followers. Any questions on that?"

He waited a few moments for questions. There were none.

Karus looked around at the centurions. All of them were battle-hardened veterans he had known for years. They were solid men whom Karus felt could be relied upon to do their duty under the most trying circumstances. In the early morning gloom, he could easily read the weariness and the strain etched upon their faces. The march, two weeks in, was wearing everyone down, including the officers, who worked the hardest.

"The First Nervorium and Second Vasconum Cohorts will provide skirmishers along the left flank of the line of march; the Fourth Delmatarum and Raetorum Cohorts will handle the right."

Karus looked up at the prefects in question. All four allied cohorts were light infantry, perfectly suited to the task that Karus had assigned them. More importantly, they were all veteran formations.

"As usual, the cavalry will provide a screen beyond our skirmishers. Unfortunately, due to increasing contact with the enemy, we will not risk sending them farther afield than a mile from our lines."

"I don't know about that," Prefect Valens drawled. "Those barbarians audacious enough to hop onto a horse are no match for my boys. We've not been licked yet."

Though he was bone weary, Karus shot an amused look at Valens. The prefect and his cavalry seemed to be the only ones enjoying themselves. Then again, Valens only enjoyed himself when the opportunity to kill Celts presented itself.

"Nevertheless, you shall wander no farther than a mile," Karus said firmly. "The legate left strict orders for you to stay close and within easy contact. He also said to tell you he will likely have orders for you around midday, consolidating your cohort. I have no idea what he has in mind, so be ready for that."

"What of my scouts?" Valens asked.

Karus sensed that if he gave too much, the prefect would take advantage of the situation. Karus was in no mood to play games.

"Send out no more than ten scouts," Karus said. "I want no reconnaissance in force, if you understand my meaning. You do, don't you?"

"I do." Valens actually looked crestfallen.

"And you are not to personally join the scouts," Karus added as an afterthought.

Valens had the grace to frown in disappointment. "I wish the legate would free me and my boys," he said. "We've been held too close to the column to do much, if any, good. Free us, and we will sweep those hills of the enemy's eyes."

"I have no doubt you would," Karus said. However, in truth he did harbor doubts. From all indications, the enemy was preparing something. The last thing the legion needed was for the entire cavalry wing to go haring off after a group of enemy horsemen on a fool's errand.

"Karus," Flaccus spoke up. "My boys were roughly handled yesterday."

Karus nodded. The legate had dispatched the Fifth after a small body of enemy infantry that had come near enough to be spotted by the cavalry scouts. Expecting to outnumber the enemy, Flaccus had run into a well-executed ambush, sprung by a superior force.

Valens had pulled Flaccus's bacon out of the fire by concentrating much of his cavalry and rescuing the Fifth, turning the tables on the enemy. Karus was confident Flaccus's cohort would have been annihilated had the cavalry not relieved them. As it was, Valens had arrived none too soon, and it had been a close thing at that.

"We will move your wounded back to Eboracum when the opportunity presents itself," Karus said, hoping to sidestep Flaccus. He well knew the senior centurion of the Fifth was hopping mad. Last evening, Flaccus had unloaded on him about it. Karus had hoped Flaccus had just needed to vent, but from the man's thunderous expression…

"That's not going to happen," Flaccus snapped, and everyone present straightened up. "The last two resupply runs meant to refill our train never arrived. Without them, we can't send our wounded back now, can we?"

"Calm yourself, Flaccus," Varno, the senior centurion of the Seventh, said. "They are likely fighting their way through the mud, just as we have done. Sooner or later they will catch up."

Karus caught Valens's eye. Three days ago, the legate had ordered two cavalry squadrons to go and find the missing resupply trains. The squadrons had returned with the news that both trains had been ambushed, and destroyed. The legate had subsequently ordered Karus, Valens, and the men of the squadrons not to breathe a word of the misfortune.

"I will not remain silent," Flaccus said with heat. He glared at the other centurions. "This country is crawling with enemy. Any chance of surprising the bastards has passed us by. I tell you, we are marching toward disaster."

There was a moment of stunned silence as several of the centurions shifted uncomfortably. Though many had expressed their concerns in private to Karus, none had dared say so publicly. Such things, amongst a legion's senior officers, just did not happen. Flaccus was straying onto dangerous ground, and everyone present knew it.

"Flaccus," Dio said carefully, "we have our orders."

"Our orders?" Flaccus spat. "When was the last time we went over to the offensive before the ground was firm? Or, for that matter, marched off to campaign early, and without support?"

An uncomfortable silence greeted those words.

"I wonder," Flaccus hissed, "if the governor even blessed this ill-conceived expedition."

"Flaccus," Karus said firmly. The salty old centurion turned his angry gaze back to Karus. No matter how much Karus agreed with him, he was well out of line. It was not his place to question the legate. "That is enough."

Flaccus took a deep breath, and for just a moment Karus was concerned he might press the issue, but then conceded and bowed his head. Thankfully Flaccus remained silent, his hands clenching and unclenching.

"Right," Karus said. "I think it is fairly obvious we are in hostile country and that the enemy has something planned for us. I need all of you to stay ready and sharp." Karus paused, allowing that to sink in. He then clapped both hands together. "Very good. Now, let's get the legion moving."

The officers broke up. Karus watched them go, and then noticed that Flaccus had hung back. The other centurion drew nearer.

"Karus," Flaccus said. "I bet—"

"It is not our place to question the legate," Karus interrupted in a hard tone.

However, Flaccus was too enraged to take heed of the warning. "This entire expedition has been ill-conceived, ill-planned, and poorly executed from the very start."

"We have our orders."

"Even if it leads us to defeat and disaster?"

"Even then."

"I lost over a hundred men yesterday with another thirty-two wounded," Flaccus said, his voice catching slightly. The tough old veteran's shoulders sagged, and a heavy breath escaped that almost sounded part sob.

"I know." Karus had read the casualty reports the night before. The Fifth was lucky they had returned at all.

"Good boys." Flaccus glanced down before looking back up, an intense look in his eyes. "They should not be used in such a way."

Karus sympathized deeply with the other centurion. If Karus's own cohort had been so callously dispatched into a hostile wilderness, he would be just as bitter. But there was nothing he could do.

"My boys should not have been used in such a way," Flaccus said again, shaking his head slightly.

"What are you saying?"

Flaccus locked eyes with Karus.

"The legate is a fool. We should do something before it is too late. Before he gets us all killed."

Karus sucked in a startled breath, wishing he had never asked the question.

"You are talking…" Karus stopped, cleared his throat uncomfortably, and then began again. "You are talking mutiny."

Flaccus said nothing and stared intently at his immediate superior. Both had served together for a number of years, and though they were not the best of friends, each respected the other.

"Karus, it would be crim—"

"I will pretend I did not hear that," Karus interrupted him, his own voice sounding harsh.

"Mark my words, Karus, this will not end well."

"For our years of shared service, I will also pretend I did not hear that," Karus said. "Say any more and you will force my hand."

Flaccus stiffened and held Karus's gaze, anger burning in his eyes.

"I need to see to my men," Flaccus said finally. He glared at Karus for another long moment, then turned away and stomped angrily off.

Karus watched him go and then, with a heavy feeling in his chest, made for his own cohort to check on their progress. As he was the acting camp prefect, his responsibilities had multiplied, especially since he had not been relieved of the command of First Cohort. It was time he checked in on his own.

When he arrived at the spot allotted to the First, Karus was pleased to find that the tents had been broken down. They had been loaded onto the mules assigned to his cohort. The men were now gathering their gear and kit. A few centuries had already begun to fall in.

"Pammon," Karus greeted the centurion of Second Century. Next to Karus, Pammon was the most senior centurion in the legion.

"Karus," Pammon said, turning to see his boss striding over to him. "About time you joined us. If I did not know better, I would think you had been loafing."

Pammon was a small, muscular man with a confident manner that bespoke a tough, no-nonsense attitude. He had sharp brown eyes that seemed to miss nothing. His hair, cropped short, had long ago turned prematurely gray. Pammon's nose had been broken several times, and it showed the damage.

Whenever duty called him elsewhere, Karus leaned heavily on the centurion of Second Century to fill in for him and command the cohort. So far, Pammon had done an excellent job of it. If the legate ever got around to making Karus's position as camp prefect permanent, Pammon would most likely replace him as senior centurion of the First. He was a good man, and Karus liked the tough old salt.

"How many on the sick list today?"

"Thirty-two new," Pammon said, checking a small wax tablet in his hand. "That makes sixty now."

"Not good," Karus said. The cold and wet conditions were taking their toll on his men. Across the entire legion, the number of sick was now in the hundreds. It had become so acute that supplies had to be abandoned and destroyed to make room on the wagons and carts for those too ill to march.

"We had one die today," Pammon said. "The fever took him."

"Who?"

"Saccus."

"Damn." Karus rubbed his jaw. Saccus was a long tenure veteran. He had been due to muster out and retire just as soon as this summer's campaign season concluded. Saccus had survived not only the legion's harsh discipline, but many difficult campaigns. He did not deserve to go out the way he had.

"You know, I thought that old bastard would outlive us all," Pammon said.

"Damn." Karus punched a fist into his palm. "What arrangements have been made for his remains?"

"The surgeon will be burning his body and several others who passed during the night. Second Cohort has seen to the funeral pyre."

"You have collected his kit?" Karus asked.

"Yes," Pammon said. "His armor and sword are being carried by the mules. His family is another matter."

"Saccus has a family?" Karus asked in surprise.

"He took Illya as a wife earlier this winter, when her man died with the Sixth."

"Illya..." Karus tried to remember the woman, but failed. Legionaries were not permitted to marry, so she would have been his unofficial wife. "I don't know her."

"Ugly as a goat," Pammon said. "But she's really good at laundering tunics. I think that's why old Saccus married her."

"For the money or for the clean tunics?" Karus laughed. Knowing Saccus, he would not have been surprised to learn that he had married her for the extra money. Like most widowed women, Illya would have looked rapidly for a replacement husband and protector. Life as a camp follower was not an easy one.

"Extra coin to buy drink when off duty doesn't hurt none, no matter what she looks like," Pammon said. "Besides, when it's dark out, what does it matter anyway?"

"Old Saccus wasn't a looker himself," Karus reminded Pammon.

"You know, I think they actually enjoyed each other's company," Pammon said somewhat sadly. "Gave each other what comfort they could. He was also fond of her children."

"Children?"

"Four," Pammon said. "Two boys, two girls."

Karus was silent as he mulled things over. On a march like this one, it was a bad time to lose a husband. Illya and her children would not be entitled to any food from the legion, unless Saccus provided it. Without him, Illya would have to fend for herself and rely upon her own resources. Karus was unwilling to let that happen.

"See that she and her brood get fed," Karus said. "Have someone check in on them regularly to make sure they are okay. Any problems with that, come and see me." It wasn't much, but it was the least he could do for old Saccus, especially after the man's twenty-five years of good service.

"I've already seen to it," Pammon said. "Saccus's portion of the funeral fund went to her instead of one of those money-grubbing priests that came along with us."

"Good."

"Karus." Pammon hesitated, almost as if he was unsure. It was very unlike him.

"What is it?"

"There is serious discontent in the ranks," Pammon said. "I would not speak of it were I not so concerned, but I fear it is spreading."

"I know," Karus said. "Just a few more miles up the road is all."

"Then what?"

"Then... hopefully the legate will see that we can't crush these Celtic tribes by ourselves. With any luck, we march back to Eboracum and wait for the other legions to come up."

"You really think so?"

Karus shrugged, not willing to lie to Pammon.

"That's what I thought." Pammon let out a long breath.

"We've been through worse," Karus said, "and if I have anything to say about it, we will get back to Eboracum."

The two centurions were silent as they watched their cohort, having packed and stowed most of their gear, begin to form up. Pammon's century was already in position, standing loosely in formation, heavy marching yokes resting on the ground by their feet as they waited for inspection. The night before, the men had painstakingly cleaned all the dried grime from their armor. They looked presentable to Karus's critical eye.

As Karus stood there watching his men, he silently fumed. Flaccus was bloody right. These were all good men. The legate was leading the Ninth to disaster. It had become more than a gut feeling. He had never been more sure of anything in his life.

"Where is my kit?"

"My boys have it over there," Pammon said, gesturing toward a pile of gear, including a shield in its canvas covering.

Karus was already wearing his armor and sword. "Good, keep an eye on it. I am going to speak with the tribune."

"Saturninus?"

"Yes. I will be back shortly."

Karus left Pammon and made for the tribune's tent, which was located right next to the legate's. Both tents were still standing, but a party was ready to bring them down as soon as they were no longer required. Outside of Saturninus's tent, a slave was readying the tribune's horse, a fine brown Numidian stallion that was worth a small fortune. The tribune had brought several horses with him, but this was the first time that Karus had seen this one being saddled. He knew it was Saturninus's pride and joy. An animal like that attracted a lot of attention.

At the tent entrance, which had been thrown open for light, Karus stopped. Saturninus was being dressed by his body slave, who was securing his master's chest armor, tying off each strap. Once the armor was in place, the slave then tied a thin blue ribbon around the tribune's chest, signifying his rank, even though the expensively ornate armor told the same story. Saturninus looked around and spotted Karus waiting patiently as the slave worked.

"Ah, my favorite equestrian centurion," Saturninus said, eyes lighting up at the sight of Karus. "You have brightened my otherwise gloomy morning. So good of you to pay me the courtesy of a visit."

"I am the only centurion of the equestrian class in this legion," Karus said wryly and entered the tent.

"You made my point for me," Saturninus said. "And though you may be my favorite, you look very dour today. Tell me, my friend, what troubles you?"

"The position of the legion," Karus said, getting right to the point.

"Oh, not that again." Saturninus breathed an unhappy sigh. "Karus, the legate's mind is set. However, you should know that your constant nagging concerned me enough that just this morning I argued against continuing forward. I recommended we turn back to Eboracum. Our dwindling supply alone is troubling enough."

Karus was surprised by that. Perhaps there was hope for Saturninus yet, if he now recognized the legion's peril.

"What did the legate say?" Though Karus already knew. His orders had arrived from headquarters earlier this morning. The march would continue.

Saturninus made a pained face. "You have to understand at this point it is more about losing face than anything else."

"What do you mean?"

"For someone so astute and educated you can be incredibly thick at times." The tribune gave Karus a long look, sighed, and then shooed his slave away as he turned fully around. "Karus, look at it this way. If Julionus turns back now, the governor will surely have his balls for breakfast. He marched the legion into hostile territory without direct orders. Should he return now without a victory, there would be no gain to this venture. And that does not even begin to cover the material cost in terms of supplies expended and men lost. Are you following me so far?"

Karus nodded, and knew acutely where the tribune was going with his line of thought.

"Good," Saturninus continued. "Turning back would be a political mistake, perhaps even career suicide. Though, as you have so rightly advocated and articulated on so many occasions, it is the tactically correct decision. So, you see, Julionus is caught in a trap of his own making."

"He must continue to push forward," Karus said, "and hope to bring the enemy to a decisive battle."

"Which I fear," Saturninus said, "judging from all available evidence, is inevitable."

"So, if he faces the enemy in battle, and wins," Karus said, thinking it through, "he can return to Eboracum with honor and save face?"

"And the governor will have no choice but to honor our fine, audacious legate." Saturninus smiled sourly. "The governor will embrace Julionus as a conquering hero, even though he will want nothing more than to sack him for foolishly putting his legion into the field and in harm's way without orders."

"What if...?" Karus swallowed. He did not want to voice his concerns about a military defeat, and hesitated.

"Now you see the matter clearly," Saturninus said, becoming grave.

Karus was silent, his thoughts racing. This all revolved around naked ambition and saving face. The legate was leading them into a dangerous position, and it was clear now Julionus likely knew it. Saturninus had as much as hinted at it.

"Look here, Karus," Saturninus said with a disarming smile. It seemed more than a little forced to Karus. "We have over thirteen thousand highly trained and disciplined men. At the very least, this venture will end up a draw. These hairy barbarians will throw themselves against our shield wall until they come to the realization they cannot break our lines. When that happens, I will strongly encourage the legate to claim 'his' victory, and then we can all go home."

Karus was silent as he thought this through.

"Besides," Saturninus added, "when was the last time an entire legion was lost?"

"Sir, have you ever fought the Caledonian tribes?" Karus asked quietly, instead of listing a few of Rome's more ignominious defeats at the hands of barbarians.

The tribune held Karus's gaze a moment and then looked uncomfortably away. He used the opportunity to reach for his sword, which had been lying on a table in its scabbard and harness. He slipped it on before turning back to Karus.

"Karus, do you know what your problem is?"

Karus shook his head.

"You worry too much."

"It has kept me alive longer than most."

"Undoubtedly," Saturninus said. "Now, I believe you have your own cohort to look after."

"Yes, sir." Karus took the hint and saluted.

"Do try to stay out of the grime today," Saturninus called after him with a chuckle as Karus left the tent. "Equestrians should not wallow in it like the common people. You have to think about your future, Karus."

"I will try to remember that."

Karus stepped back out into the frigid morning air. The slave was still there preparing the tribune's mount, which was tethered to a small wooden post. Karus walked up and laid a hand upon the horse's neck, appreciating the fine quality of the animal. It was surely one of the fastest horses in the legion, clearly superior to those the cavalry used as mounts. Such an animal could get you both into and out of trouble swiftly.

"One day," Karus said softly to the horse, "perhaps I shall own an animal as fine as you."

"Brutus," the slave said.

"What?" Karus looked over.

"His name is Brutus," the slave said, and then went back to work.

"The name suits you," Karus said to the horse, admiring the powerful muscles. "The bringer-down of tyrants."

The horse glanced sideways at him and whinnied. He was already saddled and had a heavy load of saddlebags not only tied to the saddle, but secured around the rump. These included several tightly tied bundles of hay.

Was Saturninus planning on going out with a cavalry patrol?

Karus looked back toward the tent. Was that why the tribune's horse was so well-provisioned? Karus's orders to Valens had been clear. For a moment, he wondered if the cavalry prefect had slyly arranged an extended scouting run with Saturninus, then disregarded the thought. Even Valens would not be foolish enough to take a spoiled fop like the tribune into danger.

The slave had just finished tying off one of the saddlebags and bent down to pick up the last one, which rested at his feet. He hefted it with some effort and placed it on the horse's back. The bag chinked, and Karus's head came around, his eyes narrowing.

Saturninus was bringing his money with him.

Karus stepped back from the horse and took a deep breath as he stole one more glance toward the tribune's tent, then turned back toward his cohort. He shook his head, more deeply troubled than he had been just a few heartbeats before.

Chapter Four

With a deep sucking sound and a lurch, the wagon rolled forward, the wheels finally coming free from the mud. Karus staggered forward a step, the wagon pulling away from him. He almost fell but was able to recover at the last moment.

Resting his hands upon his knees, he breathed deeply as a cold drizzle fell around them. He eyed the back of the heavily loaded bed with a feeling of relief. It had taken him, along with eight other legionaries, a good while to free the blasted thing.

"Good work," Karus said to the winded men around him. He straightened back up. Behind them, a group of legionaries was working to free another wagon. The dour-faced Centurion Pulmonus was lending a hand.

"Right," Karus said. "Grab yokes and keep moving. It's the only way to stay warm."

There was no talking as the men moved to obey. They had stacked their yokes off to the side of the track. Karus watched them a moment. They lacked the normal spring to their step. It was a troubling sign. The march was sapping everyone's strength, but this was somewhat different. There was a lethargy hanging over the legion that Karus had not seen for years.

He chalked it up to short rations and the fatigue of the march. The legate had ordered that rations be cut by a third this morning, the second such reduction so far. It was a sign of the legion's deteriorating supply situation.

Karus's kit, which he had taken to carrying, was piled with the other yokes. All available space on the wagons and carts had been allocated to the sick or injured. There was an increasing number of the latter as isolated small unit encounters with the enemy increased the deeper the legion marched into Caledonian territory. It was clear they were nearing their destination, where the enemy's main body surely waited.

Karus hefted his shield and yoke, the men doing the same. Within moments, all were back on the muddy road, trudging along behind the wagon they had just freed. Karus shifted the yoke into a comfortable position and then shivered as a stream of rain iced its way down his back. Moving would keep them somewhat warm, but the cold drizzle seemed to counteract the effort. The reality was that there was no warmth to be had, even by marching.

Not only were his feet numb, but his hands ached terribly. With one hand, Karus adjusted his helmet strap, tightening it. Instead of carrying the incredibly heavy thing from a tie about his neck, he wore it to keep his head dry. It was scant protection against the elements, but it was better than nothing. Unfortunately, the rest of his body was either damp or downright wet, the water having inevitably worked its way through his armor.

It was one thing to be muddy, but another to be thoroughly soaked through, especially on such a cold day. He was as miserable as the men, but worked to keep it from them. Such examples gave them strength of will and helped them continue onward where others might give up.

Karus glanced up at the sky. The cloud cover hung low and seemed to cling to the small, narrow valley the legion was marching through. The last few days had seen weather just like this. Not only was the effort of the march taking a toll, but the wretched weather and now the short rations were adding to the misery. Karus blinked as a drop of water fell directly into his right eye, and then scowled. He wished the gods would send them some fortune, for nothing seemed to be going right.

To his right there was a large hill with a slope that began with a gradual grade, but within ten feet became quite steep. He followed the slope upward, to where it disappeared into grayness of the low-hanging cloud cover. Something about the hill captured his attention, and he stopped to study it further.

Karus chewed his lip as his eyes raked its slopes. He had passed a number just like it—tall, craggy, and forbidding. Winter-browned vegetation, rocks, and boulders littered its slopes. But despite his weary condition, he felt drawn to climb it, as if something were tugging him upward toward its hidden crest.

Karus almost took a step in the direction of the hill, but a crack of the whip snapped his attention away. He was in the path of a mule-pulled wagon. He stepped out of the way. A dozen legionaries were closely following the wagon, including Centurion Pulmonus. The supplies had been unloaded to make room for the sick and injured.

The wounded groaned with every bounce and jolt. The wagons were torturous for them, but there was no alternative. They could not be left behind for the enemy. The mules slogged onward, heads bowed by the effort, thoroughly ignorant of the suffering behind them as they sloshed and slipped their way sullenly along, occasionally requiring a crack from the whip.

"This cannot go on for much longer," Karus said quietly to himself as he watched the wagon and the legionaries assigned to it trudge by. Their heads were down, and they looked thoroughly beaten. It was almost as if the legion were retreating from the enemy instead of advancing to contact.

Karus shifted his yoke to a more comfortable position again. With each step forward, even he was beginning to feel its weight. His stomach rumbled with hunger. "What happens when we finally meet the enemy?"

The column, with men interspersed between the supply carts and wagons, stretched out for as far as he could see. The line of march continued forward for at least a mile, perhaps more. The supply train was moving slowly, and it was quite possible the cohorts leading the way had pulled ahead somewhat, creating a gap between formations.

Over the last few days, Karus had received complaints from the legate concerning the lagging train. But there really was nothing Karus could do to speed things up. The mud was proving a difficult obstacle. Worse, both the men and the animals were beginning to flag.

Julionus had taken to riding at the head of the column, Karus suspected, more to avoid the churned-up sea of mud than to set an example of leading from the front. Karus only saw the legate late at night, after the last of the cohorts had safely reached the fortified marching encampment. And then, Julionus only cared to vent his anger upon his acting camp prefect for the slow pace.

Karus looked behind him and ran his eyes over the column that stretched back through the rain. He was somewhere in the middle of the line of march, with the train. It was the most heavily protected portion of the column, the head and tail being the most vulnerable to ambush.

The tail of the legion was perhaps two to four miles back from his current spot. The road was so churned up where he was, Karus wondered how those behind were doing. His own cohort marched just behind the train, perhaps a mile distant.

He glanced around at the surrounding terrain. They were marching through an extremely narrow valley, perhaps three hundred yards wide at this point. Behind them, the valley widened a little more, but not much. A stream, threatening to overflow its banks with water muddied by the rain, ran parallel to the road on his right. To either side, the road was hemmed in by steep, craggy slopes and hills that almost joined together to form a continuous ridge.

Karus could see several centuries from the auxiliary cohorts working their way along the slopes. They had climbed a short way up the steep terrain and were carefully negotiating their way forward, ever on the lookout for the enemy. Though it was difficult going for the auxiliaries, Karus knew without a doubt it was preferable to struggling through the frigid, churned-up muck in the road.

"Karus."

He turned. Valens had come up behind him while he had been lost in thought. The prefect was on foot and leading his horse. Like everyone else, Valens looked worn. He had a troop of cavalry just behind him, making their way back down the column. Valens had come to a stop, holding his reins loosely. He waved his men by. They looked just as fatigued as they continued around the two officers.

Karus eyed the troopers as they passed.

"Where are you off to?"

"The legate finally gave me permission for a serious probe," Valens answered with a frown. "He's afraid of letting us go too far forward. So, my orders are to have a look behind us, and I mean to."

Karus leaned to the right a little to look past the cavalry prefect, and his eyes widened. It looked as if Valens was taking the legion's entire cavalry wing with him. To avoid complicating the march northward for the infantry, the cavalry troopers were walking their horses single file one after another in the opposite direction.

"This..." Valens paused with a significant glance behind him, "is a reconnaissance in force."

Karus said nothing.

"He should never have hobbled us," Valens said bitterly and gestured angrily about them before spitting on the ground. "We have no eyes beyond these slopes. You could hide an army behind any one of these hills, and we would know nothing."

Karus took a deep breath to say something, then let it go. Instead, he settled for nodding his agreement.

"Let me correct myself," Valens said. "I am sure there is an army out there. We just don't know where it is... yet."

"How far are you going?"

"Now, Karus, do you really want me to answer that question?" Valens asked him with a probing gaze, and waited.

Karus shook his head. It was clear that Valens intended to exceed the scope of his orders. Instead of a strong probe to the south, Karus reckoned the cavalry officer would be scouting in all directions.

"We should be back by evening."

"Watch yourself," Karus said.

"I will." Valens led his horse around Karus, who stepped back out of the way, and farther up the slope. "If I find the main body of the enemy, I will make sure you know straight away."

"I would appr—"

A distant horn ripped across the air in the direction of the front of the column. Kraus snapped his head around, as did Valens and most everyone else. The horn had an urgency to it, and sounded again in rapid succession.

It was the call to arms.

The entire column had ground to a halt, with men milling about stupidly. Karus could see nothing from where he was. He wanted a better view. He climbed the slope a few more feet and had to scramble a bit. Still he could see nothing useful as the horn sounded yet again, seemingly more insistent.

Karus spied a large boulder a few feet farther up the slope. He pulled himself up and onto it. Squinting, Karus strained to see through the rain, which had gone from a drizzle to a steady downpour.

"It seems the enemy has saved me the trouble of locating them," Valens said as he pulled himself up toward Karus's perch. The prefect held out a hand toward Karus, looking for assistance.

Karus bent down and helped the cavalry officer up onto the boulder. He then looked back toward the front of the column again. The road bent sharply around a small hill, perhaps four hundred yards to his immediate front. A hundred yards beyond that one, it bent again around another hill, like an elongated snake. This second hill was much taller, and anything past that was hidden from his view.

Between the two hills, though, a confused group of legionaries was moving back toward them. Watching them, it was clear that a gap had formed between the advance cohorts and the supply train. Karus narrowed his eyes. He could see no enemy amongst them, or, for that matter, anywhere in the immediate vicinity. Nor were they being pursued. And yet, incredibly, discipline seemed to have broken down for this cohort, likely the Third, since they were next in the line of march. The Fourth and Sixth should have been leading the column. If the enemy had struck somewhere beyond the second hill, perhaps the men from those cohorts had stood firm, unlike those of the Third, who were now rushing his way in complete disarray.

"Sweet bloody Jupiter," Karus breathed in growing alarm. He had to do something fast, before those from the Third reached his position and their fear infected the rest of the legion. It could mean the end of the Ninth.

Karus glanced around, looking for a man with a horn. He spotted one of Valens's troopers just a few feet away, a horn strapped to his saddle.

"Valens," Karus said, turning to the prefect. "Get your man there with the horn to sound the call to reform." He paused and quickly surveyed the terrain. Across on the other side of the track, just beyond the small stream, there was a bit of open ground. He pointed. "I want your cohort over there, waiting in the event I need you. Send a rider down the column alerting all units. The First, Second, and Fifth should be just down the line of march. I want them up here on the double. The rest of the cohorts to the rear are to close up and form a line of battle a quarter mile that way, falling back on our position."

"What about the auxiliary cohorts?" Valens asked. "They're likely spread to hell, stretching all the way from the front to the rear."

The horn sounded again.

Karus thought hard. The legion needed to come together, and rapidly.

"I want them concentrated and tightened up along our flanks. The entire column is to close up as tightly as possible. Those are my orders." Karus paused, and then belatedly gestured in the direction of the Fourth and Sixth, somewhere ahead, beyond the second hill. "Send someone forward to find the legate. I can't see anything beyond that hill there. I want to know what is going on up there."

"I will see to it." Valens jumped down off the rock and began shouting orders to his men as he worked his way down the slope. Karus looked around. He was pleased to see the centurions who were nearby were beginning to reform their centuries, which had been broken up amongst the wagons and carts. Once Valens's cavalry horn sounded the order to reform, things would accelerate.

"Pulmonus," Karus called, cupping his hands to his lips. The centurion turned at his name. Karus pointed ahead of them. "Get your men up there a bit, and tell the other centuries ahead I need a scratch line formed across the track. Got me?"

"Understood." Pulmonus bellowed orders to his muddy men, who were hastily discarding the canvas covers of their shields to reveal the bright red and gold bull emblem of the legion. The sudden wash of color from the shields in this drab setting was momentarily striking.

Valens's trooper blew the call to reform. Those who had still been milling about jumped into action. Discipline that had literally been beaten into the legionaries took over as Eighth Cohort, with whom he had been marching, snapped to. Prodded by their officer's direction, the cohort began to come together.

Karus climbed down from the boulder, making his way down the slope to the road, and jogged forward, pushing through several sections of men as they moved toward his scratch line. He quickly reached the point where the line was being formed. Junior centurions and their optios were hastily slotting men into position and dressing centuries, one upon the other.

The track at this point was only two hundred paces wide, with steep slopes rising up on either side. As more centuries came up, armor jingling and officers snapping out orders, Karus's line slowly extended its way up those slopes.

He stepped through the ranks to the front, counting as he went. So far, there were only four ranks of men. If the enemy was coming for them, he had to increase his depth. He stepped to the front of the line as the first of those legionaries who had broken in a panic reached the first rank of his scratch line. They streamed back through the ranks in ones and twos, but farther up the road there were several hundred panicked legionaries in a great mass coming. Many had thrown their shields, javelins, and marching yokes away. They had wild looks to their faces, and that frightened Karus more than anything else he had seen. Should this continue, it would infect everyone.

It had to be stopped now.

Two legionnaires, in their panic, jostled him roughly aside. Something inside Karus snapped. Enraged, he grabbed one of the legionaries by the back of the man's armor harness, dragged him backward, and threw him roughly to the ground. The legionary hit hard, his breath whooshing out with a grunt.

"Ready shields!" Karus roared, kicking the man roughly in the side before stepping over him. There was a clatter as the line reacted to the order. "Shields up!"

The mass of fleeing legionaries, abruptly confronted by an impenetrable shield wall and an enraged senior officer standing to their front, stumbled in shock to an uncertain halt. There was an uncomfortable moment where they appeared unsure what to do. Then a few began moving to the sides of Karus's scratch line.

"Karus," Pulmonus said. "What do you intend?"

Karus turned to the junior centurion who had come up next to him and looked back at the broken cohort. He was enraged by what he saw.

"Fall in!" Karus roared at the milling mass of legionaries to his front. He could see no sign of the enemy and was thoroughly pissed off. "You bloody heard me! Fall in!"

A few of the legionaries started to form a line, but others continued edging around to the side. He did not like that one bit, and ground his teeth in frustration. Allow a few free and this might yet turn into a disaster, as their fear and panic could easily spread to the Eighth, formed up behind him. Though it killed him inside, Karus decided the time for playing nice was over.

"Any man," Karus said to Pulmonus, "who refuses to fall in is to be cut down. Understand me?"

There was a momentary look of astonishment in the other centurion's eyes, but then the man's face hardened and his eyes narrowed with understanding. He gave a curt nod.

"Draw swords," Pulmonus shouted. With an ominous hiss, the line pulled out their swords.

"Fall in," Karus roared again at the uncertain mass of legionaries to his front. Those nearest had fallen back a few paces. "By the gods, so help me, I will send your cowardly souls into the next life if you do not heed me."

More men began to fall into line, which had grown before Karus's scratch line.

Karus looked over to his right and saw several fugitives scrambling up the slope, still intent on fleeing. He ground his teeth in frustration at what they were about to make him do. Karus took a deep breath, and slowly released it. The time to act had come. Discipline would be restored.

"Deal with them," Karus said to Pulmonus, pointing at the legionaries who were refusing to fall in. Pulmonus turned and moved rapidly to the right side of the track, where the fugitives were scrambling up the slope to work their way around the Eighth's line and to the rear.

The centurion grabbed a javelin from a legionary. He hefted the weapon confidently, took a step back, aimed at one of the fugitives, and threw it with a practiced ease. It happened so fast that those nearest could only gape, stunned. The six-foot weapon, with its triangular point of steel, punched through the legionary's back armor with a loud crack.

The momentum of the toss threw the fugitive forward into the dirt. He uttered a pitiful scream and flapped around like a fish out of water, his lifeblood spilling out in an astonishing gush. A handful of heartbeats later he stilled, convulsed one last time, and then moved no more.

Every head turned toward the drama that had just played out. Pulmonus drew his sword and, with a grim expression, advanced on the next wide-eyed fugitive, who held up his hands.

"I will fall in, sir," the legionary said hastily, backing away from the centurion. "I will fall in, I swear I will."

"Then get your sorry ass in line, where it belongs," Pulmonus said. He gestured with his sword toward the line. The man hastened around the centurion, giving him a wide berth, but never taking his eyes off Pulmonus until he was well past. The centurion turned on the next man, who, without any words, began moving to follow the first. Within a few heartbeats, all the fugitives were falling in next to their mates.

Pulmonus watched for a moment, glanced at the man he had killed, and then returned to Karus's side. The two exchanged a grim look. Karus had not enjoyed ordering a legionary's death, nor had Pulmonus liked killing a comrade. To save lives, it had been necessary. Karus nodded his thanks, then stepped through the freshly reformed ranks of the broken cohort, pushing his way roughly forward. He wanted these men to know he was enraged. They should fear him and the other officers more than the enemy. Pulmonus's recent example should have cemented that fear.

Whether through habit or discipline, around half of these men still carried their shields. Karus stepped through the last rank to the front. Except for abandoned equipment, supply carts, and a wagon or two, the road before him was empty. It bent around the hill Karus had seen from the boulder, turning sharply to the left and disappearing out of view. Karus thought he could hear the faint din of fighting, but was not so sure. Whatever was happening ahead, the Fourth and Sixth were clearly in trouble.

"What cohort are you from, son?" Karus turned to look at one of the former fugitives. He wanted to be sure this was the Third.

"Third," the man replied, his voice unsteady.

The Third had been assigned to guard the very front of the supply train.

"Tell me what happened."

"They caught us by surprise, hit us from both sides, sir." The legionary licked his lips. "We didn't stand a chance, sir."

Karus nodded. It was as he suspected. He studied the newly reformed cohort. There was no one of rank present, centurion or optio. It was hardly surprising. Officers were promoted due to their aggressive nature and willingness to take risks. It was rare for one to break and run. The Third's centurions were either dead or still fighting somewhere ahead with a part of the cohort. He felt the cohort seemed rather light, so perhaps some portion of it had stood their ground and now fought with the other two cohorts.

Conversely, that part of the cohort could be lying dead at the hands of the enemy.

"Where is your centurion?"

"I don't know, sir," the man said. "I think he is dead."

Karus glanced back up the road. Another friend, Titus, had been the senior centurion of the Third. Karus thought it would be a sad day when that tough old bastard died. He fervently hoped that his friend still lived.

"You men without shields," Karus called out, loud enough to be heard. "Move to the rear ranks. I want those with shields up front."

There was a general shifting in the ranks as the formation quickly reordered itself. Karus glanced up the road. The Fourth and Sixth Cohorts could not be that far ahead. He was considering going to find them. Before he did that, he had unfinished business.

Karus turned back to face the Third. He waited until the ranks had stilled.

"There will be no more running," Karus said, loud enough for all to hear. He paused to allow that to sink in, and briefly considered giving a rousing speech to build morale. Instead, he shook his head. These men were still frightened. An inspiring speech was not what they needed. He desired them angry, and even more scared of not holding the line. Otherwise, like poorly forged metal, they would break yet again.

"We are deep into the enemy's territory. If we break," Karus took a breath, "there is nowhere to run. You know what happens to those who are caught alive by the enemy, and if you have not personally witnessed what they do to Romans... you should have heard by now."

There was an angry grumbling at that, which had been Karus's intent. He hoped it was enough that they would think twice before breaking ranks again.

"You," Karus said to the same legionary he had spoken to moments before. "Get back to the second line and ask the centurions to come forward."

"Yes, sir." The legionary stepped back through the line.

Karus turned at the sound of the hooves. A horseman came galloping around the hill. The trooper hauled back violently, sawing on the reins when he saw the ranks of ordered men standing in the road. His horse took several sidesteps. The trooper spotted Karus and kicked his horse forward, cantering over.

"Sir," the trooper said, breathless, and pointed behind him after saluting. "The Fourth and Sixth are heavily engaged. They are fighting their way back to this position. The legate requests that you form a strong line here and prepare to receive them."

"How far are they?" Karus asked.

"Perhaps half a mile beyond that bend there."

"Any idea on the enemy's numbers?"

"Thousands, sir," the legionary said. "I think more than an entire legion. It was a little confused."

Karus had expected nothing different.

"Inform the legate that we stand ready," Karus said. The trooper pulled his horse around, kicked hard, and galloped back the way he had come.

Eight junior centurions, including Artunus, the senior officer of the Eighth, made their way through the ranks of ordered men and joined Karus as the trooper disappeared back around the bend. All of them were muddied, with drawn faces. They also had a hard look to them that spoke of grit and determination. Each had proved himself over a long, hard service, and Karus knew he could rely upon these men.

"The enemy is that way," Karus said, pointing around the bend. "The Fourth and Sixth are in contact. They are withdrawing toward us, at least a half mile away. We are to prepare for their arrival. Take these men here from the Third, break them up, and add them to the ranks of your respective centuries. Keep a tight hold upon them." Karus paused and gestured at the hills on either side of the small valley.

"This is the perfect blocking position for us," he continued in a firm voice. The nearest men in the first and second ranks of the Third were close enough that they could surely hear him, and he would be damned if he showed them any emotion other than a confident indifference to the legion's circumstance. "We will extend our line up both hills here to make it as difficult as possible for the enemy to flank our position. Any additional centuries and cohorts that come forward will be slotted into line. Artunus, I want you to see to that."

"Yes, sir," Artunus said.

"Good, any questions?"

No one spoke up, but all looked grim.

"There will be no more running. We will stand and fight. Make sure your men know that if they break, there is no place to run to. We will fight our way out of here if need be, but we will do it together." Karus paused to let that sink in. "Very good. Now, get these men moved."

The centurions broke up and began barking orders at the Third. The formation quickly dissolved and started moving toward Karus's scratch line. Feeling a little better, Karus turned and glanced back the way the trooper had disappeared. He was half tempted to follow around the bend for a look-see but then decided against such an action. He had his orders. More importantly, he had a job to do. Karus walked slowly back to his line as those of the Third melted into it.

First Cohort, his own, was just coming up. He could see the standard held proudly to the fore, battle honors fluttering in the breeze. With their arrival, he felt a definite sense of relief. These were men he had personally trained, all veterans who had survived numerous fights. They were his men, and he took pride in them.

Karus stopped just before the first rank of the line he had ordered formed. It was no longer scratch, but now had depth and a solid firmness to it that only a seasoned veteran could sense. The danger had passed.

The line had been expanded to stretch up each of the craggy slopes that hemmed in the miserable road. Karus studied the hill on his left flank. It was small, barely a hundred or so feet high. The line ran up nearly to the summit. He decided he would need to place at least an entire century upon the top of it, not only to see what the enemy was up to, but also to deny them an easy way of flanking his position.

To his right flank loomed the steep hill that had earlier drawn his attention. It was so large it could potentially be described as a small mountain. Sleet-gray clouds still obscured the top. As he studied the hill, the rain petered back to a slow, depressing drizzle.

The slope was choked with boulders and medium-sized rocks. Stunted vegetation sprouted up around the rocks. Should they wish to scale it, the hill would pose a more difficult challenge to the enemy, but not an impossible one. Karus blew out a slow, long breath. He had long since learned that underestimating one's enemy could prove a fatal mistake. No matter the difficulty, he would have to ensure he secured its summit and, more importantly, retained control. A reliable man would have to take charge of that effort, and thankfully one was nearby. He looked around for another centurion for the smaller of the two hills.

"Pulmonus, Janus," Karus called, "to me."

Both men hurried over.

"Janus." Karus pointed to the smaller of the two hills. "Take your century up to the top of that hill, secure it, and report back what you see. If you need assistance, don't be shy. Ask for it."

"Yes, sir," Janus said and hustled off.

"Pulmonus." Karus turned to the other officer, and both them looked up the steep slope of the larger hill. "Take your century and climb that beast. Let me know what's on top. If you are able, send scouts to the other side. Find out what is there."

"I will do it."

"Very good." Karus reached out and grabbed the younger officer's arm as he made to leave. Pulmonus turned back to him, an eyebrow raised in question. "I will send you an additional century or two just as soon as I am able. You have overall command of the summit. Under no circumstances are you to give it over to the enemy. Make sure we hold it." Karus paused as he thought on what he would say next. "We may need a defensive position for the legion as a whole. Give me an assessment on whether or not that hill will serve."

Pulmonus looked at him for a long moment and then nodded gravely before turning away. A solitary flake of snow drifted lazily down amidst the drizzle. Karus rubbed the back of his neck as more flakes began to fall in place of the rain. He let out a long, unhappy breath and glanced up at the sky.

The gods never made anything easy.

A distant horn from the rear of the column snapped his head around. It was the call to arms. Though he wasn't certain, he could guess what had happened. The enemy had hit them there as well. The legion was just too strung out.

Karus hustled through the waiting ranks of men to where he had placed Valens. He found the prefect sitting on a small rock, his helmet resting on a knee. Valens's men had also dismounted and were resting, their horses tied to small stakes they had planted in the ground.

Valens stood as Karus approached. The snow began coming down heavier. The horn was blown again. It sounded farther away than just a moment ago. Snow had that effect, muffling sound.

"I need to know what is going on to the rear," Karus told Valens curtly. "If the enemy has hit us there, I want the rearguard cohorts wherever practical to form a line, if they have not already done so, and stabilize our rear flank. They are to fall back toward our position. We will compact the legion as tightly as we can in this small valley. It is narrow and should make the job of holding much easier."

"We do that and it will mean abandoning much of the supply train," Valens pointed out.

"Yes, it will," Karus said unhappily. He saw no other alternative. It was either that or allow the legion to be destroyed in detail. "Move as many of the wagons and carts up as we can, along with the mules. Priority is to be given to food."

"What about the camp followers?" Valens asked.

"We have to protect them," Karus said. "Take a squadron with you and leave the rest of your wing here. I want you to personally pass along my orders. That way, there can be no misunderstanding them. We have to keep the legion intact or we will lose everything."

Valens put his helmet on, tying the straps tight as he turned to his men. "Sixth Squadron, mount up."

Helmet secure, Valens grabbed the reins of his horse from a trooper and pulled himself up. He took a moment to settle himself. The animal appeared skittish, but the cavalry officer paid it no mind. He glanced down on Karus.

"I will send word on what I learn." Valens turned and looked over Sixth Squadron, which had mounted and was ready. With his free hand he waved them forward, and the squadron set off at a trot, hooves kicking up flecks of mud.

Karus watched them go and felt a deep pang of unease. The legion was spread across several miles of shitty road. The enemy had struck to the front, and likely to the rear as well. Should they strike elsewhere, say the left or right flanks, they would be able to carve the legion up one chunk at a time. Karus's stomach clenched at the thought. He prayed that he had time to salvage the situation before it grew worse. Julionus had really screwed them something good.

He turned back to his line. The men were standing loosely in formation, their shields resting on the ground. Karus did a rough estimate and figured he had at least a thousand men blocking the small valley in ranks nearly six deep. Securing his left and right flanks behind the line was now the priority. First Cohort was still coming up, and only a few yards away. He decided to use them to provide a rough close-in screen, stretching back down the road for a few hundred yards.

One of his centurions, Ajax, spotted Karus and broke ranks. He came jogging up, Pammon at his side. Mud-spattered, they looked a sorry sight, but also a comforting one.

"There is no time to fully explain," Karus said without preamble, feeling the urgency to attend to his flanks. "We are going to bring the legion up into this small valley. I want the First to secure both flanks along each side of the road. Push out and up the slopes to the crests, going back a few hundred yards. I need our flanks covered before the enemy discovers where we are weak. Place half of our centuries on the left and the other half on the right." Karus pointed where he wanted them. "I intend for the Second to reinforce you just as soon as they come up."

"Got it," Pammon said.

Ajax and Pammon turned and trotted back to the cohort, armor chinking. Within moments, they had the First redeploying by centuries.

There was movement behind his cohort. Karus stood on his toes. He could see another formation coming up. He squinted and recognized the Second's standard. Karus was now bringing enough men on-line to give the enemy some serious pause for thought. If only he had some artillery. Sadly, much of the heavy stuff had been left behind, on the orders of the legate. What they did have was far to the rear and would be of no immediate use. After a moment, he gave a mental shrug. There was no reason to cry over spilt wine.

Thinking about Julionus got Karus wondering how the Fourth and Sixth Cohorts were doing. He heard armor jangling and saw Dio jogging up. The Second was still some ways off.

"What's up?" Dio asked, a little out of breath.

"The front of the column got hit hard. Third Cohort broke. I've managed to reform them and fit them in with the Eighth. The Fourth and the Sixth are fighting their way back to us."

"What of the rear? I heard the call to arms."

"No word yet," Karus said. "But it seems likely they were hit as well. I've sent Valens back with a squadron to find out."

"He was in a hurry," Dio said, still breathing heavily, and then took a moment to glance around at the slopes. "You know… this is a great spot to bottle us up."

"That goes both ways," Karus said.

Dio turned to him with a questioning frown.

Karus raised an eyebrow and continued. "They have to come to us if they want us badly enough. We control what little level ground there is, limiting their ability to effectively strike at multiple points simultaneously. The ground around our position is difficult, rugged, and defensible. We, on the other hand, have the good ground and, once established, can easily use our interior lines to move reserves to trouble spots."

"Any idea on the enemy's numbers?" Dio asked.

Karus shrugged. Though the report the cavalry trooper had delivered suggested the enemy greatly outnumbered the legion, Karus knew when under pressure men could easily inflate the true size of the enemy. That said, Karus figured it was likely the enemy outnumbered the legion badly, but he was not about to speculate on what he did not know for certain. He was a legionary officer, a hard-bitten veteran from hundreds of fights, and he was not about to give in to a bunch of hairy-assed barbarians. Regardless of the enemy's numbers, Karus intended to make the Celts pay dearly for the Roman blood they would spill this day.

Dio took a deep breath and then looked behind at First Cohort, which had broken up by centuries. They were now moving down the line and up the slopes to secure the flanks. "I am guessing you want my cohort to extend the flanking lines that the First are now setting up?"

"I do," Karus said.

"I will get right on that," Dio said. He was about to go, but then stopped. "Do you think Felix is all right?"

"I hope so," Karus said, thinking on the ordeal Fourth and Sixth Cohorts were going through just a short way up the road.

"Make sure you take care of yourself, Karus."

"You do the same," Karus said to his friend.

As Dio stepped away, a shout drew Karus's attention. A legionary was running down the small hill where Karus had dispatched Janus's century.

"Sir," the legionary said excitedly, "the enemy—"

"Where is your salute?" Karus demanded, poking him in the chest armor. The legionary was young and likely had been one of the fresh recruits that had arrived toward the end of the winter.

The legionary blinked, drew himself up into a position of attention, and saluted.

"Now," Karus said, regretting having left his vine cane with the baggage train. "Kindly give me your report."

"The enemy is in sight," the legionary said. "We can see them from the hilltop there. They are swarming around our boys. Centurion Janus reports that both cohorts have formed a defensive square and are moving in our direction at a steady pace. The square's lines are solid and holding. He told me to make sure I told you that, sir."

"How many of the enemy?"

"He says he estimates their number to be near ten thousand."

Karus closed his eyes for a moment. The legion with her auxiliary cohorts numbered near thirteen thousand, and the enemy was likely striking the rear of the column as well.

"How about along our flank, on the other side of the hill? Any enemy spotted there?"

"No, sir," the legionary said. "Just to our front."

"How far away are they?"

"At their current pace," the legionary thought a moment before responding, "less than a quarter mile, sir."

"Advise your centurion to keep an eye out should the enemy attempt to flank us. I want to know the moment they attempt that."

"Yes, sir," the legionary said and saluted before jogging back the way he had come.

Karus moved up to the line. The men were standing loosely in formation, the bottom of their shields resting on the ground. There was talking in the ranks, but the atmosphere was subdued and tense. Karus pushed his way through to the front and called the centurions of the Eighth to him. Once they were all present, he had them gather around. He could hear the fighting now, and with each passing moment, it appeared to get louder.

"Fourth and Sixth Cohorts are hard-pressed right around that bend," Karus informed them. "They are moving back toward us and should be here shortly. We are going to let them through our ranks and then hold the line."

Karus paused to look around the gathered officers.

"We cannot allow our line to break," Karus told them. "We stick it to them. We bleed them good."

"What about the rear of the column, and the followers?" Centurion Ganarus asked. Karus read genuine concern in the man's eyes. Ganarus had a family and had been permitted by the previous legate to officially marry. His wife was good enough, but the kids were an ill-disciplined lot.

"I've sent Valens back with orders," Karus said. "We have to concern ourselves with what is coming down the road toward us first. Let me worry about the rear and the followers. Understand me?"

There were nods all around. Ganarus gave a nod also.

"Good, then get back to your men." Karus watched as the centurions of the Eighth stepped away.

The distinct thundering of hooves against the ground drew his attention. Karus turned to see the cavalry trooper riding hard back toward them. He was pursued closely by five enemies on horseback, carrying an assortment of swords and spears. The enemy wore heavy furs and animal skins over their armor. Karus had learned long ago that the wealthiest of the enemy, typically their nobles, were the only ones who could afford horses and the expensive furs.

"You men," Karus ordered to the nearest, pointing at those he wanted. "Ready javelins."

A dozen men stepped forward a pace to make room and prepare for a toss, drawing the deadly weapons back and aiming. Each had drilled countless hours with the javelin to develop a deadly proficiency, and it was this skill Karus was counting on to make an exceptionally difficult toss successful.

"Make sure you do not hit our man."

Karus raised his hand and held it there as the trooper, desperate to escape his pursuers, leaned forward in the saddle and dug his heels in for all he was worth. A well-thrown spear sailed within inches of his head. Karus saw the trooper glance behind him for a fraction of a second and could well imagine his thoughts.

The distance closed, twenty yards, then fifteen. Karus waited, hand held up. He needed to time this toss just right. When the trooper was ten yards away, Karus dropped his arm.

"Release!"

With grunts of effort, twelve javelins arced up into the air, sailed over the head of the trooper and into the midst of the pursuing horsemen. A horse screamed as one of the heavy weapons pierced its neck. An incredible spray of blood shot up into the air as the animal tumbled to the mud, violently spilling its rider. Another javelin took one of the pursuers in the shoulder, and the rider fell backwards out of the saddle. The others hastily reined in, dragged their horses around, and kicked them savagely away in the direction they had just come, hooves pounding.

Karus let slip a slight smile of satisfaction.

The trooper pulled up hard, jerking on the reins before Karus. The horse whinnied loudly, blowing great puffs of breath as it slowed to a halt.

"Thank you, sir," the trooper said, breathing heavily. He spared a relieved glance behind him. The two downed enemy writhed in the mud. They were going nowhere fast. The horse that had been pierced by the javelin lay still, while the riderless mount slowly cantered back the way it had come.

"Report," Karus ordered.

"The Fourth and Sixth will be around shortly," the man said, pointing behind him. "Tribune Saturninus is leading the men. He wants to make sure you are ready, sir."

"We are," Karus said, surprised that Saturninus was leading. "What of the legate?"

"I am sorry to report he fell in battle, sir." The trooper glanced down for a moment as his horse whinnied again, her breathing slowing. He absently patted her neck. "They were unable to recover his body."

Despite his dislike for the man, Karus felt a heavy hand grip his heart. Julionus had been a fool, but he had still been the legion's legate. The feeling lasted only a moment, quickly turning instead to a simmering rage. Julionus had found death not just for himself, but perhaps for the legion as well.

"Shit," Karus spat in the mud. He rubbed his jaw for a moment, and then looked up. "What is your name, son?"

"Sextus, sir."

"Good job," Karus said. "The cavalry wing is just behind the main line. Go and rest your horse."

"Yes, sir." The trooper looked relieved at not being ordered to return to Saturninus. They exchanged salutes before the trooper nudged his horse forward and carefully picked his way through the ranks.

The sound of the fighting abruptly surged. Karus looked in the direction Fourth and Sixth Cohorts would be coming. He saw no sign of them, but then movement caught his eye. A barbarian appeared from around the bend, and then another, perhaps forty feet away, wearing long gray cloaks and holding swords with large elongated shields. Suddenly a great group of them emerged into view. Their attention was clearly fixed away from Karus and his legionaries, focused on whatever was back around the other side of the hill.

Karus studied his enemy carefully. Most carried the straight long sword, known as a spatha. It was a good weapon, perfectly suited for the Celtic style of warfare, where individual courage was valued over group formation fighting. A few clutched spears or the dreaded war axe, which, when wielded correctly, could easily carve a good shield to shreds.

Though the enemy all had a varied assortment of helmets and shields, some were better armored than others, wearing chainmail shirts. Those who could afford the armor had some, and those who could not did without. Incredibly, a few of the enemy went bare-chested, proudly displaying their tattoos or war paint despite the frigid conditions. All of them, however, wore varying patterned wool pants with boots. On cold miserable days like this one, Karus envied the pants and boots.

"Ready shields," Karus shouted. The shields came up from the ground. "Ready javelins."

A few of the enemy turned, having heard the shout. At the sight of the armored wall awaiting them, they nudged or called on those nearest. Most, Karus realized, were oblivious to his presence. Then he saw the first of the imperial standards and legion's Eagle as the defensive square pushed around the corner and came into sight.

Karus's heart filled with a fierce sense of protection as he took in the Eagle. The legion's standard represented their honor. Karus considered marching to meet them, but Saturninus was steadily moving in his direction. A veritable horde of Celtic warriors swarmed against the defensive square's shield wall, bashing with their own shields and swords, attempting to hack their way through it or create an opening that could be exploited.

It was a shocking sight.

The sound of the fight was near deafening as sword and spear struck against shield and armor. The shields locked together, parting periodically for a jab at an exposed enemy. Occasionally, an agonized scream rang out from the cacophony.

A defensive square movement against tremendous pressure by the enemy was incredibly difficult to pull off. It was an impressive feat of leadership on Saturninus's part, and Karus could not help but feel impressed.

As the square moved, it seemed to physically shove a great group of the enemy before it in Karus's direction. He glanced to his left, and then right. The first rank was ready with their javelins, prepared to throw. Karus simply waited, allowing the square to come closer, one steady foot after another.

As he had with the horsemen, Karus remained calm, biding his time. There was no sense in becoming agitated or anxious. He would only serve the enemy's needs should he do so, since such behavior might unsettle his men. This, the battlefield, was his element. So Karus simply stood there, a rock facing the chaos of a bitter fight.

The square pushed closer, with the mass of Celts swarming around it like an angry cloud of bees around a bear that had robbed the hive. Still, Karus held his ground. He eyed the two downed enemy horsemen. The one with the javelin in his shoulder was attempting, one-handed and with little success, to draw out the long metal shaft. The other was struggling frantically to drag himself out of the way of the fight bearing directly down upon him. It was apparent he would not be successful. Moments later the fight spilled over them, and both were trampled and lost from view.

"Release!"

Hundreds of javelins arced upward as one. They seemed to hang suspended in the air for a long second before crashing back down to the earth with shattering effect, bringing a great number of the enemy down. It was an exceptionally good toss, and for a moment, the fighting seemed to still with the shock of the throw, then quickly resumed.

Karus's eyes narrowed. A large number of enemy warriors were between him and the defensive square, which, with each step, was carrying itself closer. There was an opportunity here, he realized.

"Draw swords," Karus shouted to the left, and then to the right. The fighting was so close it was hard to be heard. He shouted again. "Draw swords!"

Those nearest heard the call and drew. The rest followed suit. Karus pulled his own sword out and raised it high, so all could see.

"ADVAAAANCE!" Karus pointed at the enemy before him and let his sword fall.

"HAAAAH!" The men shouted in unison. So loud was the shout that it drowned out the sound of the fighting to his front. The men seemed to put all the frustration and rage of the last few weeks into their battle cry. "HAAAAH!"

The wet, muddy ground seemed to vibrate as his line moved forward, feet coming down in unison as nearly a thousand men advanced.

The enemy between the legionary square and Karus's line hesitated, unsure at first just what to do. Heads swung from his line back to the defensive square. There seemed no central coordination or command of their effort to assail the legionary square. Rock-solid discipline, and good soldiers, won battles. That, and body-breaking training, which could only be differentiated from real battles by the effusion of blood. It was something these Celtic warriors had yet to figure out, and Karus aimed to show them the errors of their ways.

Someone in the defensive square saw the opportunity Karus had created. The side of the square facing Karus's line surged forward, shields bashing out. The legionaries pushed hard into the enemy at their front, who, just moments before, had been harrying them. The legionaries in the square gave a great shout and pushed again, shoving the enemy before them right into Karus's way.

Karus's line came on relentlessly, and for a few steps he marched with them as they closed on the enemy. Then he allowed the front ranks to pass him by. Karus's job was to command, not to fight in the line. The distance closed rapidly, then there was a titanic crash as the front rank met the enemy.

Shields hammered forward, bashing, before the deadly legionary short swords punched out again and again, seeking the soft flesh of the enemy. The enemy warriors were caught in a veritable meat grinder. After just a few moments of pressure, they began to panic, and that was when the real killing began. Those who could, fled, escaping to the flanks by climbing the slopes to either side of the road. Only a few won free. The rest were cut down, and almost as suddenly as it had begun, legionary met legionary, with much cheering.

Shortly after the two lines came together, a foreign horn sounded, and the din of fighting coming from the other sides of the defensive square suddenly dimmed. The horn called out again, and the fight slacked even further, as those enemy who were in contact with the other sides of the legionary square pulled back and out of direct contact. It became clear the enemy was being called off. Once they regrouped, Karus understood they would be back.

A number of catcalls were sent the enemy's way as they withdrew.

Karus called a halt and snapped an order to allow the men of the square to pass through. There were walking wounded, but he could see no seriously injured being carried or helped along by their comrades. It meant that either the two cohorts had been exceptionally lucky or the badly wounded had been finished off before being left behind. With an uncomfortable feeling in his throat, Karus suspected the latter. It would have been the reasonable thing to do.

Once the legionaries of the square had passed safely through, the line closed back up, and he stepped back to the front rank. Karus's eyes widened as he took in the size of the enemy host, which seemed to swarm up over the top of the hill to the front and out across the road just thirty yards away. There were tens of thousands of them.

The enemy milled about, silently watching Karus's men. There were no ordered ranks amongst them, just a wall of enemy warriors, all armed and armored as they wished. Unlike a legion, no thought had been given to uniformity.

Taking in the sheer size of the enemy army, Karus understood heavy fighting lay ahead. He gave the order to fall back and brought his line back to the position they had started from just moments before.

The enemy made no move to advance or follow, just stood silently watching the legionaries. Karus found it a little unnerving. It was only a matter of time until they struck, and for a moment he wondered what they were waiting for. Then he decided it did not matter. All that mattered was that he was ready when they made their move.

Karus glanced at the ground they had just fought over. Hundreds of the enemy lay where they had fallen, many still moving. Scattered amongst the bodies were a few legionaries. He turned and made his way back through the ranks in search of Saturninus.

He found the tribune with the legion's Eagle, and Felix by his side. A legionary stood next to the tribune, holding the reins of his horse. Karus eyed the legion's standard a moment. The sight of it never failed to inspire him.

"Karus," Saturninus said. The tribune's face looked drawn, and his eyes darted around to Felix before fixating on Karus. "You know, you really are my favorite centurion."

"I can't tell you how pleased I am you were here," Felix said with an exhausted look. "They were really pressing us something hard."

Karus noted that both men were splattered with blood, none of it their own, thankfully.

"Very," Saturninus said with a glance around the lines Karus had set. A legionary horn sounded in the distance to the rear. The tribune frowned, head turning in that direction. The call repeated itself.

It was the call to fall back.

"I take it the enemy has hit us there as well?" Saturninus looked to Karus, who filled the tribune in on what he knew and most of what he had done so far, including his intention to bring the entire legion up into the valley.

"So," Saturninus said, glancing down the road, "the enemy has yet to close the ring completely around us?"

"It seems so," Karus said. "But we don't know for sure. All the same, I've ordered our flanks secured." Karus pointed to the slopes, where the First and Second stood ready. "The ground up there is rocky and difficult. It lends itself naturally to defense. I have also ordered the securing of these two hills, sir. If the enemy wants them badly enough, they will have to fight for them."

"How long do you think before the enemy closes the ring around us?"

"There is no telling," Karus said. "If it were me, I would do it as rapidly as possible. That said, this is good ground, sir. We can hold here."

"They may already have closed the ring around us," Felix said, and Karus noticed Saturninus glance sharply at the other centurion.

"We don't know that for sure," Karus said, to which Felix gave a grudging nod.

"What do you think our chances are?" Saturninus tore his gaze from Felix to sweep it over the craggy slopes.

"Of holding?"

The tribune nodded, looking over at Karus.

"I have no doubt about our holding," Karus said. "Fighting our way back to Eboracum, however, is a different matter."

The tribune was silent as he absorbed this. He licked his lips, which had been cracked by the cold, before taking a deep breath. Karus thought he detected a slight shudder in the man, but chalked it up to the aftermath of the fight.

Karus himself had had the shakes after his first fight. It was only natural.

"Sounds like you have things well in hand," the tribune announced in a confident manner. "I will ride to the rear and take command. You, Karus, will command here. Once we have control of both flanks, we can decide what to do next."

Though Saturninus had very little military experience, Karus was relieved by the suggestion. Under heavy pressure, the man had successfully commanded the retreat of the two cohorts just a short while before, leading nearly eight hundred men to safety. He clearly had some worth as a military man.

"Yes, sir," Karus said, and noticed Felix frown at the tribune.

Saturninus took the reins of his horse, mounted up, and rode over to where Valens's cavalry waited.

"One squadron with me," he ordered loudly in the same confident voice and waited for them to mount up. With a glance over at Karus, followed by a curt nod, Saturninus nudged his horse forward and down the muddy road.

"You know," Felix said quietly to Karus as the two of them watched the tribune ride away, "I had to keep him from losing his head entirely."

"What?" Karus asked.

"He was ready to run, and nearly shat himself with fear," Felix said with a shrug. "I had to literally slap our valiant tribune to keep him from falling apart. And then, it was a struggle. Had it not been for his rank and station, I might have cut him down myself to keep order, as he was beginning to unsettle the men."

"Are you joking?" Karus looked hard at his friend. It was certainly a poor time for a jest.

"I wish I were." Felix shook his head. "It was me that did all the hard work after the legate was killed. And now you have handed the command of the rearguard to a spineless coward."

"Shit," Karus spat on the ground. The tribune had ridden too far to call him back. He turned to Felix, thought for a moment, and then made a decision. "Grab a horse from one of Valens's troopers and go after him. You are in command. Don't let him override what you think is good common sense. Make sure the rearguard and camp followers get up here safely. Under no circumstances is that fop to command so much as a section of men. Got me?"

"Yes, sir."

Chapter Five

Karus punched out with his sword and felt the resistance as the blade slid into his opponent's belly. This was followed by a grating of steel on bone as the sword tip scraped against the inside of the left hip bone. In the gathering darkness, Karus read the surprise etched in the Celtic warrior's eyes. The man's mouth opened, and he expelled a hot breath upon Karus's face that smelled strongly of onions.

In that moment, time seemed to have slowed, if not stopped altogether. The desperate cacophony of the fight around them ceased as their eyes met. It was an intimate moment, for one filled with the horror of impending death and the other triumph.

Karus gave a savage twist of the sword and slammed his shield into the other's body, pushing him violently back and off the steel of the sword, completely tearing open the belly in the process. The warrior collapsed to the ground, dropping both sword and shield. He writhed in agony, his entrails having spilt out around him, landing amidst the dirt and rocks of the steep slope.

The sound of the battle abruptly crashed back home. Swords clashing, shields bashing, men screaming in rage, fear, and agony. The sound of it all was nearly overpowering. Karus looked down and saw that the tribune whom he had left the protection of Second Cohort's line to rescue was still alive, though clearly dazed. The boy was one of the more junior of the legate's aides, fresh to service and barely fifteen years of age.

"Get to your feet, sir." Kraus, unwilling to set his shield down or sheath his sword to help the youngster up, instead settled for a light kick against the boy's leg.

The tribune's head snapped up to look. There was a good-sized dent in his finely crafted helmet, where Karus's recent victim had struck the boy a vicious blow. Karus read the fear and confusion in the tribune's eyes.

"Get up," Karus snapped. Farther down the steep and craggy slope, a large, heavily muscled and tattooed, bare-chested Celt roared his rage and rushed the two of them, axe raised. Karus stepped over the tribune to place himself in the path of the warrior and brought his shield up, gritting his teeth in preparation for receiving the attack.

The blow struck down savagely against the shield. Karus turned his head away as the war axe bit deeply just above his arm and shattered the top of his shield, showering his face with a spray of splinters. Karus screamed incoherently in reply as the force of the strike radiated up his arm and he was nearly pushed to the ground.

Karus was yanked forward a step as the warrior attempted to pull his axe free. The weapon was stuck fast, the sharpened edge only an inch or so from his arm behind the shield. Karus hauled back, pulling his enemy forward and off balance. He jabbed outward with his short sword, reaching around his shield and aiming at the warrior's left shoulder. Karus felt the tip of his sword find purchase. A warm gush of blood spurted out as the point of Karus's blade nicked the artery and ran down the sword to his hand. Karus blinked as blood sprayed into his eyes.

The Celtic warrior released the handle of the axe and stepped back, howling in agony, hand grabbing for the wound. Karus was unwilling to allow his opponent to go. Over the jagged edges of his ruined shield, with the axe still held fast, he advanced. The warrior, cognizant of only his pain and wound, was oblivious as Karus closed upon him. Karus punched out, sword point sliding easily through the other's throat and out the back of his neck.

The warrior's eyes opened wide, then rolled back as he convulsed once before falling backward like a felled tree. The body tumbled down the slope a few feet before a large rock checked its progress.

Breathing heavily, Karus took a step back and glanced down at the tribune. His arm still ached from the blow to his shield. Karus shook his arm to shake off some of the pain. His fingers tingled.

"On your feet, sir." Karus prodded the tribune with a foot. "Or so help me, I will leave you behind, honorary rank or not."

Even that did not get through, and Karus realized the young tribune was too dazed to properly function. Tossing his ruined shield aside, he reached down, hooked an arm under the tribune's shoulder, and hauled him to his feet. Half dragging the boy along, Karus started struggling up the slope, back toward the safety of Second Cohort's line.

In the growing darkness, Karus could just see the line up the slope, perhaps twenty yards away. The confusion of the fight raged across the slope of the hill as legionaries caught out in the open struggled to reach the safety of the line.

"Come on, son," Karus said, helping the dazed tribune up the slope.

"What happened?" the tribune asked, head lolling to one side. He almost collapsed, but Karus kept him upright and moving.

"You got clobbered real good on the head," Karus said. "Tomorrow I promise you will have one serious headache. Come on now, son, we have to climb or we are both dead."

"Where are we?" The tribune tried to shake him off. Karus kept a vice-like grip on the boy's arm and continued to drag him along as they climbed one slow step after another. The resistance ceased and the tribune began using his feet.

"What's your name?" Though he knew the boy well enough, Karus was trying to get the kid's brain working again.

"Tiberius Garius Delvaris." The words came out slurred, and the eyes rolled slightly. Karus shook him roughly to keep him from passing out.

"Tribune Delvaris," Karus said. "Keep your legs going; we need to climb."

Karus saw Delvaris glance behind them. The boy's eyes flew open. Instinctively, Karus shoved the tribune to the side and dodged right, bringing his sword around.

A spear reached out into the space where the two had just been a half second before. Karus batted the spear down into the dirt with his sword, then, lightning fast, swung it back into the face of his attacker, clipping the bridge of the man's nose. With a howl, the spearman immediately dropped the weapon and fell on his back, tumbling down the hill.

Karus stepped over to the tribune and reached down to haul Delvaris back to his feet. The line was only ten yards away. Before he could complete the motion, a powerful blow struck his side, armor absorbing the impact. Karus cried out with the pain of the strike and tried belatedly to dodge, but another hammer blow to his back threw him forward to the ground, where he landed heavily next to Tribune Delvaris. Having lost his sword, Karus fumbled for his dagger, attempting to roll away at the same time, desperate to avoid the next strike.

Karus looked up. A Celtic noble dressed in rich furs stood over him, sword raised, poised to deliver the killing blow. Helpless on his back and dagger half drawn, Karus froze.

He was about to die.

There was an abrupt, meaty *thwack*, followed by a huff as the noble's wind was forced from his lungs. Karus blinked in astonishment, not quite believing what he was seeing. A javelin had somehow sprouted from the man's chest. The Celt stared in shock at the shaft of the javelin, which had carried right through and out his back.

Dark blood trickled from his lips. The noble trembled violently. Then the sword fell from nerveless fingers, and he toppled to the side, where he lay twitching in the dirt.

A legionary horn sounded. There was a tremendous shout from just up the hill, almost immediately followed by the pounding of hundreds of feet. The legionary line drove its way down the hill in a charge, thundering past Karus a few feet, and then came to a rough halt, officers calling for their men to reform.

"HAAAH!" The legionaries shouted as their line came back together, shields aligning to form a wall with an ominous-sounding *thunk*.

"Next time you decide to take on the enemy single-handed, how about giving me a warning first?"

Karus looked up to see Dio standing over him. His friend reached down, offering a hand. He hauled Karus to his feet, a relieved grin on his face.

"I will try to remember that," Karus said. His shield arm, side, and back ached painfully.

"Do so, or I may just have to kill you myself," Dio said, then looked over Karus for wounds.

"I'm just battered, nothing worse," Karus assured him, shaking his friend off.

"You're lucky," Dio said. "Keep acting like a fool and you will never live to see the comfortable life in Sicily."

Dio turned to look at the dead Celtic noble. "An exceptionally fine toss, if I might be so bold to say so."

"Your work?"

Dio nodded.

"Thank you for that," Karus said.

"Very gracious of you," Dio said. "How about buying me a drink or two when we get back to Eboracum?"

"I will get you a barrel of wine." Karus saw his sword and retrieved it. His shield was an utter ruin. Karus felt saddened—it had served him well for a number of years. Instead, he looked around and selected one that had been discarded just a few feet away. Its previous owner lying by its side no longer had a need for it.

"The good stuff," Dio said before turning back to his line. "At the slow, and in good order." Dio shouted to be heard over the sound of the fighting to either side of his cohort. After the charge, the enemy Second Cohort had pushed down the hill had yet to reorganize. "Fall back."

The line began stepping slowly backward and up the slope of the hill, shields facing toward the enemy down the slope. Karus looked into the darkness, squinting. The enemy had been pushed down the slope around twenty yards beyond the line. The Celts appeared hesitant to move up after the legionaries who had just handled them so roughly.

Karus swung around and looked up the hill. Like a burial shroud, the cloud cover, which had hung so low all day, waited with a dull, milky whiteness around sixty yards up the slope.

"Help him along." Karus gestured down toward the still-dazed tribune, who was lying in a heap muttering to himself.

"He's useless," Dio said with a disgusted glance. "Going back for him was foolish."

"He's a Roman," Karus said. "I would no more leave him to the enemy than I would you."

Dio frowned, then bent down and helped the tribune to his feet.

"Marus, get your sorry arse out of the line. Give me a hand with this fool." The legionary jogged over. Dio handed over the boy to the legionary's care. "Help the tribune up the hill for me. Make sure he gets to the summit, and don't leave him alone until he regains his senses."

"Yes, sir." The legionary started assisting the dazed tribune up the hill, half dragging him.

Karus glanced at the two. Marus, a lowly plebeian from the worst slums of Rome, helping a fifteen-year-old patrician from one of the more powerful houses. Though the distance from their respective stations in life was as vast as could be, tonight they were both Romans. In the end, that was all that mattered.

"Where's the First?" Karus asked.

"To my right," Dio pointed. "Until we pushed down to rescue you, they were firmly anchored and holding our flank."

"Who's to your left?"

"Varno, I think, along with elements of the Fourth Delmatarum," Dio said. "It seemed a little confused. I had sent a runner to get a better idea of what was occurring, but he's not returned yet."

"I need a century of men," Karus said, looking in the direction of the left. He could not see much, but he could hear the spirited fight.

Dio's cohort line had carefully backed up the steep slope and were nearly to the two officers. Karus and Dio began climbing the hill to keep from being overtaken.

"You are intent on heading over to the left then?"

"Yes." Karus nodded.

Dio glanced around and spotted a centurion in the third rank. "Cestus, on me."

The centurion moved over to Dio and Karus. He fell in alongside as they climbed the hill.

"You and your century will be coming with me," Karus told the junior centurion. "We're going to make some sense of the left."

"Yes, sir." Cestus called his men to fall out. Karus eyed them as they broke ranks. These were the manumitted the emperor had sent to the Ninth as replacements. Muddy and flint-eyed, they looked indistinguishable from regulars who had served for years. He could detect nothing that hinted at their previous life and it spoke volumes that Dio was entrusting Karus to their responsibility.

Dio caught Cestus's arm. "Stick to Karus like flies on a three-day-old corpse. Keep him from doing anything stupid or you will personally answer to me."

Karus felt himself frown. Cestus's eyes flicked his way before returning to Dio.

"I will keep him safe, sir." Cestus flashed a grin Karus's way. "As a newborn babe in his mother's arms."

"He'd best be," Dio said.

"Permission to, ah," Cestus said, "restrain the camp prefect if I need to?"

Dio grinned at Karus. "Granted."

"Everyone's a comedian." Karus shook his head and looked heavenward. "Let's get moving."

Karus increased his pace, angling his way up the slope toward where he thought the Seventh might be. Cestus's men spread out around Karus and their centurion. A large gap had clearly formed between the Seventh and Second. In the darkness, and the harried retreat up the hill, Karus could understand why it had happened. He found it no less frustrating though.

Littered with both large and small stones, the ground was extremely rugged. Karus was careful in where he placed each foot, lest he turn an ankle. The risk was serious, for should he lose his footing and fall, he would tumble down the hill.

Within a short time, they reached the end of Dio's line, which was some ten yards beneath their current position. Dio had his entire cohort steadily pulling back, climbing the hill. Karus estimated that the spot where he now was had been Dio's original position before charging down the slope. With luck, Seventh Cohort was just ahead, simply hidden by the veil of night.

It had become so dark that it was difficult to see more than a few feet. As if to prove the point, two enemy warriors abruptly emerged from the darkness. Karus eyed the Roman-style short swords they carried. The two were armored with mail shirts and carried shields. Saying nothing, the two made a cautious approach, half crouched, shields and swords held at the ready.

"Swarm them," Cestus ordered curtly. Half a dozen legionaries broke from the protective screen and descended upon the two. With the number of bodies in the way, it was difficult for Karus to see what was happening. There was a series of hammer blows from swords on shields, then a couple of clipped screams, followed by an agonized moan. The legionaries stepped back. The two were down. So was one of the legionaries.

Cestus's optio scrambled down the slope. He knelt down beside his comrade, examined him quickly, and then looked up at his centurion. The optio curtly shook his head, then stood.

"Back in formation." Cestus's tone was hard. "And, for the sake of the gods, be more careful."

A sudden massed shout ahead was immediately followed by a tremendous clash. It told Karus that two large bodies of men had just come together. A few steps later and Karus was able to just make out the end of Varno's line.

Seventh Cohort, shields forward and locked in a contiguous line, was slowly pushing a mass of the enemy down the hill before them. At the same time, the enemy, easily several hundred strong, was trying to force their way up the slope. It meant that there were a number of the enemy trapped before the Seventh's shield wall. They were pressed in so tightly that they could barely move or even use their weapons, let alone their shields. Karus had seen such presses before and knew that dozens of the enemy were literally being crushed to death. It was a horrible way to go.

"Form a wedge," Karus ordered Cestus.

The other centurion looked over at him in surprise.

"We are going to hit the side of the enemy's line hard, and then, with luck, break it," Karus explained curtly. "Now hurry, before they realize we are here."

Cestus called for his century to form a wedge.

"Argus," Cestus said in a hard tone, "you have point."

"Yes, sir," a burly legionary said. Karus could hear the pride in the man's tired voice. It would be his honor to face the enemy first. Point was also the most dangerous spot in the formation. Normally Cestus would have taken that position. Karus wondered what the legionary had done to earn such a distinction from Cestus.

Despite the uneven terrain, the men quickly slid into position, with Karus and Cestus directly inside the formation and behind the point man. The beauty of the wedge was that it allowed small bodies of men to attack a superior formation. It placed the defenders in an awkward position, with the arrow formation generally slamming home into a solid line and penetrating it at a specific point. This meant that where the wedge breached a line, the enemy at that spot only had limited angles of attack and defense against the legionaries. The Celtic defenders would be unable to fully use their weapons. The legionaries, on the other hand, with their short swords and large rectangular shields, would have the advantage.

Typically, such formations were used to break an enemy's line into smaller parts. This was something different. Karus was hoping the shock of their attack on the enemy's flank would induce a general panic.

"Advance," Cestus ordered, and the formation started forward in a steady step, shields presented outward, the men grim-faced. Swords were held at the ready, waiting for the moment of contact and the opportunity to punch out at the enemy. "Keep those shields up." Cestus's gaze roved over his men as he kept up a running dialogue. "Steady there, careful now…I said careful. Pay bloody attention! The ground is rough. Watch your footing. Marcus, that means you. Stumble again and I will have you on a charge!"

Karus felt the thrill of the moment as they closed, fifteen feet, then ten. With each step, the din of battle became louder, almost overwhelming the senses. Shouts, screams, and a thousand other sounds blended together to create one serious racket.

Karus kept his eyes upon the enemy ahead as Cestus snapped out an order and angled his formation down the hill toward the end of the enemy's line, better aiming it. With the last few steps, the approaching formation was finally noticed. Karus could well imagine the shock of the enemy, with the legionary century appearing out of the darkness as if by magic and bearing directly down upon them. A few turned to face the wedge. Others attempted to back up, but with the press of the enemy's line, there was nowhere to go. It was too little and too late as Cestus's century smashed into the extreme flank of the enemy's line.

The legionaries to either side of the arrow point of the wedge grunted with effort as they leaned into the push, smashing and bashing their shields forward to keep the momentum going. They were rewarded with screams and cries of pain. The impetus of the wedge carried the century forward, the front rank stepping over and trampling those who had fallen under the onslaught, either stunned by a smashing shield or pierced by one of the deadly short swords.

Karus jabbed down with his sword, stabbing a warrior the wedge had passed over. The sword took the man in the side of the neck, and he immediately fell back to the ground, blood fountaining and steaming in the frigidly cold air. Cestus, to Karus's right, punched his sword into the belly of another, who let loose an agonized scream. A second stab cut the scream off.

Karus turned to his left and stabbed another man on the ground, taking this one in the thigh and opening the artery, eliciting a groan from his victim. The warrior dropped the sword he had been attempting to use to strike at the unprotected leg of a legionary, and instead reached for his own, intent upon staunching the flow of blood. Karus knew it was a futile effort, and in a few moments the man would be dead. For good measure, he kicked the hilt of the dropped sword out of reach and stepped away.

"Push," Cestus shouted, encouraging his men onward, even as he dispatched another enemy with a quick thrust. Karus looked up and saw that the forward progress of the wedge was faltering, more from the compact nature of the enemy's line than from any actual resistance. They had only traveled twenty feet so far, splitting the enemy on the flank almost in two, as if peeling back a slice of cheese.

Those who were trapped between the Seventh's line and the wedge were being rapidly cut down. Karus turned around and saw a number of legionaries from the Seventh, who had just been in hot contact with the enemy, set the end of their shields on the ground. They were taking advantage of the unexpected break in action. Cestus's initial contact had swept the enemy from the tail end of the Seventh's line. Karus estimated that there were at least seventy men who were now free to be employed elsewhere. He saw an opportunity.

"You men," Karus shouted, pointing at the legionaries with his sword. "Wrap around to the other side of the wedge. The right side. I want a line there yesterday."

"Move," a centurion amongst them hollered. "You heard the prefect. Get a move on."

The legionaries picked their shields up and hustled forward and around behind the faltering wedge, stepping over bodies and rocks. Within moments, Karus had a rough line two ranks deep. He moved behind it. The wedge to his left had only managed to advance another five or so feet in the time it took to form the new line. All forward progress had nearly been arrested. The wedge had lost its shape, forming more of a curved line now as the enemy pressed back. The men of Cestus's century had locked their shields for common defense and, on their centurions' orders, were periodically parting them to jab outward.

Karus scanned over his new line, which extended beyond the depth of the enemy's tightly packed ranks along the flank. With luck, it would be enough to break the enemy's efforts and send them running. He prayed that it would be, for he felt a desperate need to break off contact and reform the legion. He needed time to do that, and the only way to get it was to break this force before him.

"On my order, I want to hear you shout for all you're worth," Karus called. "It's time to break them. Advance!"

"HAAAAH," the legionaries shouted, and for a moment it drowned out the sound of the fighting. The line advanced.

"Push," Cestus shouted at his men, and they pushed along with Karus's new line, which joined the fight.

Karus snapped an order out, angling the end of his line so it began to wrap around behind the enemy's, effectively pinching the flank. The Celtic warriors there abruptly found themselves in an impossible position, being attacked and pressured from three sides. They were hemmed in and trapped, held in place inadvertently by their own side. In moments, as Karus had hoped, panic began to set in.

It seemed as if there was a collective groan. The panic spread and then the cohesiveness of the enemy's thrust up the hill lessened and quickly fragmented. All along the Seventh's main line, the centurions sensing the slackening of pressure ordered their men once again to push.

What moments before had been a concerted effort to shove their way up the hill tuned into a scene of panic, flight, and death. The enemy broke, turning nearly as one, and fled down the hill. Men shoved their fellows aside and were in turn tripped and then trampled. Others, in a desperate attempt to elude the wolf, scrambled back up on all fours like prey and ran for all they were worth. The vengeful legionaries surged forward. They were intent on killing all they could, mostly those who had not reacted fast enough or had fallen.

Officers bellowed orders, intent on preserving the integrity of their lines and preventing their men from becoming too caught up in the pursuit. It took a few hundred heartbeats, and a horn call, but the men of Seventh Cohort began to gradually fall back into line and return to the iron discipline of the legion.

Karus took a deep, relieved breath of cold air and savored it. The sounds of fighting all along the hill died down as the enemy broke contact, slipping into the night. He had succeeded.

"Excellent work," Karus told the nearest men, then turned to the centurion who had helped him break the enemy. He saw it was Arentus, one of the most junior officers in the legion. Karus caught the other's eye and offered him a satisfied nod. "Get your men back in line with the rest of the Seventh," Karus told Arentus. "We will be withdrawing up to the summit of the hill to tighten our defense."

"Yes, sir," Arentus said.

Cestus, just feet away, had a number of wounded. The centurion was busily attending to them along with the rest of his century. Karus let out a long breath as he looked over the scene of the battle. Bodies lay everywhere, many writhing about. Legionaries from the Seventh were moving amongst them, looking for comrades that still lived and could be helped.

Karus turned his gaze back to Cestus and sheathed his sword. Now that the enemy had broken contact, Karus no longer needed the entire century. There was much to do if he was to consolidate the legion, and he could not wait for Cestus to deal with his wounded.

"Cestus," Karus called to the centurion. "I want two of your men."

"I will give you a few more." Cestus was kneeling beside a badly injured legionary, holding the dying man's hand.

"Two will be sufficient," Karus said. "Focus on your wounded. Get your century up the hill as soon as you can."

"Yes, sir," Cestus said and ordered two men to Karus's side. Both stepped over.

"I will see you at the top."

Cestus nodded and turned back to the mortally wounded legionary. Karus saw the centurion's hand move toward his dagger before he turned away and started climbing the hill, the two legionaries following him.

Karus went in search of the Seventh's senior centurion. After a short hike, he found Varno with the cohort's standard, consulting with a number of his officers.

"I take it I have you to thank for that turning movement?" Varno said.

"Who's to your immediate left?" Karus asked. There was no time to waste while the enemy had broken off contact.

"Delmatarum, then Fifth Cohort," Varno said. "Beyond that I have no idea."

"Send a runner to Haemus and Flaccus. They are to take their cohorts up toward the summit," Karus ordered. "Also, spread the word to the other cohorts that the legion will be converging at the summit to tighten our lines and allow us to make a concerted and organized defense. Once we bring the legion back together, we are going to set strong lines and make the enemy come to us. Understand me?"

"Yes," Varno said. Karus thought he detected a note of relief in the other's voice at having been given direction.

A mule brayed a few feet away. A small mule train, with each animal tethered to the next, was idly standing behind the Seventh's line. The mules, heavily loaded with supply, were unattended.

Karus had ordered the wagons and carts of the supply train to be abandoned in the rush to seek the safety of the hill and a better defensive position, but he had made sure the mules came with them. Karus only counted ten mules. He hoped that the rest of the train had made it and was somewhere up the hill in the darkness. Now that the fighting had ceased, farther up the slope he could hear crying and wailing coming from the camp followers.

"Secure those mules," Karus ordered. "Get them and any camp followers you come across moved up to the summit as well. Make sure none of the mules get left behind. We're going to need what supply they carry."

"Yes, sir."

A horse whinnied, and Karus heard the soft thud of hooves coming down the hill. He nodded to Varno to get to work, then turned to look. Saturninus was riding down the steep hill, mounted on Brutus. Behind him came a squadron of Valens's cavalry. The tribune saw Karus, but did not stop. He kept riding slowly down the hill, leaning forward in the saddle slightly to see the ground as he steered his horse around a large rock.

"Defeated them, have you?" Saturninus asked in a deep, confident voice.

"Only shoved them back a bit," Karus said. "It's just a lull, sir. Once they overcome their confusion, I am confident they will be back. We will be ready for them."

"Carry on then, prefect," Saturninus said as he and the squadron passed beyond Varno's line, working their way down the hill.

"Where are you going?" Karus asked after the tribune.

"Back to Rome."

Karus was not quite sure he believed the madness he was witnessing. He considered calling them back, as there was no doubt in his mind that Saturninus would not make it past the masses of the enemy below. He could not see how he could stop Saturninus from taking the cavalry squadron with him to his doom.

He watched Saturninus and the cavalry squadron disappear into the darkness. Karus felt a deep revulsion at the other's cowardice. Then he shook his head. He had enough to worry about without concerning himself with Saturninus. If the opportunity ever presented itself, he promised there would be a reckoning.

Varno's line began moving up the hill. Karus turned to follow as the tired and weary men streamed around him. Just then, from out in the darkness below, there was the clash of sword on sword, and shouts. A horse screamed, followed by the pounding of many hooves that in a handful of heartbeats rapidly grew fainter.

Karus rubbed at his dry eyes. There was a crick in his neck from the weight of the helmet. He cracked it and, with a heavy breath, began working his way up the hill.

"Sir." One of the men Cestus had assigned him pointed back down the hill. A riderless horse was climbing back up the slope toward them. Karus recognized Brutus.

"Grab that horse," Karus ordered to the legionary, who hastened to comply, seizing the bridle. Karus stepped over to the animal, his eyes lingering upon the saddlebags, and then the fine saddle. There was a blood stain marring the rich leather. The enemy had deprived him of the opportunity for a reckoning.

"Legionary," Karus said after a moment's reflection. "Make sure you get that horse up the hill. You are to guard this animal. No one touches the saddlebags, including yourself."

"Yes, sir," the legionary said. "I will do as you say."

The legionary led the horse on ahead. Karus glanced down into the darkness. He could see nothing beyond the ground they had just fought over. He continued up the hill, at first following Varno's line and then passing through it. Karus trudged onward, legs beginning to ache with the strain.

It became more difficult to see. Karus realized that he had entered the cloud layer. A few steps in and it was almost so thick that, combined with the darkness, he could barely see his hand in front of his face. He stumbled along, and from the sounds of it, others were having as much difficulty.

"Keep that line together," an officer's voice rang out from somewhere off to the right. "Tighten up. If you can feel your neighbor and smell his foulness, you can't get lost."

"I can smell your foulness, sir," a voice called back, which was followed by a good laugh from a number of men.

"Don't waste your breath," the officer replied. "Just keep climbing, and smelling your neighbor."

There was another general laugh.

Karus glanced back and made eye contact with the sole remaining legionary Cestus had assigned him. Satisfied that he was keeping up, Karus trudged onward and upward.

After a while, the darkness began to lighten considerably. He could see a bright glow that he supposed was the moon, somewhere over the top of the hill. There he would finally be able to stop. And there also, the legion would make its stand and force the enemy to come to them.

With each step, it became brighter, and the misty murkiness began to thin. Karus found he could see farther, making out groups of people struggling up the hill, mostly civilians. Then, with a suddenness that surprised, they emerged onto the crest of the hill and out under a magnificent night sky complete with millions of stars and a full moon shining down upon them, like a pleased parent.

For as rough and craggy as the slope was, Karus found to his surprise that the hill's summit was extraordinarily flat. It was perhaps three hundred yards wide and just as many long. Grass stunted by winter brushed against his sandaled feet as he walked.

From what he could see, it appeared that most of the camp followers had made it to the summit. They huddled together in small groups, fearfully looking for the enemy to emerge into the moonlight.

There were a few centuries on the hill. These Karus had dispatched earlier to shepherd and protect the camp followers. He was pleased to see that someone had the forethought to position them strategically around the hilltop. A horse whinnied, drawing his attention.

Off to the far left, Valens's cohort began to emerge from the mists, the men leading their mounts. Karus turned fully around and his eyes opened wide. Under the moonlight, the tops of the clouds were illuminated brightly. It looked as if he were standing upon a solitary island surrounded by a vast white sea. Karus had never seen anything quite like it, and for a moment was moved.

The legionary with him let out a low whistle as he also took in the sight.

"Sir."

The moment was broken. Karus turned to see Centurion Pulmonus approaching. The centurion stopped, and his eyes flicked over his superior. Karus glanced down. He realized that he was covered in dried blood, gore, and grime.

"It got a little spirited," Karus said, and then glanced around at the hilltop. "You were right; this is a good spot."

"Thank you, sir," Pulmonus turned. "I have six centuries positioned around the summit." He paused to point each of them out. "Most of the camp followers have made it up, though it seems there is still a good number on their way. The majority of the mule train made it too. I've put them over there, near the center where we can better protect them."

Karus looked in the direction indicated, feeling vast relief that some of the supplies had made it. Before ordering the retreat, he had given instruction that as much food and water as possible be loaded onto the mules. At great risk, he had delayed ordering the retreat to make sure that had happened. It had almost cost him the legion, but it meant they might now have a chance if he could manage to break out.

"Continue," Karus said.

"I've set the surgeon up over there, with the Eagle." Pulmonus pointed. "By that large druid stone."

Great, Karus thought sourly as he looked at the thick stone pillar, which stood erect to a height of at least twelve feet. They'd selected a holy spot for their defensive position.

"There is a ring of them unnatural stones around the summit," Pulmonus said. "Ah…the surgeon has at least forty patients right now, mostly minor wounds." Pulmonus shifted uncomfortably before continuing. "I'm afraid those with more serious injuries did not make it."

Karus understood. In the retreat up the hill, their comrades had likely finished off those without hope or the ability to move under their own power. It was a mercy killing, for had they been left behind, the enemy would have made them suffer terribly. Only the walking wounded would have made it.

"I will check in on them," Karus said, then glanced around the hilltop. He took a deep breath. "This is really good ground."

"I think so, sir," Pulmonus said. "It's a bit windy, but we have the elevation, and the enemy has to climb to get at us."

"This spot will do nicely," Karus said. "The cohorts are pulling back up to the summit. I want you to send runners when they arrive. My orders are to form a ring of steel around the slopes. I will call a meeting of the senior centurions as soon as all cohorts have arrived."

"Yes, sir." Pulmonus saluted, and then stepped off to carry out his orders.

"What is your name, son?" Karus asked Cestus's legionary, who had listened silently.

"Legionary Drusus, sir."

"Well, Legionary Drusus, how about we go see the wounded?"

"Yes, sir."

The injured had been laid out in orderly rows, with a foot or so of space between each. It was nothing Karus had not witnessed before, but seeing his comrades in such a state always tore at his heart. Orderlies moved amongst the moaning, doing what they could.

Karus found the surgeon, a man in his late twenties named Ampelius, who was finishing up sewing a nasty wound on the arm of an unconscious man. Not wanting to interrupt as Ampelius performed such delicate work, Karus waited. The surgeon finally sat back and looked around.

"Centurion Karus," the surgeon said wearily as he stood. He wiped blood from his hands onto a very dirty apron. "Good of you to visit and check in on the wounded."

"Ampelius," Karus returned the surgeon's greeting and then gestured at the wounded man. "How is he?"

"Oh, he's fine." The surgeon offered a low chuckle that came out almost like a cackle. "As long as infection does not set in, he should regain full use of his arm. He just passed out when I rinsed the wound with a little vinegar is all. Actually, it made my job easier. I couldn't get him to stand still while I examined him."

"That tends to happen when the treatment is painful," Legionary Drusus said.

The surgeon frowned at the legionary.

"There will likely be more wounded," Karus said before Ampelius could reply. The man was known for treating his patients as if they were common farm animals. That said, he was gifted at his work and had saved many a lad's life. "Do you need anything?"

"A proper hospital ward."

"Not likely," Karus responded, "at least any time soon."

The surgeon ran a hand through his hair. He glanced around before turning back to Karus.

"I could use more help."

"You will have it."

"How long will we be staying here?" Ampelius bit his lip, almost as if he feared the answer.

"I would guess at least until morning," Karus said. "Longer if needed. Why?"

"Give me some warning if you intend to move."

"I will," Karus said. He was about to step away when he stopped. "And if we have to leave in a hurry…"

"You don't need to tell me my duty," Ampelius snapped. The surgeon took a deep breath and calmed himself. "It will be quick and quite painless. No one unable to march will be left breathing."

"Thank you."

The surgeon took a long look at Legionary Drusus before moving away as an orderly called for his attention.

Karus looked once more around the summit. In the time he had spent speaking with the surgeon, several cohorts had arrived. Under the bright moonlight, their officers were busily reforming their men.

Karus recognized Fourth Cohort's standard. Felix had formed up his cohort into two long ranks and was stumping along behind the second rank, speaking with one of his centurions.

"Felix," Karus called.

"Karus." Felix stopped and gestured for the other centurion with whom he had been talking to continue on without him.

"How are you?" Karus asked.

"My cohort is in good shape. We gave better than we got." Felix paused a moment. "I've likely lost around thirty men though."

Karus looked over Fourth Cohort and then glanced around the hilltop. Most of the cohorts had now arrived. The last few were just emerging from the clouds, almost as if they were sea monsters climbing their way out of the ocean. More importantly, there appeared to be little disorder other than from the camp followers. Unit cohesiveness looked strong and intact. It was a testament to the legion's discipline.

"What's your plan?" Felix asked and then continued before Karus could speak. "I fear there is little chance we can break out and elude the enemy. This is their ground. They know every path, rock, stream, and hill."

"I am thinking," Karus said, eying his friend. He could read the stress in the other's eyes. "We hold this hill and allow the enemy to throw themselves against our shield walls. We make sure we bleed them something good."

"We got lucky," Felix said with some heat. "There are at least thirty thousand Celtic warriors down there, perhaps maybe even forty. Most are happily looting what is left of our supply train. We were only pursued by the more disciplined of the enemy. Had they all turned their attention to us, we would not be here talking this over. When they get around to coming, it will not be as easy as you are making it out to be."

"Do you have a better suggestion?" Karus took a step closer to his friend. He waited and, when Felix said nothing, continued in a low tone so that only the two of them could hear. "For all intents and purposes, we are stuck on this bloody hill. Even if we marched down the other side and tried to escape into the wilderness, the enemy would soon catch up. Exhausted and tired, somewhere along our column of march they would hit us, or at the very least set up a blocking position to bring us to battle. As you said, we got lucky. Will we be so fortunate the next time? I don't think so. This is good ground, damn fine ground. They have to climb to reach us. We will have the advantage of strong lines and the ability to easily move reserves interiorly to where we need them. We can hold for a time, no matter how many they throw at us."

Felix released a heavy breath as he rubbed his jaw. After a moment, he glanced around the hilltop. "What if they sit back and decide to starve us out?"

"I don't see that happening," Karus said and took a step back. "This is a religious site. There are druid stones around us." Karus pointed one out to Felix. "No, they will come for us. The druids will insist on reclaiming their holy site. My guess is that just as soon as there is some light, the enemy will attack. With luck, we can bleed them good and even the odds a little."

Felix said nothing, clearly thinking it through. He continued to rub his chin thoughtfully.

"We have the mule train," Karus said. "Though we will be exposed to the elements, we will have food and water for a few days. Once an opportunity presents itself and the enemy is exhausted, we will either make a break for it or go over to the attack. If we have to, we will fight our way all the way back to Eboracum."

"Julionus screwed us good." Felix untied the straps of his helmet and slowly removed it. "You always had the better tactical mind, Karus. If there is one person who can get us out of this mess, it is you. I sincerely hope your plan works."

"It has to," Karus said, and then flashed a grin. "It's the only plan I've been able to come up with."

Felix let out a long breath, almost as if he were calming himself from the stress of battle. A lopsided smile crept up on his face. "What do you want me to do with my prisoners?"

"Prisoners?" Karus was surprised at the abrupt change in subject. He was even more surprised that Felix had bothered to take any.

"Yes." Felix gestured over to the left. Two men under a heavy guard were sitting on the ground. "Orders were to take any druids that fell into our hands. I managed to grab a couple."

"Druids?" Karus shook his head as he walked over, with Felix and Legionary Drusus following.

The prisoners looked otherworldly. They wore black robes painted over with white arcane symbols. Their arms, hands, and faces were heavily tattooed, and their long hair had been limed back. One had been hit hard on the head and held a hand up to the wound, which oozed blood slowly out between his fingers. He looked a little dazed. The other glared up at Karus and Felix with a hatred that Karus found unsurprising. Studying the two of them, Karus felt nothing but disgust. He spat on the ground.

"What with the legate dead," Felix said, "I suppose those orders no longer stand. Want me to put 'em down?"

Karus considered it. Then shook his head.

"Why not?"

"We might be able to use them at some point."

"To what purpose?"

"I don't know yet," Karus admitted. "Perhaps they will have use in barter or trade. They are holy men. We don't know their value to the enemy."

"All right," Felix said with a heavy sigh that reeked with disappointment. "I will keep them safe until you say otherwise."

The two officers walked away from the prisoners and back toward the line. Legionary Drusus followed at a respectable distance.

"I want you to begin digging in," Karus said. "Give me a defensive berm on the edge of the slope before your position." He clapped his friend on the shoulder. "Best not waste the time our enemy has foolishly given us."

"I will get right on it," Felix said.

"Good." Karus looked beyond the Fourth and saw the standard of the First Nervorium Auxiliary Cohort. "Don't let me keep you. I must speak with Pactus next. I will check in with you later."

Felix gave a curt nod and stepped away.

"Drusus," Karus said, turning toward the legionary. "I should be quite safe now. Go find Cestus and your century."

"Yes, sir." The legionary saluted and left.

Karus walked behind the Fifth's line, thinking things over as he moved in the direction of the First Nervorium. The legion was in a dire position. They were outnumbered, unsupported, and a long way from friendly territory, with limited supply. Karus could not see how he could save the legion. He looked heavenward. A miracle was what they needed.

If only the gods would grant one.

As if in reply, the wind abruptly picked up, with an incredibly strong gust that blew across the summit. The wind was so cold that it stung Karus's face, hands, and feet. The clouds, which had been lapping the crest of the hilltop-turned-island, surged over it like a great tidal wave.

Karus and everyone around him were plunged into a dark, swirling fog, thick with moisture. The wind gusted hard. Karus stumbled as his legs inexplicably became weak, and he fell painfully to his knees. He rubbed at his eyes, disoriented, and saw a bright azure light illuminating the fog just a handful of feet away, toward where the surgeon had been. He rubbed at his eyes again, not sure he quite believed what he was seeing.

One of the druid stones was ablaze in a pale blue light that pushed away the swirling fog. The stone's fire grew in intensity, and a wave of dizziness rolled over Karus. He fell over on his side and rolled onto his back, helpless to do more than blink.

Karus's thoughts had become strangely muddled and his eyes grew heavy with exhaustion. He felt himself slipping off into oblivion, even as the wind stopped and a sense of quiet settled around him. The scuff of a footstep, sounding loud amidst the silence, snapped his eyes open. A blurred form was above him. Karus blinked his eyes, tears rolling down his cheeks, attempting to focus as someone knelt beside him. His vision cleared.

"You!" Karus was shocked.

The Celtic noble he had seen in the legate's headquarters a few weeks before looked down upon him. The man put a hand upon Karus's chest armor—not in a threatening manner, but one that was filled with affection, much like a father comforting a child after a terrible nightmare. The man's eyes were kindly too.

Karus felt a wave of tiredness sweep over him, dragging him back toward that deep oblivion. His eyes closed, and though he struggled mightily, Karus began drifting off into a deep, dark void, fighting a losing battle. The feeling terrified him, even as he heard the man speak in fluent Latin.

"Sleep, Karus, for you have destiny." The Celtic noble's voice was deep and gravelly. "You shall have your empire without end."

Chapter Six

Karus opened his eyes, blinking several times under the bright sunlight. It was quite harsh upon his eyes, and his vision swam before clearing. He found he was lying on his stomach, with the side of his helmet pressed into the dirt. The smell of moist, pungent soil and vegetation filled his nostrils as he breathed in. There was also a strange tang in the air that was slightly acidic. He could not quite identify it. Wondering what had happened, he shifted his head slightly. The cheek guard of his helmet scraped against the pebbles in the dirt.

Karus groaned, shifting muscles that cried out in agony. It was as if he had not moved for some time.

Slowly, he pulled himself to his feet, and almost immediately lost his balance, collapsing painfully onto his knees. His head pounded abominably. He put both hands to the sides of his head and felt the cold metal of his helmet. Unfastening the straps with trembling hands and stiff fingers, he swayed unsteadily. Then he wrenched the helmet from his head, tossing it aside. It landed with a clunk and clatter.

His vision swam again. Karus rubbed at his eyes. His mouth was dry, and foul. A wave of nausea threatened to overwhelm him, and he almost doubled over as his stomach cramped badly. He dry retched, gagging. Nothing came up.

Had he drunk himself senseless?

Karus could not remember what had happened the previous night. It was as if his head were in a fog. Still on his knees, he shook his head to clear it, and memory returned in a rush. The ambush, the legate dead, the senior tribune fled, Karus's desperate defense of the legion, the enemy's overwhelming numbers... A wave of nausea threatened to overwhelm him once again. He recovered, and the memory continued to return in a flood.

Vision clearing, he looked up in alarm, studying his surroundings as he recalled the fighting withdrawal up the large hill's steep slope, the enemy snapping at their heels. Karus's eyes went wide as he took in his surroundings. He rubbed at them, not quite believing what he was seeing.

He was surrounded by hundreds—no, thousands of bodies. Karus glanced around the hilltop, sickened. He emptied the contents of his belly into the dirt. Taking a shuddering breath, he wiped his mouth with the back of his hand and sat back on his knees, a terrible sadness tugging on his heart at the sight of so many of his comrades' bodies.

The legion, her allied auxiliary cohorts, the supply train, and the camp followers... all dead.

Bodies were everywhere, some even lying one atop another. It was impossible to believe, to conceive even.

How had he survived?

Guilt threatened to overwhelm him, then he saw movement amongst the bodies and turned his head. Another survivor groaned, picking himself up to his hands and knees. The legionary looked wildly around, clearly disoriented. There was additional movement amongst the bodies. Others were stirring from their lifeless states.

What was going on here?

Karus dragged himself once again to his feet, struggling to focus his mind. He staggered drunkenly before managing to steady himself. He turned around in a complete circle, thoroughly astonished. He wasn't surrounded by the dead, but the unconscious.

"What magic is this?"

Karus clapped his hands to the sides of his head as the world seesawed. He staggered a few feet forward until his sense of balance returned. He blinked, clearing tears from his eyes, and found himself standing upon the edge of a steep slope. Karus froze, eyes widening. The sun was halfway up into the sky, but that was not what caught his attention.

There was a second sun, rising just behind the first.

Karus closed his eyes tight and kept them that way, hoping that when he opened them the impossible vision would pass. It did not.

He heard oaths uttered behind him as those just stirring regained their senses and took in the same sight. A woman screamed, and kept screaming. It shattered his momentary paralysis. Karus took a step back from the edge of the slope, then looked about him more carefully. As hard as it was to believe, Karus understood instinctively that he was no longer in Britannia.

What had happened?

How had they come to be here?

Karus studied his surroundings more carefully. He was standing upon the edge of an extremely large hill. Ground down by age and weather, the top was flat and smoothed out, with only grass and a few large stones dignifying its top.

The hill stood alone, shaped in the way a child playing at the beach might have molded a small wet mound of sand, and it towered over a veritable sea of trees. The forest stretched outward for as far as the eye could see. The leafy canopy, several hundred feet below the summit of the hill, was thick, nearly impenetrable. More confident of his balance, Karus stepped up closer to the edge and looked down. The slope was very steep, but manageable. It was covered with a thick carpet of green grass, the ends of which produced delicate white flowers. He had never seen grass quite like it.

The hilltop itself was bare but for the strange grass, which grew to a length of about six inches. Karus moved a foot, feeling the soft, lush grass with his toes. In Britannia, the vegetation had been browned by winter.

Karus tore his gaze from the grass. Looking down below him, he scanned the vast, unspoiled forest. There were no villages or farms that could be seen, nor were there any large breaks in the green canopy. He could see no smoke rising into the air either. Smoke was the universal sign of habitation.

Where was he?

Karus racked his memory and recalled the hill he had led the legion up, seeking better defensive ground to hold off the Celtic attackers. He recalled the flat, bald top of that hill, crowned with a large circle of stones, a holy site.

Was this Druid magic?

The hill he was standing on now was clearly not the same one he had stood upon last night, working to keep the legion together and her lines firm. The trees down the slope were different as well, not the small, stunted things that grew under Britannia's harsh climate, but giants that reached hundreds of feet into the air. Karus had never seen trees so tall.

A large-winged bird caught his attention. It was bright greenish. The bird skimmed just above the treetops, then gracefully climbed upward on a draft of air.

"Sir!" The voice was full of panic.

Karus turned to find a legionary who had dragged himself to his feet. He recognized the man as Livius Marcus, a veteran from his own cohort. Marcus had put in more than fifteen years of hard service. He was a rock, unshakable in battle, unflappable, and a steadying influence in the line. Marcus was up for advancement, which would eventually see him promoted to optio.

Karus was stunned to read the naked terror in the other man's eyes.

"Sir," Marcus said, voice quavering, "what's happened?"

"Great gods," another cried out in a half shriek. Karus looked around and saw the man cowering behind a large purplish rock. "Oh great gods, where are we?"

At the words, Karus felt as if a bolt of Jupiter's lightning had struck him. This wasn't druid magic. The druids would have done nothing for the Romans but speed them on their way into the shadow. This had to be the work of the gods. In their infinite power, the gods had transported the legion here, to this strange land. Karus rubbed his chin as the idea grew. It was the only thing that made sense to him.

Glancing around the strange terrain, he shook his head, knowing the truth when he saw it. Karus sucked in a breath, eyes returning to the strange bird. He had not expected this... to wake up somewhere else, somewhere completely different.

Yes, this was clearly the work of the gods. But which one? Jupiter? Mars? Janus? He recalled the series of stones set in a large circle crowning the hill he had selected for their last stand. A vague memory of those stones glowing a pale blue flashed before his eyes, followed by a memory of someone else. Karus could not remember clearly what had happened. Yes, a miracle had been performed. He was sure of it. The legion had been saved. The gods in their wisdom and mercy had spared the Ninth from certain defeat and destruction!

Karus blew out, and then took another deep breath, exhaling it slowly. When the opportunity presented itself, he would offer up a suitable sacrifice of thanks. The gods had done right by him, and it was only reasonable to return what little favor he could.

A panicked shout drew his attention. A legionary leapt to his feet and threw aside his shield, sword, and helmet. Screaming, he went running down the steep slope of the hill in a mad dash. He stumbled and fell, his feet caught up in a tangle of low-lying brush. Scrambling back to his feet, he plunged madly onward, and in moments disappeared into the tree-line below. There were more cries of alarm and panic after that. Amongst them, he also heard a mule bray repeatedly and a horse whinny in terror. Karus glanced around again. Most of those he had initially thought dead were now stirring, regaining their senses with a good number now on their feet and milling about in confused alarm. There was even some wailing and crying coming from the camp followers and children. The sound irritated Karus. He had never much liked children.

"Sir," Marcus said again, "where are we?"

"Discipline," Karus said to himself as he eyed his people. For with the death of Julionus and the cowardly flight of Saturninus, he was now in command.

"Sir?" Marcus asked, confused, brow furrowed under the rim of his helmet.

Karus clenched his jaw.

These men, in the service of the empire, were professional soldiers. Daily, they were worked to exhaustion, either through drill or manual labor. This made them tough, and hard. During the most stressful situations and under the worst possible conditions, it was the glue, the secret recipe, that held a legion together. It was what made the Roman legionary the toughest, meanest, and most feared soldier on the battlefield. Though the march north into enemy territory had been a brutal and taxing affair, it had changed nothing.

These men were the legion. They were its beating heart, and though, for a moment, it had stuttered to a stop, he would restart it.

Karus took another deep breath of fresh air, tasting that strange foreign tang. It was time to restore order.

"Fall in!" Karus shouted in his best parade-ground voice, which only a centurion could develop over years of service. He poured his irritation and anger into it. It cut over the cries and lamentations that filled the air.

"Centurions," Karus roared as all eyes swung his way, "optios, have your men fall in!"

Almost immediately, the cry was taken up by the surviving officers of the legion and those from the auxiliary cohorts. Standards that had been lying discarded on the ground were picked up by their bearers, brushed off, and hoisted proudly up into the air. It cheered Karus's spirit to see them, almost as if the legion had been reborn.

Perhaps, it had been?

Men trained to respond to orders moved to comply. At first it was a scene of great confusion as men sought their individual sections, centuries, and cohorts. There were repeated shouts as centurions and optios called out for their men. In short order, the legion and her attached auxiliary cohorts began to take shape on the hilltop.

Karus was pleased to see the centurions from his own cohort forming his men up, Pammon and Ajax amongst them. There was something calming about being given direction, and Karus sensed it in the air. This was only the first step to restoring order. To reinforce it, he would project a sense of control and confidence. Karus watched in silence, his face a schooled, unreadable mask as the legion organized herself. The legion needed strength right now, and Karus would lend it some.

As the legion came together, Karus noticed a set of large stones that could not be natural to the hill. Each had been placed about twenty feet apart from one another. From what he could see, the stones stretched out in a rough semicircle, disappearing around the other side of the cohorts that were forming.

The stones themselves stood only about four feet in height and were nearly uniform in shape. They likely ran around to the other side of the hill and formed a perfect circle. They were very different from the vague memory he had of the stone circle that stood upon the hill he had chosen for his defensive position. These appeared older. They had an aged look, as if the weather of countless years had slowly worn them down to the size they were now.

Karus moved over to the nearest stone and reached out to feel its cold surface. He almost immediately snatched his hand away, having felt not the cool touch of stone, but warmth. Tentatively, he placed his hand back upon its surface, which was warm, but not uncomfortably so. He stood transfixed, marveling, running his hand along the smoothed surface. The temperature in the air was that of a comfortable spring day, and yet the stone felt as if it had been heated by a hot summer sun.

The cacophony around him began to settle, drawing his attention away from the miraculous stone and back to the legion. Soon, only the camp followers were making any noise, and even they began to fall silent as the legion formed up. Karus reluctantly removed his hand from the stone. He had his duty to attend to.

Somewhere, a baby began to wail.

Karus calmly surveyed the scene before him. Three cohorts—the First, Fourth, and Fifth—were formed up to his immediate front. Behind them, in neat, orderly blocks, he could make out additional cohorts. Interspersed between the formations in untidy bunches were civilian camp followers.

They too would have to be organized, Karus thought sourly. If he ignored them, Karus would face an immediate mutiny. So, he would work to protect them as well. It was a complication, but one he was accustomed to dealing with.

Karus saw a centurion approaching him.

"Felix," Karus drawled, resting a hand upon the pommel of his sword, acting as if nothing were even remotely wrong. Karus, like most other centurions, had long since learned how to project a sense of strength and calmness when he felt anything but. He well knew that Felix would understand this.

"What is going on?" Felix said in a low tone, stepping nearer so that they could not be overheard.

Karus was silent as he considered his answer.

"It seems," Karus blew out a breath, "the gods have delivered us from certain destruction."

Felix mulled on that before looking off into the distance. He turned back to Karus. "You think so? Truly?"

"Do you doubt it?" Karus asked him. "Last night our position was hopeless. We were surrounded and outnumbered by thousands of the enemy." Karus gave a shrug. "The legate is dead, and the senior tribune legged it and took one of Valens's squadrons with him." Karus paused and took a breath, calming himself. Saturninus's cowardice bothered him intensely, even if the tribune had gotten what he deserved in the end. But Karus had to project calm before the men, so he forced himself to let the anger go.

"Those barbarians," Karus continued, "would have started in on us just as soon as it was light enough to see. Yes, I think our current position is much improved."

Felix said nothing as he considered this.

Karus glanced over the ranks of men. All eyes were on the two officers as they spoke. Karus knew he had to immediately establish that things were not as bad as they seemed. The alternative was a mutiny or, worse, dissolution of the legion. He did not much care for that. To keep such a thing from happening, he had to get the officers on his side, and he would start with Felix, a respected leader.

"Do you have a better explanation?" Karus demanded quietly, turning to fully face his old friend.

Felix gave Karus a hard look, then lowered his eyes and gave a shake of his head. "I cannot explain this. It must be as you say."

"Good," Karus said, sucking in a breath. "Together, we must convince the other officers. We do that, and they can then explain to their men that the gods, in their wisdom and mercy, have saved us from destruction."

Felix gave a curt nod of agreement.

"The Ninth Legion," Karus continued, "and her auxiliary cohorts have been blessed by the gods. We have been delivered from certain annihilation."

"I agree." Felix nodded solemnly, with a quick look behind him at the assembled ranks of the legion. He turned back to Karus. "We are gods blessed."

Karus was pleased by the response. It was a start.

"Karus," Felix said, "if the gods did save us, what price do you think they will extract from us in return?"

Karus looked sharply at Felix, suddenly going cold. His friend had a point.

"I don't know," Karus said. "Besides, we can't worry about that now."

"I suppose you are right," Felix said. "We focus on the now."

"We must ascertain where exactly we are," Karus said. He looked out at the vast forest that spread outward from the hill.

"It kind of looks like Gaul," Felix said with a distasteful glance at the dense forest, which spread out as far as the eye could see.

"It does," Karus admitted, then gestured. "What about the second sun?"

"A sign from the gods perhaps?" Felix postulated. "An omen?"

Karus nodded, considering the idea. If they were in Gaul, that could present problems. Many of the occupied tribes were less than friendly and, given the chance, would happily turn on Rome.

"We must be on guard," Felix said. "If this is Gaul, we could be beyond the frontier, maybe even in Germania, or worse, somewhere farther afield."

"I hope not. Once we know for certain, we can reestablish contact with the empire."

Karus saw another large bird in the far distance, this one red in color, gracefully skimming over the treetops. It was heading lazily in their direction.

As a fresh-faced legionary, Karus had served in Gaul. He had seen his first combat there. It had not been a pleasant experience.

His eyes tracked the bird's graceful flight. Karus could not recall seeing such large birds in Gaul. All he remembered were the mean-spirited black ravens that worried the flesh of the dead.

"Contact with the empire should be a priority," Felix said.

"Though," Karus said, "once we do reestablish contact, I will be hard-pressed to explain how we ended up here."

"I think you are right," Felix said with a slow smile, followed by a chuckle. "Better to be here than where we were."

"Though the gods seem to have smiled upon us," Karus said, "I fear the emperor may not be so pleased as we are."

"It wasn't you that gave the order for the legion to march north." Felix cocked his head slightly, an angry expression coming across his face. "Julionus gave that order, and it was a stupid one at that."

"He is beyond answering for his actions," Karus said, and ran a hand through his matted hair. "I, on the other hand, may provide a suitable scapegoat. Without us, the tribes will surely be emboldened and will push south, causing all kinds of trouble for the province and the rest of the garrison."

"Your actions last night saved this legion," Felix countered. "Had you not taken command and led us up that hill, we would be nothing more than a feast for the crows. Face it, Karus, you saved the legion ... with the gods' help, of course."

Karus nodded, but said nothing. His eyes swept the dense forest again. Why did it have to be Gaul? Why could it not have been somewhere settled, civilized? Why not Greece, or even Egypt? Karus supposed he should be grateful, and truly he was. He just had no idea which way to go other than to the west. If they were too far beyond the frontier, and indeed in Germania, moving south would not work. So west it was, back to a friendly Roman province.

Glancing up at the suns, he wondered which way was west.

The forest looked deep and impenetrable. Moving through it would be difficult, perhaps even worse than the march along the muddy road. That was the least of their problems, Karus realized with a quick glance back at the assembled legion. They had lost most of the supply train, and in the fighting retreat up the hill, Karus had only managed to bring the mule train with them. He had to find a way to feed several thousand mouths, and quickly, before the little supply they did have ran out. Discipline alone would only carry the legion so far.

The flight of the large reddish bird once again drew his attention. It was gliding toward them, riding on a current of air. Occasionally it gave a flap of the wings. The bird was incredibly graceful. Felix also turned to watch, and Karus felt his friend suddenly stiffen.

Karus's eyes narrowed. There was something odd about this bird, though he could not quite put his finger on what was off. The bird, he judged, was still around a quarter mile distant. It suddenly banked to the right and began to actively flap its wings, climbing up into the air with astonishing speed.

Karus's eyes widened.

"I don't believe we are in Gaul," Felix breathed as a distant roar reached them.

Karus agreed. They were most definitely not in Gaul. They must be very far from the frontier indeed, for they were in a place where dragons roamed the skies.

Part Two

Chapter Seven

Karus dragged his gaze from face to face. Most of the senior officers of the legion and prefects of the auxiliary cohorts were gathered around him in a rough semicircle. Karus could see Otho and Pactus making their way over to them, and so he waited. The officers wore only their gray service tunics. Dio and Felix stood off to the right with Flaccus, who shifted impatiently from one foot to the other. It had been at least six hours since Karus and the others had woken on this hilltop. Karus could read the stress and exhaustion etched in each face. He knew his was no different.

The two strange suns had climbed high into the cloudless sky above. One was smaller than its partner and yellow, while the other had an orange tinge to it. The sight of the unfamiliar suns was unsettling. A light breeze blew by and around the officers, ruffling tunics and gently disturbing hair.

The temperature was comfortable, perhaps a tad warm, but not unbearably so. Karus found the wind pleasant, even relaxing. He decided that, despite the legion's strange predicament, anywhere else it would have been nearly the perfect day. The weather here was certainly an improvement over what they had had in Britannia.

This was their second meeting of the day. Karus had seen to it that this gathering occurred near the edge of the hilltop. The closest legionaries had been ordered back twenty yards, thereby creating a bit of space so that their conversation would remain private. Each cohort was busily working away at cleaning the mud, grime, and blood off of their kit. Karus had put them to the task to bring about a sense of normalcy to this unusual situation. He had then spent the next hour speaking with his senior centurions. Karus had then cleaned his own gear. It was always good to set an example. Besides, he had needed time to think.

It had been a relief to shrug out of the heavy armor. Cleaning the grime and dried blood out of every little recess had been a chore, not to mention a near exercise in futility without the proper cleaning tools. Still, the process had afforded him time to think through what needed doing. Upon finishing, Karus had toured the hilltop, checking in on each cohort before returning to where he had left his kit, which was where the senior officers were now assembling. Karus glanced down at his armor a few feet away. He was not looking forward to putting it back on. His leg ached abominably, not to mention his bruised side and back where he had been struck blows in battle.

Karus returned his gaze to his officers. Titus from Third Cohort and Fadenus from the Eighth were the only two senior officers that had not made it. Both had fallen in battle during the retreat. Centurions Macrinus and Arrens had come in their stead to represent their respective cohorts. Of the prefects, only Valens was absent. A road had been discovered leading off the hill. Karus had dispatched his cavalry to scout it.

Otho and Pactus arrived and fell in next to the others. It was time to begin. Though under normal conditions it might not have been necessary, Karus was mindful that this was anything but. He needed to cement his authority.

"Macrinus," Karus said, getting down to business. "You will assume command of the Third. Arrens, effective immediately, you have the Eighth."

Though there were likely other officers who were more senior and experienced, Karus felt a need to get his cohorts in order sooner rather than later. Besides, he reasoned, it was likely the centurions of those two cohorts had nominated these two to represent them, which meant both almost assuredly commanded the respect of their fellow officers. Still, each would bear watching and need his personal attention to help them grow into their positions as senior officers.

"Thank you, sir," Macrinus said, a slight trace of a grin showing.

"Yes, sir." Arrens gave a curt nod that was filled with a personal confidence born through years of hard service and leadership.

"I know you both will do the legion proud," Karus said.

"Congratulations," Frontinus said, which was immediately followed by the other senior officers chiming in.

All centurions were part of a brotherhood, but the senior centurions of a legion were something altogether special. These two were now part of that fold that usually, but not always, transcended any personal animosities or feelings. These men relied upon each other, especially in battle. Old grudges and hard feelings had to be put aside. If they weren't, Karus would see that they were.

Of all the senior officers, only Flaccus remained silent, offering nothing to the two newly promoted men. Instead, he simply crossed his arms, jaw flexing, and stewed. Karus was not pleased by the display of overt displeasure. He decided that later, when he had the time, he would speak with Flaccus in private.

"Ampelius," Karus said, turning to their surgeon, who was standing off to his left, slightly apart from the officers. "Let's have your report."

The surgeon straightened his posture from a near slouch and cast a quick look at the other officers.

"I have treated one hundred forty-one that I deem walking wounded and another twenty-four non-ambulatory." Ampelius's tone was laced with a heavy weariness. His eyes were bloodshot. Karus knew that the surgeon had been working days on end without a break. He and his small staff had been stretched thin. When others turned in for the night, Ampelius frequently kept working, stitching up wounds and treating patients. The life of a legion surgeon on campaign was a hard one, and Karus respected him for his dedication to his craft.

"Two men," Ampelius continued, his voice deadened by the exhaustion, "will not make it through the day. Of the walking wounded, I have sent the majority back to their cohorts, with orders for light duty only until I say otherwise." Ampelius paused and glanced around at the senior officers sourly. "I would greatly appreciate your cooperation. I do not enjoy treating the same man twice, much as you don't like to take the same ground twice."

"Don't worry Ampe," Dio said with a sly grin. "You can trust us."

"That is precisely what I am afraid of," the surgeon replied caustically, exhibiting emotion for the first time.

"Thank you, Ampelius, for your report," Karus said before things could get out of hand. The last thing Karus needed was an argument to break out. It was important that he maintain firm control of this meeting. The surgeon's shoulders slumped back to a slouch as the eyes of the officers traveled back to Karus. "Ampelius and his staff have been greatly overworked. I would ask that you respect his order concerning light duties to the maximum extent possible."

The surgeon nodded his thanks.

Karus cleared his throat and scratched at an itch. Gods, he thought, I could use a proper bath.

"Dio," Karus said, moving the meeting along. "Give us the strength tally."

"I took a census of each cohort as ordered. Of the ten cohorts," Dio said, glancing down at a small wax tablet he had been holding, "the legion's current strength, including the walking wounded, is four thousand two hundred and two men. Of the auxiliary cohorts, there are an additional five thousand three hundred twenty-one effectives. That gives us a total strength of nine thousand five hundred and twenty-three men under arms. Do you wish a cohort-by-cohort breakdown? Some," there was a quick glance toward Flaccus, "got hit harder than others."

Karus considered it a moment, then shook his head. Their losses, though grievous, were better than he had feared. Still, it was terrible and Karus's heart hurt at losing so many fine men. "You can give that to me later. What of the camp followers?"

"The count is still underway," Dio said with an unhappy look, "but it appears they number somewhere around seven thousand survivors."

Karus clenched his jaw at the news. If correct, it meant that at least three thousand followers had not made it. There was an uncomfortable shifting amongst the officers. Karus spat on the ground in disgust. This was all Julionus's fault. The gods only knew their fate, poor souls. He let out a slow breath. There would be serious heartache amongst the ranks. Men had lost loved ones, and even entire families.

Karus could have received this information privately, but he needed the trust of the officers and so they got the bad news with the good. He could not appear to be concealing vital information. It would come out in the end. Besides, all of the senior officers had suffered through losses over the years. This had hardened them. They would endure.

"Thank you, Dio," Karus said.

"You are welcome," Dio said.

"Felix," Karus said, turning to the next matter. "Have you completed the inventory of our food supplies?"

"Yes," Felix said. "Most of the mules made it. It was a good call to delay the retreat until we could transfer what food we could from the wagons to the mules. I won't bore you with the tally of what was saved. As near as I can tell, we have enough to last us at least a fortnight. If we ration, we can probably stretch that out a few days more."

"Needless to say," Ampelius spoke up, straightening his posture once more as he addressed Karus and the senior officers, "the men have been on short rations for several days already. Strength is flagging."

"We're all aware of that," Felix said with some irritation, shooting the surgeon a black look. "My stomach is nearly stuck to my backbone."

The surgeon seemed to deflate under the look. "Karus, the real problem is water. We don't have near enough to even get us through the night."

"Well," Karus said and glanced quickly out at the forest, "I've dispatched Valens and his cohort to explore the road we found on the other side of the hill. With luck, he will happen upon a stream or small river close enough that it will not be a problem."

"That forest down there is certainly green," Mettis said with a glance down the slope. "There is bound to be a water source nearby. Speaking of which, how long are we going to remain here, Karus?"

"And go where?" Flaccus demanded harshly. "For Jupiter's sake, we don't even know where we are."

Mettis frowned at Flaccus, but did not reply.

"There seems only one possible path open to us," Otho said, drawing everyone's attention.

"And what's that?" Flaccus said to the prefect of the First Nervorium Cohort.

"The road, of course." Otho's tone made it abundantly clear he felt this obvious. "I, for one, would prefer not to have to force my way through a dense forest."

"Otho's right," Karus said before Flaccus could respond. Flaccus turned his smoldering gaze upon Karus. "As I said earlier, we need to find out where we are. The only way to do that is by marching out of here." Karus paused, returning Flaccus's heated look with one of steady strength. "All roads lead somewhere. The sooner we find out where that one goes, the better." Karus shifted his gaze around the half circle. "I need not remind you, but I will. Our overriding objective is to return to a friendly province and report for duty. We can't do that sitting here atop this hill, where we will eventually run out of food, not to mention water."

"And what if that road leads us away from friendly territory?" Flaccus asked.

"We will cross that bridge," Karus said, flashing a warning glance at Flaccus and hardening his tone, "when we come to it."

Flaccus held Karus's gaze for a heartbeat, then broke eye contact. Karus almost sighed. Flaccus would need more than a talking to. He would need to be watched. If his attitude did not improve, Karus might be forced to relieve him. It was not something he wanted to do. Though Flaccus was not quite a friend, he was a man of considerable experience and a hardened warrior. He had more than earned his position as a senior centurion and combat leader. That alone deserved Karus's respect.

"Staying here is not an option," Karus said to them all. "As Ampelius so aptly pointed out, we need to find food, and soon. The strength of our men is flagging each day we remain on short rations." Karus paused and looked around at his officers. "Our immediate priority is water."

"When do we march?" Pactus asked, clapping his hands together. "My men are almost finished cleaning their kit. We need to keep them busy and their minds off of this strange land. Marching ... well, anywhere ... will be good for them."

"Agreed," Karus said, glancing in the direction of nearest cohort, where the men were busy finishing up their work under the oversight of their junior officers in preparation for inspection. Pactus was right and every officer present knew it. "I would like to get moving within the next hour."

"What of those unable to move under their own power?" Ampelius raised one eyebrow in question. "I would like to know your intentions."

"We will have to make stretchers," Karus said. "We've lost enough men as it is. No one is to be left behind, even the two that are mortally wounded."

"Then, I most assuredly will require additional help," Ampelius said, "if we are going to march within the hour, as you say."

"Pactus," Karus said, "can the Fifth Raetorum spare a section or two to help?"

"We can," Pactus said. "As soon as we break, I will see to it. Say, forty men? Will that be sufficient, Ampelius?"

"It will," the surgeon said, looking deeply relieved and a little grateful. "Thank you."

Karus rubbed a hand on his stubbled chin as he studied the senior officers a moment. Each looked incredibly worn and tired.

"I'll say it again," Karus said, hoping that the more he reinforced it, the better. "The gods have seen fit to transport us here. I don't know the reason. Perhaps the Ninth is gods blessed. I certainly will not tempt fortune and question why. Nor should you or your men. It is enough that we were saved." He paused a heartbeat. "We should all feel extremely fortunate and grateful. If anyone disputes that, I want to hear about it now."

Karus paused again, giving the senior officers a chance to speak. All eyes were upon him. He waited a few heartbeats more and made a point to lock gazes with Flaccus, daring the other to object. Flaccus simply returned the look, eyes smoldering with unfocused anger, and crossed his arms again in a petty act of defiance. In the end, no one objected or, more correctly, voiced it. Karus glanced down at his feet and played with a tuft of the strange flowering grass that grew there. He then looked back up at the senior officers.

"We need to keep the legion together," Karus said. "For if we are in a hostile land, the only way to survive is to continue to work as a team, as we have trained. To do this, we must maintain discipline and good order. Just because the gods brought us here changes nothing. We are the legion, remember that! I will tolerate nothing less than your best. I expect you to communicate this to your officers and men."

"I don't anticipate a problem keeping my men under control," Dio said.

Karus glanced over at his friend and almost smiled. "I would be shocked if anyone here is unable to do the same," he said. "We have all put in and served long, hard years, some of us together, some not. Each of us at one time or another has suffered and been tested individually. Collectively, such trials only serve to make us stronger, and this one is no different. We senior centurions are a brotherhood and, as such, support each other. Together we are the legion, its beating heart." Karus paused and allowed that to sink in. "Now, are there any questions before I detail the order of march?"

"Yes, sir," Frontinus said. "What about the dragons?"

"What of them?" Karus said, noticing more than one set of eyes darting skyward in search of the incredible animals. "They have not harmed us, only flown overhead a few times, nothing more."

"They appear to be hunting," Felix said. "Luckily they don't seem to see us as a food source. If they did, I think they would be munching on Dio about now, though he'd likely be spit out."

There were several chuckles to that, but Karus saw more than a few concerned expressions.

"Look," Karus said. "I've never seen a dragon before and I'm sure that no one else here has either. We've all heard reports and tales for years of legionaries spotting dragons. This is just our first time, that's all. They don't seem interested in us. So, we ignore the beasts as best we can and carry on."

"Karus," Frontinus said with a glance to his left and then right at his peers. "We've all thought those were tall tales told over cups. You have to admit, it's a little disconcerting finding out that such creatures actually exist."

"I find it unsettling as well," Karus admitted. "I also find the two suns disturbing. Worse, we don't know what direction is what. I will not allow that or the dragons to interfere with my duty. We have a job to do. That job is to serve the empire, and the only way we can do that is to return to Roman lands." Karus put cold hard steel into his voice. "I expect each one of you to conduct yourself in the same manner. If you are unable or incapable of doing that, step aside. I want to know now, before we march."

There was an uneasy shifting amongst the officers as they glanced from one to the other. Slowly, their gazes returned to Karus. None appeared ready to relinquish the command they had worked so hard and so long to achieve. It was what Karus had been counting on.

"Good. The line of march," Karus said, getting down to business, "will be as follows… First Cohort will lead. Second comes next, with Third and so forth. Fifth and Sixth Cohorts will have the responsibility to protect the mule train. Tenth will organize and protect the camp followers. The auxiliary cohorts will bring up the rear, with the Fifth Raetorum holding rearguard duty. Are there any questions on that?"

"When will we be stopping for the night?" Otho asked.

"Judging by the rate at which the two suns are moving through the sky…" Karus said. Several of the senior centurions glanced upward. "It's almost noon. I expect to march for three to four hours before calling a halt and settling in for the night. The legion will construct a fortified encampment." Karus held up a hand to forestall any protests. "I know we're short of entrenching tools, but we will just have to make do. We are in a strange land and I, for one, plan on taking no chances until we know exactly where we are. Are there any further questions?"

No one spoke.

"I am sure you have a lot of work to do before we march," Karus said, keeping his tone hard. "Dismissed."

The officers turned away and made for their cohorts, a few talking amongst themselves as they moved off. Felix and Dio remained behind, clearly intent on speaking with Karus.

"Well," Felix said, "that went well."

"A bit harsh on them at the end," Dio said, "weren't you?"

"You did come off a little tough," Felix said.

"It's what they needed," Karus said, feeling his anger rising. "They aren't children. I wanted to make sure that there were no misunderstandings. We have absolutely no idea where we are or how to get back to Roman territory. I am the senior surviving officer. I had to make it plain that I, and I alone, am in command. The Ninth is not a bloody Greek democracy. You both should understand what was just done was absolutely necessary, even shutting down Flaccus."

"I got that," Felix said, holding up his hands toward Karus, "but some of the others might resent you."

"Well, they can bloody well resent me all they want," Karus said, "as long as they follow orders and maintain discipline. That is all I care about at this moment."

"Oh, they will," Dio said, "but some like Flaccus will never be satisfied."

"Flaccus will get over his anger in time," Karus said. "Julionus is dead and I did not have a hand in the misfortune that befell Fifth Cohort."

"No," Dio said, "you didn't."

"I think you should speak with him," Felix said. "Flaccus is boiling over at the losses to his cohort."

"I had planned to this evening," Karus admitted. "Once we make camp, or sooner if the opportunity presents itself."

"The sooner the better," Felix said.

Karus calmed himself. The legion's entire situation was incredibly frustrating, and Karus felt the responsibility weighing heavily upon his shoulders. Karus let out a slow breath, almost as if he were expelling his anger and rage.

"Felix," Karus said, softening his tone considerably as he thought to ask after his friend's wellbeing. "Did Keeli make it?"

"Yes," Felix said. "She's just fine, a little frightened is all. I checked in on her earlier."

"Good," Karus said, "I—"

Karus heard a slight noise behind him, a scuffing of sandals. He turned to see Tribune Delvaris. Karus had not known that the youth had joined them. There was no telling how long he had been there. It was clear that the tribune had heard everything that Karus just said. Though just barely out of boyhood, Delvaris was an officer of the legion, even if he was only a junior aide to the legate. His father, however, was a powerful senator and his rank had been conferred directly by Hadrian's own hand. As such, the boy deserved Karus's respect, even if he had not yet earned it. One day, should he survive to make it back to Rome, Delvaris might become politically powerful and rise to high office, perhaps even the command of a legion.

Karus regarded the tribune a moment. The side of Delvaris's right temple was purple with bruising. Karus felt a stab of sympathy for the boy. His life had almost ended prematurely, well before it had even begun.

"Tribune," Karus said, "since the legate is gone and I am now in command of the legion, you will serve as my aide. Do you have a problem with that?"

"No, sir," Delvaris said, drawing himself up.

Karus was impressed with the youth's tone. It was hard and firm. There was strength there, he decided. Perhaps he could teach this young pup something about leading men so that years from now he would not make the same mistakes that Julionus had.

"How's your head?"

"Hurts something awful," Delvaris said.

"It will pass, son," Dio said with a slight grin appearing on his face. "Karus here once got knocked clean out in the middle of a bad fight. Felix had to drag him to safety, and then literally sit on him 'til he regained his senses."

"Is that true, sir?"

"It is," Felix said with a smile directed over at Karus. "And I never tire of reminding him of it."

"Don't you have to organize your men?" Karus asked Felix.

"Yes, sir," Felix said, smile becoming broader. He snapped off a casual salute, jerked his head at Dio, and the two officers walked off together toward their cohorts, chuckling.

"Stick with me," Karus said, turning back to Delvaris, "and you might just learn something."

"Yes, sir," Delvaris said. "I will try."

"Good, I expect nothing less than your best." Karus paused, breathing in and exhaling out slowly, thinking on what needed doing. "First order of business, Saturninus's horse was recovered last night. I want you to find it and bring it over to First Cohort. Tell Centurion Ajax he is to take custody of the horse and saddlebags for me. No one but Ajax and the legion's aquilifer are to touch those saddlebags. Got that?"

"Yes sir," the tribune said. He saluted and then started off.

"Tribune?"

Delvaris checked his progress and turned to look back on Karus.

"No need to salute me or 'sir' me," Karus said. "You are a tribune. Tribunes do not salute camp prefects. You need only follow my orders. You may call me Karus. Got that?"

"I understand," Delvaris said, coloring slightly.

"Good," Karus said and jerked his head for the boy to move out. He watched as the tribune walked away in search of Saturninus's horse. Karus fully intended to claim Brutus for his own. The money in the saddlebags would go to the legion, as the pay chests had been lost with the main supply train. It likely wasn't much, but if the legion needed money, at some point it might come in handy.

"Excuse me, sir." Karus turned to find one of Valens's troopers approaching, leading his horse. The trooper saluted. "I have a report for you, sir."

"Go ahead," Karus said, returning the salute.

"Prefect Valens," the trooper began, "reports that about a mile and half from the base of the hill, the road crosses a shallow river. Though the bridge that was there has long since collapsed, the river is easily fordable. The water is fresh and fit for drinking, sir."

"Very good," Karus said, feeling relief that they had found a source of fresh water so close. "Anything else to report?"

"No, sir," said the trooper. "I was just told to report that to you."

"Thank you," said Karus and was prepared to dismiss the trooper when he hesitated. "Give me your impression of the forest."

"It is very strange, sir," the trooper said, and then plunged onward. "Some of the trees are familiar. Others I've never seen before. Some are so wide it seems impossible. All the trees seem very old and tall. It's so dark, there is very little brush or growth on the forest floor. It's mostly moss beds and old leaves. Outside of the road, the sun doesn't touch much of the forest floor. Oh, and the road shows no evidence of recent use."

"The road," Karus said, "hasn't been used recently?"

"No, sir," the trooper said. "It is a simple dirt road. We've seen no tracks of any kind other than those made by animals. I only got to the river before I was ordered to report to you, sir. It's possible that the scouts farther up the road have found some evidence of use."

"Thank you," Karus said. "You may return to your unit."

The trooper saluted and left.

Karus looked out at the forest and contemplated it for a few moments. The leafy canopy looked thoroughly impenetrable. There was an ominous feel to it, as if the forest was hiding something. What that was, Karus did not know. He turned around and studied the activity of the legion a few yards away. The men were rushing to finish cleaning their kit, preparing for the coming inspection by their officers, intent as they always were on avoiding a punishment detail. Several formations were already beginning to fall in.

Karus's eyes were drawn back to the forest. The road through the forest would be shaded and chill. Judging by the temperate climate on the hilltop, he suspected that the march the legion was about to make would be much easier than the one they had just endured. Warmer at least, Karus thought, and without an overabundance of mud.

His gaze returned to the legion. Though the men looked presentable, they had just been through an extremely difficult and traumatic experience. They needed an extended rest before going back into action. He did not know if he would be able to give that to them. Gods, he did not even know if he would be able to feed them.

Karus looked heavenward and offered up a silent prayer of thanks to Jupiter. Though such prayers usually included a suitable sacrifice, Karus hoped that the great God of Rome would understand his lack of one.

"Jupiter and Mars," Karus said quietly, adding to his prayer, "I have never been terribly religious, but I will do my best to honor you for this miracle that you bestowed upon the legion. I beg humbly that you continue to favor the Ninth."

It was a poor prayer, but Karus had never been one to pray much. Yes, he had offered the gods routine and regular sacrifices, but not much more. He resolved to correct that oversight. He glanced once again out at the forest for a heartbeat and then turned back to the legion. He had work to do.

Chapter Eight

"Felix," Karus called, spotting his friend just ahead. Felix had clearly been waiting for him along the side of the road. He was leaning against the trunk of a tree that was unbelievably massive. It was at least twenty feet wide and perhaps a hundred or more tall, the top of which disappeared into the green canopy above. As large as it was, the tree was smaller than those just a few yards farther away from the road.

"We've been in the forest two days," Felix said, pushing himself off the tree, "and I can't get over the size of these things. Have you ever seen the like?"

"No, and I know what you mean," Karus said, looking up and marveling. It was hard to believe this tree was just one of many, thousands even. The trees were so tall and the canopy so thick, the forest floor was dark and gloomy, shrouded in a perpetual twilight during daylight hours. At night, beyond the watch fires, it was blacker than pitch.

Almost no direct sunlight penetrated the thick canopy overhead, with the only exception being along the road, which was uncommonly wide. It was perhaps twice that of a typical Roman road. Still, with even the little sunlight that managed to filter its way down through the slim gap above the road, Karus found the forest not only depressing, but slightly unsettling, though he had to admit the gloom beat marching through mud.

Karus sucked in a deep breath of the cool, crisp morning air. It bordered on chilly, but was not uncomfortably so, particularly for men under march. The tang of rotting leaves and moist soil hung heavily on the air.

Glances were thrown their way as the legionaries marching by them eyed the two senior centurions speaking along the roadside. There was more than a little talking amongst the ranks, mostly lighthearted banter, with the occasional bark of harsh laughter thrown in. Karus found that encouraging. And yet, Karus knew they were wondering if something had happened or was in the wind. Karus sighed, understanding that the rumor mill was already at work, cooking up wild speculative stories about what the two senior centurions were discussing. Little did they know it was only the size and height of the trees. The thought almost made him laugh.

Karus had started out as a ranker. He well knew there was nothing to be done to counter this, nor even that he should attempt to do so. Men would gossip and speculate even if they knew the truth. It was just their nature and it served to help pass the time. Life as a legionary was, at most times, mind-numbingly boring, especially when on the march, where you were choking on the dust of those before you.

"Those limbs are huge," Felix said and pointed.

Karus glanced upward at the numerous tree branches far above that emerged and disappeared into the leaf canopy at random. The closest of the branches were at least seventy to eighty feet in height, easily out of reach. They looked small, but Karus understood that was deceptive due to the distance.

"My father once built me a tree house," Felix continued in a wistful tone. "It was really only several small branches nailed up a tree for a crude ladder and a rough platform above. As a child, I thought it marvelous."

"I can only imagine," Karus said, trying to picture a young Felix, unlike the tough, hardened veteran who had become a close friend. He failed utterly.

"Well," Felix said, with a heavy sigh, "envision a tree fort built up there. Those limbs are so thick you could easily walk on them. Gods, Karus, if you wanted, you could build a real house up there."

"The climb would be a bitch though." Karus looked at Felix, wondering where his friend was going with this.

"I had a couple of men report they saw people up there," Felix said, as if he sensed Karus's thoughts. "They were moving from branch to branch, and attempting but failing to keep out of sight."

Karus snapped a glance at Felix and then turned upward, studying the canopy carefully. He saw no one up there. Was it true? Were there people up there? Had the men simply seen shadows? Though Karus had only ever seen one in a cage, he had heard from legionaries who served in Africa that monkeys lived in trees. Could they have seen a monkey?

"Did you see anything?"

"No," Felix said. "I did not."

"They were just imagining things then," Karus said. "This forest is a little eerie."

"I don't know," Felix said with a heavy breath. "The boys who reported it are normally reliable and steady. I just don't know."

Karus said nothing. His friend was taking it seriously, which signaled to Karus that he should do the same.

"If you could climb up to the canopy," Felix said, "those branches are close enough together to be able to step from one to another. I would think you could easily traverse from tree to tree." Felix turned to the tree he been leaning against and grabbed at the rough bark, which grew in thick clumps that could well serve as handholds. "Though I would not want to, if you were adventurous enough a person, you could pull yourself up."

"That's a long climb," Karus said. "And dangerous."

"Dangerous, but not impossible."

Karus rubbed at his forehead. If there were people up in the trees, did they live there? Were they a threat? Or just a figment of the overactive imaginations of the men?

Karus considered this as he watched as men of Seventh Cohort marched by. It was the second morning since they had marched away from the hill. It was not even close to midday yet. A long march lay ahead as the legion moved forward along the road.

Without even the hint of any twists or turns, the road cut an unnervingly straight path through the forest. Karus had never seen anything like it. The bed of the road itself was covered over with a soft layer of dirt and decaying leaves from the previous season's fall. As the men marched, they kicked up a small cloud of dust. Had the climate been a tad dryer, the dust would have been nearly overpowering.

Karus's cavalry scouts had found no recent evidence of use along the road. There had been no tracks other than those left by the wild animals. Karus found this troubling, as he had no idea how long they would have to march before coming across people. Karus had never served in a place that was devoid of habitation.

"What do you think of this road?" Karus asked, glancing back to Felix.

"You mean that it is paved?" Felix raised an eyebrow.

"Yeah," Karus replied, not at all surprised his friend had come to the same conclusion. "It was bothering me, and I didn't even realize it."

"I had the same problem," Felix admitted with a chuckle. "I couldn't understand why the forest had not reclaimed the road. Then it hit me. Despite the dirt and leaves, we've been marching over a paved road. I even dug down to be sure and found the paving stone."

Karus had done the same. In fact, he had ordered a section of men to clear away the dirt along an entire stretch of the road, just to look at the paving. "I would love to see how it was constructed. The stones are much larger than what we would typically use. Have you noticed," Karus pointed to the flat surface of the road, "there also does not appear to be any settling? Whoever built this road knew what they were doing and meant for it to last an age."

"Too true," Felix said, glancing down at their feet. Between the two of them and years of service, they had constructed dozens of roads. When not training or drilling, the legions were employed at building, whether it be roads, aqueducts, bridges… the list ran on.

"This one strikes me as very old," Karus said, "perhaps even predating the trees here. It's ancient, I think."

Felix glanced thoughtfully over at the tree he had been leaning against. "When next we make camp, I think I will set a detail to excavate a portion along the side of road to see its foundation. I want to know how many layers there are and if concrete was used. Perhaps we can learn something."

"Felix," Karus said, changing the subject, "one of the camp followers was bitten by a snake-like creature with legs. It took her less than a minute to die."

"I had heard," Felix said. "It and the sightings were one of the reasons I decided to wait for you. Karus, I am worried. I fear we are very far from Rome."

"Far or not," Karus said, "make sure your men stay away from anything that looks dangerous or, at the very least, is something they have never seen before."

The familiar rhythm of hooves drew their attention in the direction the legion was marching. A cavalry trooper was trotting casually back along the line of march. He spotted Karus and Felix and dug his heels in a little, increasing the pace. He pulled up to a stop in front of the two officers, dismounted, and, with one hand holding his reins, offered a weary salute. Karus returned it. The trooper was very dusty, his armor fairly caked in it. Dirt streaked his face, making it clear he had ridden long and hard. Valens's men had been in the saddle nearly every waking moment since the legion had arrived in this strange place. They were Karus's eyes. This was the first messenger of the day, and Karus was eager to learn his news.

"Prefect Valens sends his regards, sir. He instructs me to report that the forest ends about forty miles ahead. Before you reach the edge of the forest, there is a medium-sized river that will need to be crossed. There was once a bridge at the spot, but only the stone causeways on either side remain. It is manageable to ford, but will slow things down a bit. Also, sir, just beyond the forest, we discovered a city."

"A city, you say?" Felix looked surprised.

"Yes, sir," the trooper replied, attempting to hold back his excitement. "It is very large, walled and about five miles from the forest. It is maybe as big as Rome even, and that's not all, sir. It's completely abandoned."

"Abandoned?" Karus narrowed his eyes. "Are you sure about that?"

"Yes, sir," the trooper said. "The city is ringed by farmland for as far as the eye can see. The farms are deserted too."

"A dead city," Karus said absently to himself, a thought prickling his memory. "Just like Xenophon."

"Who?" Felix asked.

Karus had not realized he had spoken the last aloud.

"A Greek general," Karus explained, looking over. "Xenophon led a Greek army that was part of a doomed campaign against the Persians. If I recall correctly, they were late to the war and arrived to find their allies defeated or surrendered. Honestly, I can't remember which. Anyway, while he and his army retreated back toward Greece, they came across several massive cities that had been long abandoned." Karus thought back to what he recalled of reading about Xenophon's experiences. "He never found out what happened to the people that had once lived there. It was a great mystery, one we would have never known about had he not written it down. I would have loved to see those cities myself."

"Sir." The trooper cleared his throat. "The city and the surrounding countryside were not abandoned that long ago. It seems rather a recent thing, perhaps just a matter of weeks. I've never seen anything like it."

"What you mean?" Karus asked. "Explain yourself."

"I explored a farm just outside of the city, and it's like the people that lived there simply packed up a few personal possessions and, with their animals, just walked off. Where to, I know not. They left behind whatever could not be carried. I found animal feed and a silo filled with grain and dried foods, sir."

The trooper pulled free a coarse brown bag that had been secured to his horse's rump.

"I found this at the farm, sir." He handed the bag over to Karus. The opening had been tied into a knot to keep the contents from spilling out.

Karus undid the knot, opened it, and looked inside. He saw fresh oats. He handed it to Felix, who also looked.

"Horse feed?" Felix glanced back up at the trooper.

"Yes, sir," the trooper said, taking the bag. He tied it back up and then secured the bag to its net along his horse's rump. "And there was a lot of it at that farm, enough to feed a full squadron of cavalry for a week, perhaps more."

Karus glanced over at Felix, not at all liking what he was hearing. It seemed strange that an entire people would just pick up and leave without a very good reason. He could see that Felix had the same concerns as their eyes met.

"Are you certain this city is abandoned?" Karus asked, turning his gaze back upon the trooper.

"I'm sorry, sir. I did not enter. I only saw the city from a distance," the trooper said. "A few scouts went in briefly and saw nobody about. They returned and reported to the prefect. Also, I saw no smoke coming from the city either, sir."

Had people been living in the city in significant numbers, there would have been smoke from cook fires at the very least.

"It seems we have a mystery on our hands," Felix said with an excited look to his eyes. "An empty city, just waiting to be explored. I wonder what mysteries it contains."

Karus felt that was somewhat of an understatement. He, on the other hand, found himself wondering what threats it contained.

"What does Prefect Valens intend?" Karus asked the trooper.

"He has taken a handful of scouts into the city to have a look around. The rest of the cavalry has been charged with exploring the countryside, sir." The trooper's horse tossed its head about and took a sidestep. The man absently tightened his hold on the reins and patted it on the neck affectionately. The animal stilled. "Before the prefect left for the city, he instructed me to tell you, sir, that the city is intact and has in no way been damaged by a siege or assault. The walls look strong and defensible."

Karus got the message. The city might be a good spot to hole up for a while. It might be a place for the legion to lick its wounds and recover.

"What do you think?" Karus looked over at Felix.

"Honestly, it sounds too good to be true," Felix said after a moment's thought, then turned to the trooper. "There was food fit for consumption at this farm you looked over? Besides the animal feed. Grains, I think you said?"

"Yes, sir," the trooper said, "an entire silo, almost completely full."

Felix looked over at Karus meaningfully. "The gods may have provided more than just transportation away from the Celts. They mean to feed us too."

"I don't like it," Karus said with a heavy breath. He turned to look over the men marching by. He rubbed his chin and took three steps away from Felix and the trooper, thinking. He turned back. "It seems too damned convenient."

"Agreed," Felix said, and then abruptly chuckled.

Karus looked at his friend in question.

"If you had fallen into a river and could not swim," Felix said, "and the gods sent a branch to keep you from drowning, wouldn't you grab onto it, even if a mean-looking snake was wrapped around one end?"

Karus crossed his arms. He stared down at his feet for a moment, thinking it through. His people were tired and weary. They needed a place to recover, and he couldn't see how he could pass up an opportunity like this. He looked up at the trooper, having made his decision. It was the only one he could have made.

"Advise Prefect Valens that the legion will be marching to the city," Karus said.

"Yes, sir."

"I figure, with that river crossing, we will likely reach the city by dusk on the following day. He is to report anything that would affect the safety of the legion," Karus added. He knew that Valens would do so anyway, though he felt better for having voiced it.

"I will, sir." The trooper mounted up with practiced ease. He gave a hasty salute, fist to chest, and wheeled his horse around. Nudging his horse with his heels, he began riding back the way he'd come at a slow trot.

"One more night sleeping on our arms," Felix said, rubbing his hands together. "Then a roof over our heads. A legionary could not ask for more."

"That will be a welcome change," Karus said, and meant it.

"If the people in that city did pick up and leave," Felix said, "perhaps they left more food."

"That is my thinking also," Karus said, glancing over at the men who continued to march by, sandals crunching rhythmically. "Why do you suppose they left?"

"I don't know," Felix said. "There could be many reasons."

"All of which," Karus said, exhaling a long breath, "could be bad for us. Plague, war… "

"Dragons?" Felix cast a nervous glance skyward. "The beasties have flown over us several times this day already."

"They haven't yet bothered us," Karus said.

"I wonder what they eat."

"I don't want to find out," Karus said with an involuntary look skyward, which only showed itself in blue patches through the thick green canopy high above them.

"I need to get along," Felix announced. "My cohort is well ahead and I will have a time of it catching up. It's what I get for waiting to speak to you."

"See you this evening, in camp," Karus said.

With that, Felix started up the road. The pace he set was quicker than the men marching by Karus just feet away. Karus watched his friend for a moment, and then glanced upward again. The limbs, the larger ones, at least, were thick and wide enough to easily support several men. He wondered if there were indeed people up there, concealed, covertly watching the legion march by below. If there were, did they wish ill on him and his men? Or did they just want the legion to pass through and be on its way?

Karus pinched the bridge of his nose. He felt a strong need to check in with each cohort and speak with his senior centurions. Sending runners up and down the column was not a viable communication tool either. It simply took too long. Karus would have to requisition a squadron of cavalry from Valens and use them as messengers to help him keep in contact with the entire column of march, which was strung out over several miles. Brutus was some little ways to the rear with First Cohort, which was marching just ahead of the supply train. Karus decided to go in search of the horse—*his* horse.

Karus walked back down the road, the legionaries marching by in the other direction in neat, orderly blocks, one row after another. Each cohort's century was separated by a few feet of space. The officers saluted Karus as he passed them. Occasionally offering a word or two, Karus dutifully saluted them in return.

Seventh Cohort rapidly gave way to Second, Dio marching at its front before the standard bearer. Sighting Karus, Dio stepped off the road, clearly intending to speak with him.

"The gods have blessed us once again," Dio said after Karus had explained about the abandoned city.

"You think so?" The men of Dio's cohort continued by one century after another, looking smart, sandals crunching the leaves of the previous season to dust.

"You have your doubts, I take it?"

"I do," Karus said. "Whatever happened to the people who lived there cannot be good for us. Tell me I am wrong on this."

"Well, maybe not, but it will beat sleeping on our arms." A sideways grin crept up Dio's face. "I always knew you were a worrier, but now that you lead the legion, I think it suits you."

Karus had not expected this from Dio, and judging by the grin, he felt his leg was being pulled.

Dio's grin slipped from his face and he became serious. "Julionus didn't give a denarius for the risks when he marched us from Eboracum. You," Dio pointed a callused finger, which connected with Karus's chest armor, "on the other hand, dwell on the perils that await us. Then you make your decision, having weighed what is best for the legion or your men."

Karus grunted.

"I am serious," Dio said. "I would rather have someone leading us who goes in with both eyes open and his sandals on. The other senior centurions feel as I do. Well, most of them anyway. Mind you, I have not spoken with all of them on this subject."

Karus was surprised by Dio's admission. Though he expected nearly unconditional support from his close friends, he was not so sure about the rest of the senior leadership.

"Really? The others feel so?"

"A few of us talked it over last night," Dio said, shrugging in his armor, "in camp after the men had turned in."

They had had a meeting without him. Karus found that he was even more shocked by this latest revelation than the previous one. He was even a little angered. He rocked back on his heels as he considered Dio, who clearly sensed Karus's thoughts, for he held up both hands palms facing outward.

"It was just a little talk," Dio said. "Nothing formal, and I can assure you it wasn't planned. More impromptu-like. We were sitting around a campfire and fell to talking."

Karus felt slightly better, but still he found that he was concerned.

"You have to understand, Karus," Dio said in friendly yet serious tone, "you are now the legion's senior officer, as good as if Hadrian had appointed you the legate. Being a ranker, even though that is still what you are at heart ... well, for you that life is over and done. It is time you accepted that. Karus, you are officially better than the rest of us ... you and that pet tribune of yours. Where is he anyway?"

"I sent him with Valens," Karus replied. "They had a spare horse and he can ride."

"Well, I am sure Valens will look after him," Dio said. "Face it, Karus, you are now a man apart from the rest of us."

Karus glanced down at the ground, thoughts racing, and took a deep breath. Dio was right. Karus silently cursed himself. He should have expected this. The legate and tribunes always stood apart from the rest of the legion. It was the natural order of things. Though he was still the legion's camp prefect, Karus was solely in command. He was now, as Dio had so rightly pointed out, no different than the legate.

"You are right, brother," Karus said quietly, looking back up at his friend. "I wish I had seen it sooner."

"Can you say that again?" The grin was instantly back.

"Which part?"

"Where I am always right?"

"I never said always." Karus chuckled. He felt a lightening of his mood.

"I take whatever I can get," Dio said.

"Not particular, are you?" Karus said.

"Not at all," Dio said with a loud laugh. A few of the men marching by glanced in their direction. He cocked is head to one side. "Honestly, Karus, you would have figured it out on your own soon enough."

Karus nodded in reply.

"Have your men seen anything odd?" Karus said, changing the direction of the conversation.

"Besides these massive trees and the dragons?" Dio asked, grin still plastered across his face.

"Anything else?"

"We've seen some strange-looking animals, and I got the message about the snakelike creature with legs," Dio said. "My men have been warned to avoid them. I've seen a few birds that were familiar, crows and such. Beyond that, nothing yet. Why?"

"Felix mentioned that some of his men had seen people up in the trees." Karus gestured upward toward the tree tops. "Looking down upon us."

Karus felt a chill as his friend's grin slipped from his face.

"A few of my men have said the same," Dio said. "I thought perhaps it was them seeing things. This forest has enough shadows to shake a vine cane at."

"It could be that," Karus said. "Shadows."

"Some of Felix's men might also have shared stories with mine in camp last night. You know how that stuff starts, usually at a dice game." Dio paused. "How many times over the years have our men seen things that were not there and started the alarm?"

"You are right. It is probably nothing," Karus said with a nod. "Still, I think it best to keep an eye out."

"Aye," Dio said and glanced over at his cohort. The last of his centuries were beginning to march by. "I had best return to my men before they get too far ahead and I have to run to catch up. No telling what trouble they might get into without me."

Karus nodded and Dio stepped off. He waited a moment before turning and resuming his trek, thinking on what had just been said. His conversation with Dio had only reinforced his need to visit with each cohort and be seen by the men.

First Cohort was following Second, with only a small gap between them, perhaps twenty yards of space. Pammon was marching just off to the side of the cohort. The men of the lead centuries cheered Karus as they neared one another. In the perpetual gloom of the forest, he was heartened by it.

"Karus." Pammon stepped aside, offering a salute. Karus waved the salute off.

"How is the First?"

"The boys are doing fine," Pammon said with a proud glance over at the century moving past them. By the standard, Karus saw it was the Second Century. "Marching is good for them, especially here in this gods forsaken forest."

There was heat in Pammon's voice. Karus sensed a tone of dislike.

"I served some time in Gaul as a recruit," Pammon said. "Never liked those forests much either."

"Have the men seen anything up in the canopy?" Karus asked, curious to see if the sightings had spread to his old cohort.

"Aye," Pammon scowled, "several saw a man up there just a few moments ago. I didn't see it, though they swore left and right he was up there. I thought it must have been shadows is all. Why do you ask?"

"Dio and Felix's cohorts have reported similar sightings," Karus said.

"They have, have they?" Pammon looked up, eyes narrowing as he scanned the limbs above for any signs of movement.

"It is probably nothing," Karus said, "but best to keep a lookout, particularly tonight when we camp."

"I will," Pammon said.

Karus filled Pammon in on the city that had been discovered. Pammon asked a few questions but, beyond that, had no other comments.

"Where is my horse?" Karus asked, intent on riding up and down the line. With the sightings of people above in the canopy, whether real or imagined, it would be good for his men to see him calm, collected, and in control. "I want to visit with the other cohorts, and it will be quicker riding."

"Sixth Century," Pammon said, jerking a thumb toward the rear. "That was a lot of gold Saturninus was carrying. More than I've ever seen in one place. Got a mule carrying it now."

"Good," Karus said. "Make sure none of it disappears. We may have need for it at some point."

"Aye," Pammon said. "I've got an accounting and good men on it."

With that, Karus excused himself and went in search of Brutus. A short while later he had retrieved his new horse. Karus waited while Brutus was saddled and made ready. Ignoring the stained leather, he pulled himself up on the powerful animal and settled himself in the fine saddle. It was a comfortable seat and very unlike those issued to the cavalry. He considered for a moment how he wanted to proceed as the Sixth Century marched off.

Seventh Century's centurion saluted Karus.

"Fine mount," Centurion Daemon said. "You make the horse look good, sir."

The men of Seventh Century laughed at the joke.

"Enjoy the march," Karus called back to Daemon.

"Real men march, sir," Daemon said, and then the century was flashing past, the men chuckling at the joke, pleased with their officer. Karus did not mind being the butt of the joke if it improved morale.

Pulling the horse around, he nudged the animal's sides slightly and felt the powerful muscles rippling beneath him as Brutus started, eager to be off. Riding such a powerful and finely bred animal was an exhilarating feeling. Karus put it from his mind. He had business to attend to. He would first visit with the camp followers and then work his way back forward toward the lead cohorts, spending time with each.

Chapter Nine

Holding the reins, Karus dismounted. His lower tunic was still damp from crossing the river. He stretched, working out the kinks from a long day in the saddle. His butt was more than sore and, truth be told, somewhat numb. It had been several years since Karus had spent an extended period in the saddle. Despite the discomfort, riding Brutus had been an exhilarating experience. He reached over and patted the animal affectionately on the neck.

"Good job, boy."

The horse cast a sideways glance in his direction and whinnied.

Night was almost upon them. Dusk was nearing its end, limiting visibility. On the other side of the horse, the legion streamed by in seemingly endless succession, century by century. There was little talking, as the men had been marching all day and would continue until they reached the city hours after a normal day's march would have ended.

Karus handed over Brutus's reins to the legionary who had been waiting for him.

"Where is Pammon?"

"In the woods, sir." The legionary pointed. "Just over there, where that torchlight is."

Karus could see an orange glow out in the darkness, perhaps forty yards off. As he walked toward the light, the foul stench of death hung on the air. It was something that over the years he had become more than accustomed to. Feet crunching on last season's leaves, Karus stepped past and around the giant trunks, making his way through the rapidly darkening forest. As he neared, he saw a small group gathered around several bodies on the ground. The surgeon was kneeling over one. A legionary was leaning in close with a makeshift torch that hissed and popped, providing Ampelius some light.

"Are you an idiot? Closer, man," the surgeon snapped. "I can't see what I'm doing."

The legionary brought the torch nearer, though it was apparent he wanted to be as far as possible from the corpses. He craned his head back, even as he held the torch out nearly at arm's length.

"Ah, Karus," Pammon said, sounding delighted as Karus stepped into the torchlight. Pammon gestured down at the corpses lying on the forest floor. "A couple of my men were out taking a piss and found them."

"I'm surprised anyone could miss the stench," Karus said. "I could smell them all the way over by the road. Are you sure the boys were just taking a piss?"

"Yes," Pammon said, scratching at stubble turned prematurely white. "No one's been really keen to wander too far off into these trees, if you know what I mean."

Karus did. He glanced down at the bodies. There were three of them, and they had been lined up one right next to the other. They wore black leather chest armor and brown pants with hard leather boots that had been well broken in. The exposed skin of the corpses was a dark purplish color and the bodies had begun to swell. The swelling made the leather armor and pants seem a size too small. Karus had seen the decomposition stage after this one and it was not a pretty sight.

Each dead man had a single small chest wound, almost in the exact same place. Dried blood darkened the already black leather. Flies clustered thick around the wounds. Bugs both great and small crawled over the exposed skin. One man's mouth was ajar, and Karus saw bugs crawling about inside.

He was surprised that animals had not yet gotten to the bodies. It was damn odd, but what he found even more surprising were the fresh flowers that had been laid by the dead men's feet.

"We found them like this," Pammon said. "Nothing was touched until Ampelius got here."

Karus knelt down next to the surgeon. "Well?"

"Curious," Ampelius said, looking up at Karus before returning to his work. He was probing one of the wounds with what looked like a small metal spike. "Very curious."

"Ampelius, a bit more than that would be helpful."

The surgeon leaned back and blinked, focusing on Karus, as if seeing him for the first time. He rapidly recovered.

"Each was killed by a single arrow strike to their hearts," Ampelius said. He touched the metal spike to the wound hole. "Dead four days, if I am any judge. Someone removed the missiles post mortem. They were then carried to this spot and left for their bodies to rot."

"They weren't killed here then?" Karus was surprised by this.

"No," the surgeon said, standing. Karus stood also. Ampelius wiped his probe clean with a soiled rag and then tucked both into a satchel he was carrying. "At least, I don't believe so. If they had been, there would have been some evidence of a struggle or at least an indication of where each had fallen dead." The surgeon paused a moment. "Well, I am done here. Others to see and tend to."

With that, Ampelius stepped off back toward the road, leaving Karus, Pammon, and the legionary with the torch standing there gazing down on the dead men.

"Wasn't that informative," Karus said to himself, glancing at Ampelius's back.

"Are you surprised?" Pammon said. "Our surgeon is all personality."

Karus looked at Pammon and then back down at the dead. He had been serious, but Pammon had taken the statement as irony.

"Thoughts?"

"Definitely military," Pammon said and knelt beside one of the bodies. "They still have their light packs, though their weapons are missing." Taking out his dagger, he cut the straps on one of the packs, rolled the body slightly, and pulled it free. "Scouts perhaps, judging by the size of these." He opened the pack, gazing in. "Looks like dried rations and a few personal possessions."

Karus rubbed his jaw as Pammon dumped out the contents of the pack. He picked out a small purse from amongst the food and shook it a little. The bag, though mostly empty, jingled.

"Tell me, who kills three soldiers and then doesn't bother to loot the bodies?" Pammon stood and tossed the purse to Karus.

"I don't know," Karus said, emptying the coins into his palm. They looked to be made of bronze, but were unfamiliar in design. "And why the flowers?"

"Must'a been friend," Pammon said. "It's the only reason I can see as to why they didn't bother to take the food or coin."

"When a legionary dies, his mates usually split up his possessions," Karus said. "Why not the same with these? The money alone is worth the effort."

Pammon shrugged. "Dead men don't talk."

"No, they don't." Karus was silent for a time. "Why bother to move them?"

"Someone must have wanted the bodies elsewhere," Pammon said and spat on the ground. "Out of the way, perhaps where they couldn't be found."

"Maybe," Karus said, closing his fist around the coins. They felt cold against his palm.

"I wonder who killed them," Pammon said, then absently glanced upward and into the dark canopy above.

"Not you too," Karus said with some irritation.

"This is a damn strange place, Karus," Pammon said with a shrug. "The men might be onto something."

"I seriously doubt there are people in the trees above," Karus said. "If there were, more of our boys would have seen them. I've yet to run across an officer who can confirm a sighting with his own eyes."

"About that," Pammon said and shifted his feet uncomfortably.

"You've seen them?" Karus was highly skeptical.

"You know that feeling you get when someone is watching you?"

Karus nodded.

"Well, I had it earlier today." Pammon fell silent a moment. "When I looked up, for half a heartbeat I could have sworn I saw a man studying me. He vanished before my eyes, almost as if he were a wraith."

"And he was up there?" Karus gestured with a thumb.

"No," Pammon said. "He was standing next to a tree about twenty yards off the road."

Karus remained silent as he considered Pammon's words.

"Did you try to find him?"

"How long have you known me?"

"Seventeen years," Karus said.

"Eighteen," Pammon said with a hard look. "Seventeen serving together in the same cohort. Between us, we have nearly fifty years of combined experience. I've stood and fought at your side more times than I can recall. You've saved my life and I yours. We've faced odds that should have seen us long dead and fodder for the worms. Instead, we survived and came out on top. Through all that, have you ever known me to jump at shadows or give in to fear and superstitious nonsense?"

Karus shook his head. "No. You are as steady as they come."

Pammon eyed Karus a moment longer, then let out a long, slow breath. "When I looked, and I took a century with me, we found no tracks," Pammon said. "I don't know how he did it, but there was someone or something there. I am sure of it."

"Something?" Karus did not like the sound of that, especially coming from Pammon.

"Can't you feel it?" Pammon asked, glancing around. "We don't belong here. We shouldn't be in this forest. These sorry sods didn't belong here either, and they paid the ultimate price."

Karus rubbed the back of his neck. Though he wanted to disagree with Pammon, Karus felt the same. There was something about this forest. There was a darkness to it that had nothing to do with how much light managed to creep its way through the thick canopy of leaves. The forest was hiding something and had secrets Karus knew he wanted nothing to do with.

"We will be out and onto open ground soon enough," Karus said, clapping Pammon on the shoulder. "Just a few more miles, is all."

Pammon nodded. He looked as if he wanted to say more but then shrugged. Instead he turned and started back for the road, motioning for the torch bearer to come with him. Karus returned the coins to the purse. As the torch bearer strode away with Pammon, the shadows cast by the bodies lengthened. It was as if the shades were straining for release from their mortal remains. Karus regarded the dead for a moment, then tossed the purse down onto the chest of the man to whom it had belonged.

"To pay for your crossing, friend," Karus said and then turned to follow Pammon.

Karus saw motion out of the corner of his eye off to the right. He turned, hand going for his sword. There was someone there, less than ten feet away and standing just next to the trunk of a tree. The darkness seemed to swirl. He blinked. The figure was gone, vanished into thin air as if he had never been.

Karus drew his sword, the blade hissing as it came out.

"Karus?" Pammon had stopped, looking back. So too had the legionary with the torch.

Karus motioned, pointing at his eyes with two fingers and then in the direction he had seen the figure. He made a fist, opened it once, and closed it again, signaling that the enemy was ten feet away.

"Go get help," Pammon said quietly as he drew his own sword.

The man obediently ran off for the road.

Karus pointed at the massive tree trunk and made a motion for Pammon to move around to the right while he went to the left. Pammon nodded and moved in that direction as Karus started toward the opposite side as quietly as he could, which was no easy task wearing armor. Karus breathed in deeply and had to refrain from sneezing from the close proximity of the stench of death. Careful where he put his feet, he ignored the bodies underfoot and continued on.

The trunk of the tree was a giant wall of darkness as Karus slowly approached, sword held ready. He worked his way around to the other side, pausing every couple of steps, eyes searching the darkness, ears straining for the faintest sound. He came fully around and saw Pammon. Stopping, Karus searched the darkness. Taking a deep breath, he slowly let it out, shaking his head in irritation.

"I thought I saw something," Karus said, becoming angered with himself. "I think the jitters are getting to me too."

"Was it a man?" Pammon asked. "Was he wearing a brown cloak and carrying a bow?"

Karus felt himself frown, thinking. In the gathering darkness, he could not tell the color of the cloak, but he seemed to recall the man holding something.

"It could have been a bow," Karus said, sheathing his sword. "Jupiter, those three back there died by one."

The sound of many feet coming their way at a run interrupted further discussion. With a parting glance into the darkness, Karus led the way back around the tree.

"We are not alone here," Pammon said, lowering his voice and sheathing his own sword. "We have to get out of this forest."

"Soon enough," Karus said. "A few more miles of road and we will be out."

The legionary carrying the torch ran up. He had brought an entire century.

"Are you all right, sir?" Ajax asked as his century fanned out protectively around the other two officers.

"Thought I saw someone," Karus said, loud enough for all to hear, and forced out a laugh. "It was an animal, a bear I think." He gestured toward the three bodies. "It was most likely following the smell."

Ajax glanced down at the three dead men with some distaste and then back at Karus. "Yes, sir."

Karus felt that Ajax sounded far from convinced and Karus did not blame him.

"Well, enough excitement for one night. Back to the road," Karus said loud enough for everyone to hear. "We've got more miles to cover. We're not spending another night sleeping on our arms. I, for one, want a roof over my head."

Ajax's century gave a cheer to that.

Nothing further was said as they made their way back to the road. Karus took the reins from the legionary holding Brutus. He pulled himself up into the saddle, settled himself comfortably, and then scanned the trees once more. He saw nothing.

Was someone or something out there? He suspected he knew the answer to that question.

"Pass orders back down the line," Karus said to Pammon. "No one is to leave the road under any circumstances, even to take a piss or shit."

Pammon nodded his understanding.

"Whoever killed those three may still be about," Karus said, tightening his hold on the reins. "We've lost enough good men that I don't want to take the chance on losing any more."

"I understand," Pammon said. "Your orders will be passed along."

"Good. See you later tonight," Karus said to Pammon

"Right." Pammon nodded. "When we get to the city then."

"Send word if you need me." Karus nudged Brutus into a slow walk and then a trot. He glanced to the side, scanning the darkness once more and knowing his search would prove fruitless. He could see no one, but could not shake the feeling that someone was watching and had their eye upon him.

Chapter Ten

Karus stepped out of the vestibule, hobnailed sandals with each footstep cracking sharply on the shaped stone in the early morning quiet. He halted before the flight of stairs, a half dozen that led down to the street. Karus placed his hands upon his hips and felt the cool touch of his armor as he glanced around.

The two suns, which had been the legion's constant companions since they came to this strange land, had yet to rise. The sky was beginning to lighten as dawn neared. In an hour, the first of the two suns would be up and the crisp night air would begin its daily retreat as the land warmed.

Karus surveyed the scene before him. Across the street lay a public park. The grass in the park had the look of having once been groomed, but it had grown long with neglect. The park's shape was that of an elongated rectangle. It was bordered on all sides by cobblestone streets that showed the wear of excessive use. Tenement buildings varying in height from two stories to four lined the street.

In the early morning murk, Karus thought the buildings on the far side of the park looked like broken teeth. The buildings were wooden structures, with an outer covering of decorative stone. Karus had seen similar buildings back in Rome and across the empire. However, most nonpublic Roman buildings were faced with plaster instead of stone. It was cheaper and more practical. Besides being decorative, plaster helped to act as insulation against the cold.

With a scattering of trees for shade, the park had a pleasant look to it. Karus could well imagine the former residents of these buildings enjoying the well-manicured grass and open space on public holidays. He could almost imagine the children playing tag, running about with reckless abandon, screaming wildly.

Almost.

The park and street were strewn with personal belongings that had clearly been discarded when the city had been abandoned.

Karus's old wound throbbed. Absently, he rubbed at it and kneaded the area with a fist.

This was his first real look at the interior of the city. The legion had arrived late the night before. Crossing the river before exiting the forest had taken more time than expected. When they had arrived, it had been impossible to see much beyond what was lit by torchlight or signal fire. As such, this was Karus's first opportunity to get an idea of what the city looked like. Though the buildings were constructed in a similar way to those in Rome, they were very different in both look and feel. It was a subtle difference, in the shaping around the edges, the fittings, materials used, and facings. Style, Karus decided. It was mostly all style. The people of this city had clearly preferred things their way. It was that simple.

Movement caught Karus's eye. A patrol emerged from around a corner and marched into the street on the other side of the park. It was likely a section of men from Ninth Cohort, whose duty it was to provide the watch.

Karus had ordered his people to settle into the buildings nearest the gate through which they had entered the city. Once in the buildings, Karus had left strict orders that nobody was to emerge until morning. A perimeter had been set up around these buildings, and patrols kept up through the night to ensure that no one snuck off or, more importantly, anyone with ill intent slipped in.

Each cohort supplied a century of men to every building the camp followers had been settled in for both their safety and security. They were also to make certain that nobody left during the night. Though Valens and a handful of scouts had initially scouted the city, they had not done a thorough search. There was no telling what dangers lurked undiscovered.

Karus glanced back behind him. Despite the facing of the building, the people who had lived here had led an extremely humble life, very poor and without much in the way of creature comforts. The room he had taken for himself had once housed an entire family. It had been dirty, and not just from dusty neglect.

The room was a far cry from the worst Karus had ever seen. Still, it was the first time in weeks that Karus had had a roof over his head and he did not begrudge the filth of the previous occupants. Surprisingly, the room had had a small fireplace, likely used for cooking. It had provided him his first comfortable evening in a good long while. Karus had fallen asleep on a blanket before the small crackling fire. He had slept soundly enough, even if he barely managed three hours.

Part of First Cohort had shared the building with him. He could hear the officers' muffled shouts as they rousted their men with a combination of threats and curses. The heavy wooden door scraped open. Pammon emerged. Karus nodded a greeting to the centurion.

"Sleep good, Karus?" Pammon stifled a yawn with the back of his hand.

"Yes," Karus said. "The straw mats that came with my room looked a little dubious, so I settled for the floor with a blanket next to the fire. It beats sleeping on the cold ground with the rocks and my arm as a pillow."

"Hardwood instead of the hard ground is always preferable," Pammon said with a disgusted look. "The people that lived in these buildings were not terribly sanitary."

"Not everyone," Karus said, "is as forward thinking and enlightened as we are."

"Agreed." Pammon made a face as he glanced around at the buildings that bordered the park. "I think this surpasses the worst of the slums of Rome. Thanks be to Fortuna I was able to escape from such poverty by joining the legions. I don't think I could ever go back. We occasionally bathed, but the legions showed me real cleanliness."

Karus grunted to that. It was a story that was far too common.

"These people have built a great city." Pammon took a deep breath of fresh air. The tenement smelled poorly. "Yet they are barbarians. Perhaps one day we will bring them the gift of true civilization."

"If the gods will it," Karus said, "then it will be done."

"Karus," Pammon said, brow furrowing, "perhaps that is why we are here."

Karus considered what the centurion had said, and nodded. "It is possible. However, we don't know for certain what plans the gods have in store for us. Even the money-grubbing priests have difficulty reading their intentions."

"Whatever their plans, they seem a sight better than what the Celts had in store for us," Pammon chuckled darkly.

"Undoubtedly," Karus said and hesitated a moment, swallowing. He studied Pammon for a long heartbeat.

"Effective immediately, I am promoting you. The First is now yours."

Pammon seemed surprised and at first said nothing.

"You deserve it," Karus continued. "Had we made it back to Eboracum, as the senior most centurion, you would have naturally succeeded me."

"Primus pilus." Pammon rolled it over his tongue. A broad smile grew upon his face. "Primus pilus. Thank you, sir."

"You've more than earned it." Karus meant that. Pammon had proven an extremely able leader. First Cohort would do well under his leadership. Karus was sure of it. "I've sent word for all senior centurions and prefects to join me shortly on the wall above the gatehouse. I will see you there."

"Yes, sir," Pammon said and snapped off a smart salute. Karus drew himself up and returned it just as smartly. He then reached out and shook Pammon's hand.

"Congratulations, Senior Centurion Pammon."

"Thank you, sir," Pammon said again, eyes shining with pride.

With that, Karus started down the steps, hobnails cracking loudly in the quiet early morning air. Giving up the First left him with mixed feelings. The cohort had been his pride and joy. The legion was now his, and the First deserved a senior centurion who could focus all of his energies on it. That was now Pammon.

Karus strode down the paved street, moving in the direction of the city wall and gatehouse. He walked quickly, passing by the park and following the street as it took him through two rows of attached buildings. The structures seemingly crowded forward, sandwiching the street. Karus eyed them as he walked by. These had the appearance of tenements, like the one he had just spent the night in, perhaps a bit meaner. They had a slightly dilapidated feel to them, with several suffering from clear neglect.

A few hundred feet farther along and the street emerged into a cleared space that separated the city's walls from the city and ran outward in either direction, disappearing as the walls curved around and out of view. Karus approved of the cleared space. Grass grew thick and tall in the gap. It meant that, should the city ever come under siege, enemy missiles and shot sent over the walls would have to travel farther to inflict serious damage upon the city. Only the most powerful siege engines would be capable of such a feat, and the stone thrown would likely be of a lesser weight, limiting any potential damage.

The gate by which the legion had entered stood some forty yards off. The previous night, Karus had ordered its massive wooden gate closed. Two sentries stood to either side of the entrance to the gatehouse and a dim light glowed from within. The sentries snapped to attention and saluted as Karus approached. He returned their salute and entered the gatehouse without stopping.

A single oil lamp hung from a hook in the ceiling. It burned dully, shedding a pale yellow light throughout the interior of the gatehouse. Karus took a moment to survey his surroundings. A battered old desk had been pushed against one wall, a chest on another. It was a small room and meant to only hold a handful at a time, likely the city's taxing agent and a small guard.

An optio sat in a rickety chair before the desk, his back to Karus. The optio glanced around. Seeing Karus, he jumped to his feet and saluted. Karus waved the junior officer back down and turned to the open stairwell to the right. He had climbed these stairs the night before. They led up to the top of the wall. Unfortunately, it had been overcast and the moonlight dimmed considerably. He had seen little of the city.

As Karus climbed the stairs, he realized that since they had arrived in this strange land, he had not seen the moon. They had spent two nights in the forest under the heavy canopy of the trees and another marching under an overcast sky. Was the moon different? Would it be as unfamiliar as the two suns? It was a troubling thought, and it worried at Karus. All legionaries were superstitious. He realized that he had to prepare for any such further surprises.

The stone steps were bowed in the center, worn down by countless feet over the years to a point where the rough stone had been polished smooth and shone with reflected lamp light. Karus was forced to place a hand against the wall to keep from slipping on the stone.

Someone had found another lamp and lit it at the landing that led to the next set of stairs. The lamp mounted in a small recess carved out of the wall provided just enough light for Karus to see as he climbed the second flight. Wearing his armor, Karus's legs burned as he took each step. His old wound ached terribly. On the subsequent landing that led to the third set of stairs, there was yet another lamp guttering with a draft from above. It shed a flickering yellow light across the ancient stone of the steps.

Karus climbed two more flights of stairs before emerging into a roofed guardhouse that led out onto the walls. On either side, small windows had been set into the walls. The shutters on these windows had been thrown open to admit both light and air. The door that led to the walls was also wedged open. Karus could see two legionaries manning the wall just beyond the doorway, one staring outward into the countryside and the other overlooking the city. Until they knew otherwise, threats could come from either direction.

Karus paused a moment and looked around. The guardhouse clearly served as a mini-armory and break room for those charged with manning the walls. Surprisingly, it was fully stocked with arms, but no armor. On his left, resting neatly in a battered wooden rack, were at least forty unstrung bows lined up one after another. The bow strings were coiled tidily on top of the rack. Next to each bow sat a quiver thick with arrows.

In the far corner of the guardhouse, by the door, there were two large barrels filled with additional arrows. One of the barrels had been used to prop open the heavy reinforced door. Karus crossed over to one and removed an arrow. He felt the iron-bladed tip. It was razor sharp and easily pricked his finger, drawing a small drop of blood. He returned the arrow to the barrel.

On the opposite wall was another wooden rack, heavy with nicks and dents delivered through years of constant use. This one held a like number of long swords, which meant that the soldiers of the city manning the wall would have carried both a bow and sword. He saw no spears or javelins. Karus moved over and examined one of the swords. It was nearly as long as a spatha, but the blade was thicker and heavier. The edge of the weapon he picked up was sharp and well cared for. A jug of oil with several soiled rags sat atop the rack, as did a bag of sand. Karus returned the weapon to the rack.

A long wooden table with four battered chairs occupied the center of the guardhouse. The table had been stained by drink and oil. It was also pitted and had numerous indentations, likely made through the maintenance and care of the weapons that were stored here. The surface had also been carved into in several places, likely by bored guards. One was phallic in nature. Some things were just universal.

Another carving seemed to have letters. Karus ran a callused hand over a few of the carvings of what he thought was writing. He could not recognize any of the letters and symbols though. Expelling a long breath, he glanced around the guardhouse once more. It was neat and organized. Karus decided that the soldiers who had once manned these walls were a professional, longstanding force.

His eyes roved over the two racks. The weapons stored here represented a considerable expense. Karus could not understand, nor imagine, why someone would have left them behind. Running a hand through his short-cropped hair, he turned and made his way out onto the wall. One of the sentries glanced his way and then quickly returned his attention back to his duty, as he should. There was nothing more important than manning the watch, and it would not be interrupted for honoring rank.

"See anything?"

"No, sir," the sentry looking out over the countryside said. "The night passed peacefully enough."

"I've not see anything that should warrant sounding the alarm either, sir," the other sentry said.

"Carry on, then," Karus said.

The wall, an impressive sixty feet high, was around twelve feet wide. The walkway at the top allowed the guards only four feet of space. It meant that, should the wall be successfully scaled at any one point, a handful of defenders could hold until reinforcements arrived.

Crenulated battlements lined each side, and a wooden canopy topped with clay roofing tiles ran over the top of the wall. This served as missile shelter for the defenders. It rose around four feet above the battlements and was supported by thick oiled posts set ten feet apart. The shelter also served to provide the defenders with limited protection against the elements. However, there was no way to shutter it. The wind blew and whipped through the gap.

Karus moved along the wall some twenty feet from the sentries before he turned toward the city. He rested his hands upon the cool stone, looking out between the merlons.

The sky had lightened considerably, and though the city was still heavy with shadow, Karus found the view remarkable. The reports he had received from Valens were true. The city was large, very large, perhaps even as sizable as Rome. Though, if he were honest with himself, it had been many years since he had set eyes upon the mother city, so it was possible that he was wrong. But then again, maybe not. Either way, the city that was laid out before him had to have been home to more than a million people, perhaps even two.

Thousands upon thousands of buildings crowded tightly in upon each other, working their way up from near the walls to over a series of small hills. A central hill larger and broader than the others towered over them all. On the incline of this hill, there was what appeared to be a temple district with large brilliantly white marble-columned buildings. Just beyond that, near the summit, an impressive inner wall stood above all the other buildings below. This wall surrounded a palace and fortress that crowned the hill, both jointly rising above everything else. The two buildings communicated both power and wealth to the onlooker, and Karus could not help but feel impressed, awed even.

If Karus were any judge, the city appeared to have grown up around the inner walls. Perhaps the fortress had come first, before the palace. Karus could not see everything that was beyond those walls, but what he could glimpse was grand. He turned his eyes away and back to the main city wall, following them out first to the left and then right. Karus could identify two other gatehouses in the distance. Likely, there was a fourth somewhere out of view behind the central hill. All of them would need to be secured.

"Oh my," a familiar voice came from behind.

So wrapped up in his own thoughts, Karus had not heard anyone approach. He found Dio stepping up beside him, Felix at his side. Both looked out at the city.

Felix let out a long whistle. "That is one fantastic sight."

"Yes, it is," Karus said simply.

"Empty, but for us." Dio leaned upon the wall with his elbows, cupping his chin with one palm. "How very unnerving and exciting at the same time."

Karus could not help but agree. Silence fell amongst them. The three friends surveyed the empty city, each lost to their own thoughts. The only signs of habitation were just beneath them, where the legion had quartered for the night. Smoke rose lazily into the air from several chimneys.

Karus was once again reminded of Xenophon. Had the Greek general all those years ago had similar feelings of wonderment mixed with shock? What had it been like to happen across numerous dead cities grander than anything he had ever set eyes upon? Now having tread in the Greek's sandals, Karus found it a very sobering experience.

Otho joined them, followed by Pactus. The remainder of Karus's senior officers arrived shortly thereafter, including Tribune Delvaris, who came last. They all looked exhausted, but each reacted to the sight of the city with a mixture of shock and amazement. Karus gave them a few moments to look things over and absorb what they were seeing.

"Gather around," Karus said after a time. "Our first night under a roof in weeks. I trust everyone managed to get plenty of sleep."

A chuckle ran through the assembled officers. Like Karus, they had managed only a few hours' rest, three at the very most. Settling the men, establishing the watches and patrols would have taken time. Not to mention the hundred other headaches and problems that had likely popped up that needed personal attention as they settled their men in.

"I found a bed," Otho said as he scratched at his left thigh. "It was most comfortable. However, I believe I shared it with some unwanted guests."

Pactus took a half step away from Otho, who turned a sour face at the prefect of the Fifth Raetorum.

"You can keep your bedbugs, Otho," Pactus said with an amused expression.

"I had a bed in my room too," Dio said. "I elected the floor with a blanket. Seemed somehow safer."

"I must remember that," Otho said ironically. "When sleeping in a new place, take the floor over the comfortable-looking bed."

"That about sums it up," Dio said. "Let others make the mistake first."

There was general laughter to that. Karus waited until it died down.

"Right then, let's get down to business," Karus said and, with that, everyone sobered. He noticed that several curious glances were thrown Pammon's way, undoubtedly wondering what he was doing here. "This city must be thoroughly explored. We must confirm that it is empty. That means every room, basement, sewer, and attic has to be checked." Karus gestured behind him at the city. "Third, Fourth, and Fifth Cohorts will secure the walls. If you look…" Karus pointed and waited for his officers to get a better position where they could gaze outward into the city. "There are two other gatehouses in view. Third will have the responsibility for the left side of the wall and securing that gatehouse there. Fourth will take the right side and that gatehouse. I am guessing that on the other side of that big central hill there will be a fourth gate. Flaccus, Fifth Cohort will have the responsibility of securing that one."

"There is one," Valens confirmed, speaking up. "I've ridden around the entire city."

"I will do it," Flaccus said, without any of the hostility that he had exhibited of late. Though his eyes were red-rimmed and bloodshot, he seemed to have himself under control. Karus found it an encouraging sign.

"I want all gates closed and sealed," Karus continued, looking to the officers in command of the Third, Fourth, and Fifth, who nodded their understanding. "Report to me once that has been accomplished. I expect lookouts to be posted above each gatehouse and sentries walking the walls. The entirety of the wall must be patrolled. No one gets in and, more importantly, out."

"That is a long-assed wall," Macrinus said. "There are bound to be gaps in our patrols."

"Yes," Karus said. "I understand. Once the city is searched, we will have to figure out a system to secure the walls in their entirety."

"What of the rest of the legion?" Didius said.

"The remainder of the cohorts, except for yours, Didius," Karus said, "will explore the city. The Tenth will be responsible for providing security over the camp followers. Under no circumstances are they to be allowed out into the city to wander around."

"Got it," Didius said. "I will make very sure they behave themselves and stay put."

"Thank you." Karus paused a moment. "There is to be no looting. In my experience, where there is looting, there is fire." Karus pointed out into the city. "Those buildings are made of wood. Should a fire break out, a good portion of the city could very well be destroyed. Our main objective here is to search the city to confirm that it is empty. Anyone you come across is to be detained for questioning. Our secondary objective is to locate supplies that we can use, including food. There is reason to believe we may find grains and flour throughout the city."

"Why do you think there would be stores of food here?" Pactus asked with a curious countenance.

"Our cavalry scouts," Karus said, nodding to Valens, "have reported many of the outlying farms still have stores of food and dry goods. It appears that the people who lived here left quickly. Meaning that if they could not take the food with them from the farms, then there is a good chance the same may be true for the city. With any luck, we will find a large public grain supply."

"Like the dole in Rome?" Valens said.

"Exactly," Karus said. "With luck, the leaders of this city bought off the poor with a free grain ration. We can't be the only ones who do it."

"Do you mean to stay?" Flaccus asked. His voice filled with a deep weariness that Karus could sympathize with.

"I don't know," Karus admitted. "We've all been through a lot over the last few weeks. The men need an extended rest, a place to recover…" Karus paused. "I think if there is sufficient food here, we will stay for a time. At least long enough to figure out where we are in relation to Rome."

"We could use a rest," Flaccus agreed. Several of the other officers nodded with him in agreement. Regardless of the reason, Karus was grateful for the support from the cantankerous centurion. It was a sight better than the resistance he had shown to everything as of late.

"We don't know why this place was abandoned," Karus said, looking from face to face, "but if at all possible, we need to find out. Advise your men to keep their eyes open. There is no telling if anyone is hiding out. They could be armed and dangerous. As I said, anyone you come across in your search is to be taken prisoner for questioning. We need intelligence. Be on the lookout for maps. If you locate any, they could be the key in pointing out the way home."

Karus paused a few heartbeats to let that sink in.

"On other business," Karus continued and gestured at Pammon, "I've promoted Pammon to command of the First. Does anybody have a problem with what I've done?"

Karus looked again from face to face. He made a point of checking Flaccus. Surprisingly, there was no rage in his eyes, only a weary expression. The position of primus pilus was a coveted one and effectively made Pammon the legion's number two. However, Karus did not expect to be challenged over his decision. Pammon was a highly respected officer and an exceptional field commander. No one, as he expected, voiced an objection. In fact, several offered their hearty congratulations.

"Very good," Karus said. "First Cohort will explore toward the center of the city, making a beeline toward that temple district over there, then the palace and fortress. Second Cohort will take the left side of the city, along with the Sixth and Seventh. The Eighth and Ninth, along with the Fifth Raetorum, will take the right side of the city. The First and Second Auxiliary Cohorts will explore outside of the city, say, within four miles, checking on each farm, building, and structure to ensure that they are also empty. The Delmatarum will man this gatehouse and this section of the wall." Karus paused and glanced around at his officers. "Catalogue anything you discover that could possibly be of use. Later this evening, give your report to Tribune Delvaris. He will send word to your cohorts on his position."

"Where will you be, sir?" Dio asked.

"I will accompany the First," Karus said and pointed toward the center of the city. "If you need me, you will know where to find me."

"What of my cavalry?" Valens asked, speaking up for the first time. Unlike the other officers, the cavalry prefect was wearing his service tunic. Karus had ordered the cavalry into the city when the legion arrived. Not only had Valens's men needed a brief rest, so too had their horses.

"When your horses are sufficiently rested…" Karus said, turning in the opposite direction to look out at the countryside. Karus could see the deep dark forest just a few miles off. In the early morning light, it looked like a smudge on the horizon. Nothing had ever come of the reports of people in the trees. "You are to begin scouting the countryside around and beyond the city. I need to know if there any threats out there."

"We've already explored out to ten miles. How far do you want your eyes to go?"

"As far as you deem reasonably necessary," Karus said, mindful of Julionus's mistake of holding his cavalry too close to the legion. "But not too far that your men can't be easily recalled."

"Thank you," Valens said with a pleased nod. "I shall leave a squadron here to act as messengers, and I will also forward word of where I am."

"Good," Karus said and then turned to the other officers. "I want to make this very clear. There is to be no looting. There are no exceptions to that order. The consequences of violating it will be dire. Make sure your men understand that. All food stores and supplies are to be catalogued and noted. Anything that we can consume or could possibly use should be reported to Tribune Delvaris."

"Sir," Otho spoke up.

"Yes?"

"Might I suggest," Otho said, "that the cohorts searching the city be on the lookout for wagons and carts that can pressed into service? In the event we need to leave in a hurry, we will be able to take whatever we can with us."

"Very good idea," Karus said. "Any wagons that are located are to be moved to this area, near this gate. There is plenty of space between the wall and the city. Let's use it. Barrels or jars that can be utilized to transport water are also to be gathered up. Concerning food stores, once we have identified them, I will make arrangements to have them moved to a central area for accounting, storage, and ultimate transport for when we march. Think of it as our supply depot."

"What of any weapons we find?" Pactus said. "That guardhouse was chock full them. I imagine that we will find additional caches of arms."

"Note whatever you find," Karus said.

The edge of the first of the two suns peeked up over the wall and shined brightly in Karus's eyes. Blinking, he stepped aside so that the merlon blocked its direct light.

"Has anyone here heard of Xenophon?" Karus said and was almost immediately answered by several frowns.

"That Greek general from antiquity?" Otho asked.

Karus turned to the prefect of the First Nervorium with raised eyebrows. He had not expected anyone other than Felix, whom he had already told, to know about Xenophon's experience. Otho was clearly well read and possibly even educated. His respect for the man increased.

"Yes," Karus said and then returned to addressing the other officers present. "Xenophon came across an abandoned city that was larger than any other he had ever seen back in Greece. It shook him to his core. My point here, gentlemen, is that this," he gestured out at the city, beyond the battlements, "is not a unique occurrence. It has happened to others before us. We have a mystery on our hands, and, if possible, we need to un-puzzle it. Keep an eye out for clues." Karus paused, noting several of the centurions nodding. Karus clapped his hands together. "I think we have taken enough time here. We've all a lot to do today, so let's get to it."

The senior officers broke up, moving past the two sentries and into the guardhouse, heading back to their commands. Tribune Delvaris remained behind.

"What of me? Where should I be?"

"You," Karus said, "will stick with me and the First. Now, what say we explore this city and see what we can find?"

Chapter Eleven

The street was unnaturally quiet. Even the men of the First were hushed, the only sounds being their sandals cracking and smacking on paving stones. That and the occasional clipped order from an officer. Karus walked in the middle of the street, Delvaris at his side. Stone faced buildings lined both sides of the street, which seemed to be the main way up to the crown of the central hill.

First Cohort, operating by centuries, had broken up to search the buildings to either side and those just adjacent stretching outward several streets. The cohort was spread out both ahead of Karus, behind, and off on the side streets. An hour before, they had entered a more affluent section of the city. Unlike the humbler areas, many of the doors had been locked and required a forced entry. A fence around a garden was dismantled and several men from each century now carried a stout support post which acted as a makeshift battering ram. Two or three determined blows was all it usually took to break a lock or shatter a barred door.

Karus had entered a few of the larger residences himself. Filled with luxury and splendor, he found himself wondering what it would be like to have such a carefree lifestyle. At first, he figured it would be great, having to do no real labor yourself, with slaves at your beck and call. But then what?

Karus thought, without anything to do, he might be bored. He had once owned a slave, a kindly older German by the name of Baalow, who had acted as his manservant. It hadn't lasted. Karus led a simple life, with few possessions. There had not been enough for Baalow to do. Besides, Karus preferred to do his own cleaning and maintenance of his kit. So, he had sold the German.

Karus had also found the experience of exploring these empty homes unsettling. Treasured personal possessions, including jewelry, had been left behind. Karus had even seen folded laundry, tunics fresh from cleaning left out on a table in a bedchamber's anteroom. It was as if the people had just walked away only moments before. The thin layer of dust that coated everything gave lie to that feeling. There were no people, no animals, no pets, and, surprisingly, no real pests. There were bugs, but Karus had not once seen a rat, or even the commonplace droppings from rodents. It was damn strange and added to his unease.

"Any city or town I've ever visited," Karus said to Delvaris, "has more rodents than people."

"There are no cats either," Delvaris said. "Back in Eboracum, the garrison was overrun with cats, but here … "

"Have you ever been bitten by a rat?"

Delvaris shook his head, looking horrified at the prospect.

"I have," Karus said with some distaste. "Their teeth are sharp as knives and they usually get you when you are sleeping, exposed fingers, toes. Black rats are the worst, always chewing, always on the hunt for something edible. They and the mice get into our stores. Not only do they eat our food, but they can gnaw their way through leather fittings and ropes, doing serious damage to a man's equipment. Cats keep the rodent population in check. It's why most legionaries are overly fond of the furry little bastards. There is not a century in the Ninth that has not adopted a cat. The men name them and treat them as pets, though a cat will likely scratch you for petting it half the time."

"I never knew," Delvaris said.

Karus wasn't surprised. The tribune was just a junior aide. He was still extremely green and had not been with the legion long enough to understand why things were done a certain way. Most officers of his rank cared only for their careers and sucking up to the legate. They rarely, if ever, took time to pay attention to the men. It was up to the centurions to keep order and interact with the legionaries. To tribunes like Delvaris, the men of the legion were only a means to an end, which was the ultimate furtherment of his career.

"I thought they were just pets," Delvaris continued with some surprise, "kept to dull the boredom and take the harsh sting out of their miserable lives as rankers."

Karus glanced over at the tribune. As a ranker himself, Karus found the tribune's attitude deeply offensive. But that did not mean he failed to understand the honesty behind the statement or where it came from. Delvaris was born into a class of rank and privilege. A life Karus would never know. His contact with the lower class had been limited. He could not be blamed for that, but perhaps he could be shown that those of his social station were not so dissimilar to those in the ranks. It was something to think on.

"Cunning, sharp-witted little critters cats are," Karus said, recalling a few of the cats he had personally adopted over the years. "One cat can kill hundreds of mice and rats every year. That saves on stores, equipment, and bites. So, the legion imports cats and the legionaries value them not only for the service they perform—prevention of sickness, as bites can go bad and make a man sick—but they identify with them as crafty hunters skilled at their craft."

Delvaris said nothing. However, he seemed to be hanging on every word Karus said.

"Wherever the legions go," Karus concluded, "you typically find cats."

"I guess the legions just haven't been here yet," Delvaris said with a cheeky look.

Karus chuckled, but it got him to thinking again.

What happened to the people? The rodents? The legions weren't the only ones who kept cats. They were widely used everywhere, just more so in legion camps. So, where were all the cats?

Thud!

Karus turned at the sound. A century was working on smashing open another locked door. Painted a bright red, the door had a solid look to it. With two men on either side of the makeshift ram, they swung the stout post while the rest of the century stood by at the ready, swords drawn, shields up.

Thud!

The four swung back again and then forward. With a loud splintering crack, the door crashed inward, revealing a darkened antechamber beyond.

The breaching party dropped their post and stood aside. Their comrades, who had been waiting, moved cautiously forward. Following each other, they entered one by one.

Karus studied the exterior of the building. The closer they got to the city's center, the more upscale and grand the residences became. He figured it had something to do with the proximity to power, in that those with money wanted to be near the ruler of this city. It was a social class thing. Yet,

Karus understood they were in a strange land, where one was sure of nothing.

Karus turned to look on the opposite side of the street. A similar scene was occurring there too. A century was moving up several wide marble steps that led to a set of large double doors. The junior centurion leading the century tried the door and surprisingly it swung open. Karus looked over the building they were about to enter. To either side of the entrance, great rounded marble columns rose twenty feet in height to support an arched roof that was tiled over in red. The marble columns were exquisitely carved and shaped. The roof sported two statues near the summit that looked like representations of the gods, somewhat like what Karus had seen in Roman cities. What gods they were, he could not discern. The shrines that had been found in every home were nothing like the ones Romans kept.

Karus's eyes roamed over the exterior. The residence was massive. Though now, he suspected, like the others it was an empty shell. The family who had once spent their days living in comfort and ease amidst fabulous wealth was gone. Only the possessions they left behind remained, a hint to whom they had been, nothing more. Movement drew his attention back to the open doors.

"Come on, you maggots," the lead centurion called. Sword and shield at the ready, he stepped through the entrance. Like the tail of a great serpent, the entire century followed, one man after another disappearing into the building. Karus had seen this happen dozens of times as the First worked its way deeper into the city. The searching of each building was time-consuming. Worse, frequent halts were called to keep the cohort from becoming too strung out, as the larger structures sucked up more time and attention.

Karus had been sorely tempted to speed things up by giving the order to push forward directly to the palace district. He had never been inside a palace and he could not deny that he was more than a little curious. Despite personal interest as to how the powerful lived, he hoped to find answers to some of his questions there, as it was the logical place to look.

Karus tapped a sandal, his irritation growing again.

"What is my rush?" Karus asked himself, frustrated with both his impatience and the time it was taking to make progress toward the center of the city. At this pace, they might arrive by nightfall.

"Karus?"

He turned to look at Delvaris, realizing that he had spoken the last aloud.

"Nothing," Karus said, annoyed with himself that he had let his impatience show. "It's nothing."

"Our progress is maddening," Delvaris said, clearly having taken the measure of Karus's thoughts.

"Get used to it," Karus said. "That's one thing serving in the legions will teach. To do anything right, or even, for that matter, wrong, takes time. Heck, anything the army does takes time."

A century just ahead entered the next building. Up and down the street it was the same scene. Karus began moving with the hopes that it would lessen his exasperation. Several buildings farther up the street, they came to a large open market in a square, complete with stalls and businesses. Advance centuries had already searched through it, as evidenced by the large chalk X that had been placed on the front of each building. Karus could see the lead centuries just beyond the market, continuing the advance up the main street lined with what appeared to be well-to-do residences.

Karus made his way over to a stall that fronted what appeared to be a leathermaker's shop. The smell of new leather and open curing vats was strong, even before he entered. A few samples of the goods produced by the leathermaker hung in the stall, though it looked as if both the stall and shop had been picked over by looters. What was left were only scraps.

Karus stepped through the stall and into the workshop. He paused in the entrance as Delvaris moved past him, probing deeper into the darkened workroom. Karus glanced around. The workshop comprised a single large room with a few long tables, workbenches, racks, and vats for curing. It was a mess. Discarded sandals, boots, and scraps littered about the floor as if they had been tossed there by a maddened crowd of children.

He bent down and picked up a sandal. The leather felt different than he was accustomed to. It was softer, smoother. Perhaps it had been the craftsman who made the difference. The market was located near those of means. As such, it likely catered to the wealthy. Those with money, Karus considered, were used to the finer things in life. He turned the sandal over in his hand. It was of an unfamiliar design. Karus reasoned it had been made for a civilian and comfort, not for a soldier like him. There were no hobnails for gripping. Losing interest, Karus tossed the sandal aside. It landed with a soft *thwop* on the floor.

"What respectable craftsman would leave his tools behind?" Delvaris asked. The tribune was standing before an old table heaped with scraps of leather. He was holding up a pair of rough scissors that were made from one piece of metal. He tested the edge. "Sharp too."

Karus moved over to where Delvaris was. A series of brackets affixed to the wall next to the table held a varying assortment of tools. He picked up one that looked like a miniature war hatchet. Karus turned the tool over in his hands, wondering on how the leathermaker used it. After a moment, he gave up but recognized from the well-worn grip it was a tool that saw frequent use.

"You are right," Karus said. "A master takes years to accumulate tools like these. It is what sets him aside from others, apprentices and journeymen. These," Karus gestured to the wall rack, "represent a life of hard work."

"Then why just leave them?" Delvaris's brows drew together. "If it takes a lifetime, why would the master not take them along?"

Karus tossed the tool on the work table. It landed with a muffled clang. He held the tribune's gaze a moment and shook his head. He did not have an answer. Karus took one more look around and then left the workshop with Delvaris following.

They entered the next shop, a smithy. A wide range of finished products were scattered around the floor. More had been set on crude wooden shelving that not only ran the length of smithy, but also went from floor to ceiling. Despite the abundant amount of shelving, nothing had been arranged neatly. Karus suspected that this was not the result of looting, just the smith being a disorganized fellow. Blacksmiths were notorious for this sort of thing.

Karus sneezed. The shop stank of burned coal and old wood smoke, specifically ash. There was also something sweet on the air that he could not quite identify. It smelled a lot like beeswax.

Karus moved around the shop. He recognized wagon wheel hinges and pins. There were door handles, nails, and even weapons, some of which were only partially completed or looked to have been forged with flaws and then discarded. The latter, Karus decided, was the work of an apprentice. Karus glanced into several large wooden bins along the back wall. These were filled to varying degrees with ore.

Karus picked an ornamental bronze door handle off one of the shelves. It had been polished to the point where the metal gleamed. Despite the disorganized nature of the shop, the craftsmanship was notable. It spoke of a smith who was quite skilled, if not a master of his craft.

"Look at this," Delvaris said, having approached the main forge, which had gone cold long ago. The tribune pulled an unfinished blade from a bucket of brackish water and held it up. Water dripped from the sword. "Why start something you are not going to finish?"

"Everything we've seen so far would indicate that the evacuation of this city was not well planned." Karus paused. "It might have been made quickly."

"What were they fleeing?" Delvaris asked.

"I wish I knew," Karus said with a heavy breath. "I really wish I knew." He surveyed the interior once more, then turned and exited the shop.

In the middle of the market square was a large communal fountain. The centerpiece of the fountain was a heavily muscled nude man. The statue was exquisitely carved. In one hand he held a trident, and in the other a scepter. Jets of water sprayed forth from the tips of the trident, falling into three arcs that cascaded down into the pool of water below. Clearly, this was a representation of a god. Though there were similarities, it looked like no statue of Neptune Karus had ever seen.

He approached the fountain, studying the god carefully, almost warily. The sound of the falling water was relaxing. The pool into which the water fell was a good ten feet around and two feet deep. The water was clear and free of major debris, a sign of recent maintenance. Karus dipped a cupped hand into the water, which he found surprisingly cold. He tasted the water. It was fresh, and clean. He could well imagine slaves crowding around the pool and drawing water into jars, casks, and barrels for their masters.

Standing back, Karus looked over the statue of the god once more. It was an impressive piece of work. The cold, clean water could only mean one thing. The fountain was aqueduct-fed. Somewhere, fresh water was carried into the city. Karus wondered if this city had bathhouses. He certainly hoped so—it had been weeks since he had properly bathed.

Karus turned around in a circle, looking over the square. Delvaris was just emerging from another shop. He ducked into the one next to that, which, by looks, was some type of rug merchant. Karus studied the square. At least five large streets converged upon it, likely feeding customers to the craftsmen and merchants that had set up shop here. Besides his soldiers, the place was thoroughly deserted. Again, he wondered where all the people had gone. Did the gods transport them away even as they brought the Ninth here?

A shout up the street drew his attention. Pammon was standing just beyond the square, shouting at a legionary who had appeared on the roof of a building opposite to him. The senior centurion of the First tapped his foot impatiently. Two centuries stood with him in the event there was trouble.

Karus made his way over to Pammon.

"Find anything?" he asked.

"Plenty," Pammon said, with a sour look. "Just no people."

"Make sure your men stay alert," Karus said. "It will be easy to become complacent."

"They are on edge as it is," Pammon said. "I don't think we have to worry about that, at least not for an hour or two. Then they will become tired and lazy."

"Still," Karus said, "better to remind them anyway."

Pammon let slip a slight scowl, then nodded. He glanced up at the suns, which were now sitting high above them. "We can speed things up a bit by not being as thorough picking through these buildings."

Clearly Karus wasn't the only one frustrated with the slow, painful progress the cohort was making.

"No, we continue as is," Karus said. "We do this right. I want to make sure there are no surprises."

"Do you expect any?" Pammon asked.

"Do we dare take that chance?" Karus asked. "Are you willing to bet your life or those of your men?"

Pammon said nothing.

"I thought not," Karus said, then patted Pammon on his shoulder armor. "This snail's pace is getting to me as well. Best to suck it up and not to give into it."

Pammon gave a curt nod, a sour expression on his face. He stepped away, bawling the men of a century out for their laxness.

"Stop dragging your asses," Pammon shouted. "Get in that bloody house or so help me I will kick your sorry butts in there."

Karus watched for a moment and then started up the street. With each step, he noticed the grade was ever so slightly increasing. They were beginning the climb up the central hill.

Throughout the afternoon, the progress of the cohort was excruciatingly slow as they worked their way toward the center of the city. Karus waited as patiently as he could, occasionally entering buildings, but more as not standing outside with Delvaris. He did not want Pammon to feel like his heels were being dogged. Nor did he wish to undermine the newly promoted officer's authority.

Eventually they came to the temple district. The buildings, like those in Rome, were designed to impress and awe the populace. Karus felt small in the shadow of these grand temples. The marble columns before each were nearly as wide as the massive trees in the forest. Karus stopped to look over one such temple. He followed the mighty columns up to the roof, a height of at least seventy feet.

"Makes one feel kind of tiny," Delvaris said, coming to up Karus.

"Compared to a god," Karus said, "I guess we would be rather small, perhaps petty even, in their eyes." Karus looked over at the tribune before resuming his pace. Delvaris fell in beside him as they moved down the wide avenue, temples to either side. Karus counted thirteen grand temples. Romans honored twelve gods. He counted again to be sure his math was right. One of the temples at the far end looked to have collapsed into rubble.

"The priests teach we were made in the gods' image," Delvaris said.

"Do they?" Karus said. Never having been terribly religious himself, he could see the logic. "I guess that makes sense. Just by living our daily lives, we, in a way, honor them."

"I've never looked at it that way," Delvaris said.

A legionary, red in the face, hustled up. He stopped before the two officers and came to attention, saluting.

"Sir," he said, breathless yet excited. He pointed up the street. "Centurion Pammon requests your presence. We've found some bodies."

"Inform him I will be along presently," Karus said.

The legionary saluted and jogged back the way he had just come, armor chinking. Karus and Delvaris picked up their pace. They found Pammon and a century of legionaries standing before the temple that had collapsed. Close up, it was apparent it had been razed.

The columns had been pulled down and, with them, the roof had collapsed. A few of the ropes that had been used lay in the street. One was still wrapped around a column, which had fallen into the street and split into several large sections. The once grand building was now an extremely large pile of rubble sitting upon a raised foundation. Whatever it had looked like previously was now completely unrecognizable.

Several bodies had been staked out before the ruins and rubble.

"That is a terrible way to go," Pammon said to Karus in almost a whisper.

The dead had their hands tied behind their backs. They had been spitted upright through the asshole by a large sharpened stake that Karus assumed penetrated through their lower bowls. Karus was sure they had been allowed to slowly die, in agony without their feet being able to touch the ground.

"Death is always ugly," Karus said, "whether one dies peacefully in bed, on the battlefield or," he gestured at the miserable-looking bodies, "like this. There is really no good way to die."

Pammon said nothing.

Karus turned from the nauseating sight and glanced over at Delvaris, who looked pale but had not turned away. He gazed on in what appeared to be a morbid fascination mixed with horror. Once again, Karus was impressed with the mettle of the young man.

Karus walked up to one of the bodies, which had been stripped naked. The smell was horrendous. Though their flesh had blackened as the bodies bloated, Karus had the impression they had been old men. Flies were thick upon the corpses. Karus waved a hand to shoo them away so he could better see the body. It helped a little. He figured these poor sots had been staked well over two weeks ago, perhaps three, which gave him an idea of when the city had been abandoned or, at the very least, the last time people had been here.

He stepped between the line of stakes to better look over the ruined temple. Whoever had set to work on it had done a thorough job. There would be no searching it. Sending legionaries up to poke through the jumble of destroyed masonry would be dangerous. A scrape behind drew his attention as Pammon came up.

"This is something the druids would do," Pammon said, holding a hand close to his nose and looking over one of the bodies close up. "What do you think happened?"

"I don't know," Karus said, thinking it through. "Since we have happened across no other such scenes, I suspect," he jerked a thumb at the row of staked bodies, "their god fell out of favor."

"I guess," Pammon said, turning his gaze from the bodies to the ruins. "Though this looks more than a simple falling out of favor. There is serious hate tied up in what was done here."

Karus agreed. He regarded the bodies once more, eyes swinging over the ruins of the temple and then back to the dead.

"Take them down," Karus said, "and see that they are buried. The last thing we need is an outbreak of disease."

"You men," Pammon shouted to the century that had been standing by. "Bury them."

Karus's eyes met those of Delvaris as he moved back toward the street. No words were exchanged, just a silent mutual understanding that the world they lived in was a hard one. It was a tough lesson to impart, but the trials of the last few weeks had begun the lad's lesson. Perhaps, Karus thought, the staking out of the men had completed it. Karus understood that the tribune would forever after look at the world differently, as he himself had long ago.

Karus left the century and Pammon behind as he walked farther up the street. Delvaris followed. The grade increased with each step, more so than before. On either side, additional centuries from First Cohort were sweeping the temples. Karus considered going inside one but decided against it. He was more interested in what lay ahead just up the hill within the inner wall.

Glancing down a side street to his left, Karus saw legionaries in the distance. These were likely from one of the three cohorts charged with exploring that side of the city. Karus watched for a moment, then continued, moving up the street, which became even wider, broader, and steeper. It was slow going, but they finally came to the inner wall and a large, imposing gate.

Karus stopped before the broad gate. It took up much of the street. The gate was part fortification and part artwork. As such, it had an ornate, almost delicate look to it. The outer façade around the heavily reinforced gate was covered with carvings of soldiers fighting great battles. Though Karus had seen such things before in Rome, he found it very interesting. A coat of arms rested above the center of the gate. It had two golden birds to either side of a blue shield topped by a gold crown.

"Those carvings," Karus said to Delvaris, pointing at the images of soldiers, "tell a story."

"A military one," Delvaris said, eyes roving the carvings. "That's for sure. It's like one of the monuments back in Rome celebrating a victory."

The gates had been left open, and several centuries had already passed through. Despite the ornate appearance of the gate, Karus sensed real strength in the defensive works. The inner wall and gate would, he felt, withstand a serious assault. The wall, though smaller than the city's, was around fifty feet in height and, judging from the open gate, at least ten to twelve feet thick.

"In Rome," Delvaris said, glancing to his left and then right, "the buildings are built right up to the defensive walls. They did not do that either here or at the outer wall to the city..."

Karus looked. Delvaris was right. There was thirty yards of open space between the buildings of the city and the wall. At least knee-high grass grew thick in the open space.

"That's because...." Karus stopped, studying the wall. He noted several patches along part of the wall. It had the appearance of having been recently repaired and maintained. A wooden barricade sat atop the wall. It also looked relatively new, as in the wood had not yet had a chance to gray over with age and the weatherproofing stain was still a dark brown. "That's because it's been a long time since Rome has been threatened militarily. The rulers of this city were taking no chances."

"Then there must be a serious threat nearby," Delvaris breathed in understanding. "Why else leave such a great city as this? Especially with such solid defenses?"

"That," Karus said, starting forward again, "is the question. One I think Valens and his cavalry will likely answer for us if we don't find it in there."

He and Delvaris passed through the gate and emerged into a wide open, paved space that looked like a parade ground. To his front, on a rise, loomed an incredibly impressive white-marbled palace that gleamed brightly under the sunlight. At least four stories in height, it towered above the parade ground. Hundreds of wide steps led up to the main entrance.

The structure was unlike anything Karus had seen. There were over a hundred windows, each filled with real glass, an incalculable and extravagant expense. Several balconies with stone railings overlooked the parade ground. These appeared to have been strategically placed to gain the best views.

Lawns and gardens graced the sides of the palace, disappearing around the back. A single tower in a skinny minaret rose behind the palace. Karus presumed that it would provide a perfect vantage point. He made a note to climb it to get a better sense for the city.

To his right was the fortress, large and imposing. There was nothing ornamental in its appearance. Next to the fortress was a large building with wide doors that had been shuttered. A century of men was busily working to open the doors. The exterior gave it an appearance that looked like it was a combination barracks and stable. Karus judged that the palace guard likely lived there. To the left of the palace was a three-story building rimmed with windows that had all been shuttered. It seemed an administrative building.

Karus continued toward the palace. Delvaris followed along behind him. Another century was working their way up the steps ahead. As Karus placed his foot on the first step, the men above were already disappearing inside the palace.

Slowly working his way up the steps, Karus felt like the conquering general. A breeze caught his cloak, ruffling it slightly. He glanced back. Delvaris was still with him. Karus continued until he reached the top step. He then turned and surveyed the scene before him. He was higher than the lips of the inner wall. The city spread out in a magnificent display. From his vantage, the city seemed far larger than it had from the main wall several miles below.

Where he should have seen tens of thousands of smoke trails lazily rising upward to form an ugly blue-gray cloud above, Karus saw only a few hundred coming from the part of the city where the legion and camp followers had spent the night.

In the distance, he could see the three gates along the city's main wall. The fourth would be somewhere on the other side of the palace behind him. Karus was gratified to see tiny figures on the walls of all three gates that granted access into the city. His men had taken possession and secured them.

"Karus," Delvaris said, drawing his attention. A man was running from the building that looked like a barracks and combination indoor riding arena.

Karus took a deep breath. They had found something and Karus feared it would not be good news. He considered going down to meet the runner, then dismissed the idea. He would not undermine himself by showing concern or weakness of will.

"Sir." The legionary stopped on the second to last step and offered a hasty salute. His chest was heaving. Running in armor and then climbing the steps to the palace at the pace he had done was exhausting.

Karus looked down upon the man and nodded for him to continue, though inside he worried about the messenger's portent.

"That building, sir," the legionary turned and pointed. "It has an indoor parade ground that is packed to the ceiling with equipment, and rations, sir."

"What?" Karus snapped, not quite sure he had heard correctly.

"There is more supply in there than I ever saw at the depot in Eboracum," the legionary said, gulping down air. "It's all been packed neat and orderly like."

"Are you certain?" Karus was still having trouble believing the man's story.

"Centurion Ajax said it could feed an entire army for months, sir." The legionary paused, making a strong effort to catch his breath. "We opened a few of the barrels and crates, sir. Wheat, salted meat, spirits, and some stuff we don't recognize, but it's food."

Karus rocked back on his heels and closed his eyes briefly. The gods had provided again. Felix had been right. Karus took another deep breath and exhaled it slowly. He would be able to feed his people for the foreseeable future, and that did not even consider any supplies they could scrounge from the city and surrounding countryside.

"An army's worth?" Delvaris said in a quiet voice that was speculative. "I wonder whose army it belongs to."

Karus's turned to look at the tribune. Truer words had not been said, he decided.

"Whose indeed?"

Chapter Twelve

"My men would like to kill the druids," Flaccus said.

"You mean *you* want to kill them," Karus said.

Dio, Felix, and Delvaris looked on in silence.

"Yes," Flaccus said, gaze flinty and unblinking. "They deserve to die."

"No."

Karus could well read the exhaustion, hate, and anger warring on the other's face. It was clear Flaccus had not yet recovered from the loss of so many of his men. He hungered for revenge, even if it was sated on a pair of helpless prisoners. For a moment, Karus considered giving in to him in the hopes that the steady, cantankerous combat leader he had known for years would return. No, Karus decided, he would see this through.

"Why ever not?" Flaccus demanded.

"We may need them at some point," Karus said.

"Mark my words," Flaccus said heatedly, "keeping those bastards alive is a mistake."

"Then it is mine to make. Can I trust you and your men to guard them?"

"Yes," Flaccus fairly ground out through gritted teeth. "They will come to no harm."

"Very good," Karus said. "Then you may relieve Felix's men and assume responsibility for their care."

"When it comes time for them to die," Flaccus said, "I want to do it. Give me your word on that."

"You have it, if it comes to that."

"I will hold you to that, Karus." Flaccus gave a curt nod, turned, and left the room, stomping out.

"He has become a problem," Felix said, breaking the silence that followed. "You should relieve him."

Karus stared at the empty doorway and rubbed his jaw, wondering if he had done the right thing. He turned to the others. All wore grave expressions.

"No," Karus said. "I will not relieve him."

"Do you think it wise for his men to guard the prisoners?" Dio asked. "They've been through a lot."

"Flaccus will follow his orders," Karus said, although he was not altogether sure he would.

"A test," Felix said, snapping his fingers. "There was no reason to change the guard to his cohort. You are testing him with the druids then? You don't really care if they live or die, do you? All you want to know is whether Flaccus is steady enough to follow orders, even those he feels are patently wrong."

The room became silent. Karus was not at all surprised Felix was onto the truth. He almost opened his mouth to reply, then stopped himself. It was time to move things along.

"Let's have it." Karus looked over at Delvaris, who held a good-sized wooden tablet. Felix held a similar tablet and had made notes on its wax face using a silver stylus held loosely in his other hand. Karus had set each of them specific tasks, and they were here now to report back.

They had gathered in a spacious room Karus had selected on the second floor of the palace to serve as a temporary headquarters. The space had been devoid of furniture. Instead, sturdy shelving neatly stacked with hundreds of scrolls lined each wall. It was one of the reasons he had chosen the space. Many of the other rooms were cluttered with gaudy pieces of furniture, both large and small. This, he was sure, was a library. It also had a small adjacent antechamber that had likely served as the librarian's office. He had decided it would serve well enough for the legion's headquarters.

The shutters to three of the four large windows had been thrown open, allowing in plenty of the late afternoon light and a gentle breeze that periodically flowed into the room. The fourth shutter's hinges were rusted stuck and so remained closed. Two heavy wooden tables had been manhandled in. A sturdy but battered-looking stool had also been found for Karus. A pile of parchments was stacked neatly atop one, along with an ink bottle, stylus, and feather pen. These writing supplies had been found in the administrative building next to the palace. The other table held a suit of dull gray armor. Next to the armor sat a small metal lantern that Dio had brought in. The flame, protected from the breeze by glass panes, burned bright and yellow.

Karus glanced around at the neatly stacked scrolls that cried out of great age. Unfortunately, the neatly flowing script within the scrolls was indecipherable. Based on how they had been stored, he had decided that they were important works. Why else keep them in a library?

The sight of the scrolls ignited a fire that burned within. What great knowledge did they hold? Karus felt a pang for his own collection, which had been left behind in Eboracum. Would he ever return?

Delvaris cleared his throat.

"Near as I can tell," Delvaris said, glancing down at his tablet, "with the stockpile of supplies discovered here in the palace district, we should have food to last us at least eight months. To be sure, I confirmed this figure with Felix."

Scratching away at parchment, the clerks could be heard through the open doorway as Delvaris fell silent. Karus's staff, all three of them, were working diligently at rebuilding the legion's books, meticulously listing out the active legionaries and auxiliaries of each cohort. These men had been pulled from the First, men Karus knew to be literate. The legate's staff and slaves had not made it through the retreat. Karus wasn't surprised. The slaves had likely run off when everything had gone balls up.

The scratching was interlaced with the occasional comment, question, or arriving messenger delivering a report on strength totals or counts.

"That's right," Felix said. "He did the math using an average-per-day ration allotment based upon an estimate of what was found. We're guessing, because the stock of supplies is so large we haven't sorted through it completely yet. But going off what we've found, there is plenty of flour, grain, barley, salted beef, and pork that we won't be wanting for anything for some time."

"There is also a large stash of salt," Delvaris added, having consulted his tablet, "and a type of grain that we've been unable to identify, but since it's been stored in quantity, it is most likely edible. We've got a cook with the camp followers experimenting."

"Oh?" Karus asked, curious, turning his eyes on Felix.

"Marci's wife," Felix explained.

"Elena's a good cook," Karus said. Marci was a junior centurion in Fourth Cohort. He had never officially applied to marry the girl, but they had been together so long she was considered his wife by one and all. Such things were common in the legion.

"If anyone can make something tasty of it," Dio said, "it will be her."

"What else?" Karus asked.

"We have begun gathering food stores discovered in the city." Delvaris paused to take a breath. "You were right about a grain storage. It seems there was a public dole."

"Hah!" Karus grinned, slapping the side of his good thigh. "It's always good to be right."

"Well," Felix said, "it's not all roses. The bloody storage is only a quarter full. We think that when they city was abandoned the warehouses were opened to the public. There was grain scattered all over the ground and street leading from the warehouses for at least two blocks."

"So…" Karus said, thinking it through. He had found no answers as to why the city was emptied here in the palace. If anything, the mystery had only deepened with what had been discovered. When they were done here, he would show it to Dio and Felix. "The evacuation was hasty and authorities opened the food supply for all to take what they could carry?"

"That sounds about right," Felix said.

Karus nodded for Delvaris to continue.

"The grain from the warehouses should give us an extra two months at best. I have taken the liberty of ordering that it be moved to the indoor parade ground with the rest of the stockpile. It's the perfect place for a centralized depot. There are barrack cells in the building that can be used for offices, record storage, and to billet a guard."

Karus raised his eyebrows at the tribune, surprised with the initiative. He very much doubted whether Julionus would have permitted a junior tribune to make such decisions in his name. It told Karus that Delvaris was not afraid to make decisions that he felt were right.

"I would have consulted you," Delvaris added hastily, "however, it seemed prudent to move things along and order the concentration of our food stores. At the time, I also could not find you. I did consult Felix."

"I was in the minaret overlooking the city," Karus said. "I should have left word where I was going. It's all right. Excellent thinking. I would have made the same decision."

"See?" Felix said with an amused chuckle. "I told you he would be fine with it."

A relieved grin spread across Delvaris's face before he colored in sudden embarrassment. Karus realized that the boy had been agonizing over how he would react. If Karus wanted to develop him further as an aide, Delvaris needed to feel confident when he had to give orders in Karus's name.

"We will need an officer to oversee the depot," Felix said. "Someone who is good with organization, having the ability to say 'no,' and counting above the number ten, I think, would be a prerequisite." Felix paused and turned his gaze to his fellow centurion. "Sorry, Dio, that rules you out."

"Well," Dio said, with an overdramatic sigh, "I am a man of action, a fighting man, not a clerk."

"You'd pass up a cushy job like that?"

"You know how much I hate the bureaucracy." Dio paused and turned to look at Delvaris. "Those are the blokes whose job it is to make sure things get done, but then happily stand in the way of allowing someone else who has to do the job from doing it. Remember that when you become a legate."

Karus chuckled and just shook his head slightly.

Felix was right about Dio, but for a more serious reason. He needed his cohort commanders to lead without the distraction of a second job. It couldn't be the tribune either.

Delvaris's rank was too high to serve as a simple supply officer. Delvaris was from a senatorial family; the position was simply beneath him. No, it would have to be a centurion, and a junior one at that.

"Who do you suggest?" Karus asked of Dio and Felix. "It must be a junior officer. I can't afford to replace any senior officers right now. Nor do I think that wise, as they are our most experienced combat leaders."

"What about Janus?" Felix said. "He is good with numbers and seems organized enough."

"I think he could do it," Karus said. "He's got a good head on his shoulders."

"I hate to lose him, but Cestus might be the better choice," Dio put in. "Prior to getting posted to my cohort, he served a stint in supply."

"And you've never held that against him?" Felix asked.

"If he wasn't such a good officer, I might have."

"Cestus then," Karus said, making up his mind. "At least until we find someone better."

"He won't like losing his century," Dio put in.

"He can keep his century." Karus did not want to take the man's command away from him. Men who made it to Cestus's rank worked hard for it over many years. It would be cruel to snatch that away. "They can help him manage and secure the depot. Dio, will you notify Cestus of his new responsibilities? He is to begin immediately."

"I will," Dio said, a relieved note in his tone.

"Good," Karus said. "My clerks will provide him with a strength total for each cohort. The same will be done with the followers. Accordingly, he will need to provide a weekly ration draw and account for it."

"I will make him aware."

Karus turned to Delvaris. "Continue."

"A list of additional food stores is still coming in," Delvaris said. "However, my best guess is these will extend our stores at least another two months. This is, of course, dependent upon what Valens finds in the surrounding countryside and if we can properly store it all before the food spoils."

"As long as the aqueducts continue to flow," Dio added, "we should have plenty of water too."

"Speaking of which, has a bathhouse been located?" Karus asked. "There is one here in the palace, but it is rather small and not suitable for large scale use."

"We've located several throughout the city," Dio said.

"Is one near the palace district?" Karus asked.

"Yes," Dio said. "A bathhouse is just a few blocks over from the palace gate and, like the fountains, is aqueduct-fed. No need for any manual hauling of water from the fountains."

"Good," Karus said. Bathhouses were important to legionaries. Many forts and garrisons included such amenities in the towns that inevitably grew up next to them. Using fountain-drawn water for bathing was not the same thing. "Dio, I want you to get it operational as soon as possible. Delvaris, once the bathhouse is ready, come up with a rotating schedule for the men and camp followers."

"It shouldn't take too much work," Dio said.

"I want to ultimately move our people to the area just outside of the palace gatehouse," Karus announced. "The accommodations in this area are nicer, more spacious, and close enough that if we need to pull everyone inside the inner walls on short notice we will be able to do so."

"Karus." A troubled look washed over Felix's face.

"Speak your mind."

"This cache we found. It was stored in a similar manner to how we would prepare a depot." Felix paused a heartbeat.

"What I mean is, well, this is how a disciplined force would store supplies."

"I know," Karus said, understanding Felix's concern. "I took a look myself and found it all very orderly. Our supply clerks back in Eboracum could learn a thing or two."

"I suspect whoever left it did so after the city was evacuated," Felix said. "Otherwise I think those stores would have been picked over and looted. It's fair to expect whoever left them to come back. I mean, why bother organizing supplies you would be abandoning?"

"We will burn that bridge when we come to it," Karus said, having already come to the same conclusion. Felix was right, but his people had an immediate need. There was simply no telling how long it would take or how far they would have to march to return to friendly lands.

"Thing is, Karus," Felix continued, "just by taking advantage of it, we may burn your bridge beforehand."

"We need that supply," Karus said in a firm tone that was hard with certainty, "and it is gods sent."

"I agree with Karus," Dio said. "You really expect us not to use it and rely upon what can be scrounged up in the city and surrounding countryside?"

"I did not say that," Felix said. "It seems to me that it was put here for a reason. Someone will come looking for it. Someone who right now may not be our enemy."

"That can't be helped," Karus said, having felt the tension in the room grow with the exchange. "We found it and will use it to keep our people fed."

Felix bowed his head in acknowledgment of Karus's decision. The room was silent for a few moments, then Karus looked to the tribune to continue.

"That armor there," Delvaris said, nodding to the table where the suit of armor lay.

It had been brought in by a pair of legionaries before the meeting. The two legionaries had struggled just carrying the chest armor in alone. Karus turned his gaze to the armor, which had been found amongst the supply cache. He had already briefly examined it.

"I would not," Delvaris continued, "want to encounter whoever that was meant for."

Karus agreed, though he did not say so aloud. He walked over to the armor and studied it again, contemplating the impossible size of the chest plate. It was very thick. The person it was made for would have been short in stature, but broad-chested and incredibly strong.

Below the chest plate was a skirt of mail that hung down under the waist, and it would have been a very large one at that. It was almost as if the armor had been made for a very short, fat man. The helmet that had been placed next to the armor was also too wide and twice the weight of a legionary's. The shield was smaller than those used by the legion, but it was made of all metal, save for the leather brace secured behind for an arm. There would be little if any cushion for blows. There were arm and leg greaves as well. All of it was incredibly heavy.

The armor had a plain look that disguised its quality. Karus judged that it was superior to that of the legion's standard issue. His critical eye was sure of that. He reached out a hand and felt the cold touch of smoothed metal. It had been wrought by a master armorer.

"How many more sets like this did you find?" Karus asked, turning to Delvaris.

The tribune moved over to join Karus, glancing down contemplatively at the impossible-looking armor. He consulted his tablet.

"Four hundred and twelve."

"And all are about the same size?" Karus looked to Delvaris for confirmation.

"More or less."

Dio let out a low whistle at that. "Not only do we have to worry about the bastards that fit this armor, but if these are spares and with the sheer quantity of the cache … "

"How large," Karus finished as Dio trailed off, "is the army that stored these here?"

"Another thing," Delvaris said and pointed at a mailed hand. "One of the men noticed this. Each hand has six fingers, not five. Every set is the same. I checked."

Karus glanced down sharply and counted. He had missed it, but sure enough, there were six finger holes in the armor. He chewed his lip a moment as he considered, not liking what he was seeing.

"I've never met a six-fingered man," Dio said, his voice sounding troubled. "Kind of like a woman with a slanted vagina. They don't exist."

Karus shot Dio a look which said, "You are not helping."

"A 'round-the-clock guard has been placed on the depot," Delvaris said, changing the subject. "On another troubling note, we've also found large quantities of spirits in the city. Felix suggested that the spirits be secured. I concurred, so I've passed along orders that all such drink is to be confiscated and moved to the depot."

"That said," Felix blew out an unhappy breath, "we're still having a problem."

Karus could well imagine. The life of a legionary was generally dull and difficult. Drink took the edge off. Legionaries were allotted a standard two-pint daily ration of wine. They were accustomed to drinking and, when off-duty, imbibed freely. With what had been found throughout the city, there was no doubt in Karus's mind that there was a great deal of excessive drinking in the evening hours.

"What kind of spirits?" Karus said.

"We found hard stuff and some beer, sour tasting shit that's worse than what the Celts drink," Felix said. "Surprisingly, no wine."

"Delvaris, sour or not, coordinate with Cestus to arrange for each cohort to begin receiving enough beer to meet the two-pint ration," Karus said, knowing the rank and file of the legion were not discriminating drinkers. "Dio, set up several drinking establishments for off-duty hours. Get a few of the followers to run them at no charge to our men. See that the amount consumed is limited. The cohort commanders can work out a schedule for their men to frequent these establishments on a pass basis. That should cut out some of the unauthorized drinking. Once we have that in place, punishments are to be handed out to violators that are caught pilfering drink from the city."

"We can easily get this up and running," Dio said, "by tomorrow night at the very least."

"That sounds good." Karus had placed Dio in charge of compiling reports of the exploration of the city. As Karus's second, Pammon was responsible for executing the search of the city, which was why he was not present. "Dio, I would like an update on how the search of the city is progressing."

"It is a big city," Dio said. "Searching it is taking some serious time. That said, we have yet to find anyone skulking about. When the city was evacuated, it seems that no one was permitted to remain. We did find a series of mass graves just outside the walls. Whoever buried them did a shitty job of it, and it was relatively easy to dig up a few of the bodies. They are fresh to within the last two weeks, maybe just a day or two longer. This matches with the bodies that were staked out in the temple district." Dio paused to scratch an itch on his cheek. "I would guess that there are at least several hundred bodies in the one that I looked at, judging by the size of the pit that was covered over. We've found five others just like it."

"Several thousand then," Karus said.

"Yes," Dio said. "We've also found an extensive dungeon right under the administrative building here in the palace district. We have only just begun exploring the first two levels, but it is possible that the bodies in the pits are the prisoners that were held there. No sense in bringing the criminal element with you when you're fleeing."

"It could also be," Karus said, "that the bodies were stragglers."

"You mean the populace had a choice?" Felix's eyebrows drew together. "Either evacuate with everyone else or be executed?"

"It would explain why we've not come across a soul in the city," Dio said. "You'd think someone would have stayed behind for the loot."

"We just don't know yet," Karus said. "Speculating is about all we can do. Tell me about this dungeon."

"There seems to be a large network of underground spaces honey-combing the palace district," Dio said. "We think they go down maybe ten stories. A few cells are occupied by bones of prisoners left to rot. There are rooms for torture too." Dio paused to suck in a breath. "We've also found catacombs under the city, with at least seven entrances identified so far. Otho and his cohort are exploring them, but just like the dungeons, they are extensive. He believes there are more entrances, and I agree. These both will take time to search and map out. It is possible the dungeon and catacombs may even connect somewhere. At this point, we just don't know, and that does not even take into account the sewers, which we haven't gotten around to yet."

Karus did not like the sound of that. The city was far too large to search quickly. He knew that criminal elements in Rome used the catacombs and sewers as hideouts, as did runaway slaves. Karus rubbed at his forehead with the palm of his hand. He felt a headache coming on.

Though they had explored much of the city, Karus was becoming convinced that there was a solid chance no one was hiding out in it. That did not mean he would allow himself or his men to relax.

"I want those dungeons explored immediately," Karus said. "If for whatever reason we need a secure place to fall back upon, I want to be sure that we know every nook and cranny of the palace district. We can afford no surprises."

"I knew you would want that done," Dio said with a sudden trace of a grin. "I've dispatched two additional centuries to help scour the dungeons. With luck, they will ferret out any tunnels running under the walls and out into the city. I was thinking of assigning two of the auxiliary cohorts to explore the sewers. Also, with your permission, I will detail a century to look for hidden passageways concealed behind the walls of the palace. Wouldn't want anything to happen to our 'acting' legate."

"Camp prefect will do," Karus said, wishing he had thought of searching the palace for hidden passages sooner. Who knew what secrets the palace held? "Do it."

"One other thing," Dio said and reached for the lantern. He handed it to Karus, who was surprised by its weight. "We found a number of these in the dungeon."

"It is an oil lantern," Karus said and set it back down on the table next to the armor.

"Blow out the flame," Dio urged.

"I don't have time for games."

"Do it," Dio said and opened the glass panel that provided access to light and extinguish the lantern.

Slightly irritated, Karus bent over and blew the flame out. As he was straightening back up, the lantern reignited. Karus blinked. He blew it out a second time and the flame relit.

"I've even used water," Dio said, "and doused it. The flame always comes back."

"Magic?" Karus found it difficult to believe.

"That is extraordinary," Delvaris breathed.

"Quite," Felix said.

"Magic," Dio said. "There are about forty such lanterns in the dungeon. We've also found a few in the palace and throughout the city. There must be some trick to turning them on and off, because we've found ones just like this that are not lit."

Karus rocked back on his heels. He had never seen true magic before, only sleight of hand performed by charlatans. Then again, he thought back to the glowing druid stones and those warm ones on the hilltop above the forest. There were so many things he just did not have the answers for.

"What more have you got for me?"

"Karus, there are plenty of tools and equipment that were left behind," Felix said, "much of which we can use. Four blacksmiths made it through with the camp followers. I've had them study the smithies that we happened across. They feel they can easily work them. However, some of the ore and metals were unrecognizable."

"What do you mean unrecognizable?" Karus was surprised by this revelation.

"Just that, stuff they've never seen before."

"Huh," Karus said, not knowing what to make of that.

"We've also found several woodworking shops," Felix said, "complete with tools and a saw mill just outside the city, near the forest. Between the smithies and these woodworking shops, we have the craftsmen amongst the followers, not to mention our own men who can make whatever we need."

"How many wagons and carts were found?" Karus asked, thinking ahead. If they needed to leave the city for whatever reason, he felt it was important to begin planning for the worst.

"We found no serviceable wagons and carts," Delvaris said. "They were likely taken when the city was evacuated."

Karus crossed his arms and looked down. Then glanced up at Dio and Felix. "We should be able to easily make wagons, right?"

"Yes. As I said, we have the craftsmen. We also have the manpower to get it done."

"Good," Karus said. "I want you to get started on that immediately. Felix, oversee this. If we need to leave the city, I want to take as much with us as possible."

"There is another problem," Delvaris said.

Karus gestured for him to continue.

"We don't have the draft animals needed to pull any wagons that we build."

"Feel free to rain on my parade, will you," Felix said.

"We have the mules, and can dismount Valens's troopers, if necessary," Karus said.

"He won't like that," Dio said.

"I know," Karus said. "Let's hope it does not come to that. Delvaris, see that word is sent to the cavalry to be on the lookout for oxen and mules. Valens's scouts are bound to happen across people at some point."

Delvaris nodded.

"Felix," Karus said, "see that we begin making wagons immediately."

"I will get on that as soon as we finish here," Felix said.

"Delvaris," Karus said, "I want an inventory taken of every cohort to determine what materials are in need of repair or replacement: swords, shields, sandals, whatever. A priority will be given to replacing equipment over wagons."

Delvaris inclined his head in understanding.

"I also want javelins," Karus said to Felix. "We used all that we had."

"It will be done." Felix made a note on his tablet.

"What of the walls and the city gates?" Karus asked. "How are we progressing on that front?"

"The walls are patrolled," Dio answered. "The gates are secured, and each one is strong and defensible. Currently we have an entire cohort on each, which helps covering the gaps between the gates. Two men are posted every seventy-five yards, and we have sections of men regularly walking the walls, patrolling. Still," Dio expelled a frustrated breath, "the walls are damned long. It would take the entire legion to properly man them, and then we'd still likely be short on reserves should it come to it. Beyond that, I don't see what more we can do at present. Oh, and as ordered, we're not allowing anyone other than Valens's troopers in and out of the city without express orders from you."

"Very good," Karus said. "I know you are doing what you can."

Karus walked to an open window, Felix and Dio following him over. From it, he was able to look out upon a good portion of the city. He studied it, silent for a few heartbeats. For the moment, his people were safe, in a strong, defensive position. They also had plenty to eat and, for the first time in weeks, a solid roof over their heads rather than a flimsy tent or being forced to sleep on their arms.

Karus let out a long, soft breath that was partially a sigh. This unknown city was a temporary refuge. It was not a permanent home. Something was terribly wrong in this land, and eventually it would look his way. Karus was sure of it.

"Our overriding priority is to return to Rome."

"That," Felix said, from behind, "may not be possible."

Karus looked over at his friend and felt saddened. If only his Felix knew what he had seen just a few rooms over. Well, he would, Karus thought, shortly at any rate.

"We've been in this strange land," Felix said, "for five days. With the dawn of each new day, we find the same two suns still overhead. The moon isn't even right. Our moon is white." Felix paused, sucking in a low breath. "Karus, we are very far from home."

Karus was silent. He considered his friend's words. Free from cloud cover, the moon had finally emerged the previous evening, and as Karus had worried, it caused quite a stir. It was slightly orange, and far more pockmarked.

"Still," Karus said, "our overriding objective is to return to Rome. If it comes to pass that this proves impossible, we will deal with it then. The last thing we need is the men concluding that they will never return home. If that happens, discipline will break down and I fear we will lose the legion."

"That would not be good," Felix said.

"The men might surprise us," Dio said. "For most, the legion is their home. The only one they have known for many years."

"We cannot count on that," Karus said. "They are exhausted and morale is poor. We've all been through a tremendous ordeal. However, given enough time to rest, they will recover." Karus paused and took a breath. "The quickest way to build morale and maintain discipline is through training. I will call a meeting of senior officers this evening. A schedule will have to be drawn up. Each cohort will implement a training regimen that is to be executed once every three days. On days where there is no training, they are to be doing work in and around the city or standing duty. We keep our boys busy and we keep them active with as little downtime as possible. That, and the training, will see a return to normalcy."

Karus turned his gaze back out into the city. "My friends, we are in a strange land. We need to hold together or we may lose ourselves amongst its mysteries."

"Just a tad optimistic today, aren't you?" Dio chuckled, though Karus felt he could detect a hint of worry in his friend's tone.

Karus glanced at Dio. He noticed that where his friend normally had something in his hands, they were empty. Dio's fingers were instead fidgeting with his tunic. Karus crossed over to one of the tables and picked up a gold coin that had been found in the city. Karus turned the coin over in his hand. It was well-worn and in places chipped where someone had carved pieces off. A strange face graced one side and a bird of prey the other.

"What happened to your lucky coin?" Karus asked Dio, turning around.

"I lost it," Dio said, a melancholy look to his face, almost as if he had lost his favorite cat.

"Here," Karus said, tossing the coin to Dio, who caught it with ease. "I have a feeling that soon we may all need some luck."

"Thanks," Dio said.

They were silent for several moments, then Karus cleared his throat.

"Delvaris," Karus said, "please see to the tasks I set you."

Delvaris clearly understood Karus wished to speak to Dio and Felix alone. He gave a curt nod and stepped out of the room. Karus waited a moment. When he heard Delvaris speaking with the clerks, he turned to his two friends.

"Now," Karus said, "I have something for the two of you to see."

Chapter Thirteen

"Now *this* is interesting," Dio breathed, staring down at the floor as he slowly walked in a large circle around the mosaic map. "We've not found one map in this the entire city, and here you find the only one that could not be taken with them when the people here fled."

Karus, Dio, and Felix were in the palace hall that served as the main throne room. Two other lesser rooms containing thrones had been found, but these were nowhere near as grand. Over one hundred fifty yards long and another fifty wide, the rectangular-shaped hall was vast. At one end, two massively thick wooden doors allowed entrance. At the other, the throne, a large gilded, high-backed chair that sat upon a raised platform. This would have been where the leader of this city held court, dealing with major functions of state, receiving envoys, and conducting diplomacy.

To either side, slender marble columns flanked the length of the hall, rising at least sixty feet in height to where they supported an arched ceiling covered over with colorfully painted frescos. Suspended by ropes, great candle-bearing iron chandeliers, each separated by ten feet of space from the next, hung in a long line down the center of the hall. Between the columns, colored glass windows beginning at shoulder height reached nearly up to the ceiling. These cast much of the interior of the hall in a muted light.

The throne had been positioned directly under a large dome set high above. The dome was multi-tiered with clear-paned windows, allowing the sky to be seen. The flooring throughout much of the hall was stone, yet around the throne it gave over to polished white marble, likely designed to further accent the natural light radiating down.

But all that and the grandeur around them was not what was interesting to Karus, Dio, and Felix. A mosaic map had been laid out upon the floor ten yards before the throne. Karus had never seen such a work of art look so detailed and perfect. The map depicted continents, islands, seas, mountain ranges, countries, and cities. It was at least ten yards around. Yet all of it was unfamiliar and unrecognizable as could be.

"We are very far from home," Felix said in a tone that expressed extreme unhappiness, almost bordering on despair. Like Dio, he began walking around the edge of the map, looking at it from different angles. As if by unspoken agreement, no one tread on the mosaic. Instead, they moved around the map, careful where they put their feet. Both were silent for some time as they examined it.

Karus said nothing. He just waited.

When Felix finally looked up, there was something akin to pain in his eyes.

"Very far," Felix said in a ghost of a whisper, before returning his gaze back to the floor.

Dio stopped his circling. He now stood as if rooted in place, his eyes continuing to sweep across the map. The gold coin appeared in his hand. Absently, he began rolling it over his knuckles, again and again. Karus simply watched, allowing them time to gather their thoughts.

"I think," Dio said slowly after some time, "that the worst thing about discovering this is that, even with it, we still have absolutely no idea whatsoever where we are on it."

"That was Pammon's thinking as well," Karus said, catching Felix's eye. "Still, it changes nothing."

"How so?" Felix asked. The look of pain that had filled his eyes moments before had lessened considerably. There was almost a resigned look to him, as if he had accepted what fate had thrown his way. Felix was like that.

"We still need to find our way home," Karus said, matter-of-factly.

Felix pursed his lips. He appeared as if he was going to say something, perhaps even object. Instead, he simply gave a slight shrug and returned his gaze to studying the map. Dio did the same.

Karus took a step back and allowed them the opportunity to continue to study the map. When Karus had told Delvaris that he had been in the minaret, he had been here scrutinizing the map for something, anything, familiar. It had been both fascinating and frustrating.

He glanced around the hall. It spoke not only of vast wealth, but power, military prowess, and strength. The colored glass windows were thick with imagery, each telling a distinct story. They recounted battles, the history of this land, and the wise and benevolent nature of its leaders. Cruelty and suffering were also on full display. Several windows were devoted to detailing what clearly appeared to be punishments directed at defeated and broken enemies. Karus was familiar with such brutality. It was nothing that Rome had not done to those she vanquished, and would continue to do. It was the best way to communicate a simple message to those who contemplated resisting the will of the empire.

Karus shifted his gaze from the glassed windows to the columns. From each one hung battle standards that Karus assumed had been taken as prizes. There were hundreds of the captured standards. Some were damaged, the wood staffs cracked, shattered. The fabric of many were torn and ripped. One was spattered with dried blood. Like the rest of the hall, these additions were designed to impress, and intimidate.

Karus's gaze fell upon one particular standard. It looked uncomfortably like an imperial legionary Eagle, though cast in silver instead of gold. Upon closer inspection, the bird, however, was not an eagle, but a hawk.

"We need a shrine for our Eagle," Karus said to himself as he looked upon the silver hawk. Wherever a legion went, a shrine was set up, whether permanent or tent-based. This hall was a shrine to power. It would be fitting to place the Eagle and the rest of the legion's standards here. This city now belonged to Rome, as did her past victories. "Yes, this will be our legion's shrine."

Satisfied with his decision, Karus considered the glassed window directly behind the throne. It provided a view of the city. Karus could not imagine the cost it'd taken to construct this hall, but he was confident the expense had been steep and the people of this city and others had paid for it.

Leaving Dio and Felix behind, Karus walked up to the throne, which was on a raised dais. With each step up to the great chair, his hobnailed sandals echoed off of the marble flooring. Once he reached it, he contemplated the dais and throne. He turned and gazed back across the entirety of the rectangular-shaped hall. In his mind, Karus imagined it filled with courtiers, petitioners, supplicants, and ambassadors from other nations, each one having come to seek something, to pay homage to greatness, to beg, to be close to power…

What would it have been like? Slaves to cater to your every need, people honoring your greatness, praising your magnificence at every turn…

The two wooden doors at the far end of the throne room opened. Hinges badly in need of an oiling cried out in protest. The sound echoed through the hall. Karus looked up, as did Dio and Felix. He had left orders not to be disturbed.

Irritated, Karus almost barked an order for the junior centurion who had entered to leave. He bit back on it, as he saw it was Crix, from Dio's cohort. They would have only been disturbed for a very good reason. Karus also realized that he could not be perceived as hiding the knowledge of the map. Word of it would get out eventually, if it hadn't already.

Crix quickly scanned the hall, spotted Karus, and walked purposely over. He came to a position of attention and saluted fist to chest. Karus returned the salute. Felix and Dio, curious, moved up behind.

"Sir," Crix rasped in a scratchy tone. The junior centurion had suffered a grievous wound to his throat several years before in a minor skirmish against a Celtic raiding party. He had recovered, but his voice had never been the same. "We discovered a prisoner being held in the dungeons under the administrative building."

"A prisoner?" Karus was surprised. He had begun to believe the city was empty. Apparently, it was not completely so. He noticed Dio and Felix sharing a look.

"Yes, sir," Crix rasped. "A woman in her early twenties. It appears that she was locked up, chained, and left some food and water. However, I estimate that she ran out of both a couple of days back."

Karus was even more surprised by that. Someone had wanted her to survive, at least for a time. The question was, *why*?

"What is her condition?"

"Passable," he said. "The prisoner will live."

"Where is she now?" Karus rubbed his chin. He wanted to speak with her.

"Just outside, sir." The centurion glanced behind him before returning to look at Karus. "I thought you might like to see her straightaway, though she doesn't seem to speak any Latin."

"Very well," Karus said, resisting the urge to frown in disappointment, "bring her in."

The centurion turned on his heel and began walking toward the far end of the hall. Karus moved up to Felix and Dio. He glanced at both of them before taking a few more eager steps toward the door, curious about the prisoner. He stopped just before the mosaic and waited.

"An entire city abandoned," Dio said, coming up next to him on his right, "and we only find a single prisoner?"

"I wonder why she alone was left behind," Felix asked. "And why bother to leave her with any food?"

"To suffer a slow death," Karus said, "I would think."

A section of legionaries entered the hall. Amongst the chink of armor, there was the heavy clinking of metal chain. Surrounded, the prisoner shuffled awkwardly forward. Not only were her hands manacled, but so too were her ankles.

Karus carefully studied the prisoner as she approached. It was clear on first glance that this was no slave or petty criminal. Her white dress which had once been well-cut from fine material was now ripped, torn, ragged, and badly stained. She was covered in grime. Karus could not be sure, but her skin under the filth appeared to be an olive color. Her long hair was matted and greasy. He could not see her eyes, which she shielded with a hand that was heavily manacled at the wrist; the other, supported just below it by the chain, hung limply. It was apparent she had not seen sunlight or, for that matter, any type of light for some time.

One of Crix's men supported her about the waist. The way he leaned his head away as he helped her along one struggling step at a time communicated how he did not think such close proximity a pleasant experience.

Despite her wretched appearance, Karus found he was intrigued. Though he could not put his finger on it, there was something about this young woman. It was a gut feeling, and Karus had learned to trust his instincts. She was important. He was sure of it.

Led by Crix, the section stopped before Karus, Felix, and Dio. The legionaries in front of the prisoner stepped to the side, yet remained within easy arm's reach, their attention fixed upon their charge. The man supporting her hastily took the opportunity to also step aside. Startled by the move and suddenly without his support, she almost collapsed. Karus resisted the urge to move forward to assist her, but in the end, she managed to maintain her feet, swaying slightly from the effort. Chains clinking dully, she slowly lowered her hand. Blinking several times before squinting, her gaze settled upon Karus.

He was immediately struck by her dark eyes. There was an intensity to them, which, after a moment, wavered as she glanced first at Dio and Felix and then at the legionaries who had become her guards. It was almost as if she was sizing them up.

"Do you understand me?" Karus asked, hoping Crix had been wrong.

Her gaze slowly returned to him. Karus could read what he took to be a deep sadness within her bearing. Yet despite her condition, the gaze she locked upon Karus was strong. Prisoner or not, he sensed that there was strength to this woman who stiffened her spine before him. There were veterans who had difficulty meeting his eyes. He had the feeling that if she cleaned up, she would look quite fine, regal even.

"Do you understand me?" Karus repeated, putting emphasis on his questioning tone.

She looked him over, eyes traveling from his feet to his head. After a moment, she shook her head, though he thought there was recognition in her eyes, which widened slightly as she studied his face.

Karus switched to Greek and again she shook her head.

He stepped up to her, looking her up and down, studying the woman before him. She smelled horrid. Karus resisted the impulse to pinch his nose. Raw sores and cruel bruises were visible where the manacles contacted her skin. Without a doubt, he was sure she was infested with pests. Such was the way of things with prisoners.

She spoke, and it came out in a croak, almost a whisper. She closed her eyes, swallowed, and spoke again, this time stronger, in a tone that cracked with a dry throat unaccustomed to speaking. Karus did not recognize the language, but to his ear it sounded a little rough, almost like one of the harsh Germanic languages. He looked to Dio.

"Don't look at me, I only speak Latin, and bad Latin."

Karus shifted his gaze to Felix.

"That's no tongue I know," Felix said.

Karus's eyes flickered downward. She and Crix's section were standing upon the mosaic. A thought occurred to him, and he turned to Crix.

"In the headquarters with my clerks, there is some fresh bread. Kindly go and get some. Bring some water as well."

"Yes, sir," Crix said, promptly spun on his heel, and began moving briskly down the length of the hall, hobnails cracking loudly on the stone.

She watched the officer leave, clearly wondering where he was going.

Karus drew away from her and motioned Felix and Dio closer.

"What do you think?" He kept his tone low in the event she understood Latin.

"With those manacles, she must be dangerous," Dio said, voice just as quiet.

"I don't know." Felix glanced over at her. "She does not appear to be too strong. I doubt she could best any man here."

"A murderess then?" Dio postulated.

"No," Felix said firmly, "I don't think so."

"Why not?" Karus asked. Though he privately agreed with Felix, he wanted to hear the other's reasoning.

"Look at her bearing," Felix said and waved a hand in her direction. "She stands like a patrician, not a beaten-down plebian from the slums of Rome. Despite the filth, I would say that long hair was once well cared for. Her hands are too refined to have toiled at cooking and cleaning. No, she is not some common criminal or murderess. She is something else."

"A political prisoner then?" Karus said. "Someone who was meant to suffer from isolation and then a slow death from starvation?"

"That sounds plausible," Felix said. "She may have been someone's wife who was put to death."

"Those chains say otherwise," Dio countered. "Why bother to chain a prisoner after you have dumped her in a perfectly good dungeon?"

The sound of Crix returning drew Karus's attention. The centurion was carrying a hunk of bread. He also held a ceramic cup. Karus motioned him forward and took the bread. The prisoner eyed the bread hungrily.

"All of you," Karus ordered, looking at the guard detail, "step back and off the mosaic."

The legionaries did as bid. The woman looked about nervously before fixing her gaze squarely upon Karus, her eyes darting hungrily to the bread.

"You," Karus said, pointing at her, and then down at the mosaic, "show me where we are."

She looked at him and then down at her feet. She looked back up again, her face full of confusion. She tilted her head to the side slightly, and it was clear she did not understand what Karus was asking of her. Karus pointed once again at the mosaic. She looked down and then back up at him. He held his free arm out in question and then pointed back down.

"Where are we?"

Karus took his sandal and touched the mark that he assumed was a city and then another and held his hands out wide in question. She looked down again and up. Her brow furrowed. She bit her lip as she contemplated him with those strikingly dark eyes.

Karus pointed at the bread he held, and then down at the map. He gestured his arms wide and then once again at the map. Her eyebrows rose in sudden understanding. She looked down at her feet and shuffled around, moving to the side a little. With her left foot, she touched the representation of a city nearly in the center of the map that was marked with a strange script. Karus stepped closer to her. Once again, he resisted the impulse to hold his nose against her stench. She looked over at him, pointed downward, and spoke a single word.

"Carthum."

Karus pointed with the hunk of bread and then gestured about him and repeated what she had said. She nodded enthusiastically and then gestured toward the bread. Karus handed it over. He stepped away from her, more to distance himself from the reek than anything else. She tore hungrily into the bread, jamming it into her mouth and chewing voraciously. As she ate, she watched him like a starving dog.

"Well," Dio said, looking down at the map. "We now know where we are, but wherever that is in relation to Rome is beyond me."

Karus felt himself frown as he looked over at his friend. He glanced back at the young woman devouring the hunk of bread. He wondered why she'd been incarcerated. Was she a political prisoner, as Felix had postulated? The heavy manacles seem to indicate otherwise, as Dio had suggested. Looking her over, despite the grime and her distressed nature, he decided she certainly did not look dangerous. The more he studied her, the more confident he was that, cleaned up, she would be quite beautiful.

Karus tore his gaze away from her and brought it down to the map, studying the terrain around the city she had identified as Carthum. He could see a shaded green area that was most likely the forest. Judging by the distance from the forest to the city, Karus could now extrapolate distances from Carthum to other cities and points on the map. Knowledge was power, and he now knew where to better to direct Valens's scouts. They were in a strange land, and even though he now knew where he was to some degree, the legion was still lost.

Karus looked back up at the woman. He needed information that she had and this woman. Dangerous or not, there was an opportunity here, and Karus would be damned if he passed it up. He would either learn her language or she would learn his, but regardless, he would communicate with her and discover what she knew.

Karus moved closer. Still hungrily devouring the bread, her eyes fixed on him and she froze in mid-chew.

"Karus," he said, and tapped his chest. "I am *Karus*."

He pointed toward her ample chest and then held his arms out in question, palms up. She chewed the last of the bread in her mouth and swallowed. Tilting her head to the side slightly, her eyes narrowed, and she pointed back at him with her free hand, manacles clinking solidly.

"Karus," she said, as if testing the name out.

"Yes," Karus said, pleased, and nodded, before tapping his chest again. "I am Karus."

He then pointed at her and held his arms out in question again, palms upward.

"Amarra," she said, and touched her breast. "Amarra."

"Amarra," Karus repeated, to which she nodded, her eyes guarded.

Karus reached out and took the cup of water from Crix. He handed it over to her. Amarra gulped greedily, water spilling from around her mouth and down onto her soiled dress and the floor. Finished, she said something in her own language that sounded like a thank you and handed the cup back.

"Crix." Karus gave the cup back to the centurion. "See that she gets cleaned up, fed, and watered. Have those manacles removed too."

"Are you sure, sir?" There was doubt on the junior centurion's face, not to mention his tone was heavily laced with skepticism.

"Very," Karus said. "I believe she has intelligence that we need. We will treat her with respect until she proves otherwise. She is to remain under close guard at all times. Also, have the surgeon examine her and treat those sores."

"Do you want my men to clean her up?"

"No," Karus said firmly. "In no way is she to come to harm. We need to earn her trust, not her enmity. Choose a suitable woman from the followers to attend her."

"Yes, sir," Crix said. "Where do you want her held?"

"Pick a room in the palace that is secure, where she cannot easily escape, preferably one with no windows. I want her close, so that I can question her when needed. Speak to the tribune to arrange a more permanent guard detail."

"Yes, sir," Crix said and snapped an order to his men.

Once again, the section of men fell in around her. Supported by the legionary who had helped her in, the prisoner was led toward the doors, both armor and manacles chinking and clinking as the small party made their way from the hall. Bread in hand, and still chewing, she glanced once back in his direction, and then she was gone. The doors closed with a screech and bang that echoed around the hall.

"Are you sure about this, Karus?" Dio asked. "Someone put her in that dungeon for a reason. You don't usually end up in those places without good cause."

"Yes, I know." Karus expelled a heavy breath. "She could be dangerous, but at all times she will be under guard. As I said, she has information and intelligence locked up in her head. I aim to get it."

"Well," Felix said with a sudden amused grin, "I knew you occasionally enjoyed the intimate company of women, but I never thought I would see you so emotionally taken with one. Before we know it, you'll be wanting to raise a family."

Karus glared over at Felix with a sour expression, then chuckled. "Feel free to have some children for me with Keeli."

"Oh, I plan to," Felix said, grin becoming even wider. He then leaned forward conspiratorially. "You know, Karus, the best thing about having kids is the practicing at making them."

"Well," Karus said, amused, "it's good to know you can still get it up. I thought you might be too old for that sort of thing."

"Better watch who's calling who old," Felix said.

Dio barked out a laugh, clapped Karus on the shoulder, and started walking from the room. "I have things to do. I will report back later this evening on my progress."

Chuckling, Felix joined Dio, leaving Karus alone in the throne room. Karus thought about Amarra. He could still smell her foul stench on the air. Everything in this land was a mystery to him. With each piece of the puzzle he uncovered, it seemingly became more confused. He glanced down at the city indicated on the map.

"Carthum," he said quietly to himself. It was a strong name for a city. A worthy name for this great city, he decided.

"Carthum," he said again, rolling the name across his tongue, and then left the throne room, intent upon returning to his headquarters. Like Dio had said, there were things to do.

Chapter Fourteen

"And how exactly do these tools differ from the ones you are accustomed to working with?" Karus turned his gaze from the toolbox to the blacksmith, a middle-aged Gaul name Harikas.

The air inside the smithy was uncomfortably warm, the byproduct of an active forge. Karus had only stepped inside a few moments before, but already he felt the first beads of perspiration dot his forehead. Despite the shutters and doors having been left open, the smell of smoke hung heavily on the air, along with the acrid smell of sweaty bodies.

The blacksmith was a tall, imposing middle-aged man. He wore a heavily stained tunic over a growing paunch that spoke of a fondness for beer. His arms were thick with muscle but showed the first signs of flab. Even for a Gaul, Harikas was exceptionally hairy. He was known affectionately as the Bear amongst the legionaries, most likely from the hair on his arms, which grew thick like fur. Streaked with gray, his beard climbed higher than most, partially concealing a heavily pockmarked face.

Karus had known the man for years. Despite the forbidding exterior, Harikas was a kind man, a veritable gentle giant. Amongst the rank and file, the smith had a reputation for fairness, in that he did not overcharge.

Behind the smith, one of his assistants hammered away in spurts at a glowing piece of metal. The smith had four assistants, all young boys from the followers. They were hard at work, busy around the dingy and disorganized shop. One, using a set of long prongs, plunged a glowing piece of metal into a bucket of water, where it hissed menacingly and threw up a cloud of steam. Karus was well pleased with what he was seeing.

"These four beauties…" The blacksmith's voice was deep, drawing Karus's attention back to the matter at hand. He spoke good but heavily accented Latin. Reaching into the tool box, Harikas removed and laid out the tools on a battered table, one after another. "I've never seen them before." He pointed to another set of tools that he had left in the box. "These others are similar enough to those I've worked with." He picked up a miniature hammer and hefted it. "A hammer is a hammer."

Karus studied the tools on the table as the smith tossed the hammer back into the box, where it landed with a clatter. They were each around ten inches long. Two appeared to have ends that made them look like large screws, the only difference being the size of the grooves on each. The handles were well-worn. The other two had the appearance of being oversized keys; the teeth of each, varying in magnitude, were shaped into a hammer's head.

"Do you have any thoughts on their purpose?" Karus asked with mild curiosity. He had seen Harikas do his work, but he did not pretend to understand the man's craft.

"I have my ideas." The smith touched the two key-like tools with a callused and scarred hand. "These seem to be made to help better temper and shape iron. The other two have me a bit stumped. They could be for drilling, but with the size of each, I am at a loss for the practicality of their purpose. When I get some time, I plan to experiment."

The hammering of the smith's assistant paused before resuming once again, this time with a measured beat. The sound drew Karus's attention. The hammering continued. Karus moved closer to observe. The assistant was working a piece of heated metal that shone a bright orange-yellow. He held it in place against a black anvil with a pair of medium-sized tongs. Using a small hammer, he painstakingly shaped it one hard blow at a time. Sparks flew with each strike.

"What are you working on at present?" Karus asked as another of the smith's assistants shoved a lump of ore into the heart of the forge using a long pair of tongs.

"Pins," the smith said, coming up next to Karus, "for the wagons, one for each wheel."

"How many have you made so far?"

"We got the forge fired up yesterday afternoon. It took several hours to achieve the right heat," the smith said and moved over to another table where a battered crate held a bunch of pins. "Finished about a couple dozen so far. By this evening, I should have another dozen. I was asked to make around three hundred pins and a thousand three-inch nails."

"How long will that take?"

The smith thought for a moment. "With my assistants and working day and night… we should have the pins done by tomorrow evening. The nails will be ready the day after."

"What will you be working on next?"

"Ah." The smith scratched his chin. "Heads for javelins, I believe, is the next project. After that, repairs to swords and armor."

"You have sufficient material to make all that is needed then?" Karus asked.

"Oh yes," the smith said with a pleased expression. He gestured toward an open bin that was chock full of a mix of ore and bars of metal that Karus assumed were ready to be fired. "Likely more than I can use. There are a number of smithies throughout the city. My assistants have found plenty of material and your boys have been bringing us all that we require. If, for some reason, we run out, I am quite confident we can scavenge metal from the city and repurpose it."

Karus glanced around the forge. Despite the windows and doors that had been thrown open, it had been intentionally darkened. There were only two lanterns that had been lit. The other four that hung overhead were dark and lifeless. Karus knew that some smiths preferred to work in low light to better see what they were shaping.

"I understand you found some metal you are unfamiliar with?" This was part of the reason for his visit.

"Yes," the smith said, "strange, but interesting material."

He led Karus over to a large wooden crate that had been shoved against one wall. It was filled with oddly formed chunks of metal that glinted a muted gray in the poor light. Harikas picked up a small chunk that gave the appearance of having been melted and handed it over. Karus was surprised how heavy it was, like a similarly sized chunk of lead. He handed it back.

"I wasn't even able to get this stuff hot enough to blush," the smith continued, dropping it back into the crate, where it landed with a solid clunk. "Very stubborn."

"Blush?"

"Glow," the blacksmith said. "You heat iron hot enough and it glows, first reddish like, then orange, yellow, and finally white. Blushing is where it goes red. When it turns a bright yellow-orange, you can shape it to your will. That's where we want it, but this is not iron. It is something different. It must have a use. Otherwise the smith that came before me would not have kept it here in such quantity."

"I see," Karus said. "You think what you need is more heat then?"

The smith nodded his large head.

"Do you feel the blacksmith that ran this smithy likely was able to get the right amount of heat?"

"He must have," Harikas said, running a hand through his hair. "For the life of me, I don't know how he did it."

"Keep at it," Karus said, "and let me know if you learn anything."

"I will, sir." The smith nodded vigorously.

"Very well then, I've kept you long enough," Karus said. He had several places he wanted to see this day, including an underground aqueduct that had been discovered. "Thank you for your time and your hard work."

"It was no trouble, sir," the smith said and bowed his head respectfully.

Karus left the smithy and stepped out into the street, where the air was fresh, clean, and cool. He had spent only a short while inside and was already drenched with sweat. Karus wondered how Harikas managed working under such difficult conditions. He figured, like being a legionary, that a person eventually became accustomed to one's profession no matter how distasteful or uncomfortable the line of work.

Karus's guard detail, which Pammon had insisted upon, were waiting just outside. The commander of each legion was always accompanied by a personal guard. The section of men that had been chosen was from Second Cohort and led by Optio Mettis. The optio straightened to attention, and so did his men.

"Optio." Karus nodded a greeting. Mettis was a veteran of fifteen years and was a good man. He had much promise, though his dismal writing ability would likely see him never make the centurionate.

"Sir," Mettis said. "We stand ready."

Karus glanced around. He was in what could be described as an upscale mercantile district. It was very close to the palace gate, several streets over, but only around six hundred yards distant. At least, Karus thought so. Outside of the main boulevards, the city was a confusing maze of twisting streets and back alleys.

The day before, Karus had moved the camp followers and the bulk of the legion to this district and the next one over, a residential neighborhood, where the homes were nearly the size of the palace. It had gone over without much fuss.

Karus pulled out a small map that one of his clerks had hastily drawn of the two districts. It was a rough sketch, which tapered off to empty areas of the outer city that had not been fully mapped out yet.

On the map, Carthum had been separated into four parts, or quarters. Karus glanced up into the sky and narrowed his eyes. Thanks to the two suns, there was no way to tell which way was North, South, East or West. The stars and moon did not help either, as they were different than those he had known. The map they had found in the hall had proven some help. What had made sense to him was the forest, which on the map was closer to the throne, meaning Karus decided that the top of the map faced the throne. As such, this was the most likely direction that was due north. Karus fully realized that he could have gotten this wrong and north as he saw it was actually south. Regardless, he had made his decision and would stick with it until proven otherwise.

The map he now held was divided into four directional quarters: a north side, a south side and east and west. This made it easier to assign patrols, areas of responsibility, and describe specific locations for supply gathering, instead of relying upon landmarks for direction. So far, it had worked out well enough.

Each of the smithies that had been set up were carefully marked on the map, along with woodworking shops where the wagons were being assembled. Stores of significant food caches and supplies that had been located within the two districts had also been carefully marked down. These were being moved to the legion's new depot, presided over by a none–too-happy Cestus.

Before stopping in on Harikas, Karus had checked on one of the food caches. It had been a merchant's warehouse a few buildings down the small street he was standing on. Hundreds of wooden barrels filled with ground flour were stacked floor to ceiling, though there had been evidence some of the barrels had been taken when the city was evacuated. Without any workable wagons, the process of moving the stores had fallen to the mules. This was proving to be painfully slow. It would speed up once the first of the wagons was completed. With luck, that would happen today.

Finding where he wanted to go using the map, Karus turned to his left and started walking. His guard detail fell in behind him. As Karus walked and moved from street to street, he was once again struck by how different the city of Carthum was when compared to those he had known.

The buildings he passed ranged from one to four stories in height, with only a handful managing to climb higher. They were all lined with windows that relied upon shutters to keep the elements out. So far, Karus had only seen glassed windows in the palace.

Nearly all of the buildings in the mercantile district were lined with shops on the first floor and residences above. Likely, the proprietor's families had occupied the space over the shops. The camp followers had quickly established themselves here and in the residential district a few streets over. Karus had seen to it that the cohorts were spread out between the two districts, not only to keep order, but to respond rapidly to any threats that might appear.

He had also established a guarded perimeter that prevented movement out into the wider city. No one was allowed beyond that line without special permission. The city had been thoroughly swept and, other than Amarra, no one had been found. The only thing that remained was mapping out the catacombs and sewers and centralizing the food stores and supplies the legion required.

In truth, Karus expected no additional threats from within the city. The perimeter was more for the legion's security than anything else, really to protect it from itself. Karus did not want to encourage or allow uncontrolled looting of the wider city beyond the perimeter. The chance for a fire to break out was just too great. As such, it was imperative to control the movement of his people and maintain strict discipline. Karus needed not only the security of the city's walls, but the resources within Carthum.

Following the map, Karus turned a corner and started up the next street. People were abruptly everywhere, going about hundred different tasks as Karus made his way toward his next destination. He passed a woman hauling a bucket of water, with two children following along in her wake. Showing no signs of the recent ordeal, they were happily playing a game of not stepping on the cracks of the paving stones and were instead hopping along from stone to stone. The mother was another story. Karus noted as the mother's eyes silently marked him. The children began to lag behind.

"Keep up," she snapped at them. "Come on, let's go."

Then she was gone.

Farther up the street, Karus happened across several people gathered around a public fountain, filling buckets and small kegs. This would be used for cooking and cleaning. Karus looked them over as he passed them by. A few heads turned his way, but when their eyes met, they quickly looked away.

"Optio." Karus glanced back at Mettis and beckoned him forward.

Mettis picked up his pace and fell in beside Karus.

"Sir?"

"How do you feel the followers are coping?"

"We're quartered in the administrative building next to the palace," Mettis said, "but we spend most of our time out in the city. I think they are adjusting well enough, sir."

"They are coming to terms with what has occurred then?" Karus seriously doubted it.

"I did not say that, sir," Mettis said. "There is a lot of heartache. A lot of people lost loved ones, and to be completely honest, they're scared, sir."

Karus had figured as much. It was only to be expected. He could not do much about the heartache, but he could at least provide security. With time, the fear would lessen as people became more accustomed to their new situation.

"The followers are used to a hard life where nothing is guaranteed," Mettis continued. "They are grateful to the gods for delivering them from the Celts."

"Good." The more they accepted that truth, the easier his job would become. "I am pleased to hear that."

"Of course, sir," Mettis said. "Oh, and my wife asked me to thank you personally, sir. For saving us, that is. They say you are favored by the gods, sir."

Karus glanced over at the optio. At first, he was not sure what to say. For a long while now, he had felt guilt at not having been able to stop Julionus's mad plan.

Finally, he cleared his throat. "I am happy she made it."

"Many didn't." Mettis's look became distant and then refocused on Karus. "But you pulled us through, sir."

"We did it together," Karus said, raising his voice so that the entirety of the guard detail would hear him clearly. "With the gods' help, of course."

"That's right," Mettis said, "and you will get us home, sir. I know you will."

Karus noticed that the optio's eyes fairly shone with belief. Karus glanced around the optio's men and saw the same. It made Karus even more uncomfortable.

What if he couldn't do it?

"We will get home by working together," Karus said, voice a little gruff.

"Yes, sir," Mettis said in the tone of a believer, "we will."

There was agreement from the guard detail.

Karus fell silent after that and, thankfully, so did Mettis. As he passed through the district, working his way past street after winding street, he noticed the eyes of nearly everyone shot his way. He could well guess their thoughts, and it weighed heavily upon him. Like Mettis, they expected him to get them home, to be their savior.

"Ampelius," Karus called, having spotted the surgeon emerging from a building carrying a bag.

"Karus," the surgeon replied, stepping over.

Karus noticed that Ampelius looked almost rested, though there was still a weary appearance about him. Gone was the haggard look that came with lack of sleep coupled with overworking oneself. He, like everyone else, was slowly recovering, and it showed.

The surgeon set his bag down on the ground and jerked a thumb behind him. "These accommodations are much more sanitary than where we were staying yesterday. You should know, I approve."

"Only the best for our people," Karus said, taking a stab at levity with the surgeon. Karus knew it was not worth the effort. Ampelius was a lost cause when it came to humor.

"It is nothing more than your duty to look after the well-being of the followers," Ampelius said, "as it is mine to look after their health. Better living conditions will make for less work."

Karus almost smiled. Out of the corner of his eye, he noticed Mettis covering his mouth.

"Have you checked in on Amarra?" Karus asked, wanting to move the conversation along. Ampelius could be boorish if he felt he was being toyed with.

"Yes," Ampelius said. "I saw her just this morning. I feel confident she will make a full recovery. The sores on her wrists and ankles will take some time to heal, of course, and truth be told, they may mark her for life. She will also have to cope with the scars of being confined for so long. Since she does not speak our tongue, this is more difficult to assess."

"Based on her condition," Karus said, "do you have any idea how long she had been locked up?"

"No," Ampelius said. "The damage caused by the manacles was relatively fresh." He paused, a hand going to his chin as he thought it through. "I'd say within the last three weeks, maybe a day or two longer or less."

"So, it is possible," Karus said, "she was locked up before the city was evacuated."

"Maybe," Ampelius said with a shrug. "I think it is safe to believe she spent two to three weeks in that cell."

"Thank you," Karus said and started to step away.

"Ah ... Karus," Ampelius said and lowered his voice, stepping nearer. The surgeon's eyes flicked to Mettis and his men. "There is something else I have to report."

Karus raised his eyebrows, but checked his progress. Karus waved Mettis back so that he and Ampelius could speak privately.

"It may be nothing," Ampelius said, "however, I have attended to several camp followers over the last few hours who have come down with sickness. I thought you should know."

"What kind of sickness?" Karus felt his blood chill a little.

"It could be a simple cold, a byproduct of the poor conditions of the last few weeks," Ampelius said. "But then again, it might be something more. There is a commonality with their symptoms: fever, cough, and a general loosening of the bowels."

Karus regarded the surgeon unhappily. The last thing he needed was an outbreak of disease or, worse, plague. He very much hoped it was a simple cold.

"Prognosis?"

"It is too early to tell," Ampelius said. "Give me a few days and I will know more."

"Very well," Karus said, hoping sickness was not why the city had emptied out. "Keep me informed."

Karus bid the surgeon a goodbye and resumed his trek, following the map. He wanted to see one of the three underground aqueducts that delivered fresh water into the city. Several service entrances had been discovered. Karus had helped to construct aboveground aqueducts, but he had never before seen an underground one. That stop would be more to satisfy his own personal curiosity than anything else.

Afterward, Karus planned to visit the east gatehouse, which was near the service entrance. Next, he would check in on Eighth Cohort before returning to his headquarters to attend to the legion's administrative business. All in all, it would be a full day.

Karus turned a corner and found himself staring at the palace gate just fifty yards away. A century from Second Cohort was marching out into the city. Wanting to curse, he studied the map and realized he had taken a wrong turn two streets back. With his finger, he traced out a new path to the service entrance. Satisfied, Karus started out with a purposeful stride, mindful to keep Mettis and his men from guessing that he had gone astray. For all they knew, he was strolling around to see how the followers and the cohorts were settling in.

As he turned onto the main boulevard that led away from the palace gate, a rider came galloping up the street. He waved and called the man over. The trooper at first did not see or hear Karus.

"Trooper," Karus called again, this time in his parade-ground voice that had been honed over years of service. "Over here!"

The man's head snapped around. He saw Karus, slowed his horse, and steered his way over. The trooper dismounted, saluted, and handed over a dispatch.

Karus opened the dispatch and read the contents quickly. He looked up at the trooper, eyes narrowing. The man was road dusty.

Karus tapped the dispatch with a finger. "When did this fight occur?"

"The day before yesterday evening, sir," the trooper replied.

"Tell me what happened."

"A squadron was scouting a village that had not yet been previously explored. They came across a party foraging about the village who surprised our men. However, the squadron was able to escape without any dead and only one man lightly wounded."

Karus could understand what had occurred. Valens's cavalry had gotten accustomed to an empty countryside and let down their guard.

"What happened next?" Karus was thoroughly irritated at the lapse in discipline. Though he was sure that Valens had already addressed the matter, he would write to the cavalry prefect all the same.

"Prefect Valens concentrated those squadrons nearest and then attempted to make contact. The result was not a positive one, sir. Our envoy, who was under a flag of truce, was attacked. At that point, the prefect decided to stop toying with them, sir. Especially after they marched out of the village and formed a line, aggressive-like. They advanced to confront us, sir."

Karus closed his eyes. He knew what was coming. Valens was as bloodthirsty as they came. He would not have backed down from a challenge like that. He would have eagerly embraced it.

"We rode them down," the trooper said simply, "and killed them all."

"How many were there?" Karus had more to add to his dispatch to Valens, as his cavalry commander should have tried to take prisoners for questioning. Karus found his rage growing at Valens's thoughtlessness.

"Somewhere around twenty."

"Any further casualties?"

"No, sir," the trooper replied. "Funny thing, sir. They didn't seem to know how to face cavalry. It's like they never saw a mounted soldier before, either."

Karus's thigh began to ache and he absently massaged it. "How do you know they were foraging?"

"Well, sir," the trooper said, "they had a wagon with them and it was piled high with food that had been looted from the village and any booty they could lay their hands on. Very much like how we forage, sir."

"I see," Karus said. He touched the dispatch, pointing to it with one finger. "And this creature that the prefect mentions, what of it?"

"Very strange, sir," the trooper said, a troubled look passing across his face. "They were accompanied by a green-skinned manlike creature with tusks in its mouth. Prefect Valens thought, based upon how it acted before the fight, that it was in command of the foraging party. It is not human, sir. It's a monster out of someone's nightmares."

Karus was not quite ready to believe that.

"I saw it with my own eyes, sir," the trooper said, clearly picking up on Karus's doubt. "The prefect had the wagon unloaded. He ordered the monster brought back here for you to see, sir."

"When will it get here?"

"It's already here, sir," the trooper said. "Once we cleared the city gate, my optio gave me the dispatch and ordered that I ride ahead and report to headquarters."

"So, it's here, now," Karus said, "in the city?"

"Yes, sir," the trooper said. "The wagon is being pulled by two oxen-like animals. I've never seen anything like them either."

"Ride back and have it brought to the palace immediately," Karus said, thinking quickly. He had to see the creature first so that he could plan his next steps before word broke out about it and the rumor mill started. "Your optio is to stop for no one, nor is he to show the creature. Is that understood?"

"Yes, sir," the trooper said. "Prefect Valens left orders for the same. He wanted you to see it first. It is covered over by a sheet."

"Good," Karus said. "Thank you for your report. Dismissed."

The trooper saluted, mounted back up on his horse, and rode back in the direction he'd come. Karus watched him a moment, then folded up his map and tucked it away in a pocket. The aqueduct and the rest of his planned visits would have to wait.

"You heard?" Karus turned to Mettis.

"Yes, sir," the optio said.

"What do you think?"

"Troubling," Mettis said, "if true."

"I am afraid it is." Karus blew out a slow breath. "Send a man to find Ampelius. I think he is somewhere back where we left him. Have him report to the palace immediately. Instruct your man to say nothing of the creature."

"Yes, sir." Mettis snapped an order, along with a terse instruction, to the legionary he had selected to keep his mouth shut. The man hustled off, armor chinking, in the direction they had just come from.

Karus glanced down at the dispatch that Valens had written, read through it a second time, then stuffed it in the same pocket as the map. He turned and made his way to the gate. The gate sentries came to attention and saluted as he passed into the palace district. Once at the steps to the palace, he sent runners to fetch Dio and Felix, whom he knew were working at headquarters. Karus would have invited Delvaris, but he had sent the boy earlier in the morning to the west gate to examine things there and report back.

Mettis ordered his men back a respectful distance.

"Stand easy," the optio called.

Dio and Felix appeared and made their way down to Karus.

"Read this," Karus said, thrusting the dispatch into Dio's hands.

Dio scanned over Valens's scrawl, gave a low whistle, and then handed it to Felix.

"The creature is in the city and being brought here to us," Karus said as Felix continued to read. "I've also called for the surgeon so he can examine it."

"It may be native to these parts," Dio postulated. "We have to remember we are far from home."

"Perhaps," Felix looked up, returning the dispatch to Karus, "you should call for Amarra. She may be able to recognize and identify it."

"That is not a bad idea," Karus said. He turned to Mettis. "Send a man to headquarters and have the prisoner brought to me."

"Yes, sir," Mettis said and snapped an order to one of his men, who began moving up the stairs.

"What do you think this means?" Dio asked Karus, gesturing toward the dispatch.

Karus turned the dispatch over in his hands as he considered his reply. He tapped it against his palm. The contents did not bode well for their current situation, especially if this was a foraging party. It meant there was a larger force nearby, perhaps even an army. Had it been that which had precipitated the evacuation of the city? There was just so much he did not know. It was maddening.

"I think," Karus said finally, "that we are in a hostile land with no friends. Do either of you disagree?"

Felix shook his head.

"I hope that you are wrong," Dio said. "But if we are in a hostile land, there are worse places to be. The walls sealing us in are quite formidable. It would take a determined enemy to overcome them and break into the city."

A wagon clattered loudly through the gate, pulled by a pair of animals that looked like oxen, but were far from it. Long haired, with great shaggy heads that hung toward the ground as they walked, they had six legs instead of the standard four and were much longer than an ox. They plodded along at a slow pace, almost grudgingly pulling the wagon. Everyone nearby stopped what they were doing to stare at the spectacle. Karus was sure it had been the same as the wagon made its way through the city. The rumor mill was likely already at work.

Karus had difficulty dragging his eyes away from the animals before gazing over the wagon. It was a rough contraption with two wheels that hardly appeared roadworthy. The wheels were larger than they should be and had been made of solid pieces of wood nailed together to form a rounded whole. A high-backed seat for the driver was positioned at the very front of the wagon. Heck, Karus thought, that rickety thing was more cart than wagon.

The wagon turned in their direction, a squadron of Valens's cavalry riding right behind it. The wagon rattled to a halt before Karus. The driver hauled back on the reins before engaging the brake, locking the wagon in place. The animals pulling the wagon began to *wuff* quietly and toss their shaggy heads from side to side.

"Sir." The optio leading the squadron dismounted from his horse and offered Karus a salute. He handed the reins up to one of his troopers. "Prefect Valens thought you should see this personally, sir."

The optio moved around to the rear of the wagon, Karus, Dio, and Felix following. He pulled himself up and into the bed. Karus saw a coarse brown canvas covering whatever was in the back. Without hesitation, the optio pulled it back, revealing a body beneath.

Karus sucked in his breath at what he saw. Dio made an exclamation that was barely audible and was more akin to choking than anything else. Felix said nothing, just stared.

The creature that lay in the bed of the wagon was manlike in that it had two arms, two legs, and a head. The skin was a pasty greenish color. It was heavily muscled and wore black leather armor that had been pierced in several places. Greenish blood had congealed and dried around the wounds.

The monstrosity was something out of a nightmare. It had two eyes, a mouth, and a nose, but there the similarity ended. The eyes were small, beady, and close together. The nose was thick, almost flat against its face. Two yellow tusks jutted from its lower jaw, which was open, revealing smaller teeth set farther back.

"I wouldn't want to come across one of those at night," Dio breathed.

"They die just like us," Karus said, dragging his eyes away from the creature. "The truth of that is before us."

"We can thank the gods for that little blessing," Felix said. "That thing must be at least seven feet tall."

Motion off to Karus's left drew his attention. A guard detail was escorting Amarra down the marble steps from the palace toward the wagon. Karus almost did a double take. He had not seen her since she had been found in her dungeon cell, two days before. The transformation between then and now was nothing short of remarkable.

She wore a plain gray dress that someone had clearly found for her. It had likely belonged to a slave or servant and had seen better days. Moving down the steps, Amarra made the dress look regal, her figure underneath fine and shapely. The grime and dirt were gone. Her jet-black hair, pulled back behind one ear, had been washed, then brushed clean and straight. A delicate ear was exposed, which only served to highlight her high cheekbones and button-like nose centered on a perfectly proportioned face. With olive-colored skin and almond-shaped eyes, he found her not only exotic, but captivating.

The manacles had been removed. Karus could see the ugly red and purplish marks about her wrists. She did nothing to conceal them. There was a braveness about that. Over the years, Karus had known many who worked to conceal their defects and scars. She wore her wounds like badges of honor.

She stepped up to him and inclined her head slightly, breaking the spell. Karus blinked, abruptly struck by the contrast between the horror in the bed of the wagon and Amarra.

"Hello," she said in broken but accented Latin. Karus found the accent fairly attractive. His heart beat a tad faster.

"Amarra," Karus greeted and gave her a slight tight smile of welcome, remembering the men around him.

"Thank you," she said in rough Latin and gestured down at her dress. "Thank you."

"You are welcome," Karus said, though he had had nothing to do with its acquisition. He hesitated a moment and turned. "Come."

He beckoned toward the bed of the wagon. With a curious expression, she followed and made her way over to it where Dio and Felix waited with grim expressions. She gazed in the back and then froze. A hand went to her mouth, a look of horror passing across her face.

"Orc."

She said the word with such disgust and revulsion that Karus immediately knew it was the name of the monster. She made a strange warding sign with her fingers, and then turned toward Karus and let loose with a string of fiery language that was thoroughly incomprehensible. Whatever she'd said was done with more than a little passion. He thought he caught the word orc at least once, but she spoke too quickly to be sure.

"Orc?" Karus pointed at the monster.

Her eyes widened with what Karus took to be surprise.

"Orc?" Karus asked again.

"Orc," she replied with a firm nod. "That, orc."

"Well," Felix said, "at least we know what it's called."

"Think there are many more?" Dio asked. His coin appeared in his hand. He tossed it into the air and caught it.

"There is a fair chance." Karus noticed Mettis looking between them, a grim expression on the optio's face. Karus turned to Felix, having made a decision. "I want this creature taken around and displayed to each cohort and the camp followers. Make sure everyone sees it."

"Why would you want to do that?" Dio exclaimed with some surprise, catching his coin and palming it.

"The men need to be made aware of the threats that are out there," Karus said. "More importantly, they need to understand that, if the legion dissolves, they may run into creatures like this one without the protection of their mates."

Karus fell silent. He saw Mettis nodding in agreement. There was nothing more important than being honest with the men.

"I agree with Karus," Felix said after a few heartbeats. "We must hide nothing from the men. If we start doing so, they will quickly lose trust in our leadership, which is even worse."

"It's decided then," Karus said. "Felix, I want you to make it plain this thing and others like it can be killed. The men must understand that."

"I will see to it," Felix said.

"That," Dio spat on the ground, jabbing a finger at the orc, "won't make anyone sleep easy, that's for sure."

"No, it won't," Karus agreed. "But that's not the point, is it?"

He turned to Amarra and regarded her a moment. Someone had clearly taught her a few words of Latin.

"It's time we learn to properly communicate," Karus said to her.

She looked at him inquisitively.

Karus stepped up to the wagon and rapped his knuckles against the rough wood. Then he looked at her. "Wagon," he said. He gestured at the entirety of the wagon and repeated the word. "Wagon."

Her eyes brightened and she nodded.

"Wagon," she said.

"Wheel," Karus said and touched the wagon's wheel.

"Wheel," she said.

He then moved to the oxen-like creatures and looked to her in question.

"Teska," she said.

"Teska," he repeated, to which she nodded.

"Karus," Felix said, amusement dancing in his eyes, "if you continue to show her the wagon, I won't be able to take this orc around, now, will I?"

Karus chuckled and stepped back from the wagon. "Very well, the wagon is all yours."

"You called for the surgeon, right?" Felix said, sobering. "Do you still want him to examine the orc before I start off or after?"

Karus glanced around, irritated that the surgeon had not yet arrived. Likely Ampelius was in some building somewhere attending to someone who was ill and had not yet been located. He considered the matter a moment.

"He can examine the creature later," Karus said.

"I will see that he has time alone with it," Felix said. "After I take it around."

"Thank you," Karus said.

Felix turned away and snapped out an order to the driver, who disengaged the brake and cracked the whip. The teska *wuffed* and lumbered forward. Felix pulled himself up next to the driver as the wagon picked up speed.

"I think I will leave you to it as well," Dio said as the wagon pulled away. Karus's friend gave a mock salute before heading off for the administrative building, where he had billeted his cohort, leaving Karus alone with Amarra, her guard detail, his guard, and Valens's troop of cavalry. It was quite a crowd.

Karus glanced at the cavalry optio, who had dismounted from the bed of the wagon before it had pulled away. The man's eyes were on Amarra. Karus thought he read suspicion there.

"How long did it take you to get here?" Karus asked the cavalry optio.

"We came straight on through the night and all of today," the optio replied, weariness etched in his tone, gaze shifting to Karus.

"Then you'll be needing some rest," Karus said with a nod. "Draw some food from the depot. Find a place to stable and care for your horses. Make sure you rest the night. Report to me in the morning. I will have a dispatch for your prefect."

"Yes, sir." The optio offered Karus a salute, which he returned.

As the optio led his squadron away, Karus turned back toward Amarra. Once again, he was struck by her incredible transformation. He reminded himself that she had been a prisoner, which meant she had likely done something to deserve being imprisoned. He could not permit her beauty to distract him from his duty. She held potentially vital intelligence locked up inside that pretty head, and the only way to access it was for her to learn his language and he to discover hers.

"Come." Karus made a gesture toward the steps, which she understood and began moving in that direction. He walked at her side, the guards falling in around them both. There were gardens behind the palace, and Karus felt it was a perfect place to begin learning, well away from any unwanted distractions.

Chapter Fifteen

Following a guide, Karus jogged down the empty street. Sweat ran down his face. His lungs and legs burned from not only the exertion, but the weight of his armor. Delvaris trailed just a few feet behind. Karus could hear the lad's labored breathing as he struggled to keep up.

Though the first of the two suns had been up for half an hour, the city was still heavily shadowed and the air chill. The guide led them through a tangle of streets and then around a corner and finally into a cross street.

"There they are, sir." The guide pointed and stepped aside.

Shields resting upon the ground, a century was lined up behind Pammon. He had positioned himself at the corner of the side street that opened up onto another street, which was more of a back alleyway. The men stood silent, tense. Heads turned toward Karus and Delvaris as they rounded the corner. They opened a hole for him, and he passed through the century's tightly packed ranks.

"Where are they?" Karus asked of Pammon, gratefully slowing to a stop. He gulped down air and for a moment was forced to bend over. Hands on his knees, Karus struggled to catch his breath. Delvaris skidded to a halt at his side. The tribune was just as winded, if not more so.

Pammon turned an amused look on Karus. "Getting too old for this kind of thing, are you?"

"When I got word, I ran all the way from the palace," Karus said. "Has to be," he paused to suck in a breath, "close to two miles."

"In our youth," Pammon said, clearly enjoying the moment and glancing at Delvaris, "we could have done that without breaking a sweat."

"Somehow…" Delvaris said, wheezing and glancing between the two older officers. He rested a hand on the wall as he worked to catch his breath. "I don't doubt that."

Pammon chuckled.

"That was many years ago," Karus said, managing to finally get his breathing under control. "But I still almost managed to run this young pup here into the ground." Karus shot Delvaris a wink, then turned back to Pammon. "Now, where are they?"

"Down this alleyway, five of them," Pammon said, becoming serious. He gestured around the corner, but did not to expose himself. Karus refrained from taking a peek as Pammon called upward, "Jarad, how far off are they?"

A face appeared from the roof above, perhaps three stories up, looking down at them. "Two hundred yards and coming fast, sir. They sure are moving with a purpose."

"Give me a countdown, starting at seventy yards," Pammon called back up.

"Yes, sir." Jarad disappeared.

"I've hidden another century a couple of streets down," Pammon explained. "Between where I placed them and us here, there are no doors or windows around this corner, at least within easy reach." Pammon paused and patted the building wall. "Large warehouses to either side. They are using this back alley that cuts between them and a lot of other buildings. When we move to block their path, so will the other century. With luck, we will have these bastards penned and boxed in neatly."

"How were they detected?"

"A bright-eyed sentry spotted them moving covert and slow-like as they crept through the fields outside the city and up to the wall," Pammon said.

"Make sure you give that man an extra ration of drink," Karus said.

"I plan to. Luckily, the centurion on duty at that section of the wall had his wits about him. He called for help and settled in to watch. I was lucky enough to be touring the south gatehouse only a few blocks away and was able to juggle around a couple of the ready-response centuries to set this trap."

Pammon seemed very pleased with himself and bounced on his heels.

"I wonder what they want," Karus said.

"Whatever it is," Pammon said, "they are up to no good. I watched them throw up a spear-like contraption attached to a rope and scale the wall, which is quite a feat when you think about it."

"The city walls are pretty high," Karus said. "That must have been some toss."

"You should know, it was also no accident that they scaled the wall where they did," Pammon said. "It was timed so that our roving patrols on that section were at their farthest points."

"So, they've been watching our boys walk the wall," Karus said. "We're going to have to mix it up a bit, randomize our patrols."

"That was my thinking as well," Pammon said.

"Could they be here to scout us out?" Karus wiped sweat from his brow and out of his eyes. He tightened his helmet strap, as it had loosened a bit during the run down from the palace. "To gauge our numbers perhaps?"

"I don't think so," Pammon said. "They are moving through the city like they know where they're going. After shadowing them, their path became predictable and allowed me to set this sweet little trap."

"Where do you suppose they are headed?" Karus was troubled by this. It meant there was something in the city they had come for.

"The palace district," Pammon answered without hesitation. "They took their spear-thing and rope with them once they were up and over the wall. It could simply mean they didn't want it found, but I believe they mean to scale the palace wall too."

"Sir," Jared called down quietly. "Seventy yards."

"Here we go, boys," Pammon said, turning to the men. "Shields up, draw swords. Time to surprise these sneaky bastards."

The shields came off the ground, and swords were pulled out.

"Fifty," Jared called down. Someone else above was giving him the distance. Karus could just hear it being relayed.

"Gareth," Pammon hissed, turning to a man standing close by. "Be ready with that horn. As soon as we go around the corner, you blow. Without you, the other century won't move. Understand me?"

"Yes, sir," Gareth said.

"Forty yards."

"Nothing like a little excitement to start your day off, eh?" Pammon said to Karus, flashing the other a confident grin. Amongst an officer core known for aggressiveness and leading from the front, Pammon stood apart from his peers. He was one of those rare officers who lived for moments like this. Pammon wasn't reckless. He just craved action and he was stunningly good at his job of being a combat leader.

"Let's make sure we take prisoners," Karus said. "I want to know what they are up to."

"That's the general idea, sir." Pammon flashed Karus a wink. "We're gonna surprise the piss out of these sneaky buggers."

"Thirty."

Pammon turned to look at his men. "On my order, we move at the double around this corner and form a wall of shields from one side of the street to the next." Pammon spoke in a tone just loud enough for all to hear. "Screw it up, let one escape, and I promise all of you will have latrine duty for life."

"Twenty yards, sir!"

"Now," Pammon shouted.

The men burst forward, rushing by both officers and out into the street, where they turned the corner. Karus and Pammon followed as Gareth blew his horn in one long loud blast that rang off the walls. In such close proximity, the horn was almost deafening.

The men were around the corner in a flash, forming a line, dressing themselves as if they had executed this exact maneuver every day. A handful of heartbeats later, the first rank was set and shields thunked together to form an impenetrable wall from foot to shoulder height. In the early morning and empty city, it was an ominous sound.

Karus laid his eyes upon those who would intrude upon his city. The five men, wearing black leather armor and brown pants, came to a surprised halt just shy of ten yards from Pammon's line. One carried a javelin-like spear with a hook on one end. The modified javelin was attached to a rope that was coiled over the man's shoulder. He held the hooked javelin out like he meant to use it as a weapon. The other four immediately drew long, wicked-looking swords that had a slight curve and were meant for slashing rather than jabbing. The intruders did not carry shields. One turned to run back the way they had come, only to have that avenue blocked as the other century emerged and formed a solid shield wall to their rear.

Pammon had chosen the ambush site well. The large warehouses to either side presented sheer walls from which there was no ready escape. Nor were any windows within easy reach, the first set being at least fourteen feet up.

The five intruders eyed the legionaries, clearly unsure what to do.

"Stay here," Karus told Delvaris, then pushed his way through the line. Pammon followed. He took several steps down the street and stopped. Placing his hands on his hips, he studied the five, who looked desperately about for an avenue of escape. There was none. One of the intruders said something in a low tone to the others and they stilled, their eyes falling upon Karus.

"Dressed just like those dead we saw in the forest," Karus said.

"I see that," Pammon said. "They must be part of some type of light infantry, scouts or a special tasks group."

Karus agreed with that assessment. These men were professional soldiers or something close to it in this strange land. Karus was sure of it. Why were they in his city?

"Drop your weapons," Karus said in his best parade-ground voice. He knew it was unlikely that they comprehended Latin, but he figured they would understand his meaning. "Surrender."

"You know, I don't believe they understand you," Pammon said when the five did not comply.

Karus switched to what he knew of the language Amarra called the Common Tongue. She had taught him a little over the last few days.

"Drop. You drop."

He pointed at them and then gestured to make his point, as if he had a sword in hand and was dropping it into the street.

One of the five snarled something back, which was lost on Karus. He suspected he had just been cursed at.

"Whatever you told them," Pammon said, "failed to have the desired effect."

"Tell me about it," Karus said with a heavy breath. "Nothing is ever easy. I guess we do this the hard way. Order your men to move in. We will disarm them by force."

"On my call, we will advance," Pammon said, half turning to his men. "I want them ali—"

At that moment, three of the five rushed at Karus and Pammon. Surprised by the move, Karus instinctively reacted and pulled out his sword. He dropped into a one-on-one combat stance, sensing Pammon doing the same, just before the first sword came slashing down for Karus. Then there was no longer time to think.

CLANG!

Blocking the strike set his hand tingling. To his side, Pammon faced off against two of the attackers. He blocked a sword strike from one and slammed an armored shoulder into the chest of the other, knocking him roughly back.

Karus tightened his grip on the pommel and jabbed out for the arm of his opponent, who dodged and swung lightning fast. Karus barely got his sword back up in time to keep from losing his head.

CLANG!

Small sparks flew from where the two blades met.

Karus shoved back with his sword and was about to jab again when he was roughly knocked aside as the century exploded forward, roaring as they came in.

"I want prisoners!" Karus shouted, attempting to get their attention as the men bashed with their shields and stabbed their way forward. Karus understood that, having witnessed the attack on their officers, the men were in a murderous mood. He knew it was too late, but he tried anyway. "TAKE PRISONERS!"

"Hold!" Pammon shouted. "Damn you, hold! I said hold!"

It was over in a flash. The three had been brutally and efficiently cut down. The other two down the street had retreated a few yards, but were unharmed. With Pammon screaming invectives, the legionaries seemed to abruptly come to their senses.

"Form a bloody line," Pammon angrily roared at the men. In an almost sheepish manner, they did so, though some clearly wanted to finish things and looked hungrily down the street.

Karus looked past the reformed line. The remaining intruders were still trapped between the two centuries, including the one with the hooked javelin. The century behind them was now slowly advancing up the street, steadily closing the distance.

"I want these two taken prisoner," Karus said, loud enough for all to hear. "We need intelligence, and they have it."

At that moment, the one carrying the sword swung around and slashed the other's throat, almost decapitating his companion. The javelin-like weapon fell from nerveless fingers as a fountain of crimson shot into the air. The stricken man toppled over backwards onto the stone paving, where he lay twitching as his lifeblood flowed out in a rush and ran into the gutter like rainwater.

The sole survivor dropped his sword and turned his eyes on Karus. He then calmly pulled out his dagger and, to everyone's utter astonishment, cut his own throat, gritting his teeth while he did it.

He stood there, balefully eying Karus as his blood poured out and down his chest. Several heartbeats later, the bloodied knife fell to the street with a clatter. The life dimmed and then altogether left his eyes. He fell forward, landing hard on paving stones already stained brightly red.

If a single denarius had dropped, Karus knew he would have heard it at twenty paces.

"That was some wild shit," Pammon breathed, breaking the prolonged silence. "I've not ever seen anything like that."

With a heavy breath, Karus stepped through the line of silent legionaries and over to one of the dead men. He looked down.

"Why would they do that?" Delvaris had come up next to Karus. The tribune's eyes were almost impossibly wide.

Karus was silent as he considered the dead man.

"Why?" Delvaris asked again.

"If I had to make a guess," Karus said quietly, "religion drove this, a fanatical belief in what they were doing was right."

"Like the druids," Pammon said, and spat on the corpse.

Karus sheathed his sword. He had so many questions, it was maddening.

"Who are you," Karus said under his breath, "and what were you after?"

"I think I will double the watch on the walls," Pammon said, turning to Karus. "We need to do more than just vary and randomize our patrols."

"The city needs to be swept again," Karus said. "If these got over, more may have as well. We may have just gotten lucky here."

"What about the inner walls?" Delvaris said. "If this bunch was headed there, we should secure those as well."

"I don't think we can completely cover all of the walls. We simply don't have the manpower," Pammon said. "But we can take steps that will make another attempt at scaling the city walls more difficult."

"Let's do it," Karus said. "As soon as we get back to headquarters, I will cut the orders."

Karus looked down at the dead man at his feet.

"Pammon," Karus said, "search them and see if you can learn anything."

"I will," Pammon said and snapped out orders for it to be done.

"The city may no longer be safe," Delvaris said.

"Whoever suggested it was?" Karus gave Delvaris a meaningful look, then turned to go, thoroughly disgusted with how things had just turned out.

Chapter Sixteen

"This my home," Amarra said in broken Latin as they strolled through the palace gardens. She held her arms out, gesturing around them. "My home."

The air was a comfortable summer day. It was neither too hot, nor too cold. Bees and other insects buzzed busily around the neglected beds, which were becoming thick with weeds, crowding the decorative plants. Some had flowered.

Karus had never been one for gardening, nor, for that matter, enjoying gardens. Yet here he was, taking a pleasant turn through the palace grounds with a beautiful woman by his side. He glanced over at her. She flashed a happy smile back at him.

"My home is Rome," he replied in Common.

Amarra frowned at him and Karus knew he had not said it correctly.

"My home is Rome," he said changing to Latin. "I am a Roman."

"Ah," she said with a slight nod, switching back to Common, speaking slowly and carefully so he could better follow. "My home is Rome."

Karus repeated it in Common. The smile returned and for a moment he thought it more radiant than the suns high above their heads. Amarra turned away and picked a delicate white flower, brought it up to her nose, then sighed in pleasure.

Karus fell back a step as she continued walking. Why was he so fascinated with her?

Amarra was picking up Latin quicker than he was her Common Tongue. It had been slightly over two weeks since their language instruction had begun and ten days since the intruders into the city had been ambushed. Karus had kept at it day after day, whenever duty permitted, spending several hours with her each day. Though they were getting much better at communicating, he still had no idea why she had been confined and left to rot. It troubled him that he did not yet know the answer to that question. However, the more time he spent in her company, the more he doubted she was a threat to anyone.

Karus glanced around at Amarra's guard, positioned about the gardens, not too close nor too far. All eyes were upon their charge. There was no shirking, and it had nothing to do with orders. Karus knew the men were wary of her, perhaps even afraid.

Dio had even told him that there were wild rumors beginning to spread about Amarra. She was the prisoner so dangerous she had been left behind to die chained up like a dog in the deepest, darkest part of the dungeon. Another had her a murderess, having killed her own babies without showing remorse. She had also been branded an evil witch and was using her magic on him, bending Karus to her will.

His eyes roved over the guards. They clearly did not trust her. Karus knew he should feel the same, but for some reason he could not. If anything, the more time he spent with her, the more impressed he became with her inner strength. Anyone else who had been imprisoned the way she had been would have taken weeks, if not months, to recover from that horrendous ordeal, perhaps even years. For Amarra, it seemed she had recovered in just days. She was strong, resilient, and he admired her for it.

Karus understood this had something partly to do with her faith. She seemed exceptionally religious and prayed regularly to a god that, as near as he could tell, roughly translated into the Father, or High Father. He was not quite sure, as their communication was still fairly basic. Karus did not understand exactly what her god stood for, only that he was incredibly important to Amarra.

As he watched her continue to walk ahead, Karus found himself wondering about the gods. Barbarians he had encountered over his long years of service had worshiped gods other than those honored by Rome. The Celts were a perfect example. They had their own set of gods, like Cailleach, the Caledonian goddess otherwise known as the Veiled One. Like many such gods, they were incredibly evil and not fit for a civilized nation. Was Amarra's god one of those evil deities? Or was her god a different shade of one of Rome's own and honored deities? It was an interesting thought.

"Excuse me, sir."

Karus turned to find one of his clerks, Serma. The clerk snapped to attention and offered a salute.

"What is it?"

"You asked to be notified when Prefect Valens returned," Serma said. "He has, sir."

"See that he is escorted to the great hall," Karus ordered. "Ask Centurions Dio and Felix to join us."

"Centurions Felix and Dio took Prefect Valens there immediately after he presented himself to headquarters, sir."

"Very, good," Karus said. "I will be along presently."

The clerk saluted and left.

"Must you go?" Amarra had come up behind him. She had done it so quietly he had not heard her.

Karus turned to face her, noting the pouting expression.

"Yes, I must go."

"May I... how you say... stay?" He noticed her eyes flick toward the nearest of her guards.

"Here?" Karus asked. "In the garden?"

"Yes," Amarra said. "Garden makes happy. My room..." She trailed off and shook her head. "No happy."

Amarra's movements about the palace had been restricted. She was as much a prisoner as she had been, just under better conditions and without manacles. He nodded his approval.

"Thank you, Roman."

Karus was amused by the last. She had no idea what the Roman Empire was, nor where it was. Heck, he did not know where it was either. But she knew he was Roman.

"Karus," he said. "You will call me Karus."

She gave a slight nod of acceptance, and with that he stepped past her and up to the commander of her guard, Optio Ternus. The optio stiffened his back into a position of attention.

"She may remain here," Karus told the optio. "When she is ready, escort her back to her room."

"Yes, sir," Ternus said.

Karus made his way into the palace. He passed by the door that led to his headquarters. There were two guards out front. Both snapped to attention, as did a messenger who was coming from the opposite direction. Then Karus was past them, striding down the corridor toward the great hall.

Two more guards stood to either side of the double doors to the great hall, which had been left open. They smartly snapped to attention at the sight of Karus. With a nod, he brushed by them and found Valens inside with Felix and Dio. The three were farther down the hall, standing around the map. They had been talking with Valens, who was pointing down at the map.

The hall now served as the legion's shrine. As such, Karus had ordered the removal of the throne. Occupying the dais now was the legion's Eagle. Karus sucked in his breath at the sight of the golden bird, which glittered magnificently under the bright light cascading down from the dome. Every other remaining standard from the cohorts and centuries had been arranged neatly before the Eagle.

The sight of the standards gathered together reminded him that a few centuries had lost theirs. The punishment for such a disgrace was usually very severe. So far from home, Karus needed every man. He could not afford to punish those centuries, at least just yet.

Four guards stood to either side of the Eagle. Their kit had been so highly polished, their armor gleamed in the sunlight. Their eyes were watchful, for here rested not only the legion's honor, but that of Rome.

"Karus," Valens said by way of greeting as Karus made his way up to them. He offered a hand, which Karus shook. The cavalry officer's grip was firm and hard. From Valens's arm, a thin mist of dirt and dust rained slowly to the floor.

There was a weary look to him, but there was also something else there. Valens looked more alive, animated, more so than when Karus had last seen the cavalry officer. It had been a good long while since he had seen the prefect exhibit any emotion other than frustration, hate, or the anticipation of a coming fight.

"Valens," Karus said. "It seems you have been keeping yourself busy these past three weeks. How are you?"

"Tolerable," Valens replied, then a grin sketched its way onto his face. "Truth be told, my men and I are just fine. Stretching our legs has been grand."

"Out from the confines of the legate's clutches, eh?" Dio's coin appeared in his hand. With a thumb, he flipped it up into the air and deftly caught it with his left hand and then slapped it on his right forearm and checked which side had landed upright.

"Something like that," Valens replied as Dio flipped his coin again. "Though I admit regret at being away from my men, even to make a face–to-face report."

"It was necessary," Karus said, brushing aside the prefect's concerns. "Dispatches can only tell me so much."

Valens glanced down at the mosaic. "Felix was showing me where you got the map you sent me."

"I had one of the clerks draw it," Karus said. "I assume it helped?"

"Immensely," Valens replied. "Once we knew where we were, I could dispatch squadrons to each city, and town within fifty miles." Valens paused and pointed at a city near Carthum, perhaps thirty miles distant. "This city, which you tell us is called Caradoon, is just as empty as this one. Caradoon has been picked over and thoroughly looted. Half of the city has also been torched."

"Was it sacked then?" Felix asked.

"I don't think so," Valens drawled. "This is only speculation, mind you, but we've come across tracks of large groups moving through the countryside and along the roads." He paused, looked down, and pointed at the map. "They seem to be moving in the direction that you designated west, Karus. By the way, that helped simplify things by choosing a direction. What with those two suns and the stars being different, it has been a bit of a bitch telling my men which way to go."

"These large groups," Karus said, not liking the sound of it, "armies perhaps?"

"I am fairly certain not," Valens said. "More like migrating peoples. Some numbering in the hundreds, other groups the thousands, perhaps even tens of thousands, all on the move. Wherever they go, almost always traveling west, they pick things clean. Before I returned after receiving your summons, I got word of a band of four thousand coming this way. I figured I would bring the news personally."

"Here?" Karus said, surprised. "What is their position?"

Valens turned his gaze back to the map, took a step back, and touched a spot with his foot. "Right about here, perhaps forty-five miles distant. At the pace they are making, perhaps five to six days away. The report from my scouts said they were mostly civilians, though there are armed men mixed in amongst them. My boys are shadowing them and will provide you regular reports on their movement."

"Have your men been spotted?" Felix asked Valens.

"No," Valens said. "At least, I don't think so. They have orders to stay out of sight."

"Do you think this bunch are connected to that armed band you encountered?" Felix asked.

"No," Valens replied. "Those were something different, much more organized. They were clearly a foraging party. They were also trained to fight as a cohesive force."

"For an army?" Dio asked, catching his coin in midair. He did not check to see which side had landed up.

"Seems that way," Valens said. "We've not found it yet."

Valens paused and made a large circle around the City of Carthum with his hand. "My scouts have gone around fifty miles in every direction and found nothing else but abandoned countryside, and bodies."

"What do you mean bodies?" Felix asked.

"Everyone in this region got up and outright left," Valens said. "There is no telling how far it goes, but it seems that entire peoples are on the move. Where smaller bands stumbled upon one another, there appears to have been some fighting, perhaps over food. My scouts have come across a number of such sites where skirmishes occurred. We've found bodies in various states of decay, from weeks to months. Whoever won did not seem very interested in burying the other side."

Karus nodded. The explanation made sense. Whenever people struggled to survive, there was killing. It was unfortunate, but nothing he had not seen before.

"The nearest such skirmish that we've found is to the east, by this town here." Valens gestured down at the map. "There were no bodies, but several damaged war chariots like the ones the Celts are fond of using. Grass and the like had grown up around them, so the fight occurred some time ago, months even."

"We also," Valens continued, "followed the paved road that leads from Carthum and heads west." He paused and touched the map again with his sandaled toe. "About here we happened across the remains of a large camp, and then again another one farther down the road, here at forty miles."

"How large?" Karus asked.

"Big enough to hold several hundred thousand people," Valens said. "I saw it myself."

"That must be the direction the people from this city fled," Felix concluded.

"It would seem so," Valens agreed. "They left a trail of discarded trash and debris, easily marking their path."

"So, the question that comes to my mind," Dio said, glancing from one to the other, "if these other towns, villages, and cities in this region were picked clean of food stores, why wasn't this one?"

Karus looked over at Dio and then Valens, who shrugged. Dio had a point.

"I have no idea," Felix said when Karus looked for his opinion. "Something must have kept the city from being looted."

"These supplies you found," Valens looked to Karus. "I understand they were stored like a depot? Almost as we would?"

"That's correct," Karus said. "It was well-organized."

"It is possible an army was here at some point," Valens said. "Carthum might have been a base of operations after the people here fled, hence the lack of serious looting."

"Then why leave their supply behind?" Felix asked. "You'd think they would have at least left a guard company."

"With much of the countryside empty and already fled, they may not have seen the need, especially if they intend to return." Valens turned back to Karus. "One of my scouting parties found tracks to the east. The decurion in charge thought them to be from an army on the march." He paused and used his toe again to indicate a point on the map. "The paved road ends at this small city here. This is where they found the tracks moving eastward." Valens looked up at Karus. "I would like permission to explore beyond the fifty-mile radius you mandated, particularly to reconnoiter farther in that direction."

"Granted," Karus said without hesitation and then remembered to whom he was speaking. "I don't want my eyes wandering too far to be useful. You are to send only a handful of squadrons with your best officers. They are to avoid all contact."

"Two squadrons then," Valens said. "Will that be acceptable?"

"Yes," Karus said, "but I don't want you with them."

"Understood," Valens agreed. "I will regrettably remain behind and direct operations."

"Good." Karus let out a long breath. "How are your men holding up? They've been in the saddle now for some time."

"My boys are getting more than a little saddle weary," Valens admitted. "I was going to request this, but now that you have brought it up, we could use a rest. On a rotating basis, with your permission, of course, I would like to send a quarter of my command back to Carthum to enjoy the fruits of civilization. That way," Valens continued, "at any time, Karus, you will have a force of cavalry at your disposal."

"I like it," Karus said.

"Dio tells me you have a functioning bathhouse. The last one I saw was back at Eboracum. Bathing in frigid rivers and lakes just doesn't cut it."

"It's divine," Dio grinned. "You're gonna love it."

"I can't wait," Valens said and then his brow creased. "One other interesting thing, Karus. It may be nothing, but we've found no evidence of any stables for horses. We've seen plenty of animal stalls, but none made for an equine. For that matter, we've come across no saddles or harnesses that would fit a horse anywhere so far. The closest we've seen is tackle for those oxen-like creatures we sent back."

"They are called teska," Karus said. "We've learned that from the woman that was found in the dungeon."

"Is that how you found out the name of Caradoon?" Valens asked.

"I am learning her language," Karus said.

"I bet he would like to learn something more," Dio teased.

Karus shot his friend a heated look before turning back to Valens. "So, what are you saying about horses in these parts?"

"I think it is a very real probability that the people who live in this region know nothing of horses or cavalry."

"How is it possible?" Dio asked.

"I don't know," Valens admitted, "but that foraging party we wiped out had no idea how to defend themselves against a massed cavalry charge." Valens got a faraway look. "We rode them down like a farmer harvests wheat in the fall. I swear, not one of them had ever seen a horse before. Which makes the discovery of the war chariots all that more interesting, don't you think?"

"Next time," Karus said, feeling irritation at the reminder of Valens's thoughtlessness, though it seemed the prefect was on to yet another mystery, "I would appreciate it if you managed to take a prisoner or two."

"Your note to me," Valens actually managed to look abashed, "made your feelings on that matter plain. I won't make that mistake again. In the future, we'll do our best to grab prisoners for questioning."

"Very good," Karus said, suddenly feeling tired. "Your report is something to think on. Is there anything else?"

"Yes," Valens said. "My scouts found and explored a dirt road leading into the forest several miles to the west. It led to a small temple that is really old. After hearing their account, I went and looked for myself. There was a statue inside. I swear by the gods, Karus, it looked like the spitting image of Jupiter. I am sure you've seen his statue back in Rome, at the Temple of Jupiter Optimus Maximus."

Karus nodded. On his last visit to the mother city, he had paid a priest to help him make an offering before the great god's statue.

"It was complete. Jupiter had his lightning bolt, beard, and everything. Karus, there must have been Romans here before us." Valens paused. "What's even odder, the forest's grown up thoroughly around it. However, there were fresh offerings inside. My scouts saw no one, nor evidence of tracks anywhere outside. Someone had left fresh offerings, but how they got in and failed to disturb the dust is beyond me."

"Really?" Felix said and shot a glance to Karus.

"My boys," Valens said in a near whisper, "think the people living in the trees were responsible."

"Valens," Felix said, exchanging a look with Karus, "have you seen them yourself?"

Valens shook his head curtly. "That doesn't mean they don't exist, and it would explain who left the offerings before the altar."

Dio abruptly laughed at the prefect. "By Mars and Jupiter, Valens, I never thought to see you visiting a temple. Ever. You of all people."

"Well," Valens replied, turning a serious look upon Dio that caused the other to still his mirth. "A man changes, especially after what we've been through."

There was an uncomfortable silence after that. Karus cleared his throat. "I think you need some rest and the opportunity to bathe before you set out again."

"I would appreciate that," Valens said. "The bath alone is worth coming all this way."

"Speak to the clerks," Karus said. "They will find a room for you. The palace has a freshwater bathing house. It is aqueduct-fed. The hypocaust heating system is not working, but the water's not too terribly cold."

"That sounds heavenly," Valens said.

"Would you join me for dinner?" Karus asked. It was anything but a request. "I would like to hear of your travels and will likely have more questions."

Valens nodded and, with Karus's permission, excused himself.

After he was gone, Karus turned to the other two. "What do you think?"

"Someone will be returning for that supply," Felix said. "I am sure of it."

"Agreed," Dio said, then hesitated abruptly, becoming gravely serious. "Something is happening in this land. Entire peoples don't up and leave unless there is some serious threat."

"Dio is correct," Felix said. "Our deliverance from the Celts will, I fear, come with a price. We were brought here for a reason, Karus. I feel it in my bones."

Karus rubbed his chin as he considered what Felix and Dio had said. They were right, of course. The gods gave nothing freely, least of all good fortune. Karus's thoughts turned dark. There was no telling what threat lay out beyond Carthum's walls.

"How is the wagon construction coming?" Karus looked at Felix.

"We've finished thirty-four as of this morning," Felix reported. "I've got two centuries assisting in the construction. I think we will need at least two hundred, bare minimum, if you are planning on moving the legion anywhere."

"How many are we making a day?"

"Two to three," Felix answered.

Karus did rough calculation in his head.

"Almost three months, then, until we have enough." He was frustrated by the progress. "Is there any way to increase production?"

"Yes," Felix said, "I will assign more men. We are constrained by the number of wood workers we have, but even so, I think we can speed things up."

"Do what you can," Karus said, feeling an urgency he did not want to voice.

"Oh, before I forget," Dio said. "You asked me to look in on Macrinus and Arrens. I spoke with a few friends, junior centurions and optios I know well."

"Yes," Karus said. "How are they doing with their new commands?"

"Well enough, it seems," Dio said. "Both are popular men and inspire confidence, though I suspect you already knew this."

"Aye," Karus said. "I did. So, no complaints then?"

"There are always complaints," Dio said. "But I judge them to be doing an acceptable job."

"Excuse me, sir."

Karus turned to see Serma standing respectfully a few feet away. He motioned the man over.

"The surgeon is here to see you, sir," the clerk said. "He was quite insistent. Shall I send him in?"

Karus nodded, and the clerk stepped off, walking back down the hall.

"Ampelius," Karus said, greeting the surgeon as he entered the hall and walked over to them. Karus noticed the tired look to the surgeon's eyes as he scanned the room. The last he had seen the man, Ampelius had seemed almost rested. Something was wrong.

"Ambitions on becoming emperor?" Ampelius asked, glancing around the hall, eyes settling upon the legionary standards.

"Ah, no." Karus decided it had been an attempt at humor, rather than a barb. The surgeon, though acerbic by nature, was without guile. Until this moment, Karus had thought him incapable of jest.

"This hall contains a detailed map." Karus pointed down at their feet. "Valens had just presented a report on his scouting efforts out in the countryside. You missed him."

"So it does," Ampelius said with no little amount of surprise and began studying it curiously. "Can't say I recognize anything."

"You requested to see me?" Karus asked.

"Yes," Ampelius said, looking back to Karus with unblinking eyes. "That sickness we spoke on."

"What about it?"

"It's spreading," the surgeon said.

"Plague?" Dio asked. There was a pang of concern in his tone.

"I am not sure," Ampelius said. "It does not have the hallmarks of plague, yet. The victims suffer mainly from fever, cough, and severe intestinal distress."

"Could it be the food we are eating?" Felix asked.

"I've thought about that," Ampelius said, "but ruled it out. Too many are eating the same and have yet to fall ill."

"What of the water?" Karus asked. "Could it be diseased?"

"Everyone is drinking the same water." Ampelius shook his head. "The water is clean and fit for consumption. There seems to be no causality to the sickness other than close contact. So far, around thirty of the camp followers have fallen ill, many members of the same family. Also, one century has ten men on the sick list with the symptoms. One of the men in that unit has family who have fallen ill, a wife and child."

"Which century?" Karus asked.

"Second Century, Eighth Cohort," Ampelius said. "It may be spread by the breathing in of contaminated vapors."

"What do you recommend?" Karus did not like what he was hearing. The last thing he needed was to have to deal with mass sickness, plague or not.

"Well," Ampelius said. "I've selected a large building as a hospital and had my patients moved there to keep the sickness isolated. Once someone shows signs of illness, they should be moved there forthwith. I would appreciate your support in this."

"I will give orders to that effect," Karus said, though he knew that word of the sickness would rapidly spread. Fear would soon set in. He was working to rebuild the morale and discipline of the legion. This would surely chip away at what he had accomplished so far, much like water undermining a poorly built dike. "What else do you require?"

"A century to act as assistants, and another to guard the hospital."

"Guard it?" Dio seemed surprised by that. "Whatever for?"

Ampelius turned his unblinking gaze on the centurion. "Why, to keep my patients in, of course. If you were sick with a potentially fatal disease, would you really want to remain with others who may make you sicker?"

"Of course not," Karus said, cutting anything further off from Dio with a hard glance. "I will see that you have what you need. Anything else, please don't hesitate to ask."

"Thank you, Karus," Ampelius said and started to shuffle off, before stopping and glancing down at the mosaic. "You know, I was in Athens years ago studying medicine. While there, I saw a map of the lands east of Asia, beyond provincial Roman control. I always wanted to go there, but I was told the peoples in that land were savages beyond compare who drink fermented goat's milk." The surgeon shuddered with disgust. "Parts of this look somewhat like that."

Ampelius turned on his heel and, without another word, left.

Karus blinked and glanced down at the map. Could it be? Were they beyond the province of Asia? The lands and peoples east of the province were reputed to be violent barbarians. Karus looked up at oH

Dio and Felix.

"Well," Felix said, with a heavy breath, "if we are beyond our province, we need to find out which way leads back to Rome, and fast, because the peoples who live out here are, as the good surgeon said, barbarians. Not likely the friendliest of neighbors."

"Crassus," Karus said in a near whisper.

"The bloke," Dio said, "that was part of the Triumvirate, with Pompey and Caesar?"

Karus looked over at Dio with more than a little astonishment. It must have been evident, for Dio gave a shrug.

"Karus," Dio said, "we've been friends for more years than I can count, and you talk incessantly. I do listen, you know."

Karus gave a chuckle. "All these years and I thought it went in one ear and out the other."

"Some days it does," Dio said. "Other days it gets stuck inside my head. Now, what of Crassus?"

"Well," Karus said, "if we are beyond the province of Asia, we could be in the general area past Syria. That is where Crassus, with seven legions under his command, was soundly defeated."

"And we have only one," Felix said, looking meaningfully at Dio. "You should really listen more, you know."

"I will take that under advisement," Dio said and fell silent.

"Karus," Felix said, "in addition to wagons, perhaps we should build some artillery as well. A few bolt throwers on the walls would be a nice comfort. The city has everything we need: boards, rope … I don't believe it would impact the wagon construction very much."

"Very well," Karus said. Each cohort was trained in building artillery from scratch. What Felix had just suggested made good sense. If it came to defending the walls, artillery would come in handy. "Have each cohort get on it and see that they are placed on the walls around the gatehouses. Dio, make sure that Ampelius gets the men he requires."

"I will," Dio said. His brow furrowed. "Karus, are you all right?"

"Just a little tired," Karus said. The truth was he felt weary. He had been working himself hard and getting very little sleep.

"You should get some rest," Dio said.

Karus nodded and, without saying another word, turned and left his two friends. The legionaries guarding the door snapped to attention as he passed. Karus made for his quarters, moving through the room where his clerks worked away diligently. They stood to attention as he passed.

Karus's quarters were just beyond the room he had designated as his headquarters and adjacent to the library. He entered and closed the door behind him. The room contained a large feather bed, a trunk someone had found for his personal possessions, and a desk with a stool. He glanced over at the bed and rubbed the back of his neck. Sleep beckoned. A gentle breeze blew into the room, drawing his attention to the large open balcony that overlooked the gardens. He stepped out onto it, rested his arms on the stone railing, and took a heavy breath.

Karus's thoughts were dark and troubled. The fate of his legion weighed heavily upon his shoulders, and it was keeping him up at night. Movement below drew his gaze. Amarra was still strolling through the gardens. She had picked several flowers, forming a bouquet. The sight of her lifted his heart, and his troubles receded just a little.

She looked up, saw him, and waved. Karus gave a small wave back and caught himself smiling. She turned away and continued making her way through the gardens. Her guard trailed a few steps behind. Karus's thoughts darkened again. She, like everything else in this land, was a mystery that needed solving. Karus sensed that he was rapidly running out of time.

Chapter Seventeen

Blood slicked the floor. There was so much of it, Karus could taste copper on his tongue when he breathed in. Karus's gaze drifted around the cell, his rage growing with each passing moment. A legionary lay dead at his feet. His throat had been cut nearly from ear to ear. The sheer amount of blood told Karus that there was another wound he was not seeing.

The air was cold, even on this first floor, just feet beneath the surface. The dungeon reminded Karus of the catacombs in Rome, though here small cells had been cut into the rock, instead of shelves for the dead.

Karus turned around. Outside the cell was another body, and beyond that, Ampelius was treating a gravely wounded man. Judging from the tear to his belly, and the dark blood that oozed out, he would not long survive. The sight angered Karus even more.

The cell door lay open, and beyond it, Delvaris, Pammon, Flaccus, and half a dozen legionaries from the Fifth looked on in dismay. Two of the magic lanterns hung from chains in the passageway outside the cell. They provided just enough light to see by. A couple legionaries held torches that hissed and lightly popped.

Shouts and calls could be heard in the distance, as a search was being conducted of the entire dungeon. The two druids who had occupied the cell were on the loose. They were being hunted.

"I thought I could rely upon you," Karus spat at Flaccus.

"I don't know how they managed to escape," Flaccus said with a helpless look that only served to anger Karus further.

"That's not what I meant." Karus moved by Delvaris, who was intently studying the metal door's lock, and out into the corridor. He stepped up to the senior centurion of the Fifth. "You were charged with holding those two damned druids." Karus turned around and pointed at the dead man in the cell. "What was he doing in there?"

"I don't know," Flaccus said.

"Don't you?" Karus roared, the sound of his voice echoing off the stone walls. "I will tell you. Your men thought they'd have a little fun, maybe rough them up a little? Helpless, defenseless prisoners. I mean, what could have gone wrong?"

Flaccus remained silent, a muscle in his jaw flexing.

"They escaped," Karus said, lowering his voice an octave. "Two of your men are now dead and likely a third. All because orders would not be followed."

"Karus," Pammon said in a cautioning tone. "We don't know that happened."

"I gave strict orders on that," Flaccus said, becoming heated. He took a step nearer Karus. "I made it plain."

"Then you can't control your men," Karus said. "Can you?"

"Why, you dirty…"

"Karus," Delvaris exclaimed in a shout of surprise. "You have to look at this."

Karus and Flaccus turned. Half bent over, Delvaris was holding one of the magic lanterns close to the lock. Unlike everyone else, the tribune had not been following their exchange.

Pammon brushed by Karus and Flaccus. He examined what the tribune had been studying.

"The locking mechanism is melted," Pammon said, sounding astounded.

Karus stepped closer. Flaccus too. The metal from the lock had run like water, leaving a large round hole where the keyhole had been.

"I once saw a building that had burned down," Pammon said. "The metal from the locks ran like this. But I don't understand. There's been no fire here."

"How did they manage that?" Karus asked, anger abruptly fleeing.

"No idea." Pammon shrugged.

"My boy was dragged into the cell before he was killed." Flaccus shot Karus a heated look.

Karus held Flaccus's gaze for a moment, then turned and moved over to where Ampelius was tending to the mortally wounded legionary. The surgeon had removed the man's chest armor, and it was lying next to him. A sword had penetrated clean through it. Either the blow had been particularly forceful or, more likely, there had been a defect with the lad's armor. Ampelius had just finished wrapping a bandage tightly around the man's stomach. Blood leached through to stain the gray fabric a dark red.

"Can he speak?"

"He is beyond my skills," Ampelius said. "It is a kindness he lost consciousness. With luck, he will pass from this life without waking and suffering further torment."

Karus considered the unconscious legionary a moment and weighed his options.

"Can you wake him?"

"Karus, it would be a mercy to let him go without the pain consciousness would bring," the surgeon said.

"I need answers. I must know what happened here," Karus said. "Can you wake him?"

"Yes," Ampelius said, looking none too happy. He rummaged through his satchel, which lay at his side, muttering under his breath just a tad too loud. "And people feel I am the heartless one."

Karus ignored the surgeon's comment.

Ampelius finally found what he was looking for. "Are you sure you want me to do this?"

"Yes," Karus said. Though he did not wish to have the lad suffer, he needed answers.

"Very well," Ampelius said and waved a small packet under the man's nose.

At first, there was no reaction. Then the man stirred, coughed, and turned his head away. Ampelius's hand followed. He kept the packet close to the man's nose. A moment later, the legionary's eyes fluttered open. Ampelius drew his hand away.

The man immediately grimaced and cried out, bearing his teeth. Bloody spittle frothed to his lips.

Karus knelt down next to him, feeling terrible about what he had done.

"What is your name, son?"

"Severus," he said. A spasm of pain wracked his body. When he recovered, sweat slicked his brow and he shook ever so slightly. "Am I done for, sir?"

"Yes," Karus said, deciding to go with the truth. "I am afraid there is nothing we can do for you."

Severus stilled, locking onto Karus's eyes before his gaze slid over to Ampelius. "The pain hurts something awful. Will it get worse?"

The surgeon nodded. "Undoubtedly."

Another spasm of pain struck. It left the legionary panting.

"Mommy," the legionary whined in a soft, pitiful voice. "Mommy, help me."

Karus had seen hundreds of fights and their aftermaths. He had witnessed numerous comrades and friends breathe their last. Some had even died in his arms. More often than not, grievously wounded with the sands of time running out, they called for their mothers. Karus let out a heavy breath. It never got any easier. He carried them all with him still and, soon, this one as well.

"I don't want to feel the pain." Severus focused on Karus. "Can you finish me, sir?"

"I will," Karus said, voice gruff with emotion. "I will speed your way to the afterlife and give you the coin to pay the ferryman."

Flaccus knelt down opposite Karus.

"No, Severus," Flaccus said, hand going for the hilt of his dagger. He took a moment to clear his throat before he continued. "I will give you that mercy myself. It would be my honor."

"Thank you, sir," Severus said and then closed his eyes. "I'm ready, sir."

"Not yet, son," Karus said, placing a hand on the lad's shoulder. "We need to know what happened here."

Severus's eyes snapped open.

"Monsters," he said in a whisper, gaze becoming wild and unfocused. "Monsters came for us."

"What do you mean 'monsters'?" Flaccus demanded.

"Like in the back of the wagon." Severus's breathing became heavy, abruptly coming in great gasps. Another spasm gripped him, and he screeched like a dying calf. "Like in the back of the wagon, sir. We all saw it, monsters… "

"He is mentally disoriented," Ampelius said. "Sometimes it happens with mortal wounds, lack of blood combined with the shock."

"Calm down, son," Karus said, patting Severus on the shoulder.

"They are coming for us all," the legionary screamed before yet another spasm took him and he arched his back. When he recovered, he retched up thick dark blood onto his chest and bandaged stomach. After a moment of panting, he wiped his mouth with the back of his hand and relaxed. The legionary's eyes found Karus. He grabbed at Karus's chest armor with a bloodied hand and pulled him close. The grip was surprisingly strong.

Karus offered his hand and the legionary took it, pulling Karus closer. Severus trembled slightly. With a gasp, he whispered. Karus leaned his ear close and Severus whispered again. A moment later he went limp, the hand going slack as his shade crossed over to the other side.

Karus closed Severus's eyes and sat back, looking at the legionary's blood on his hand.

Ampelius checked for a pulse. After a moment, the surgeon shook his head and stood.

"What did he say?" Flaccus asked, standing with Karus.

"He said, 'They came out of the walls'," Karus said. He took a deep breath and then looked around the small corridor.

"What does that mean?" Flaccus glanced downward at Severus's body.

"I think…" Karus stopped, spied a legionary holding a torch, and held out his hand. "Give that to me."

The legionary passed over the torch. Karus's eyes swept the corridor once again. The cell that the druids had been kept in was one of four on this level. It was also at the farthest end, and the last cell. Karus paced a few feet beyond Severus's body, holding the torch near the floor.

"Ha!" he said with triumph, spotting a large bloodied boot print. None of Karus's men had been wearing boots. They wore only sandals. He spun on Flaccus. "Were the druids wearing boots?" Karus asked. "Think, man, this is important."

"No," Flaccus said, brows drawing together. "I don't believe they were."

Karus turned back, studying the floor. The intruders into the city and those dead that had been found in the forest had been wearing boots. With everyone watching curiously, Karus followed the prints. After a few feet, by the main door that led up to the administrative building, he noticed a blood trail.

"Flaccus," Karus said, stopping suddenly. "Are you missing any men?"

"No," Flaccus said. "The druids were locked up in that cell. Those three were the guard detail for their shift. The rest of the century was quartered on the floor above. When they heard the commotion, they rushed down here. By the time they arrived, it was all over. Karus, I swear, the door leading down here was locked. Those druids could not have gotten out and to the surface."

Karus nodded as he thought it through. He studied the blood trail again. It continued on past the door. He pointed it out. "Maybe your boys got in a few licks of their own."

Flaccus studied the floor.

"I think," Karus said, kneeling beside one of the boot prints and placing a finger on it, "the druids had help escaping." Karus gestured at the blood trail. "This, I think, is proof one of your boys stuck one of them before he went down, possibly Severus there."

Flaccus nodded at that, but Karus was still deeply troubled. Somehow, he suspected the intruders had known about the druids and had come to free them. Karus did not yet understand how or why, but his gut told him it was so.

He continued to follow the tracks, working his way down the corridor. He checked each cell for tracks or blood. He found nothing but years of grime and mold. The blood remained confined to the corridor. Delvaris, Pammon, and Flaccus trailed behind him, along with the men. Everyone was hushed and quiet.

Karus stopped. Without any of the magical lanterns nearby, this section of passageway was darkened and it was harder to see. He held the hissing torch closer to the ground. The boot prints were becoming fainter, yet the blood trail was still easy to see.

The trail ran up to an alcove with a set of stairs that led downward to the right. Karus started to move down them, but then stopped. There was no blood on the steps. He retraced his path and looked around. The trail led right into the alcove and then stopped cold.

"What is it?" Flaccus asked.

"The blood trail," Karus said, rubbing his jaw. "It stops here."

"Surely it goes down the stairs?"

"No, it doesn't."

Karus's eyes narrowed. He waved the torch around the alcove, then bent over and studied the floor more carefully. A draft caught the torch, and the flame fluttered ever so slightly. Karus put a hand out to the floor and felt a cold breeze upon his fingers.

"There's a door here." Karus straightened. "I feel a draft. Get me more light."

There was a scramble, followed by someone handing forward one of the magic lanterns. Karus handed the torch to Flaccus, who began to examine the wall with him.

"Look." Flaccus pointed.

There was a bloody handprint on the rock about waist high. Karus felt it, hoping there was a secret lever. He gave the spot with the handprint a push. Nothing happened. It was just solid rock. They began exploring the entire wall.

"This appears to be a seam," Flaccus said, running a finger down the wall.

Karus looked closely and agreed. "Yes, but how do we open it?"

"There must be a mechanism," Flaccus said to those behind them. "Look around."

They searched for several moments, but found nothing.

"What about this?"

Karus turned completely around. Delvaris was pointing at a chain affixed to a small ring on the opposite wall. It was the kind of ring manacles were secured to.

"This is a landing for a stairway," Delvaris said. "Why put a ring for manacles here?"

Delvaris gave a small tug on the chain. Nothing happened. He tugged harder and the chain, secured to the wall, moved just a bit. There was a loud click behind Karus. Delvaris let go of the chain. There was another click.

Karus turned and pushed on what he thought would be the door. It didn't budge.

"Pull it again," Karus ordered.

Delvaris gave the chain a hearty yank. When the first click sounded, Karus pushed his weight onto the door. With a grating sound, it slowly began to shift.

"Throw your weight into it," Karus grunted to Flaccus, who leaned forward and pushed with him.

Hinges screaming, the door slowly opened. When it was wide enough to admit a man, Karus stopped and grabbed for the lantern. He shined it into the darkness. A small passageway that was thick with dust stretched out before them. Karus lowered the lantern to the floor. The dust had been recently disturbed. More importantly, the blood trail continued.

A sound echoed back to them from farther up the passageway. Karus looked to Flaccus.

"Let's get some payback for your men," he said.

"Aye." Flaccus drew his sword. "Let's go get the murderous bastards."

"Sir." Pammon stepped forward. "Let the men go first."

Karus thought on it a heartbeat. He was angry over the deaths of Flaccus's men. He looked over at Flaccus and then firmly shook his head.

"This is something that I need to do," Karus said, "for our boys back there."

"We need to do this together," Flaccus said, clapping a hand on Karus's shoulder armor. "The men can follow behind us."

"Pammon," Karus said, "we will take Delvaris and five of these men with us. Summon help and follow as soon as you can."

"Yes, sir," Pammon said, sounding not particularly happy.

"Let's go," Karus said and ducked into the passageway, holding the lantern forward. It was only wide enough to admit one man at a time, and his armor rubbed and scraped against the tight stone walls. Behind, he could hear Flaccus and then the bulk of the men following. The noise they made in the tight confines of the passage was surprising. As a result, he could no longer hear anything ahead. Karus advanced, sword ready and lantern held out before him lighting the way.

The passage smelled old and musty. It had an unused feel to it, and with each step, centuries of dust kicked up and tickled at his nose. Two hundred paces in, it made a slight curve to the right. Karus began encountering a step down every few feet. Thinking on the terrain above, and the distance traveled, he decided the tunnel was taking them downward from the palace district and into the city.

Seeing something, Karus paused and held the lantern to the floor. The blood went from a light trail to a heavy flow. It also looked fresh and glistened with reflected light, meaning they were gaining on the escapees and whoever had helped them. Karus continued on, counting his steps.

At four hundred, the tunnel led them to an abrupt turn. Karus stopped before making his way around it, careful lest someone was lying in ambush. It was clear. He paused and motioned for everyone behind him to quiet down.

Once everyone had stilled, noises and voices, sounding somewhat desperate, could be heard ahead. By the sound of it, they appeared not too far off, though Karus realized that the acoustics of the confined passage could be deceiving and likely were. Once around the bend, the passageway opened up a little. Karus found he was able to move quicker and easier, setting a faster pace. Flaccus followed close behind.

"Chavak!"

Karus was abruptly slammed into the wall, and hard. The breath whooshed from his lungs with the impact. Something connected painfully with the armor on his lower chest and grazed off. Karus went down in a tumble, losing his sword and the lantern.

He tried to roll to his side to see his attacker, but he was kicked hard in the back, sending him down again. Something wet sprayed across the side of his face. This was almost immediately followed by an animal-like roar of pain, then the repeated clang of sword on sword.

Struggling to get air back into his lungs, Karus drew his dagger. He rolled to the side and saw the leg of his attacker. He struck, neatly hamstringing the ankle. There was another roar of anguish, and the attacker went to a knee. Karus struck again, this time in the meat of the leg, eliciting another roar. This was followed immediately with a meaty *thwack* above, and the body of his attacker crashed down atop him, once again forcing Karus back down.

Finally, Karus's lungs started working again, and despite the weight on his back, he sucked in sweet air, relishing it.

"Come on," Flaccus said and rolled the body off. He helped Karus up with a hand. "Are you all right?"

"Only my pride is damaged," Karus said, sucking in a deep breath.

He looked down at the body and saw it was an orc. The creature wore black leather chest armor, brown pants, and boots like the intruders who had tried to sneak their way into the city and those in the forest.

"What is going on here?" Karus said to himself. He wondered how it had gotten into the city. Had it come over the walls? Or had it and others been here the entire time? How many others were there?

"That was a nice hamstring," Flaccus said. "Until you struck, that beast had me on my heels. It was frightfully powerful."

Karus picked up his sword and retrieved the lantern. One of the glass panes had shattered, but the flame still burned brightly. He glanced behind Flaccus. There was some distance between him and the others, who were led by Delvaris.

"How about we call it a team effort," Karus said, "and not mention how close we both came to being fodder for the worms?"

"Agreed." Flaccus chuckled and kicked at the dead orc. "We could say we just killed that big old bastard with no trouble at all, like right proper officers."

Karus shot the cantankerous centurion a slight grin and chuckled.

"It's a deal." Karus looked over Flaccus's shoulder. "Stop dragging ass and keep bloody up."

"Yes, Karus," Delvaris said.

He spared the tribune a withering look and then turned and continued, with Flaccus right behind, staying close. They moved quickly and with purpose. A glance behind, and he saw Delvaris lagging again. Karus considered reprimanding the tribune, then shrugged and turned back to the task at hand. He did not want to slow his pace and allow the druids to get away.

Fifty feet farther on, Karus thought he detected a reflected flash just ahead in the darkness. Possibly from a blade. There looked to be another hidden alcove. He slowed, turned slightly, and pointed two fingers at his eyes and then ahead. Flaccus nodded his understanding, and together they crept forward.

When the attack came, Karus was more than ready for it. He had expected an orc, but this time it was a man. Karus dropped the lantern and blocked with his sword as Flaccus reached over his shoulder in a deft move and jabbed the attacker in the chest, eliciting a grunt.

Wounded, the man stepped back. Karus pressed forward and punched out with his short sword, aiming low.

The sword slid easily into a thigh. Karus twisted the blade as he pulled it back. Blood sprayed across his hand and arm. An artery had been nicked. The attacker stumbled to his knees. Though he would be dead in mere heartbeats, Karus did not want to take a chance and thrust his sword into the other's exposed neck. The man gagged before falling backwards, dead, his blood pooling out around him in the dust.

"Nice work," Flaccus said, admiring Karus's work. "Would you mind leaving the next one for me?"

Karus picked up the lantern and shined it over the body. He wore black leather armor, brown pants, and boots, like the others.

A noise ahead drew his attention back to the task at hand.

"Let's go," Karus said. "They can't be too far ahead."

Another fifty paces farther on, light began to illuminate the passage. Karus could see what looked to be an exit in the distance. He and Flaccus picked up their pace. Once they reached it, Karus cautiously poked his head out into the afternoon light. In their haste to flee, the door had been left open.

Judging from the massive buildings to both sides, Karus realized they were in the temple district. Specifically, in a narrow alley between temples. Twenty steps forward, a man was half-carrying and half-dragging one of the druids. Spying Karus and Flaccus, he carefully laid the druid down. Then, calmly, he drew his long sword and moved toward them with confident intent.

"This one is mine," Flaccus said. "Do you have a problem with that, sir?"

"No," Karus said, hearing Delvaris and the others emerging from the passage. "Take him."

Flaccus moved forward, sword held lightly in his hand. The man sprang at him. It was over in the blink of an eye.

Flaccus dodged right and away from the strike, even as his own blade punched forward and deeply into the other's belly. Flaccus stepped in close and drove the sword deeper, right up to the hilt, before giving it a savage twist. His opponent let out an agonized cry, sword clattering to the stone.

Flaccus held the man there for a moment, then roughly shoved him back and off his blade. The man fell to the pavement, intestines landing around him. Flaccus drove his sword viciously downward into the other's neck. The strike was delivered so powerfully that the tip rang on the stone paving.

Flaccus strode over to the druid, who had rolled onto his back. Karus stepped up next to him. The druid looked up at them. Like Severus, he had been stabbed in the gut, and the front of his black robes glistened darkly.

The druid's face had been blackened by something. Karus thought it might be ash, but it could simply have been a mixture of dust and grime. Underneath the coating, the face almost looked pockmarked, as if it were going through the beginnings of a dreaded disease. Karus found it was hard to focus on the druid's face. The druid glowered back at them menacingly.

"You should have let me kill them," Flaccus said.

"You are right," Karus said. "I should have. I should not have accused you of failing in your duty either. I will not make that mistake again. You have my word on that."

"That's enough for me," Flaccus said, glancing over at Karus, face hard. "I will not hold back on my opinion, when I think you wrong."

"I expect you to give it to me straight."

Flaccus nodded, then his gaze turned back on the druid. "Can I kill him now?"

"Yes," Karus said. "Send this piece of shit on his way."

"My Lord is coming for you, Karus," the druid said in bad Latin. "He will take—"

Whatever the druid was going to say ended abruptly with a sword thrust through his throat.

"I always despised those who spouted on and on about religion. They always seem to think they know better than the rest of us," Flaccus said. He used the druid's cloak to clean his sword. "Better that he talk to his god directly than with you and me, eh?"

Delvaris came up, along with the handful of legionaries from Flaccus's cohort.

"I only see one druid," Delvaris said. "Where do you think the other one's got to?"

Karus and Flaccus looked at one another, rushed to the end of the alleyway, and looked out onto the empty boulevard that ran through the temple district.

"Wouldn't you know it," Flaccus said with palpable irritation, "the bugger got clean away."

"He probably left the other behind and legged it," Karus said. "There likely was never any real chance we'd catch up to him."

Flaccus sheathed his sword.

"We'll search the city for him," Karus said and turned to Delvaris. "Send a man to each gatehouse with word to double our patrols on the wall and keep a sharp eye for anyone trying to leave the city."

Delvaris nodded and turned away.

"With your permission, Karus," Flaccus said and breathed in deeply, "I am going to muster my cohort and start turning this city upside down."

"Granted," Karus said, "and good hunting."

Chapter Eighteen

Karus turned as Amarra descended the steps from the palace, her guard trailing a few steps behind. She wore the same plain grey dress that had clearly seen better days. He was sure that, with all that had been found in the city, there were better available than those a servant or slave had worn. He decided he would speak to Delvaris about finding her better wear.

Karus shrugged his shoulders, shifting his armor about for a more comfortable fit. He had left his helmet and shield behind. He had not worn his kit for a few days, and under the morning suns, the heat was building inside. Perspiration began to bead his forehead.

Karus's escort waited at a respectful distance; the men without their shields stood at ease. Under the watchful and stern gaze of Ipax, there was no talking. The hard-faced optio had taken a position to their side. He had remained there, motionless, as if rooted in place. Karus almost smiled, but refrained. One thing service with the legions taught was how to hurry up and wait.

"Are you sure this is wise?" Dio asked him quietly. "Because I am not. With people falling ill, they have become scared, and the men are talking about her."

"Are they saying anything new?" Karus asked absently. His mind was on the trouble in the dungeon and the druid on the loose. Despite turning the city upside down over the last week, the bastard had yet to be found.

"No," Dio said, "but it is getting worse. You know how this sort of thing goes."

"She's a witch and I've fallen under her spell, is that it?"

"Yes," Dio said unhappily. "Well, that is one of the more common claims flying about. There are also people saying she is responsible for the sickness. Add to that the escape of the druids, the death of Flaccus's men... With everything that has happened, Karus, we really don't need this sort of thing right now. Pammon and Felix agree with me on this."

"Nonsense." Karus let out an exasperated breath. "I am learning her language to gain intelligence. That is all."

"I know that," Dio said. "Karus, the men love you, especially after you held the legion together against the Celts. In their eyes, you can do no wrong. It's her they are concerned with. Think about how it looks. We find only one person in this entire city and she's a prisoner. No one knows why she was imprisoned. Next thing, she is your guest, living in the palace alongside you and secluded from view. The circumstances she was found under are mysterious. We have been transported to a strange land, empty of people, with two unfamiliar suns, an odd-looking moon, and stars that don't match our own. Add to that, sickness is running through the cohorts and followers. People are scared, and trouble may come of taking her out into the city."

Karus turned a sour look on Dio. "Then they will see her. That will help put these *rumors*," Karus said the word as if it were distasteful, "to rest. She is flesh and blood. Nothing more. She has nothing to do with anything. By the gods, they will see her."

"That's what I am afraid of," Dio hissed. "Taking her out into the city is a bad idea, especially now with the sickness.

The legion's been through a lot lately. We need to find a better way to handle this, to introduce her so that she is accepted."

"My mind is made up," Karus said, tone becoming hard. "She offered to show me the temple district. I would learn more about their gods and, through them, her people."

"Her people," Dio scoffed, becoming heated, "where are they? Certainly not here. What do they matter now?"

"Everything," Karus said. "I've heard enough. Our people will see her one way or another. They will adjust. It is that simple."

Dio looked as if he wanted to argue, but clamped his jaw shut as Amarra descended the last few steps and approached, her escort trailing.

"Karus, Dio," she said, bowing her head slightly. "I believe you say, uhm... greetings."

"Amarra," Karus said, switching to her language, at which he was still a poor speaker. "Good morning."

She gave him a faint smile, and Karus felt his heart warm slightly.

"Will you excuse me?" Dio said stiffly, declining to return Amarra's greeting. Without waiting for permission, he stalked angrily off in the direction of the palace.

Karus noticed Amarra's brow furrow slightly as she watched him go. Karus let out a soft breath. He would have to speak to Dio later and make things right. He glanced over at Ipax, wondering what the optio thought of Amarra. Did he consider her a threat? Bad luck? The optio's face was an inscrutable mask. Karus was sure he had heard everything that had transpired, as had his men. They scrupulously avoided Karus's gaze. So be it, thought Karus as he beckoned Optio Ternus over, who was in command of Amarra's guard this day.

"Sir?" The optio straightened to a position of attention.

"You and your men are dismissed," Karus said. "Ipax here can manage."

"Yes, sir," Ternus said. "When will you return?"

"I expect to be back in four or five hours," Karus said. "You may resume your duties then."

"Thank you, sir," Ternus said. Karus thought he saw the optio flash a smirk at Ipax before forming his men up and marching away. Ipax showed no reaction, as would Karus had he been in the other's sandals.

"I am looking forward to the tour of the temple district," Karus said, switching back to Latin. She had proposed this excursion last evening, and at the time, Karus had thought it a good idea. The more he learned about this land, including the people's beliefs, the better. Having heard Dio out, he now questioned that decision, though only a little.

"It will be my fun," she said, though she appeared a little nervous, or perhaps simply ill at ease. Karus chalked that up to having been confined, first in the dungeon and then in the palace for so long. She had spent very little time out and about. Whenever she had, it had been closely supervised and limited to the palace gardens.

"Pleasure," Karus corrected. They began walking toward the gate. Ipax snapped out an order, and Karus's escort formed up behind them into a double line of four each.

Eighth Cohort was using the parade ground. It was one of the largest open spaces in the city and perfect for formation drill. Centurion Arrens stood to the side with another centurion, critically watching as his cohort began to move through the drill. Karus noted Amarra's eyes on the Eighth as they maneuvered smartly from a marching column into a battle line six deep.

"Yesterday," Karus said, drawing her attention away from the Eighth, "we spoke of your people and why they left the city. You said they fled. Why?"

"Yes," she said, eyeing him with what he thought might be guarded caution. "They leave, fled, you say."

"It was not sickness then," he said, wishing to confirm that yet again. Ampelius had stopped by a short while before. Dio's words and what Ampelius had told him had it at the front of his mind. The sickness was spreading at an alarming rate, and if it continued, the surgeon assured him a quarter of his men would be down, ill within a week. More after that. Worse, several of those who had been stricken first had died, with only a handful managing to recover.

"Sickness?" she asked in her thick accent.

Karus made an exaggerated coughing sound.

"Ah," she said with a shake of her head, "no, no sickness."

Amarra said something further in her own language, which he did not understand. He must have frowned, for she tried again. A look of frustration furrowed her brow. Then, she snapped her fingers, face lighting up.

"Orc," she said, "many orc. That right word? Yes? Many."

Karus stopped in his tracks just before the gate and turned to her in astonishment, pieces of the puzzle finally sliding into place. "Are you saying that the people of your city left because orcs are coming?"

She paused a moment, as though thinking through what he had just said, mentally translating Karus's words. Amarra pointed at him. "Soldier just like you. Many orc come…" She made a funny screwed-up face as she struggled and said that strange word again, scowling, then seemed to settle for another word. "Come, they come."

"Here?" Karus asked, alarmed, and pointed at the ground. "They are coming here?"

"Yes," she said with a firm nod and a pleased expression. "I pray to god, High Father, for help. He show me you, not Dvergr." She pointed at the legionaries acting as their escort. "And you and you and you. Dvergr, they no help, no friend."

Karus wasn't sure what Dvergr meant in her language, but he rocked back on his heels, stunned at what he had just learned. The people of this city—no, of the entire region—were fleeing over the creatures. More incredible, she believed that the Ninth had been sent by her god, the High Father. Karus did not like the sound of that.

His thoughts trailed back to Felix and his comment on the price the gods would extract for their deliverance. Was this it? He hoped not. How could one legion stop what so many were fleeing? Surely the people of Carthum had an army, a professional military force beyond the city guard? The walls of this city were strong and sound. He had seen the captured standards in the great hall, the martial images in the colored glass. They bore mute evidence to this city's military prowess. Besides, a city as large as Carthum would have plenty of young men to call into service. It made no sense to flee from such a defensible position.

Karus rubbed at his jaw and considered canceling their visit into the city. He was so alarmed that he thought of immediately calling for Felix and Dio to get their thoughts. Then, with a glance to Amarra and her eager look, he changed his mind.

Karus had learned over the years not to overreact. There was no immediate threat on the doorstep of the city and hence no emergency. Valens was out there. He trusted his cavalry commander to spot any threat long before it neared Carthum. He should have some warning in advance. The key there was *should.*

He would have to alert Valens though. The next dispatch rider was due to leave tomorrow morning. With him, Karus would send word of what he had learned. When he returned from seeing the temples, Karus would solicit Dio and Felix's opinion on the matter and then write his dispatch to Valens.

"We go? Now? I show you High Father's temple," she said, eyes shining with excitement.

"So," Karus said to confirm what she had said as they resumed walking toward the gate, "an army of orcs is coming, here?"

"Army?" She seemed confused by the word.

"Me and my men," Karus gestured wide with both arms encompassing the area around him and then pointed at the sentries standing before the gate and the cohort drilling. "Army."

"Ah," she said, with sudden understanding. "You army…yes, orc army, man army coming. People leave, hurry."

"That must be some army, sir," Ipax commented from behind. "To get an entire people to up and flee, to leave the protection of these stout walls."

Karus glanced over at the optio, forgetting he and his men had been within earshot and listening.

"Yes," Karus said, suddenly conscious again of his escort. He could tell the men were hanging on every word, "but I bet they didn't have legionaries manning the walls."

The men of the escort abruptly let out a hearty cheer. Amarra jumped and a few nearby people glanced their way, including the guard at thc gate.

"Karus," a voice called from behind. Tribune Delvaris was hustling up. "I understand from Felix you will be visiting the temple district?"

"That's right," Karus said, stopping. Amarra and the escort came to a halt also.

"Might I accompany you both into the city?" Delvaris looked eager. "I would be interested in seeing the temples." He paused and suddenly gave a sheepish shrug. "I've been locked up in the palace with the clerks these last few days. If I don't get out, I think I will go mad. It's really an excuse to stretch my legs."

"I'm not one for ledgers and accounting either, sir," Ipax said to Delvaris. "I'd rather be on my feet and out and about. Exercise is good for the constitution, sir."

"Very well," Karus said, somewhat amused. Ipax was a taciturn type and Karus thought that last might be the most he ever heard the man say at one time. With a shake of his head, he started forward once again.

The optio on duty at the palace gate called his men to attention as the party passed. Karus's thoughts quickly returned to the orcs. It had always been a possibility that the legion might have to leave the city sooner than desired. But now, Karus suspected that time was fast approaching.

Where could they go?

Karus glanced over at Amarra and wondered where her people had gone. It was clear the people of Carthum had fled west. Scouts had seen other peoples—small groups, really—moving in the same direction too. Was there a refuge to the west? Allies to be gained? Perhaps he could find a safe harbor out there, somewhere they could go, at least long enough for him to learn of a path that would take him back to Rome.

Karus's thoughts remained turbulent as they worked their way down the street, passing civilians, who moved aside to make way.

People stopped what they were doing to watch Karus and his party pass. Amarra was their focus. Some of the looks were downright hostile, angry even. Keeping hold of his temper, Karus had to remind himself that his men and the followers were still scared. They had settled in rapidly enough, but there was still the fear of the unknown and what the future held. The sickness was not helping either. When people were afraid, they looked for someone to blame. That had clearly become Amarra. Perhaps, reflected Karus, this had been a mistake. Dio may have been right.

"Witch! Dirty whoring witch!"

Karus spun angrily around. His escort ground to a halt. Karus scanned the street but could not identify who had shouted. There were just too many people about.

Amarra rested a hand upon his arm.

"It be fine," she said to him. "I been called badder."

Karus looked into her eyes. He found them filled with a deep hurt mixed with a terrible sadness, of which he understood so little. It pained him that she was hurting so.

"I can see if I can find the offender, sir," Ipax said, though, by his tone, he sounded doubtful that any search would prove fruitful.

Karus, already angry, turned it upon himself for not listening to Dio's council. He balled his fists.

"No," Karus said, unclenching.

"It might be wise to return, sir."

"No," Karus said. To return to the palace now would undoubtedly be wise, but it would demonstrate weakness. Karus could not afford to be viewed as weak. "We continue on."

"Of course, sir."

A century of men turned a corner and began marching up the street toward them as they started forward. Karus recognized Pulmonus to the side of the formation. He held up a hand to stop them.

"Halt," Pulmonus grated, and the century came to a stop.

Pulmonus snapped off a salute, which Karus returned.

"Stand easy," Karus called to the century. As the men relaxed, he noted how more than a few eyes darted toward Amarra.

"How are your men settling in?" Karus asked him.

"All right, sir," Pulmonus said. "We've taken a home a few streets over. It's a little too plush for the likes of these maggots, but better than no roof over our heads."

"Good then?"

"Fine, sir," Pulmonus said, glancing over his formation with obvious pride. "We've got plenty of food. What with stomachs full, it's just like being back in Eboracum, but less crowded and without the cold, mud, rain, and fog, sir. Can't say I'm missing Britannia much."

Karus chuckled, as did a number of the men.

"Now that there are drinking establishments," Pulmonus continued, "and a regular liquid ration, I've got relatively happy boys."

"Good to hear," Karus responded, looking over the legionaries, who appeared fresh, their armor clean of both rust and dirt. It was a far sight from how they looked just a few weeks ago. Then they had been muddy, hungry, and tired. "Where are you off to?"

"Drill and training, sir," Pulmonus replied with no little amount of gusto. "We hit the posts first for sword drill, then some formation work with the rest of our cohort, and finally," the centurion paused and looked back over at his men with an evil smile, "we will have a good run, sir." There were several groans at that and for good reason. Pulmonus was well known for his fondness of jogging in full kit and forcing his men to do the same. "Busy boys are happy boys, sir. I expect a good day of it."

"Very well," Karus said, well pleased with the centurion's attitude. Training was a regular part of a legionary's life. Now that Karus had seen it reinstituted, he had hoped it would bring back a sense of some normalcy. Judging from the looks of Pulmonus's men, Amarra was unintentionally undermining that effort. "Carry on, then."

"Century," Pulmonus called after offering Karus a parting salute, "forwaarrd maaarch!"

Pulmonus's cohort resumed their march. Karus watched them pass, very pleased with their look and attitude, though he continued to notice a few concerned glances thrown Amarra's way. It troubled him. He would have to do something to diffuse the situation before it became worse. The problem was, Karus just did not know what he could do to fix it. Perhaps Dio or Felix would have some thoughts.

Farther up the street, Karus came across a woodworking shop. Several wagons were lined up out front, all in various states of assembly. There were both legionaries and civilians working on them. The staccato of hammering and sawing filled the air. The scene was one of chaos, but Karus had long since learned that such things were often deceiving. He was sure there was a system to the madness.

Across the street, several finished wagons were parked, awaiting removal to an open space near the palace gate that Felix had settled on as a collection point. The sight of the wagons brought Karus back to his concerns about having to leave the city before they were ready. He did not know how he was going to pull off getting the Ninth home. Keeping her intact was proving a tough enough job as it was.

There was an abrupt whooshing sound overhead. Karus and everyone else looked up. A gray shape flashed by, one of the dragons skimming the rooftops. In less time than it took to register what it was, the dragon was gone and out of view.

Karus shook his head as he glanced around. No one on the street had shown any terror or fright at the fearsome creature's passage, only curiosity. After a moment, they simply returned to what they had been doing. The red, green, and now a gray dragon had been flying over the city for days now. So far, they had shown absolutely no interest in the Romans. Four weeks ago, a dragon would have been an impossible thing, a creature from myth and tale. Now they were a common sight. Karus was about to start forward. Then, he spied Amarra and the look of shock and horror sketched across her face. A cold feeling slithered down his spine.

"You've not seen a dragon before?"

She shook her head an emphatic no.

For a moment, Karus wondered how she had not yet managed to see one, as they were always over the city. Then he understood. Under guard, she had spent limited time outdoors, and generally those precious few hours as Karus's companion. He could not once recall seeing a dragon while in her company. Karus's eyes narrowed. She had grown up in this land. Why had she not seen a dragon before?

Since the legion's arrival, the dragons had been ever-present companions, randomly appearing and troubling no one. Karus, along with everyone else, had begun taking them for granted as having been normal animals of these parts, like deer were common to the forests of Gaul. Studying her now, Karus realized the mistake he had made. Much like the legion, the dragons were recent arrivals too.

What did they mean?

"Try not to worry about them," Karus told her, though he was now very much worried. "They've been around for days and they've not hurt anyone."

She swallowed and then nodded, but looked far from convinced.

Karus shot another look at the sky before continuing on. The day was not going as he had foreseen. He was in a mind to get this expedition done.

A guard detail stood farther down the street, checking anyone who was moving out into the larger city for an approved pass. Karus and his party were waved through the checkpoint and into the temple district.

Amarra's pace picked up and she led them down the street, moving by several temples. She idly pointed each out as they passed. "Temple to Maas. That one Arrak, Valoor over there. That one honors Castor, very bad god. No good."

Karus looked to the temple in question. Like the rest, it was an imposing building. However, unlike the others, Castors's temple was faced with black marble. Karus had to admit, it had a sinister look to it.

"You honor the dark gods too?" Karus asked. "You said Castor, right? We Romans know of that god."

"Yes," she said. "Better than angry."

"You mean your people respect them all, even the ones you don't want to or, for that matter, like?"

She nodded. "Castor bad god."

"Better safe than sorry," Delvaris said. "Keep all of the gods happy."

"I guess," Karus said. "Though you would not catch me honoring the barbarian gods, especially those savage Celtic ones."

Karus turned his attention back to Amarra, who was leading them down the street. She seemed incredibly focused. He figured she likely wanted to show him the temple of the High Father first, before the others. Karus followed, his guard detail trailing behind. Not unsurprisingly, he reflected with no little amount of hindsight, the temple in question that she led them to was the one that had been razed.

Amarra slowed the last few steps as it became clear to her what she was looking at. The final steps were almost a stagger. She stopped and stood gazing upon the destroyed temple, her face a mask of devastation. It was one that matched the complete destruction before them.

At first, she remained perfectly still, with only a muscle flexing along her jawline. Then, she tentatively moved toward the posts, where the bodies of the men had been staked out. She approached one, tears running freely down her face as she took in the blood stains. Her shoulders shuddered. Karus moved to comfort her.

"I think we should head back," he said, reaching out to take her hand. He saw no point in continuing.

Her back straightened and she pulled away from him, half turning. There was a hard look in her eyes, full of a single-minded determination Karus had not seen before.

"No. You come," she said insistently and pointed at the ruins. "We must see if," she said a word in her own language, "lasts. We are called. You feel." She pushed a finger into his chest armor. "You feel High Father's call. I know you can."

"What?"

Amarra ignored him and turned running to the wall of ruble. She moved so quickly, it caught him off guard. Hiking up her dress so that her legs showed, she scrambled and climbed up into the rubble. A few feet up, she stopped, looking back at Karus with a quizzical expression.

"You come, now." There was a fierceness to her tone that was almost commanding. "Now."

Karus glanced over at Delvaris, who had moved to stand by his side. The young tribune shrugged. Karus turned back to her, and their eyes met. He did not feel like climbing through a pile of loose debris, especially with his armor on. It would mean hours cleaning his kit free of dust. Yet, at the same time he also felt somehow called to follow her. It was hard to describe, more like a gut feeling that it was the correct thing to do. No, that wasn't right. It was stronger, almost like something was tugging him after her, pushing him forward. He needed to go with her. He had to go with her.

The call had been there since she had first suggested this visit to the temples. Why had he not noticed it before now?

"Stay here," Karus said to Ipax. "I expect we won't be long."

"Yes, sir," Ipax said. The optio looked relieved at not being required to climb through the ruins of the temple. "Be careful, sir. It may be dangerous."

"I will come with you."

Karus looked over at the tribune with some surprise. He was clearly eager to explore the ruins. Karus supposed that, as a youth, something like this would pose a near irresistible draw. He gave a curt nod and then followed Amarra, who had scrambled up farther onto the remains of the temple. A moment later, she pulled herself up and over a large column. Then she was lost from view.

Karus began climbing. He found he had to be careful where he put his feet and hands, as a lot of the debris was loose and shifted easily. He climbed ten feet before he could pull himself over the top of the pile, where he had seen Amarra disappear. He glanced back and saw Delvaris following.

"Watch your handholds," Karus advised. "It's very unstable."

"I am," Delvaris said as a piece of roofing tile he had grabbed onto pulled free and crashed down to the ground. The tribune glanced down at where it had smashed into a thousand pieces. He was more careful after that, testing each hold before using it.

Karus stood atop the debris pile. A column that had fallen diagonally blocked his way. It was as thick as he was tall and smooth all around. When it had been pulled down, the column had cracked into several large, uneven segments. Using one of the cracks for purchase, Karus carefully scrabbled atop. Breathing heavily from the exertion, made worse by the fact that he was wearing armor, he took a moment to catch his breath. Karus offered a hand to Delvaris, pulling the tribune up.

Around the fallen column, the debris field from the collapsed roof was fairly level. Standing atop, Karus was able to get a true measure for the size of the building. If he was correct, this temple would have been far larger and grander than the rest. Even in ruin, he could not help but be impressed.

"I am beginning to regret coming along," Delvaris said, rubbing sweat away from his forehead with the back of his arm. "Climbing in armor is overrated."

"No truer words have ever been said," Karus said. "Wait 'til later when you have to clean your kit free of the dust. Then you will truly be sorry you asked to come along."

Delvaris glanced down at his chest with a sour look. "I think I already am."

Karus looked for Amarra. She was just a few feet ahead, working her way toward the center of the temple. He considered jumping down, but the mess below was uneven. It would be easy to turn an ankle, perhaps even break one. A more cautious approach was required.

Using the same crack that split unevenly through the column, Karus climbed down the other side. Once down, he waited for Delvaris. Together, they began moving forward over the uneven pile, which seemed to shift with every step.

Karus paid close attention to where he planted his feet before taking the next step. Even so, a clay roofing tile slipped loose from under his left foot and he lost his balance. Karus teetered forward toward a gaping hole that he had not seen a moment before. Karus's arms windmilled as he attempted to avert disaster, but it was too late. He fell forward into the hole. At the last moment, Delvaris gripped his shoulder, checking his forward progress and keeping Karus from tumbling into the blackness of the hole.

"Regrets aside, I am rather glad you came along," Karus said and wholeheartedly meant it as they both peered down into the hole. He figured they were at lease twenty feet up. There was no telling how far down it went. Had he fallen in, the walls of debris might easily have collapsed and crushed him. Karus puffed out his cheeks. He should never have agreed to follow Amarra.

He paused and looked for her. She was around twenty feet ahead, scrambling over the debris in a frantic manner, clearly searching for something. After a moment, she disappeared once again, lost from sight.

"Amarra," Karus called. There was no answer. He cupped his hands. "Amarra, are you all right?"

"Here," her muffled voice could be heard. "You come."

Karus exchanged a glance with Delvaris. More slowly than before, he started forward, with the tribune close behind. A piercing scream rang out overhead. Startled,

Karus almost lost his footing as he looked up to see the red dragon circling several hundred feet above, every few moments giving a great flap of the wings.

It was the first time he had had a close-up, unobstructed view of the dragon that lasted longer than a few heartbeats. From head to tail, the dragon was longer than several of the larger residences in the city. Karus had the feeling that the magnificent creature's attention was focused exclusively upon them. Fear gripped his heart and left him wondering if the animal was going to dive and attack, but it continued to circle. Another more distant cry carried on the air. One of the other dragons was out there too.

Spell broken, Karus started forward.

"Come on," Karus said to Delvaris, who had also stopped. "Let's go."

The path forward was not an easy one. Karus had to scramble and pull himself over fallen columns and blocks of toppled marble as he made his way to the spot where Amarra had disappeared.

Finally there, he blinked, looking down. Some fifteen feet below, the center of the temple, an area with a thirty-foot radius, was almost completely free of debris. Amarra had ducked under an intact column, which had fallen against the far debris wall. It had come down in such a way that it was suspended over two other smaller columns. There seemed to be a space, or really a recess, underneath the collapsed column. Amarra, with a rope in her hand, appeared to be tugging upon something on the floor. She could not budge it and came back out into the light.

"You help," she said with a look of frustration that made Karus chuckle with amusement.

"Give me a moment," Karus said, planning out how he was going to make his way down to the floor below without breaking his neck. Satisfied that he had found a safe route, he started down, only to catch movement out of the corner of his eye that drew his attention back toward Amarra. He froze, eyes narrowing.

From under the column, in the recess where she had just been, the darkness moved. Something was following her out into the light. Karus saw the glint of a metal blade. His hand shot to his dagger. Yanking it out, with a deft flick, he reversed his grip to the blade and threw. Clearly horrified at what he was doing, Amarra froze, eyes wide in shock at his seeming attack on her person. The blade thrown in her direction flew past her face, with only inches to spare, and impacted just behind her with a solid, meaty *thwack*.

Time seemed to stop.

Then Amarra turned, breaking the moment.

An orc, sword poised and prepared to strike at her back, gagged. It was choking on its own blood, for Karus's knife had sunk deep into its neck. The orc opened its animal-like mouth in a silent, horrified scream, green blood bubbling up, before it dropped its sword, which landed with a clang on the marble. A moment later it toppled heavily to the ground, landing with a solid-sounding thud.

Heedless of his own safety, Karus was immediately moving. He scrambled down to the floor and yanked his sword out. Where there was one, he knew there was likely more.

Amarra was staring at the twitching orc as another emerged from under the column. It wore black leather armor that only covered its chest and black pants with brown boots. White swirling tattoos ran up and down its muscular green arms. The orc's hair had been limed back and tied off in knots with coarse rope. It eyed its fallen comrade for a heartbeat and then drew a wicked-looking long sword. Ignoring Amarra, the orc rightly guessed who had killed its companion. It bared its tusks at Karus and uttered a deep guttural growl filled with rage and hatred.

"You big ugly bastard," Karus yelled back, moving forward and gesturing at the creature with his sword. "That's right, I killed your friend. Now it's your turn."

Shoving Amarra behind, Karus put himself between her and the creature as it advanced. A third orc stepped out into the light. Karus could hear Delvaris scrambling down from behind. Delvaris was but a youth, and Karus had no illusions about who would do the brunt of the fighting. He knew he had to act fast before the two orcs could combine forces and rush him.

Lightning fast, Karus lunged forward, jabbed out for a leg, and missed. The orc danced aside, sword flicking out. It connected painfully with Karus's chest armor. Before the orc could react, Karus stepped inside the creature's reach and thrust, this time aiming for the stomach. He was rewarded with an *umff.* The short sword went in deep. He gave it a savage twist as the tip of the blade grated against the spine. Karus yanked the sword out, trailing greenish gore. He stepped back and away. The orc collapsed.

Without hesitation, Karus spun to face the other orc and brought his sword up just in time to ward off a blow. The two blades met with a ringing clang that instantly set his hand tingling. Karus tightened his grip and jabbed, but the creature managed to get its sword around and deflect. At that moment, unexpectedly, a sword strike jabbed shallowly into the orc's side. The creature roared in pain and bared its tusks at its new tormentor, Delvaris.

Karus, taking advantage of the opportunity, punched forward, taking it in the throat with the tip of his blade, which traveled upward into the brain. The savage roar was almost instantly silenced. He stepped back as the lifeless body hit the temple floor, which had once been polished marble but was now dusty and cracked like dry mud in summertime. A pool of green blood rapidly spread out from under the body and across the marble.

Karus turned at a noise to his right. The orc he had taken in the stomach was still alive. On its belly, it was struggling, clawing its way toward its discarded blade, leaving a trail of green blood. Karus had clearly severed the creature's spine, as the legs were slack and apparently useless. Karus stepped up behind it and stabbed down with his sword into the back of the creature's neck. The orc twitched once, issued a gurgling sound, and then fell still.

Karus glanced around. All three of the creatures were down and unmoving. He looked to Delvaris, whose arm was drenched in green blood. He nodded his thanks. Then he turned to Amarra. She looked a little shaken but had herself under control.

Karus was about to say something, but stopped himself. The air around them abruptly cooled, dropping to that of a frigid winter day. He turned toward the darkness from which the orcs had emerged. A cold fog rolled out of the space under the column, and frost spread across the cracked marble. Karus stepped back, as did Delvaris. Something was coming slowly out of the darkness, and whatever it was, it wasn't an orc.

The demon that emerged was hideous. It clawed and shuffled its way out from under the column. Even in his nightmares, Karus had never imagined something so terrible. It had two arms, two legs, and a head, but beyond that it looked nothing like a man. For some reason he could not name, Karus felt it once had been human. It was hideously deformed, tortured even, and Karus's brain had difficulty making sense of it as it shuffled and crawled forward. It wore the remnants of a black robe that looked suspiciously akin to those the two druids had been wearing.

When the light from the suns hit it, the demon stopped, shivered, and then turned its gaze toward Amarra, slit opening where a mouth should have been. Black saliva drooled out, falling to the floor, where it sizzled upon contact with the marble. The demon hissed, and Karus felt his skin crawl as it turned red eyes upon him.

Karus dropped into a close combat stance.

"Back," Karus snapped. "Delvaris, Amarra, get back!"

The tribune hastily scrambled backward and grabbed at Amarra, tugging her with him. She resisted.

"High Father," she said in the Common Tongue, the rest of which was lost to him, but sounded like a hastily uttered prayer.

The demon reacted to whatever she had said and let loose a long hiss that was clearly directed at her.

Karus quickly glanced around for fear of taking his eyes off the demon for too long. They were in a confined space, and the pile of rubble ringed neatly around them like a gladiatorial arena. Karus judged that he could not climb the rubble in time to escape, but perhaps the others could.

"Climb!" Karus shouted. "I will hold it. Climb!"

Delvaris, a look of horror on his face, glanced behind and then back, his expression hardening. His sword, however, wavered slightly.

"I will not be called a coward," Delvaris said, a tremor in his voice, but there was also steel there.

The creature began to again advance, shuffling forward.

"Amarra," Karus shouted, half turning, "damn you, climb, woman!"

"No!" Her voice was firm. "I stay."

There was a flash, followed by a powerful explosion. Karus was knocked back and to the ground. An intense wave of heat rolled over him. This was followed almost immediately by a tremendous *thud*, which shook not only the ground, but shifted the pile of rubble, which began to cascade down around him. Karus dropped his sword and covered his head with his hands as debris rained down from above.

From the corner of his eye, he caught a glimpse of a massive red form on the rubble directly above the demon before an incredible blast of flame shot down upon it. The heat from the flame was intense.

Then the heat was gone. When he looked, the demon still lived, but its attention was focused elsewhere. Karus caught a glimpse of a huge head, jaws open, with rows of serrated teeth that snapped closed upon the demon with a loud *clap*.

The demon screamed.

The dragon, for that's what Karus realized it was, reared backward, with the demon struggling trapped within its mighty jaws. Like a dog that had caught a rat, the dragon shook the demon violently, swinging its head from side to side. Through it all, the demon screamed.

Then the dragon extended its wings and, with a great flap that kicked up the dust, took to the air, its prize clutched firmly within its mouth. A few powerful wingbeats later, both the dragon and demon were lost from view.

Silence settled around Karus.

Stiffly, he sat up and glanced around. The marble just feet away was glowing an angry red from the dragon fire. Around the edges, the marble was blackened and had a glasslike look to it. Like a badly roasted goat, one of the orcs had been thoroughly burned. The smell was awful.

Delvaris and Amarra pulled themselves to their feet. Karus just sat there, enjoying the moment. He looked up at the clear blue sky and smiled to himself.

"I'm getting too old for this," he said. "But it's a good day."

"What was that?" Delvaris asked, looking over.

"We survived," Karus said. "That makes it a good day. Always is… surviving that is, when you really shouldn't."

"So," Delvaris said, looking a little dazed, "this is a good day then?"

"Another good day was when I rescued you during the retreat up the hill," Karus said. "You should have not survived that either."

"I don't remember that," Delvaris said with a frown.

"I do," Karus said and grinned at the tribune. "And I won't let you forget it."

Amarra stepped over to him and looked down before offering a hand. Karus allowed her to pull him upright. She pulled him in close, and kissed him soundly, her soft lips pressing passionately against his. Shocked, more than he had been when confronting the orcs, Karus stiffened. Then he gave into the moment. He kissed her back.

"Brave man," she said, pulling back and wagging a finger in his face. "Brave, but stupid."

"I think Dio and Felix would agree with you on that point," Karus said with a half smile.

"What was that thing?" Delvaris asked.

Amarra stepped back toward the space under the column. She was careful to move around the marble that still glowed a deep, angry red. The spot radiated heat like a smithy's forge. She also gave the dead orcs space. Amarra hesitated, peering into the darkness. Karus was ready to object, then decided against it. The danger was past. He was sure of it.

"I have absolutely no idea," Karus said instead as Amarra ducked back into the hole. He followed her over. Karus saw that one of the large columns had fallen upon a stone altar, which, surprisingly, had held. Underneath the altar, on the other side, was a trap door of some sort. The space ran farther back into the darkness, primarily along the length of the column. Karus surmised that was where the orcs and demon had come from.

Amarra picked up a stout rope that was attached to the door and attempted to tug it open. Fallen debris was preventing her from succeeding. Karus eyed the darkness beyond what he could see and hoped no more orcs were coming, nor anymore demons. Facing off against one had been enough.

"Help me," she said. There was desperation to her tone.

Expelling a heavy breath, he moved over. Grabbing her arm, he pulled her out from under the debris.

"We need to clear this first," he said and turned to Delvaris. "Give me a hand."

Most of the debris preventing the trap door from opening was easily enough moved aside and cleared away. Both he and Delvaris worked diligently at it. A few hundred heartbeats later, all that remained was a fallen beam, the end of which was buried farther back in the rubble.

"I think," Delvaris said, wiping sweat from his brow with the back of his arm, "we might be able to push it over to the side a bit, enough so that we can open the trap door."

"Let's try," Karus said, and together, with not an inconsiderable effort, they pushed from one side, inch by inch forcing the beam away from the trap door. Rubble from where the remainder of the beam was buried groaned, cracked, grumbled, and shifted. Smaller bits and pieces cascaded down from above to the floor.

"That should do it." Karus let out a relieved breath as Amarra scrambled forward and pulled on the rope that was attached to the trap door. As if they had not been used in an age, the hinges groaned loudly, but the door moved. He bent down and helped her, grabbing the edge of the door and hauling it back until, with a crash, it came to rest against the altar. Karus peered downward. A set of marble steps led into darkness. He wondered why she had been intent on opening a crypt. What was hidden down there? More troubling, what was so important that orcs and a demon would come for it? Surely the encounter had not been a coincidence.

Amarra started down the steps, but Karus grabbed her arm, checking her progress.

"It could be dangerous," Karus said. "With all that debris, the roof could cave in at any moment."

"It be fine," she said. There was that single-minded determination in her eyes again. "It be fine."

Karus was unsure about that, but before he could stop her, she wrenched her arm free and plunged down the steps. A cry from above drew his attention. Karus stepped back out into the light. The green dragon was now circling above. The red dragon was nowhere to be seen.

Why had the dragon saved them? He had so many questions. Would he find the answers he sought down in the crypt?

Karus looked over at Delvaris, who shrugged, as if having read his thoughts.

"Wait here," Karus said, poised to start after Amarra. There was no sense in risking Delvaris's life too. "If something happens, go for help. Under no circumstances are you to follow until you've summoned aid. Understand me?"

The tribune nodded.

"And keep an eye out." Karus gestured toward the darkness that ran the length of the fallen column. It had come down nearly intact, and there was clearly a space that ran along its length. "There may be more trouble coming. If it does, go for help. Don't be a hero."

"Perhaps I should go for help now, sir." Delvaris had a grim expression on his face.

"After the dragon," Karus said with a sudden grin, "Ipax is likely already on his way and has summoned help from half of the legion."

As if in reply to that, a shout could be heard from the direction they had just come.

Satisfied, Karus made his way down the steps, footsteps echoing loudly back at him as he descended into what he assumed was a crypt.

Chapter Nineteen

It surprised Karus that the farther he went, the light did not fade as he had expected. The brightness seemed to increase with each step downward. There were no torches or lanterns. It was only as he neared the bottom of the stairs that Karus realized the walls themselves were emitting an ethereal bluish light.

"What magic is this?" Karus's voice was barely a whisper as he felt the walls, which were warm to the touch. He had the sudden feeling that he was descending into the depths of the netherworld, crossing over into the world of the dead. Instinctively, he knew he should flee, but something, some force, tugged him onward, deeper into the bowels of the temple.

Amarra waited at the bottom. She looked serious yet exultant as she held out a hand to him, which he tentatively took. Her flesh was warm and tender in his callused hand. He rubbed his fingers over her soft skin, enjoying the feel. Her eyes captured his and seemed to pierce his soul. Then, with some effort, he pulled away and studied their surroundings.

They were in a small rectangular chamber that was most definitely not a crypt. There were pedestals lining the walls with strange devices sitting upon each. At the back wall was a statue of a warrior god holding a spear. Without question, Karus knew he had seen that likeness before.

It was Jupiter.

But that was not what caught his attention. Like the walls, the statue was emitting a bluish light, but more brilliant, and it seemed to be increasing in luminosity. The statue pulsed with a power that Karus could almost feel. The small chamber throbbed with each pulse, and they were getting stronger, faster.

The statue shifted, moving, coming alive. Karus's vision swam, and his knees gave out as the presence of an incredibly powerful mind swamped the room, rolling over his thoughts as a cavalry charge rides over disorganized infantry. Karus fell forward, catching himself painfully on his hands. His heart fluttered with fear as his mind screamed in panic. He was in the presence of a god.

There was a deep rumbling as the Jupiter took a step forward, toward Karus and Amarra. On their knees, her hand found his, and the fear, though still there, receded a little. The god advanced, towering over them in all his magnificence and splendor. So intense was Jupiter's penetrating gaze that Karus could not help but avert his eyes.

"Look upon me," a deep voice commanded. Though he wanted to do anything else, Karus could not but help look. He was commanded and his body obeyed, though his mind could only shudder in fear.

A gilded throne materialized behind the god, upon which he seated himself, planting the end of his golden spear on the polished marble with a *crack* that seemed to vibrate the air. The god's eyes locked upon Karus, and in that intense gaze, he sensed time beyond end.

Karus was entranced. He became lost, drawn in, and yet at the same time, the eyes vanished. Karus found himself flying. He was skimming over the land, as if he were one of the dragons flying high in the sky. The feeling was exhilarating.

Things looked very different from the air. Great grasslands, saw-toothed mountain ranges, snaking blue rivers, forests, swamps, lakes and oceans, he flew over them all.

Without quite knowing how, Karus understood he was soaring over a world different than his own. He had never guessed such a thing possible, but it was. His flight slowed, and a great empire stretched out beneath him. Time passed with each mile. Cities rose from small towns and villages before crumbling to dust. The empire came and went. Kingdoms sprang forth from its ashes, followed by yet another empire that unified them all. An age was passing before his eyes.

Is this how a god sees the world?

"Yes," came the reply.

His path took him along a river where a small town was nestled securely in a bend. The town became a city, sprawling across both banks of the river and the adjacent hills. It looked like Rome, but was not. A flight of golden eagles flew above the town. Somehow Karus understood he was looking upon a possible future. Then, with a snap, he was back in the chamber with the god seated upon the gilded throne and leaning forward to look down upon them both.

Karus felt small and insignificant in the god's presence. The god's mind pulsed in near-overpowering waves, beating down upon his mortal soul. The strength of it drove rational thought from his mind, and he groveled in terror.

"Roman," the god spoke, booming, "hear me well. You know me as Jupiter, but on this world, Tannis, and many others, I am the High Father."

Karus abased himself, whimpering like a chastised child who had displeased a parent. His mind screamed that he was unworthy to be in the presence of the great god Jupiter, ultimate lord and master of the Roman Empire.

Karus had never known such fear. The power of the god's mind washed over him like a series of tidal waves of pure will. He whimpered in terror, tears stinging his eyes, running down his cheeks. Then the waves of power abruptly and without warning ceased.

"Rise," Jupiter commanded. "Rise, my favored son."

Karus struggled unsteadily to his feet, his legs seeming to defy him. Had the god not commanded it, he would have gladly continued to cower and grovel. He understood he had no power here. It was a sobering realization.

"This bastion of faith is one of the last refuges of my *will* upon Tannis." The god abruptly became sad, and Karus felt a terrible wash of anguish roll over him, bringing fresh tears to his eyes. "Soon even this shall be gone, for my flock here hath dwindled. The faithful have been cast aside like grains of sands on a strong desert wind by those who should know better."

A sob escaped Karus's throat, the grief of the god beating down upon him. To his side, Amarra unabashedly cried.

"Hear me," Jupiter boomed, and the sadness lifted from his soul, "for your people's arrival upon this forsaken world has awoken my strength and *will* in this place, if only for a short time." A measure of the god's infinite power surged again, and Karus struggled to remain on his feet as it buffeted him. "You were brought to this world against my wishes, but I shall use you just the same. It is not my desire to command it, so I ask you, Lucius Grackus Lisidius Karus, Roman warrior, will you do my bidding of free will?"

"I will do as you command, my Lord," Karus said, surprised the words escaped his lips, before his brain caught up.

"Good, for I set you holy tasks." A fire ignited in front of Karus. Out of the flame came the image of a sword, a legionary gladius. "Find Rarokan, the Soul Breaker, and take it with you when you travel from this world. Though you may wield it, you will never fully control it. Rarokan is not meant for you, but another in a different time. It should be handled with extreme caution, as this weapon has a *will* of its own. Without the Soul Breaker, victory will ultimately prove impossible. Should this powerful relic be left behind, it will be lost to the shadow that is even now sweeping across the face of Tannis. It will be claimed by the enemy."

"How can I find it?" Karus asked, again surprising himself that he had the courage to question Jupiter. "I know not where to go."

"You have the last of my faithful on this world." Jupiter gestured over to Amarra, who was still kneeling. "She alone honored me when others turned aside for fear of carrying my standard. She sacrificed all that she had and was for me. For that act of love, I reward thee, Amarra."

Amarra pressed her forehead to the stone floor. She trembled.

"Rise, my favored daughter."

Amarra sat back up and then stood on legs that were wobbly. She looked straight at the great god before her, eyes fierce and proud.

"I bless you, Amarra. I make you High Priestess of my flock. When I leave this place, take my spear as reward for your faith. It is imbued with a semblance of my *will.* Use it well and squander it not. Go forth with these Romans and feed them the mana of my wisdom and teachings. Be their spiritual strength, as Karus lends them strength of will. Bring the free peoples of this world back into the fold and the full measure of my power shall be restored."

With tears of joy brimming her eyes, Amarra said something in Common that Karus took to be an affirmation. Whatever she said, Jupiter seemed pleased.

"Your journey shall be very long and fraught with difficulty. There will be much danger. Success is not even certain. Together, support each other, lean upon the other's shoulder, spread my word and my *will.*

"Karus," Jupiter said. "Know that you have been torn from your world against the order of things. You have been cast adrift in the middle of a great war that has raged eons."

"Why?" Karus asked, thoroughly confused. "Who did this?"

" 'Who' matters little," Jupiter said. " 'Why' is the real question. You are now a central figure to that struggle, for another has tied you to destiny."

Karus was suddenly ripped away from the temple and plunged into yet another vision. He moved through space and time. Hundreds of worlds flashed before him, each one distinct and different from the other. They moved past in a blur that was almost dizzying in its speed and intensity. Karus found himself shocked and amazed by the wonder of it all… the sites and incredible scenes.

The vision closed upon one world. Cities, towns, and villages flashed before him. There was yet another shift. Karus could see the people, some like him, others alien, hideous in shape… going about their daily tasks, living in peace. It was fascinating.

The vision changed again, and this time he was presented with something he knew only too well: war. A battle was raged, with thousands struggling against one another. There was a flash of lightning and Karus found himself flying again.

"Behold the Horde," Jupiter said. Karus felt a measure of the god's deep burning anger wash over him.

An army marched in great long columns and blocks, spilled across the countryside below. The army must have numbered hundreds of thousands. The might of so many was an awe-inspiring sight. The Horde was marching toward a great citadel defended by short, squat figures. Karus sensed that he was looking upon the opening of a war very different than those he had known. This was a terrible war that would be waged on an unimaginable scale from one world to the next, burning like an out-of-control forest fire.

There was another shift. Karus once again found himself looking upon world after world. Fighting raged across each. Creatures, some familiar and others not, struggled against one another or fought as allies in purpose, which was dominance. Karus sensed some of those he saw were aligned with Jupiter and others most definitely not. He realized that what he was being shown was not a war of peoples, but a war of the gods. The thought terrified him.

With an audible crack, the vision was abruptly snatched away. Karus found himself back in the temple. Staggered, he stumbled a step, breathing hard, as if he had run a great distance.

"My son," sadness laced the god's tone, "my time here grows short, as does my power to influence events. When I leave, you both shall be on your own. Already our enemies know of your presence and purpose. They move to stop you." Jupiter paused. "Karus, for you and your people, there is no going back. You cannot return home, ever."

Karus felt his shoulders sag at those words.

"Your legion will march forward, toward destiny," the god continued, voice rising. "You knew me as Jupiter, now know me as the High Father. Amarra and Karus, this day I give you both gifts to help you on your journey... including the Key to one of Tannis's World Gates, which, when opened, will give you access to a new world for your peoples, a new home. Use my gifts well. Find your way from this world before it is too late. Should you pursue it, there is help here on Tannis. Forge new friendships and alliances, and escape before the shadow falls across everything that was once fine and fair. Find Rarokan, which was placed in the Fortress of Radiance and is protected by those who willfully stand apart. Do all this, and I shall reward thee. Karus, should you prove successful, you Romans shall finally have your empire without end. Fail not, for it will mean your death and the destruction of the legion you so love."

There was a thunderclap, followed by a flash of blue light, almost like the burst that accompanied a lightning bolt. Karus knew Jupiter had gone. The vast presence had left the chamber.

It took Karus a moment before he could see. He slowly fell to his knees, overwhelmed. After a time, he looked up. Before him on the floor was a silver scepter, about three feet long. It had not been there when they entered. It was the kind, he imagined, a king would carry. Karus looked at it for a long time, his breath coming hard and ragged. Was this the Key Jupiter had spoken of? It certainly looked like no key he had ever seen.

Karus sat back on his heels and glanced over at Amarra, who was standing. He rubbed his eyes, wondering if he was seeing things. Standing next to him, she was gazing at the statue of the High Father in awe, which had returned to its original position. She wore a long flowing snow-white dress that was very different from what she had been wearing when they had entered the chamber. Emblazoned upon the side of the dress from the hip down was Jupiter's lightning bolt, emanating from the beak of an imperial eagle. Karus corrected himself. It was Jupiter's eagle, the High Father's.

She turned to look at him with impossibly large eyes. She looked radiant… magnificent to Karus. His heart swelled.

Amarra held out a hand, which he grasped. Once again, he felt the warm, comforting touch of her skin against his callused palm. His heart quickened and Karus knew without a doubt what had been missing from his life. With a firm grip, she pulled him to his feet.

"I…"

Amarra placed a finger to his lips. Her touch felt like fire on his skin.

"High Father show me where you from, Roman…" she said, withdrawing her finger. "We do this, you and me." She clasped her hands together before him, an earnest look upon her face. Amarra brought her hands together a second time, fingers intertwining. "We do, you and me, yes?"

"Aye," Karus said with conviction. "Together, that we will."

She gave him another smile that warmed his heart more than he wanted to admit.

"The Horde," Karus said, thinking through what he had been shown by Jupiter. "It is coming here, still?"

"Yes," Amarra said with a curt nod.

"Karus," a voice called down to them, breaking the moment. It was Delvaris.

Reluctantly, he drew away and went to the stairs, looking up at the worried tribune.

"Thank the gods," Delvaris said. Karus's escort was with him, Ipax and another legionary.

"Sir," Ipax said, "are you okay?"

"I am fine," Karus said and for the first time in weeks realized that he was. He now had purpose and direction beyond that of trying to get home. He knew what needed doing and he had a mandate from Jupiter to get it done. It was now time for action.

"We heard strange sounds," Ipax said. "Some invisible force prevented us from coming to your aid."

"We were visited by Jupiter," Karus said. "This is his temple."

Ipax and Delvaris straightened up, glancing at each other and then back down at Karus.

"Truly?" Ipax asked.

"Yes."

"We go," Amarra said, coming up next to him. She held the scepter. She handed it to Karus, who took it reverently and was surprised by the lightness of the object. Then, she walked up to the High Father's statue and knelt before him briefly. Karus watched silent as she prayed.

When she stood, Amarra reached forward toward the god's stone spear. With a deep grating sound, the statue's hand released it to her. As she took hold of the spear, it transformed from carved white marble to a spear of azure made completely of solid crystal, with the exception of the wicked-looking point, which was made of a silverish material. Karus realized he was witnessing another miracle.

The spear flared brilliantly as she took firm hold. A great deep bell rang throughout the chamber, causing dust to fall from the ceiling. The bell tolled a second time. Karus shielded his eyes from the light with his hand as it became intense. After a moment, the light died away and Amarra stood before him, crystalline spear slowly pulsing with power.

"Sir?" Ipax called down. "What was that flash?"

Gaze fixed upon Amarra, Karus did not reply. When she turned, there was a dazzling smile upon her face as she held Jupiter's spear. The ground trembled beneath their feet. Dust and pieces of plaster cascaded down from the ceiling as the floor vibrated. One of the pedestals toppled over, crashing to the floor.

Karus knew it was time to go. The chamber they were in was unstable. Amarra came up to him, flashed a wink, and then started up the stairs. Karus's eyes followed her. The men above drew back and away, as if she were a serpent slithering out of a hole.

Karus turned to look upon Jupiter's statue. The room around him seemed to be darkening, the shadows creeping up the walls with every passing moment. The floor trembled again.

"Thank you, great Jupiter," Karus said. "Thank you for saving my people and for this opportunity. I shall not fail you. Though I do not know how, I will find Rarokan and take it with me when I lead my people from this world. On my life, I swear it."

If Karus had expected one, he did not receive a reply. Clutching his prize, he started up the stairs after Amarra. As he climbed out, there was another rumbling behind him, then a crash, which was immediately followed by a blast of dust that blew past him and up into the air above. Karus closed his eyes until the dust cloud dissipated. When he looked back down, he saw that the chamber had collapsed in upon itself and the stairs were now blocked halfway down.

The men around him had drawn back a few feet and away from him and Amarra. Their gazes shifted from one to the other with frank astonishment.

"What's wrong?" Karus asked.

"Besides that crystal spear?" Ipax said in a near whisper. "I'd say that award on your chest, sir."

Karus glanced down and stumbled back in surprise, almost falling down the stairs before he caught himself. A new phalera hung from his armor, just above the others he had won for acts of valor. The newest addition to his collection was gold and made in the face of Jupiter. It shone brightly under the sun, glinting with reflected light. Twin lightning bolts to either side of the god's face throbbed with light. Karus touched it, and found the phalera was warm as fresh bread. Within a handful of heartbeats, the light slowly faded away, matching the burnished gold of the god's face.

"Jupiter, you say?" Delvaris said, looking to Karus.

"Yes," Amarra answered. She rapped her spear on the marble with a crack, and it flashed with light. "Jupiter is High Father."

"The Ninth," Karus said, "has been given a holy task by the great god himself."

"Gods blessed," Delvaris whispered.

There was silence to that, then Ipax went to a knee. His men followed. Only Delvaris remained standing, clearly either too stunned or unsure what to do.

"Don't do that," Karus snapped. "I . . . "

There was a loud flap of wings from above, buffeting them with a strong gust of air. Karus glanced up in surprise as both the green and red dragons, flapping their great wings, slowed their descent. They landed, claws seeking purchase on the ruins of the temple. Karus's men scrambled back.

Claws digging deeply into the pile of debris, the rubble shook and shifted under the dragons' weight as they settled down. Karus looked up at the massive creatures and was awed not only by their size, but their fearsome beauty. As if planned in advance, both lowered their heads to the ground in unison.

"Hail daughter of the High Father," the red dragon spoke, but Karus heard it not with his ears, but in his head. The dragon's jaw opened slightly as the creature breathed in, revealing long rows of serrated teeth, each nearly as tall as a man. There was a jagged tear about three feet long on the dragon's lower jaw, which bled freely and spilled great droplets of blue blood onto the marble. "Long have we waited for your coming, as our god has commanded. We are ready to serve."

End Book One

Author's Notes:

A lot of research went into writing this book. As such, there are bunch of historical facts, thoughts, and ancient attitudes thrown in. At the same time, it is also important to note I have taken more than a few historical liberties. I hope you will be kind enough to excuse me for these. It is very easy to lose oneself in the weeds of history. I know some of you would have loved that. However, I wanted to keep the story fast-paced. That required a little trimming and modification of the historical record. I did not want to lose the average reader amongst Roman ranks, titles, and organizational structures of the legion. I also used javelin instead of pilum to limit potential confusion with too much Roman terminology… again apologies. One day, I promise I shall write such a book. Perhaps a historical fiction around Pompey, or another fascinating figure that helped to shape the world we know today. Until then, I hope the hardcore Roman history fans cut me a little slack and enjoy the Karus Saga.

Historical Background: The disappearance of the Legio IX is one of history's greatest mysteries. The Ninth Legion (Legio IX, Hispana) disappeared somewhere in modern day Scotland, along with all of her auxiliary cohorts. This occurred sometime around the year 122 AD, shortly after or just before Emperor Hadrian visited Roman-controlled Britain. The loss of the legion and all of her auxiliary cohorts (the Ala Agrippiana Miniata, First Nervorium Cohort, Second Casconum CR Cohort, Fourth Delmatarum Cohort, and the Fifth Raetorum Cohort) represented a considerable portion of Roman military power in occupied Britain. The men in these formations were highly trained professionals serving significant terms of service. The absolute loss of so many professional soldiers (many of whom were battle-hardened veterans) could not be easily or readily replaced.

What happened to the Ninth? The most widely accepted theory as to the legion's disappearance is that the tribes (Celts) in Scotland annihilated the legion along with her supporting auxiliary forces…though it is important to note there is no supporting historical evidence to conclusively determine what actually occurred. The site of a final battle has never been located and perhaps never will be. One moment the Ninth was guarding Rome's most extreme frontier, and the next, nothing. To give you a little context, she dates to the time of Caesar and Pompey and simply disappears from history somewhere around 122 AD. There is some fragmentary evidence (but not conclusive) she, in her entirety or in parts, may have been transferred to present day Holland. A number of historians believe she was ultimately moved to Judea, where the Ninth was destroyed. This is a distinct possibility, but again, there is no real hard evidence to support such a movement.

The truth is no one knows for certain what exactly happened to the Ninth, and that's what makes her plight so fascinating, though if we look hard enough, there are a few breadcrumbs to be followed.

Additional historical evidence to support a military disaster: The legion's second in command, Lucius Saturninus, is the last known senior officer to serve with the legion and have a subsequent political career that is specifically mentioned and detailed by classical historians. Interestingly, as senior tribune and second in command, his career was put on hold shortly after his term of service with the Ninth ended. Perhaps his service with the Ninth ended unexpectedly and in a way he did not anticipate? This is all speculation, but what is known for a fact is that Saturninus did not receive a public appointment for the next twenty-five years. His career literally hit a brick wall, while many of his contemporaries flourished.

Saturninus would eventually go on to the command of a legion. Yet such a hiatus is very unusual, but not without precedent for someone having been involved in an embarrassing military disaster. Saturninus would have to wait for a new, friendly regime (Emperor Pius) before his career got back on track. This is one of the reasons some believe that the destruction of the Ninth was covered up and intentionally erased from history by Emperor Hadrian. The emperor would have wanted news of the military disaster to be kept from the mob in Rome, as it would have reflected badly upon his stewardship of the empire. So, efforts might have been made to silence and punish those who had survived.

Saturninus's career path potentially backs this theory up. It is very possible that Saturninus fled from the Ninth's final battle and was one of the few who survived or perhaps was even captured and then ransomed back to Rome. (Either outcome would have been catastrophic for his career in Roman public service.)

It is important to note that the Saturninus in my book is purely fictional and a creation of mine. That said, I might have still done the man a disservice. If I have, I am profoundly sorry and apologize to his shade.

Around the time of the Ninth's disappearance, Hadrian soon began construction of his famous wall (Hadrian's Wall) that would see the separation of Roman Britain from the northern unclaimed lands of modern day Scotland. This may have been a reaction to the destruction of the legion and the emperor becoming resigned to the fact that subduing the northern tribes was not worth the expense and trouble. Then again, this may have simply been coincidence.

Another legion late in 122 AD was transferred, along with supporting auxiliary cohorts, to England. This legion took up the Ninth's previous post at current day York (Eboracum). It is possible the Ninth was simply disbanded by Hadrian. Yet, with the trouble Rome was having with the tribes, the disbanding of an entire legion, along with all of her cohorts, would not have been likely. At least in my mind.

Perhaps until some new archaeological evidence is unearthed that sheds light on this mystery, we shall never know the truth. Until then, I, for one, believe a troublesome Dvergran wizard transported the Ninth from Earth to the world of Tannis and set Karus on the path to destiny.

Best regards,
Marc Alan Edelheit

A Note from the Author

I hope you enjoyed *Lost Legio IX.* It has been my pleasure to introduce you to the start of Karus and Amarra's adventures…A positive review would be awesome and greatly appreciated, as it affords me the opportunity to focus more time and energy on my writing.

Care to be notified when the next book is released and receive updates from the author? Join the mailing list!

http://www.MAEnovels.com

Facebook: Marc Edelheit Author

Also:

Listen to the Author's Free History Podcast at

http://www.2centhistory.com/